The Fugitive's Son

By

Bruce Kemp

ISBN: 978-0-9737885-2-5
U.S. Library of Congress Registration Pending
Number: 1-8040147401

Cover Illustration by Graham Thomas
gra44thom@gmailcom

Waypoint Press
Box 312
Merrickville, Ontario
Canada
K0G 1N0

www.brucekempphotography.net/waypoint

This novel is dedicated to
my mother
Dinorah Kemp,
who taught me the importance of the
romantic intellect,
and
my father Howard who never got the
chance.

PROLOGUE

September in Detroit is a transitional month. Not a month of extremes, but one of variability nonetheless. Throughout September, summer and autumn struggle to agree on an old age for summer or premature youth for fall. When Dr. Richard Jenkins rolled away from the warmth of his wife Connie and lifted his sleeping mask to let in the light, he was pleased to see that summer would be allowed to acquire a few more wrinkles. Reaching across the bed he placed his hand on her butt. Normally she wore a nightgown to bed, but with the girls at his sister's house and Richard junior luxuriating in the independence of his sophomore dorm at Wayne State, the pair had killed a bottle of Sauvignon blanc and two of Shiraz with their meal. When they fell into bed, they spent the evening doing things that would cause their children great embarrassment if those things were ever made public.

"Come on girl. The day's wasting."

"I hurt."

"Doesn't matter. The monarchs are waiting and if we don't get moving we'll miss them again this year." He had been obsessed with seeing the migration of monarch butterflies since reading an article in National Geographic and discovering something so rare happened only a few miles away in Canada.

"Let's just stay in bed."

"No deal. It's a beautiful day and we're going to enjoy it." Then he employed a line he'd heard on some television show to make her smile. "Besides, this is the worst you're going to feel all day."

She did smile.

An hour later, Richard was loading their new Range Rover then they caught the I-75 and drove through the middle of the Motor City heading for the tunnel under the Detroit River to Windsor on the Canadian side.

At the customs booth the Canadian agent pounded in the license plate number on his computer keyboard then waved them through without looking at their passports. Green highway signs attached to lampposts pointed them in the direction of Highway 401.

From Windsor the 401 escapes across some of the flattest country in North America. Except for the disruption of distant woodlots, the horizon is almost an inverted bowl curving downward into the haze at its ends. Energetic sunlight danced across the corn and soybean fields bordering the roadway.

Another green sign, this time for Point Pelee National Park, caused Jenkins to flip on his right turn signal indicating he would be heading off the highway toward the north shore of Lake Erie.

Richard booked the bed and breakfast room two months earlier. Built by a local farmer turned newspaper publisher, the house was a fine old Victorian home. When the Thompson's, who owned the Migratory Arms B&B, offered him his choice of rooms, Richard chose the Tower Room that had part of a two-and-a-half story turret in one corner and an en suite in the other.

Shortly after one o'clock Richard and Connie were back in the car heading to the national park. The sky on the five-mile drive to the park entrance was a swirling tapestry of orange and gold and black against a background of crystalline blue. Butterflies were everywhere and Richard turned on the wipers several times to clear dead insects from the windshield.

It turned into a splendid afternoon with Richard giving his new Nikon a workout. Connie was happy just to see him happy. Suddenly she began to enjoy herself even though the tiny fliers were Richard's passion. When they first got there, she spent a frustrating hour trying to reach their oldest daughter Shannon on her cell phone, but the number was continually busy. She did not even try to contact their youngest girl, Christine, because Christine's plan for the day included shopping and a movie at the mall with her cousin Lemoyne and Lemoyne's mom. Finally, Connie got through to Shannon.

"Hey baby girl. How are you?" The relief in Connie's voice was tangible.

"Hi mom. I'm fine and you? It's like only twenty-four hours, not twenty-four months since you saw me and the kidnappers let me go early." Connie could hear mall sounds in the background. "How's the trip? Are the butterflies really cool?"

"Fine honey. The butterflies are so beautiful. There's just millions of them and daddy's so happy. He's taken like a ka-jillion pictures with his new camera."

While they were talking the wind shifted subtly to the north. Connie didn't notice it at first, but the butterflies did and as if one command swept through their squadrons, the insects lifted off, turning south toward Ohio across the lake – the next step in the implausible transcontinental flight that would carry their great grandchildren to the Oyamel rainforests in central Mexico.

"Oh my! Baby I've got to go. This is so beautiful I wish you were here to see it."

"That's alright mama. I've seen butterflies before."

Then the butterflies were gone with only weak and dying insects remaining. In the end the remnants were merely elegant corpses whose colour began to dissolve within the hour.

"Did you see that? Did you see that honey?" Richard chanted over-and-over as if it had been a celestial vision instead of a natural phenomenon.

He was still testifying when they swung into the Migratory Arms' drive. Mike and Joanne were busy seeing the bed and breakfast's other guests off, which left Connie and Richard as the establishment's sole tenants.

Before turning back off their front porch to go inside, Mike asked Richard about their experience.

"Pretty impressive huh?"

"Never seen anything like it. I can't wait to get home to get my pictures downloaded."

"Got lots?"

"Two memory cards full. It's going to take a month to sort them all out and process them."

"Don't start tonight. Joanne and I thought you might like to join us for dinner at the Skein Of Geese. Kind of a tradition with us. We're closing for the season on Sunday so we always take our last guests out for dinner."

Connie didn't let Richard answer. She was convinced he would somehow bring in the butterflies instead of accepting the invitation. "We'd love to. Just let us get cleaned up."

It was one of the most relaxed evenings Richard had ever spent. Mike asked intelligent questions about ophthalmology and Richard, in turn, talked about his time in the Navy treating eye injuries during the first Gulf War. When the bill came Richard tried to pick it up, but Mike insisted they were his guests and paid the two hundred and thirty dollar bill – more than twice what Richard spent for their room.

When they were putting their jackets on Mike told Richard. "There's an estate auction on tomorrow at a century farm near here. The newspaper said there'll be some nice antique walnut furniture."

Turning to Richard, Connie asked, "Are the butterflies finished? Because if they are, I'd really like to go."

The yard in front of the farmhouse was packed with tractors, cultivators, wagons and manure spreaders. It was obvious that the late farm owner had a passion for tractors because the machinery collection included antique machines with solid iron wheels, two with bulldozer treads and four Mc-Cormick utility tractors of varying vintages, the most recent of which had not been made for at least a half a century. Some of the less valuable tables, chairs and wardrobes were set out on the lawn in front of the house, and on these the auctioneers had placed boxes of dishes and cutlery along with the assorted bric-a-brac farm wives collect to ameliorate the loneliness of their lives. A line of cars stretched back from the edge of the yard along the maple-bordered drive. It was a good place to park because the canopy of trees kept the direct sun off the cars' dashboards and leather seats.

Richard was about to abandon the idea of finding a space in the lane when a young couple appeared carrying an oak-framed mirror and a kerosene lamp. The lights on a Nissan Maxima flashed indicating a keyless entry and Richard positioned the Range Rover to block any would-be trespasser from occupying what would soon be his space.

Inside the house there was an astounding collection of high quality, mid-nineteenth century furniture. One walnut bed in particular, with a hand carved head and footboard caught Connie's attention and she whispered to Richard that she wanted to bid on it. When he saw the reserve bid, he sucked in his breath then decided it would be okay. After all, she had stood by him through med school, internship and his stint in the navy so this was payback he could live with.

People stared at the couple as they browsed. Not because they were black, but because Richard could have been Colin Powell's twin brother. He was tall and his slightly graying hair gave him dignity and appeal that caught envious stares from most men and lust-filled glances from any woman who had taste. Connie, on the other hand was a butterball. Everything about her was short including her hair. Her only features that weren't diminutive were her bust line and her smile. Her smile arched across her face with genuine pleasure and made everyone she met feel good.

The house had the peppery smell that marks the stain of long human habitation. Dowdy floral print wallpaper covered the parlor walls and didn't match, or even compliment, the upholstery of the furniture. By far the largest room in the house was the kitchen. Its walls had been overlaid so many times with glossy, white enamel paint the detail in the wainscoting virtually disappeared in places.

Connie noticed it first, but it didn't take long to register with Richard, there was a distinct lack of femininity about the house. The pictures remaining on the walls were men's pictures – photos of navy ships, lithographed hunting scenes and a Ford tractor calendar. Among the boxes on offer only two contained woman's clothing which told Connie the late owner's wife had died before he did, leaving him to shuffle and shift in an attempt to create a new world as a replacement for the one his unknown wife made for the both of them.

It all made Richard feel melancholy and he found himself hoping that when he passed on the kids, and not strangers, would want his things.

One of the tables in the yard supported a box of old record albums which he began going through. He fantasized about finding a set of pristine Ellington or Callaway 78-rpm recordings. Mostly, the records were Lawrence Welk or Montovani LPs with a few country music albums thrown in.

Below the table were three more boxes with their flaps folded shut. Kneeling down, Richard slid the first one out and heard glass tinkle gently as he lifted it onto the table. It contained a set of cranberry-coloured juice glasses.

The second box held photographs. Several were tintypes and old-fashioned albumen studio prints. There were also seven books that looked like ledgers, and three packets of letters tied together with ribbon. Richard gently lifted one of the tintypes.

It was a photograph of an ageing black woman. She was thin and her dress was dark and it was definitely taken in the 1860s or '70s. It was plain just by looking at her reluctant face that the picture hadn't been taken by her own choice. There was no smile on her lips or in her eyes. Hers was a tired and angry face laced with sadness.

Three other tintypes were pictures of black soldiers in Civil War uniforms. Each was posed beside a freestanding Union standard and each held both his Enfield musket and regimental colours. Two of the battle flags, Richard recognized as being from the 54th Massachusetts.

The taller of that pair, whose head came to within inches of the flagstaff's head, had fierce eyes with vengeance radiating from them. Staring into those eyes gave Richard a rush of pride linking him unexpectedly to this unknown soldier who may have forfeited his life for a country that still had trouble recognizing blacks a century and a half after the end of that war.

Turning his attention to the second 54th soldier, Richard paused then brought the tintype closer to his face so he could inspect it. Apart from the age difference, the young man's face was an exact duplicate of the woman's who first caught his attention. "Brother and sister or mother and son…" he thought.

Instead of glaring at the camera, the soldier stared timidly into the lens, uncertainty writ across his face. Moisture threatened the luminous black eyes and the mouth waited for any word that would give it some kind of shape. He was no more than fifteen or sixteen years old and skinny. His uniform hung off him like washing pegged onto a clothesline. Where the first soldier had his head almost completely shaved, indicating he had been in camp long enough to have suffered from lice, the second soldier had a short crop of curls flowing out from under his kepi.

The third soldier wore the stripes of a master sergeant and had a scar running from the ridge of his nose and across his left cheek that was a deeper tone than the rest of his cream-coloured face. The background of the photo was subtly different indicating that it was not taken by the same photographer. The soldier's look was placid, neither challenging nor frightened, but experienced. His posture was graceful and easy, one that Richard had seen before in professional soldiers. This man could respond in a second to the long roll of the drums calling him to battle or be instantly asleep with the sound of light's out. It did not matter to him, which he had to do.

Digging further into the box, Richard saw that the bundles of letters had not been untied for a long time. The ribbons around them had permanently adopted the sharp angles created by the top and bottom edges of the packets. He gently worked some of the letters loose from their bundles and on one envelope discovered the return address of the Office of the Commanding General of the United States Army.

"How much for the boxes of these old records and pictures?" he asked the auctioneer's assistant who was standing guard over the materials in the yard. Richard asked about the records hoping to conceal his interest in the pictures and letters. It was obvious no one had gone through the box very thoroughly and when the assistant flipped off a price, "Twenty bucks'll take all three," Richard pealed off a bill without hesitation.

To Connie's disgust, Richard made a big deal out of getting a receipt. "You think you're going to write that off of your taxes? You can't write everything off, you know. You're not a dentist."

"Honey we just need it to get these things back to the States without a whole bunch of bullshit at the border."

"Well, you just make sure you get a receipt for the bed."

In his excitement he had forgotten the antique bed. He went back to the assistant and asked if he could buy it before the auction and was delighted to find he could.

Getting everything back to Birmingham was easier than expected. They paid a small duty and the customs agent didn't even bother to look in the boxes. At home, Richard got his neighbor to help carry everything in from the garage. They put the bed in the spare room. Connie would have to give away or throw something out to make room, but the bed was magnificent and worth it. They put the boxes on the island in the kitchen.

"Don't leave that stuff here honey..." she protested.

"It's okay, I'm just going to have a quick look to see if there's much I want to keep, then I'll put it all away." It was a white lie, one that you tell your spouse when something has taken your fancy, but which you don't want to talk about until you've had the chance to understand what it was that grabbed you. He knew he wanted to keep every scrap – except the records and juice glasses.

Of the seven ledgers, four were actual financial ledgers with business information. They could wait. The remaining three were some form of diary or memoir. A quick look through gave him the date on which the writer had started recording his thoughts: 1878.

It was late when Richard made a decaf green tea for himself and told Connie he was going to stay up for a while. He took his tea and the first ledger into the den, sat in the wing-backed chair that he liked to sit in while he read, adjusted his reading glasses, took a sip of the tea and started to read.

BUXTON
BOOK ONE

CHAPTER ONE

June 2, 1878

Albert once told me that if I climbed high enough, into a tall tree or the steeple of our church, I would be able to see the path of the storm that tore through our township the year I was born. So I climbed into one of the black walnut trees along our lot line. It took what seemed like an hour until I got to branches that were so thin they wouldn't support my weight and I was terrified from the height. The thin, whip-like new growth, driven by a wind I had not felt on the ground, raised welts across my face and arms. I thought the burning must have been like my father's pain when the master whipped him. Along with the flailing limbs the entire tree moved, sawing with the breeze. I held on to whatever larger branches I could reach despite the fact my hands were awash in sweat. When I finally steadied myself enough to look out across the top of our bush lot, I could see the track of shorter trees that grew up after the storm and realized they hid the real destruction caused by the whirlwind. It occurs to me now that I only partly knew the extent of the damage because I had personally visited the wind-felled trees and ruins of unfortunate homes to see for myself.

Maybe because I had lived with stories of that storm all my life and heard them whenever my birthday came around, I expected more and could not understand or interpret what I was seeing, so I only attached limited historic import to the broader destruction it wrought. That was how I felt about the Insurrection and my role in it for a long time after coming home, but now my view is changing.

Despite all the miles I tramped and my naïve eagerness to enter battle I personally, did not see the worst of it and I am thankful for that. I suspect my wife Eunice knows those things more than I although she has not revealed what she did during the war. The things I saw and was part of terrified me to the very roots of my soul. Yet, it was very little and it was my duty. This I did as well as any man.

There is another reason that I now indite this diary. It is the tree from which I hope to gain the height of time to look down upon the course of those events. I wish to have a clarity of mind before committing myself to the instruction of the lady. I would not have undertaken such a thing, but for the letter. I am unusual in that respect. Many other veterans have expended countless hours and vast amounts of energy writing their memoirs. There are those who are proud of what they did and I cannot blame them for their pride because I share in it. Others have attempted, in the darkest hours of the night, to do what drink could never do: bring peace to their souls. Being a trained newspaperman, I did file dispatches home to The

Planet, but I should probably have entertained a history of the conflict and my contribution before now. However, until recently I have had nothing but the desire to forget our victory, and with the innumerable pages out there, it seems futile to add one more account to what many would rather put behind them. If I ever finish this, I will show it to Rufus for his opinion.

On that morning, four days ago, when the first letter arrived from the General, I had gone to the southeast field to get it ready for planting. We planned to grow ten acres of sweet corn, but to make sure the seed went into the ground in proper time to have it mature before the fall frosts, I first needed to drain the saturated soil. Absolom had ditched the edge of that field twenty-five years before, but little has been done since his death. The ditches needed to be cleaned and deepened. After I got them in good working order again, I planned to dig some lateral channels to speed the run-off. It was a big job and we hired Benjamin Munro to help. Like me, Benjamin elected to return to British Canada rather than disappear into the graveyard that was the United States in the years following the Civil War.

The spring weather was good for working. It wasn't too cold and no fog came up from the lake to dampen our clothes. Benjamin walked down from the village arriving in our yard just as night was greying into dawn. Eunice gave him coffee while I was in the outhouse. He said "Hello," but Eunice, as always, did not say anything. She just set the coffee on the table in front of him and returned to whatever work she was doing. When I finished my business and went back into the house it was darker inside than out because she tried to keep the curtains closed permanently and there was only one lamp burning. Eunice would not tolerate more than the barest amount of light to see by. She horded every penny, despite our owning another property that we drew a good income from. It was quiet in the kitchen even though there were three of us sitting around the table.

Of recent years, Eunice has become a pall falling over a room whenever she enters it and the shroud that trails behind her has become heavier. As it is, I am glad to escape her sobriety, but it would make going to work much more pleasant if there was the noise of a contented woman or happy children. However, Eunice and I were never able to have a baby.

Benjamin and I collected shovels, rakes and axes from the barn and loaded them in a barrow. It is not a very long walk from the house to the southeast field and before ten minutes were up we were working. This was our third day and already the ground was draining faster. On the higher rises you could see the difference in the colour of the soil. It was lighter than the deep black where water still saturated the earth. I figured this would be the day when we finished the main ditch that ran along the edge of the concession road. There were a hundred and fifty yards to go, and between Benjamin and I we could get that cleared by mid-afternoon.

"This reminds me of Petersburg. We spent more time with a shovel than a goddamned gun. And cold! God it was cold. Then it was hot. Never any in-between." He laughed grimly.

My service had been in a combat regiment under Col. Higginson, then with General Sherman's army in Georgia and the Carolinas. What I saw was mainly fighting and travelling. When they gave Contrabands uniforms a lot of our men in the Army of the Potomac were treated like workhorses and are still bitter about that. Benjamin figured someone had to dig the pits and build the barbettes. He watched as many of the white soldiers shouldered that burden too, so unlike other coloured soldiers, he never complained.

Benjamin had a beautiful face for a man, but sometimes it lost its momentum. I often wondered where he went when that happened. His shoulders would relax, losing all the tension in them, his eyes would fix on a point and he wouldn't speak or move for five or ten minutes, then he would set back to work without saying anything to me. His wife, Mary, told me he did not sleep well. He suffered from bad dreams and wandered the house at night constantly checking on his two sons.

Eunice later narrated how Lincoln arrived at the yard door looking for me.

"He was all excited. He kept saying there was a big letter from the president of the United States in his father's store and that you had to come quick. I didn't know what it could be. I thought we were shut of those people. I don't want anything to do with them so don't include me in any foolishness."

By the time she told me this, I thought I knew what the letter said and that I would not refuse its request.

Instead of crossing the fields, as he would have done in high summer when the ground was dry, Lincoln went back out from our house to Wellington Street then came by the longer route, following the road along the front of the farm and turned right onto Dillon Road. He did this to avoid getting his school shoes muddy. Had he crossed the fields we would have seen him almost as soon as he came out from behind the barn. We could have gone to meet him. Instead, he just appeared on the road above the ditch and his appearance startled both of us causing Benjamin to jump.

"Mr. Frederick, there's a letter for you at the post. My daddy sent me to get you 'cause it's from the president of America and important."

"How d'you know it's from the president?" Benjamin teased him.

"Cause it says so on the front, and there's a eagle an' a star," he breathed excitedly.

16

John Edwards, the Buxton postmaster, would not have sent his middle son to fetch me if it had not seemed important, but then he would never have delivered it personally even it had been from the Christ child himself unless there was some payment tied to it.

"You go ahead Frederick. I'll keep working on the ditch," Benjamin said midway through a lift of his shovel.

Stacking my rake on the side of the drain, I climbed up onto the road. We headed toward the barn where I changed out of my work clothes before setting off for the village.

"What do those damned people want?" Eunice was in the middle of the yard as I emerged from the barn.

"I don't know. Probably something about pensions or a meeting for veterans."

"Well I don't want anything to do with them. We are British subjects an' they can go to hell."

Lincoln turned to look at her with amazement. It was probably the longest speech she had ever made within his earshot and undoubtedly the most profane. She planned to make soap that morning and had an armload of firewood for the fire already burning beneath the big soap kettle. Eunice flung the quarters of split hardwood at the foot of the tripod on which the kettle was suspended and turned away angrily.

I remember feeling that I didn't want to waste time on some veterans' business that could be accomplished on Saturday when we went into Buxton to purchase our necessaries at the Edwards' store. But a man of my station never gets letters from the president of America or a summons that even suggests he might have one waiting for him. The fact that there was an official seal, even if it wasn't from the president, convinced me there was more to it.

"It's 'cause you were a soldier I bet." Lincoln was feeling very important and wanted me to know how important he was to be delivering messages on behalf of his father.

"Probably." Certainly I was curious too. I was confident I had shut out the war from my day-to-day existence. As I told Benjamin, it was probably something from the offices that administered veteran's affairs or some association of former soldiers. I didn't want to talk about it with anyone – particularly Lincoln – but I also didn't want to ignore the boy. This was, more than likely, one of the first real conversations in which he saw himself equal to a grown man.

"Maybe it's a medal for killin' lots of Secessionist rebels."

"I don't know that I killed any enemies, Lincoln." Which was not true. "When you were in a battle, the smoke and confusion made it hard to tell if you hit whatever you were shooting at."

"I bet you hit lots of 'em. I bet you killed the fellow who hurt your face." There was the slightest tinge of curiosity in his voice as he referred to the scar that marred the left side of my face.

"That was done by a piece of a canon shell that exploded near me. I never even saw the canon that fired it."

"Okay. But I bet you killed lots of others."

Letting his prompt go, we walked along in silence for a few minutes before he tried a different line of questioning. "Maybe it's from the office of slaves?"

"I don't think there is such a thing Lincoln. Besides, I was born here in Buxton.'

'Well maybe it's about you're daddy. He was a slave wasn't he?"

"Yes, he was, but like your grandfather and Mr. Munro, he ran away from the plantation where they kept him. But you know my daddy's been dead for a long time so I don't think it would be about him."

"Maybe you've got a aunty you don't know about that's trying to find you? We get letters from people looking for people all the time." He could have had a point, but the letter would have been from a private address, not one with an official government seal.

"I guess we won't know until we get there, huh?" By the time I said this we were already inside the southern boundary of the village and heading toward the general store that is its heart.

Since the war our village has shrunk. At one point more than two thousand people lived and worked in the settlement. We had businesses and a small furniture factory and an ash works. After 1865, my neighbors headed south in flocks trying to find whatever relatives may have survived the four war years. We rarely heard from any of them even though they had been good friends and found safety here in Reverend King's settlement.

Lincoln bounded ahead of me so he could herald my arrival. Part of his importance was to hold the door of the post office open for me while yelling "Daddy we're back."

Edwards looked up from the pile of mail he was sorting. His speech rumbled out like a distant summer thunderstorm "You have a letter from Washington – from the Office of The Commanding General of the United States Army. Which general is that?"

"Sherman."

"What's he want with you?"

"No idea." And I took the letter and slid it into the pocket of my shirt.

"Aren't you goin' to read it?"

"Of course I am. But, it's probably just some form I have to sign and I've got to get back to work. But while I'm here I'll take any other mail that has come for us." Usually I pick up mail once a week, but I didn't want to make it seem like I was anxious to read the letter. I knew who it was from and was startled he would write after thirteen years.

Closing the door to the post office behind me, I paused long enough to open the letter and read through it.

The mile-long walk between Buxton and our home farm soured with memories of months of hard campaigning and the death they brought. I thought a lot about Albert while I walked. Because he was bigger than me, I admired him for his size and strength and depended on him to protect me from the other older boys. It was only as we began to grow up that I absorbed the fact he was barely nine months my senior. His life had been substantially different than mine. Albert had been an actual fugitive where I was only a fugitive's son. Albert escaped from Missouri and made it safely to Amherstburg with his father Aaron, mother Tibby and two brothers.

When I arrived back at the farm Eunice was upwind of the soap kettle staring into the bubbling lye. I yelled to her that I would take our lunch with me when I went back to work. She looked up, nodded then prodded the burning logs beneath the kettle with the long stick she used as a poker. After a short search in the secretary, I found an empty ledger of the kind we used to keep track of all our businesses. Using a new nib in my pen, I carefully copied the letters into it, not wanting to miss anything in the transcribing. When I finished, I slid both letters into their envelope, searched Eunice's sewing basket for a length of ribbon to bind the two letters.

The first letter was addressed directly to me. It was short and to the point. Like the General. The second was a copy of a letter he sent to the widow committing me to this mission.

Gen. W. T. Sherman,
Commanding General,
United States Army,
Washington, D.C.

Mr. Frederick Douglass Macdonald,
Buxton, Ontario
Canada

Thursday, May 2, 1878

Dear Sergeant Macdonald,

It is my privilege to greet you fondly as an old comrade in arms. Years have passed since we last spoke and yet I remember you as if you had just left the room. Over the intervening time, I have often wondered how fortune has treated you. I know, left to your own devices, you would have succeeded in any time and any place, but I believe your decision to return to your native country was sound and for that I have missed you. Unfortunately for our friendship, life has taken me on new campaigns and away from that last May morning we shared in Washington.

I have often wondered whether you were able to make a return to civilian life. Did you marry and have children? What is the nature of your occupation now? I always pictured you as a teacher or man of letters. It is strange to think about you this way as all of my breeding and training has been that those of the colored race are inferior to the Northern European, but you have proven that wrong so many times over.

Prior to writing this correspondence, I reviewed your file. It presents a man of truly sterling qualities and advanced intelligence. It is because of this I turn to you, with one last request for a volunteer to face hazardous duty.

Recently, Major Rathbone wrote to me with a request on behalf of Mrs. Lincoln. She has become fascinated with understanding all that transpired in the Rebellion, particularly its affect on the colored people whom it freed and with the soldiers of color who saw service under our flag. She has asked in particular if there was a colored soldier capable of reading and writing to whom she could direct her questions.

I shall warn you, if her treatment of others in the late president's circle is any indication, she may be difficult to deal with.

As I say, this is a request for a volunteer willing to face hazardous duty, but one that I hope an old friend will not avoid.

I look forward to your response and to hearing the details of your current situation in Canada.

Sincerely,
Gen. Wm. T. Sherman,

The second letter was a copy of one directed to the presidential widow.

Mrs. Abraham Lincoln,
Pau, France

Thursday, May 2, 1878

Dear Mrs. Lincoln,

A number of years have passed since I had the privilege of addressing you in person and rarely since then by correspondence. It is my pleasure to do so once again and I hope this communication finds you well.

Major Rathbone passed along your desire to speak or correspond with one of our former colored troops. I was lucky enough to have a colored associate in the closing days of the war who would make a good informant.

Frederick Douglass Macdonald rose to the rank of master sergeant and I would have offered him a field commission had others not intervened and the conflict not drawn to a close.

Macdonald originally hails from British Canada and is, I believe, a second or third generation fugitive slave. He was well schooled and has quite a lively story.

When he first came to me, I doubted if he could read or write, but his diction was impeccable and his cursive hand among the best I have ever seen. My credulity was strained when he calmly announced one day that he had studied both Latin and Greek. This, I also found to be true, upon testing.

It has taken me some time to locate an address for him through the various veterans' organizations and for this delay I do apologize. Master Sergeant Macdonald can be reached at:

Frederick Douglass Macdonald,
C/O General Delivery,
Buxton, Ontario,
Canada

If I can be of any further service it would be my honor as it was to serve your late husband.

Sincerely,
Gen. Wm T. Sherman

CHAPTER TWO

Mr. Frederick Douglass Macdonald,
C/O General Delivery
Buxton, Ontario
Canada

Gen. Wm. T. Sherman,
Commanding General
United States Army
Washington, DC

Sunday, June 2, 1878

Dear General Sherman,

Thank you for your letter May 2nd instant. You do me great honour to even mention my name in the same conversation with that of Mrs. Lincoln. Of course I will write to the lady and provide her with whatever information she wishes. However, I believe there are others better equipped and who saw more of that war than I. The battles I participated in do not come quickly to mind even though many fine men perished in them, and I did not rise to either the heights of bravery or responsibility. Those others would be more suitable correspondents. I am now just a rough-handed farmer and sometime cabinetmaker and schoolteacher, but will do my best to answer any and all of her questions.

General, you are correct it has been too long since we last spoke. It is coincidental that your letter should arrive when it did and its timely arrival now prompts me to say this to you. I miss the life of a private soldier and I miss the conversations you and I indulged in. It seems to me that although the war terrified me, it also gave me a sense of the world and of fine men like yourself. I developed an admiration for General Johnston, even though he was our enemy and worked to keep my people enslaved, and I often believe that I may have even understood General Lee and could have forgiven him his stance enough to admire him.

Your letter caused me great upset. It is not that I did not wish to hear from you, but lately I have been feeling the call of the long roll. As I am married and settled in life, these challenges to the spirit do not serve me well. This is not meant to be reproachful, I say this with all love and admiration, but with the first glimpse of your letter I became as terrified of what it would stir up in me as I was at any time in line of battle. Now after calm reflection and the passage of a few days I can only welcome with happiness the renewal of our friendship.

I have followed your career through the news dispatches we receive here in Canada West. Among the items mentioning you, are reports suggesting you be nominated for the presidency and I must say that I believe the United States could only profit from your leadership.

As for me, I have endeavored to lead as normal a life as possible. I remarried when I returned to my home. My wife Eunice is the widow of a fellow soldier, Albert Watson, with whom I was raised and about whom I spoke to you in Atlanta. The three of us have known each other since childhood. He was a member of the Mass. 54th and was lost at Fort Wagner. We have no children and I believe this may be a good thing for I fear that much of what we have done for the Negro race is being eroded with time.

I live on the farm inherited from my father and raise wheat, corn and tobacco. We also raise our own livestock. With the help of another veteran, former Private Benjamin Munro, our barn has been partly converted to a cabinetmaking factory. My father, Absolom, was instructed in the trade while still a slave and he taught me those skills.

Before the war, he had a small manufactory in the village proper, but business fell off when people from the village moved back to the United States. Still there is some call for the trade outside our community. We produce fine furniture. The land here abounds with excellent hardwoods for this task. There is oak, walnut, maple and ash. Though, our primary business is agriculture, between Benjamin and I, we build any number of bedsteads, tables, chairs and chests of drawers a winter when the farm is dormant.

Eunice and I also own a boarding house in the nearby town of Chatham. We have an older couple who clean and cook the meals. With Chatham as a growing centre for business, we rarely have an empty bed and the property turns an excellent profit. I also teach history at our local school.

We instruct the students in the basics of reading, writing and mathematics, but we also continue to teach Latin and Greek to equip our young men for higher education. It is my belief that if our children can learn the history of recent years from those who experienced it, then they will remember it. I talk about you at great lengths in this class and what you accomplished. The children are anxious to learn of our battles, but more from the childish fascination with muskets and canon than what winning in Georgia and the Carolinas actually meant.

Because I knew you personally, they also assume I met President Lincoln and General Grant. They do not hide their disappointment well when I explain that I knew neither gentleman. Still, I attempt to give meaning to the Insurrection and the years leading up to it. I tell them about John Brown, what he fought for and his time here in Canada. I also try to paint a picture of Dr. Martin Delany, but Delany's efforts lack dash and the sounds of battle, and I cannot speak of him with the same admiration I hold for Brown.

When I talk about either man I am not sure I have ever been in total agreement with their different plans.

The weather here has turned favourable and I spend most of my days in the fields. I still keep Sunday and as today, use it to maintain my personal correspondence and other matters not related to the farm.

I look forward with genuine anticipation to hearing more from you and hope this finds you well.

Sincerely
Frederick MacDonald

June 9, 1878
I made breakfast this morning before Eunice and I went to divine services. I like to cook, but she doesn't like my coffee. 'Too strong' she says. However, she says she love my eggs, pork and biscuits, but usually does not finish a plateful. Despite this, the gratification I feel when I cook for her is that which should come from those small services you provide for someone you love. Others would call it unmanly, but I freely admit that she has been the star of my affection since we met as children. I make nothing fancy, but I like cooking and other people, especially Benjamin, eat it and rarely leave anything on their plates.

The kitchen is the room Eunice and I share mostly. Not only is it shared between us, but we share it with friends and members of our congregation. Eunice has the parlor and her sewing room while I have the small office off the kitchen and the barn. So, the kitchen becomes our meeting ground and with the most life to it.

Our kitchen measures ten feet by twenty-four making it the biggest room in the house. It runs the entire length of the original structure on the building's back side. My father wanted a big second family to ease the pain of losing the entirety of his first and he prepared for it with this kitchen. Maybe his seed was spent, or maybe, someplace deep in his heart, he feared bringing more children into such an uncertain world and my sister and I were only accidental. We will never know because he treated us with a great love and gentleness that betrayed nothing. Our house was the first frame home on our concession line. All of the rest are log homes.

I must have been seven or eight years old when he painted the kitchen. That would make Harriet about ten. The walls are divided horizontally by an oak chair-rail. Above the rail the wall is limestone plaster and below there is carefully fitted wainscoting that Absolom made. He painted the plaster a very light yellow, "To bring sun into the kitchen – even on dark November days." The wainscoting was stained to a golden colour then shellacked to withstand all the bumps and scrapes of reckless children my dad hoped he would have to repair.

Mother was very neat in everything she did and one of the jobs she set down for Absolom was to make frames for the Berlin wool work she and Harriet sewed in the evenings. It was not long before the walls were covered with all kinds of samplers portraying themes ranging from scriptural verses to the names of the boys Harriet liked at school. When Absolom painted the kitchen, Harriet could not contain herself and used it to lord over the other girls in our school. The boys were unimpressed and more than one told me he thought it made her less of a catch because she would be wanting too much of a man.

Absolom made the table and chairs for the kitchen. It was one of the first things he did when he set up as a furniture maker. Already the oak top of the table has darkened with age. The wax he coated it with seems to have mellowed from what I remember of the table's first entrance to the house and now contributes to its depth of colour. My father took his time and made this table a showpiece to attract business. The grain ends have been sanded so smooth they are as even as the top and sides. As a child, I remember wondering how my daddy could take something as rough as a board and turn it into a mirror in which I could see myself. When no one was looking, I would fog its gloss with blasts from my nostrils just to see its depth re-emerge.

At the time, they did not seem to be of any great import, how could they be if they were in Buxton and not America, but the people who sought out Absolom and his table were as lustrous as the finish. I like to think that something of their human stain has soaked into the soul of the table making it even more special.

Harriet Beecher Stowe once rested her teacup on it when she visited with my mother Martha and Dr. Delany sat on its chairs and argued with Absolom trying to gain my dad's support for Delany's plan to return all the slaves to Africa. Reverend King was always at our house and still visits. I would listen as he talked about the settlement and the problems made by the influx of people we underwent before the Insurrection. They were not bad problems and he was glad to be doing God's work, still it seems to me that God left him alone to figure out too many of the solutions. People of all stripes came and went and sometimes Harriet and I were not allowed to see them. One of those who did sit at our table was none other than Osawatomie Brown.

I have not told General Sherman about my career as a newspaperman and wonder if I should tell him even now. I was in Savannah when the general read about the death of his infant son in a newspaper. The news came even before a letter from Mrs. Sherman arrived containing this dark intelligence. He had never even seen this child and it was a time when I witnessed true tears in his eyes. But even before the death of his son, the General's volcanic reaction to any reporter who entered our camp frightened me and still frightens me now. At one point I was afraid he would order a newspaperman from the New York Times to face a firing squad for spying. He certainly railed at the man and promised execution if he ever returned. Benjamin and I talked about all of this yesterday, as it was a problem that has been bothering me since I first encountered the General and it fills me with a profound sense of deceit. This feeling has become worse with the arrival of his letter. I thought those emotions would fade over time, but just as they dimmed to near oblivion, I would begin thinking of the General and his kindness towards me and they would well up again.

"Frederick," Benjamin said, "those days are long past. The General has come looking for you because he likes you and wants you to do something for him. He don't worry about what you done when you was a kid. He don't worry about nothing because he's the number one boss. But if it bothers you that much, write to him and tell him you didn't spy on him or write anything for the newspaper that wasn't true all the time you was a soldier."

The problem was I did write about my experiences and that is a large part of what's been bothering me. I sent reports from the field back to the Chatham Planet as regularly as I could and Rufus published them. But, I never told Benjamin this. He only found out about it because his mother cut the stories out and saved them for him.

Shortly after I started working for Rufus Stephenson, John Brown arrived in Chatham and I met him through Dr. Delany. General Sherman does not know I knew Brown as well.

Sometimes it is hard to love Eunice. It has taken three days to calm herself over the letter from General Sherman and in those three days she has sorely tested my affections – slamming pots and doors; and on occasion cursing the General under her breath as a 'son-of-a-bitch'.

She makes life miserable. Yet, her distress is understandable as she loved Albert a great deal and had he not been one of those killed, I would find myself alone today. Because of this, I cannot turn to her for advice in these matters, so I will follow Benjamin's council and make my confession.

CHAPTER THREE

Mr. Frederick Douglass Macdonald,
C/O General Delivery
Buxton, Ontario
Canada

Gen. Wm. T. Sherman,
Commanding General of the United States Army
Washington, D. C.

Sunday, June 9, 1878

Dear General Sherman,

I have been mulling over your request for information about my life here in Canada West and realize the letter I sent you last week was not sufficient. Compared to what we shared, farming is pleasant tedium. Nonetheless, there is enough change and momentum with something as simple as the swing of the seasons.

The weather here is much like that of northwestern Ohio though fractionally colder, but the topography is astoundingly similar. That is, broad and flat without hillock or rise to interrupt the horizon. After the war, I was able to buy acreage at a very good price so now I farm one hundred and fifty acres. Most of what I have planted is wheat and corn. There is a growing demand for tobacco and I anticipate selling all that we can grow and will raise more if sales live up to my expectations. Because of the strong market, I considered planting all tobacco, but that is wherein the danger of farming rests. It isn't a blatant danger, as in buck and ball, but an infestation or blight could wipe out everything that my parents; and Eunice and I have worked for.

As I mentioned in my earlier letter, I also teach at our school, which I helped to build in 1861. Sectional School #13 is a frame building large enough to accommodate more than one hundred students. Most of the children share their desks, and when I attended our earlier school in the 1850s our teachers, Reverend King and Mr. John Rennie, provided such quality that a number of white families sent their children without worrying about the fanciful issue of white and Negro children playing together.

The school is something we are extremely proud of and there is foundation for that pride. You are already familiar with Dr. Anderson Abbott who served the Contraband Hospital and was a friend to President Lincoln. Dr. Anderson was among the first six graduates of our community's school although his graduation preceded the current building by several years.

Our community once contained two thousand people and it has alternately been referred to as the Elgin Settlement to honor the Elgin Association who purchased the land through the Presbyterian Church and the King Settlement after Reverend King. Most of us just call it Buxton because that was the name of the church mission here.

Reverend King was very specific when he set up the community and was clear as to what he envisioned, but first you need to know a little about him.

Born in Ireland, he was educated in Scotland, so for all purposes he is a Scotsman and has seen his own share of the world. The name of our settlement's mission, Buxton, comes from Reverend King's great influence, Lord Buxton, who marched the Emancipation Act through England's parliament in 1833. King came here by a circuitous route that saw him marry and lose a wife in South Jackson, Louisiana then return to his home over the seas.

By a curious serendipity, the Presbyterian Church posted Rev. King back to Canada to do missionary work. He was about this business when he learned his father-in-law died leaving Reverend King his late wife's inheritance. Included in this were the family plantation and fifteen slaves. He sold the plantation and brought the slaves to Upper Canada where he freed them.

Freeing slaves was certainly a dangerous act in South Jackson, but he has often told me that it was not out of fear for himself that he brought them north. "This is the only place I could guaranty the sanctity of their freedom. If manumitted in Louisiana, someone would have captured and sold them off to Georgia or Texas and their rights would never have been respected."

These newly liberated souls constituted the basis for the settlement and it grew from there. By the time I was fifteen years old, the town had progressed to the point that we had nearly one hundred and fifty students in both schools (our school had two buildings: one for the boys and one for the girls). There was a post office, two-story hotel, a blacksmith, my father's carpentry, a lumber mill and bank.

Each farm was laid out according to a prescribed plan.

Firstly, the farms were neatly ordered on fifty-acre plots over fourteen concession blocks. The long side of the settlement ran north for six miles from Lake Erie's shore to Granville Street, which paralleled the Grand Trunk Railway. In all we had close to 9,000 acres. Part of it is under the plough and the remaining hardwood forests provide lumber for the mill.

Homes were not allowed to be put up haphazardly or be left in a slatternly condition. Reverend King knew that order had to be imposed to keep the Settlement moving in a forward direction. All houses were to be at least twenty-four feet long by eighteen wide and a minimum of twelve feet to the ridgeline of the roof. Each house had to be set back precisely thirty-three feet from the road and had to have a front porch and a flower garden facing the street.

The more I think of it, the more Reverend King reminds me of another old friend. Both known to be miserable sticklers for the smallest detail.

Perhaps the most important condition for the success of Buxton was the prohibition of spirits. No one complains as they would in a military encampment as this ensures peace throughout the settlement. People here have had enough sorrow.

We are located twelve miles from Chatham. It is easy enough to get over there during the summer and then we usually go once a month, but spring and autumn are another story. Eunice and I often wait until the cold weather has set in so we can use our cutter. Then we spend two weeks or more in town at our boarding house on King Street. I decided to keep one of the six bedrooms for us and we let out the other five. Mrs. Bell and her husband, who manage the house for us, live in a set of rooms I built above the carriage house.

Chatham lies along the Lower Thames River which threads its way down from above London and ends in Lake St. Clair. During the War of 1812, there were a number of battles fought in the region and local stories hold that a gunboat from Detroit made its way up the river where it was descried and destroyed before its intended attack could be made. Several older men who saw its wreckage have told me roughly the position where it finally sank and out of curiosity I have looked, but now nothing shows above the water.

It is also near to where your namesake, Tecumseh, was killed in that war.

Prior to the Insurrection this city, which lives beneath a canopy of beautiful maple and chestnut trees, was a hotbed of the Anti-Slavery Movement and northern terminus of the Underground Railroad. Chatham was generally considered a safe destination for fugitives because it is far enough from the U.S. border that slave catchers slinking over the line balked at the distance which made escape with their victims most unlikely. This allowed a large Negro community to spring up and at one point as much as a third of the city's population were fugitives. Not only were they present in growing numbers, but many were well-respected members of the community. Some being like my father, a trained and valuable tradesmen, while others like Dr. Martin Delany were professional men.

Dr. Delany was the physician and community leader who advocated a return to Africa for all former slaves. He advised President Lincoln in this and the good president believed him somewhat. Dr. Delany did not have such a constituency with the Negroes of Chatham. Absolom called him "… one of those men who sought to become the sole purveyor of the Negroes' salvation."

"We are no more African than the American is a Britisher, this is where we were born" was my father's response when tested by Dr. Delany. "What we lost by being drug into slavery, we're slowly getting back under Queen Victoria. Any man who has the will to work can own his own home and land. Nor, do we have to step off the sidewalk at the first sight of a white man. Yes, it is true there is hatred for us, but it is also a fact that because of our industry many of our white neighbours simply accept us and little more you can ask."

Needless to say Dr. Delany never listened to these arguments. He was, however, the instrument of my introduction to Captain Brown.

I will confess this now, as it has bothered my sleep for some time and it could become an impediment to our friendship, which I wish it to be no further. I know you have regarded all newspapermen as treasonous spies and held the view that they should be treated as such, but in my youth I was a reporter for the Provincial Freeman and the Chatham Planet.

Even as children, my wife's former husband, Albert, and I used to discuss the goings-on in Washington, York and London. We were keen to see the end of slavery with our own eyes. The Mexicans outlawed it first, then the British and then the French. We waited for the United States to drive the final knife deep into its guts then twist it so hard slavery would never rise from its grave. But that, as you know, failed to happen. We followed every report and rumor with unbridled interest. Reverend King must have taken note of our discussions, because in my final year of Common School he recommended me to Mary Anne Shadd as a possible journalist.

She obviously encouraged him to suggest that I approach her, which I did. I read the Provincial Freeman voraciously. It was the only newspaper published locally which dealt in news specifically for fugitives and their children. It carried stories by the great abolitionists like Frederick Douglass, for who I am named. It also ran reports from local correspondents and this is where I fitted in.

You might say I reported on the price of grain and whoever's cat was up a tree that week. Before I reached such august heights, I was enslaved as a copy boy taking edited stories from Mary Anne's desk to the composing room. Osborne Anderson ran the composing room and printing presses and I think he may even have been a partner in the newspaper. I made tea or coffee and I delivered bundles of papers locally. In general I was the newspaper's dog's body until I had absorbed enough printers' ink through inhalation to view myself as being part of the family.

The fateful day came after I had been with the newspaper three months. Mary Anne told me to fetch pencils and foolscap then we sat down at her desk. She was, she announced, 'going to teach me to write.'

Any of us who have been to school can write A, B C, etcetera, but that is as presumptuous as saying that because we can throw a stone we are trained solders and fit for the general staff. I did not know this and bore the perceived insult only because I admired her. We began by writing an obituary. She gave me the facts of Denman Hayward's life and death and bade me set them down in the manner I thought appropriate. I began with his birth, conveniently ignoring the fact that, in three expeditions to the South, he had led twenty-seven people to freedom and died of wounds received on the last of these journeys. Mary Anne gently corrected me and showed me how to evaluate the events properly so they would make an interesting story even if it were simply one of remembrance.

From there she taught me the basics of reporting and assigned me stories of increasing importance, but never failed to pull me back to write the occasional obituary. Oddly enough, as my writing skills improved, I began to take greater pride in making a death notice as interesting as a police report or a new tax assessment.

Mary Anne was a graceful, naturally elegant woman whom I immediately fell in love with. I held her in such awe, because rarely had I met anyone so intelligent and determined to set her own course. This is what created friction between her and people like Dr. Delany and the Bibbs. Mary Anne was in the camp of full integration while Delany and the Bibbs sought segregation of the races. For this reason the Freeman was never apprised of any news by Dr. Delany until it had been reported in The Voice of the Fugitive, which belonged to the Bibbs.

I did not know it, but The Provincial Freeman was in a precarious financial position. While Mary Anne, who as the first Negro woman to publish a newspaper in either British Canada or the United States was a great crusader for the cause and a good editor, she was not the best businesswoman. With competition from the Bibb family's Voice of the Fugitive, The Freeman ceased publication.

I fretted about my future at first and did not know that I had already attracted the attention of Rufus Stephenson who owned the Chatham Planet.

Rufus was a supporter of the Elgin Settlement and a friend of George Brown, the publisher of the Toronto Globe, who was himself a committed abolitionist and, as I later found out, a good friend of Reverend King. When Mary Anne could no longer afford my wages, I was sent home.

It was one of those hot days pushing toward the autumn when the maples were just on the edge of donning their sunset hue. A few leaves that could not hang on any longer were dropping prematurely as I dragged myself back to the boarding house I lived in on Grand Avenue. Before I could finish packing; a younger, white version of me was knocking at my door with a note from Rufus asking me to see him immediately. Reporters are supposed to be acute and sensitive to the events going on around them, but to my discredit, I did not even entertain the idea he was going to offer me a position.

Rufus is a Massachusetts man by birth with Abolitionist sympathies, but like many he found greater opportunity north of the line and cast his fate here. Politically, General, you and he would have seen eye-to-eye. Rufus was a Macdonald Conservative and determined that both Canada's East and West, should stand on their own, as a united country independent of, but still aligned with England. I thought his friendship with George Brown odd, as Brown was a Liberal and in the other camp politically on all matters except confederation. This seeming chasm did not affect their comradeship to any great extent.

When I walked into his office he was expecting me and to my surprise had a docket of my writing on his desk. It contained everything that ever carried my byline and a number of stories that didn't.

"When would you like to start at the Planet?" were his first words to me. These were followed by "I can pay you four dollars a week. Take it or leave it." It was parsimonious, but it was work.

I had seen Rufus around Chatham and we had spoken occasionally when his paper was short-staffed forcing him to cover important meetings himself. His willingness to actually roll up his sleeves and fill the role of reporter even though he was publisher impressed me greatly. Along with being a good businessman and expert printer, he was a very good writer. His phrasing was always clear, concise and devoid of the hyperbole often found in provincial journals. I knew immediately how lucky I was and that I could learn a lot from him.

It did not take long to settle in and soon I was reporting on city and county council meetings. My geographic sphere extended to Buxton, which allowed me to return home for regular visits with Absolom and Martha. Absolom was beginning to complain of stomach pains and I would often bring him medicines that he could not get in Buxton. Rufus assigned me everything from cricket matches to politics, but because of my Negritude I was considered the official expert on my race, slavery and the Abolitionist movement.

One afternoon, early in the following April, Rufus asked me to interview Dr. Delany for a story about the doctor's proposed expedition to Liberia in West Africa. He wanted to find a suitable home for the former slaves once the question of slavery was answered by outlawing it. The cool, post-winter weather continued unabated and I still dressed warmly praying for the start of summer as I walked along King Street. Near the corner of Fourth and King, I encountered him and he bade me accompany him so we could talk.

It will sound cruel and mean, but Dr. Delany is a short, stump-like man with an aggressive face and eyes that warn you off taking him to task. When I stopped him hoping to set up an appointment, he recognized me and was about to send me on my way but I parried his rude behaviour by announcing I was making an official request as a representative of the Planet. Obviously he did not know I had left the Provincial Freeman and began to fall all over himself to make sure I would report his words to a wider world than that any Negro journal offered.

"When will this story appear?"

"In one of the next few editions. Mr. Stephenson would like to address your expedition before it departs and then follow it during its course."

"Well, you'd best walk along with me so we don't lose any time. Now what is it you would like to know?"

I began where the Planet's voluminous files on Dr. Delany left off. Reading them had only been perfunctory, as Dr. Delany made sure everything he did and thought was widely known.

Before I got far, a scarecrow of a Quaker in a modest dark brown suit, maniacal porcupine hair and a flowing white beard intruded. "Sir, you are Dr. Delaney?" Which Delany acknowledged. "I must see you as soon as possible. I have come to Chatham seeking you out and have not, so far, been successful in this errand but God has seen fit to bring us together now."

'We have not met, but I know you sir. Do you recognize this gentleman Frederick?' I allowed that I did not, although he looked somewhat familiar.

Then he addressed me warmly, "I must apologize for the interruption, but I have traveled a long way to finally meet Dr. Delany in the hope of enlisting his support for my work. Time is growing short for me to accomplish what needs doing and so I must beg your indulgence."

"Mr. Macdonald, this is the famous Osawatomie Brown of Kansas." With this, Brown smiled meekly, nodded his head in my direction and extended his hand. There was warmth in his handshake that had nothing to do with the day, and it pleased me immediately. He did resemble the artist's rendering of his face and mane that we used in both the Freeman and Planet.

"I must speak to you in confidence, sir. Is there someplace we might repair to where I may present my case? If you will excuse us?"

"Young Master Macdonald and I were just on our way to the Villa Mansion Hotel. Frederick is a reporter for the Chatham Planet and is about to write a great work on my impending journey to Mother Africa."

"I look forward to reading it Frederick." Paused, then "your last name is uncommon among Negroes. Are you, by any chance, the son of Absolom Macdonald?"

This caught me off guard. Strangers who had visited our home farm at night were the first clue Harriet and I had that Absolom lived another life, but in no way could we have suspected that he was in league with someone as daring and ruthless as John Brown. I replied that Absolom was my father.

"He is a good man who supports my cause in many ways. I may have even met you as an infant in New York unless you have a brother who approximates you in age." I shook my head being somewhat dumbfounded.

"Frederick should be no hindrance to what you have to say Mr. Brown. He may even find fodder for a story he wasn't expecting to write. As such I have no objection to his joining us."

The three of us made a strange looking trio as we entered the hotel, but the residents of Chatham were used to unusual goings-on, especially when it involved Dr. Delany.

When we had settled in a corner of the parlor and away from two other patrons who were conducting their own business opposite us but out of hearing, Brown began to outline his plan of establishing Kansas as the new terminus of the Underground Railroad.

"We have fought hard to keep Kansas on the side of God and I believe we may succeed entirely if we can only have the support of men like yourself. For now, my supporters provide enough money to accomplish this task, but we are desperate for men to join our ranks as settlers and soldiers. But, there is another bolder plan that I seek to accomplish.

"I believe this new plan will ignite the..."

"You are talking about a slave rebellion sir?" Dr. Delany now turned toward Brown and leaned quite close, hissing "this is dangerous talk even in a place as safe as this."

"Are you afraid? I was advised you are a fearless man. Nothing will ever be accomplished except with violence. Look what is happening today in Kansas. We are on the verge of declaring it a free state."

As children, Albert and I often fantasized about a slave rebellion and read everything we could find on Nat Turner. Albert was much more taken with Turner's story than I, having been an actual slave. He even went so far as to make a wooden sword, which he waved in every direction pretending to kill slaveholders. I must confess to you General, this turn of conversation excited me and I memorized every word said by each of the men. My blood boiled to take up the musket in aid of Brown's plan. For the first time in my life, I was part of an historic moment and preserved the memory of it until I could write it down. I felt the same way when I accompanied you in Georgia and Carolina. Those memories I wrote down in a diary at night. It is interesting that I now confess this and my pre-war experiences to you. Except for Absolom, I have never told another soul what happened that day. With Dr. Delany, there was a circumspect amount of pettifogging in later years regarding this entire incident and his recollection of the conversation. Merely to set the record straight about what I witnessed and swear to be true has been my goal.

"No man has ever called me afraid when it comes to standing up for my people" but I could smell the sour stink I would eventually know from the moment before battle and it was not emanating from Brown.

"Sir, I would not insult you so casually. Your references are of the best. If you would care to give me council after hearing me out, I will value it."

Dr. Delany couldn't refuse such a request and Brown began laying out his plan.

"Brown, this scheme is both deadly and preposterous. It will create a sentiment among the slaveholders that will lead to hundreds, if not thousands, of deaths as did the Turner Rebellion." Dr. Delany uttered "Turner Rebellion" with a tone close to reverence. He had often eulogized Nat Turner whenever he wanted to show that the Negro race held a definite antipathy toward the white man.

Time, contained within the air of that parlor, stood still. I waited for Brown to deny this charge. Instead, he nodded his head in assent. 'It is precisely this that I want. The threat of large-scale bloodshed will force slaves to rally, once and for all, to my side in their own defense and President Buchanan to act faster than he normally does.

"It is my hope that the federal government will then intervene. If they do, this will bring the question of slavery to the front and no one will be able to deny the truth of the slaves' desire to be free."

This will put shut to other plans," said Dr. Delany.

"It may..."

"Would it not be better to move at a slower, less volatile pace. The slave has waited this long. A while longer should not be of consequence. There is an election in two years and I feel Buchanan will be unable to hold his seat. Then we may see a wiser man as the head of state who will banish slavery. For this, the slaves can wait."

"You were never a slave were you Dr. Delany?' He already knew the answer. Then he turned to me. 'Mr. Macdonald, were you born into slavery or after your father made good his escape?" I told him I was born free.

"Then neither of you have any more experience of slavery than I. Yet, what I see every day is misery. Misery generated by a lifetime of toil and pain from having to leave behind family in the bid to become a whole man. I see the bodies of children lining the pitiful, unmarked graves on some unwanted piece of land at the back of the plantation. I see the women who bear mulatto children, not because they lust for their master, but because they must bend to their master's will. Can these unfortunates wait? No Dr. Delany, they can not and all the grand schemes to return them to Africa are for naught compared to the conditions they must immediately escape."

Dr. Delany's face grew even more severe than it normally was. Many people turned away from him and discounted what he said, but very few stood up to him. Even fewer mocked his Return To Africa to his face.

"I can see I have once again insulted you and I apologize. Doctor, you must understand my frustration and forgive me. I fear any progress toward the elimination of that institution has come to a halt in the Northern states. Northern men are becoming complacent and satisfied that they have done their utmost and need do nothing more. Good Abolitionists are content to cackle like crows from the safety of their pulpits with little result. If we are to make this a just world, then we must act.

"Please forgive my impetuous tongue. It is important that I do not waste my time here in Canada West. I know how well respected you are and your name would be great currency in my efforts. What I have come to ask is for your blessings to hold a conference of our movement's most influential men to be held here in Chatham where I can put my plans before them. If they deem my ideas too rash, then I will gladly listen. If not then we can all move one step closer to freedom."

General, this is how I first met John Brown. I could not then know how important his plans were to be in the shaping of our world, but I definitely felt that I had been present when history occurred.

Dr. Delany ended the meeting by agreeing to help organize Brown's conference. My feeling was that he only did this because there was no other way to terminate our discussion. Dr. Delany dismissed me with the promise that we would meet again in a day or two to discuss his African expedition. Brown rose and formally shook our hands then bade me to give his greetings to Absolom. I left the hotel after Dr. Delany. Brown settled back down into his chair to watch me go. His arms and his legs dangled and bent and the furniture appeared too small to house him.

Brown went on to hold his meeting. But it is growing late and this letter is becoming a novella. I will say goodbye for now and write more about meeting Brown if you are interested in hearing the rest of this story.

I hope this finds you well.

Your friend,
Frederick

CHAPTER FOUR

June 16, 1878
Just after our first meeting I remember Brown disappeared briefly. It was reported that he had gone down to the States to raise more money. Although Brown's name was not foreign to my ear, he was the kind of man you heard more rumor than truth about. At one point, another friend and recently escaped fugitive, Thomas Bradley, told me Brown had killed a hundred men and escaped on his last adventure with a thousand freed slaves. Thomas also maintained that Brown had a fifty thousand dollar price on his head. The numbers were fictional, but not the fact that Captain Brown had killed slaveholders; nor that he had escaped with bands of fugitives; and most certainly I could not doubt the truth that he was followed everywhere by a large bounty.

While Brown was away, two men arrived at the Chatham station on the evening train. They were dressed neatly and confident of themselves. The obvious leader of the pair was a handsome, well-barbered man in his mid-thirties. Their accents proclaimed they were from somewhere in the southern United States. Later, after hearing them speak, I decided they must be from Louisiana or Mississippi. Except for their origins, there was nothing unusual or out of place about them. Yet, the nature of their business was written all over them.

Men don't habitually travel with arms in Canada. If we carry guns at all, they are long guns used for hunting ducks and geese or chasing the occasional fox away from the hen house. We found out very quickly that these two hid weapons under their coats. The leader, whose name was Henry Livermore, was subsequently discovered to be armed with a pistol and the other, a Texan called Tom Branson, had a big Bowie knife.

Immediate upon their arrival, they registered at the Royal Exchange Hotel where they began to make less than discreet enquiries about fugitives and Captain Brown.

I came to hear about them from Osborne Anderson who was delivering some printing work for Rufus.

"Two slave catchers in town. They got here last night on the train from Windsor and I think they intend to cause mischief."

While I was receiving the brown paper-wrapped package of newly printed forms from him, I asked how he knew they were slave catchers.

"You can always tell. They still think they're down south dealing with field niggers."

"Have they done anything yet?"

They had not. But, Osborne thought it a matter of sooner than later. Leaning across the counter of the newspaper's front office he almost whispered that he wished they would offer some threat, because then he would have the right to kill them. There was a lot of sentiment against slave catchers. Few ever made it as far as Chatham, but those that did were arrogant to the point of being dangerous and they were also ignorant, or contemptuous, of the fact that American laws did not apply in Canada West. Several had been caught and gaoled. In one incident irate fugitives and their white friends had subjected three slave catchers apprehended near Niagara Falls to a well-deserved beating. Slave catchers had even gone into the heart of Buxton to try to coerce people into returning to slavery with promises that life would be better and the fugitives with their families would be kept together and not be harmed if they returned of their own free will. None were foolish enough to believe this.

Livermore began walking on King Street beyond Prince, where most of the fugitives lived. I think he was genuinely impressed with the fact that many of the houses were two-stories high and equal in quality to those of their white neighbours. Indeed, he even paid compliments to some of the ladies whose homes they were. One of them was the mother of Helen Jones, a girl with whom I had become friendly. The women ignored him. Still he had a watchful eye, which would fix on one young man after another. Occasionally he tried to engage them in conversation, but they wanted nothing to do with him. This went on for a week, before he addressed me in the street as I was leaving my boarding house.

"Young man, might I have a word?" he was civil enough and I was professionally curious.

"I am sorry, but I am in a rush to get to my work. What can I do for you?" I asked almost hoping he would brazenly attempt something untoward.

"You can't be a fugitive you have neither speech nor the manner. Are you one of the Negroes born here?"

"Yes, I have the privilege of being a born subject of her majesty."

"You are very lucky in that instance. There are others hereabout who are stolen from their rightful masters. My associate and I are here to convince them to return peacefully to their obligations and you may be able to help me in that. I understand you are the leading reporter for the local journal." In truth I was not. I was still learning my trade and held out some hope of becoming proficient, but a leading light was not the best way to describe me. "May I walk with you?"

I could not refuse him as the request had been put so civilly, so the pair of us set off together under the gaze of the matrons he had previously been patronizing. I could only hope that Helen's mother was not witness to this. My eyes were constantly turning from side-to-side watching for any deception on the part of Livermore or the appearance of his partner.

"Are you asking my help?"

"In a way. I would like you to tell our side of the slavery story. It has never been put forward fairly and truthfully. Abolitionists rile up our darkies and encourage them to flee. They would have you believe life is all hell on the great plantations, but nothing is farther from the truth. We protect and look after our less gifted brethren. There are thousands of happy coloured people working profitably in the South. The South needs their labour and they are being well treated. Occasionally, I do admit, a lazy soul drives his master to distraction and needs a whipping, but then there are whites who should be treated the same way.

"An entire way of life depends on the labour of these good people. We cannot afford to lose any more to the north. So, sir, I offer myself to you as an interview subject and a witness to this much maligned institution."

I could not believe what I was hearing. Livermore was arrogant enough to think that I would accept his version of this well-known evil. Southerners themselves knew the full of it and many could not bring themselves to address it for what it was. They preferred instead to simply refer to it as "…that peculiar institution."

"You have no experience of our labour system yourself. Many of the malcontents who flee to the north carry inaccurate tales and false accusations to malign Southerners. I would submit to you that these men and women – if you can bring yourself to call them that – are lay-abouts and malcontents. They are not intelligent and educated like you. I would like to invite you Mr. Macdonald, to come as our guest to visit New Orleans and some of our fine plantations to see for yourself and to report back what you have seen."

His invitation, as reasonable as he made it sound, was not one that would afford the chance to study slavery in any other way than first hand and as a slave myself should I be so foolish as to accept. American laws always reflected the belief that the slaveholder and not the slave had all of the rights. Negroes were considered mere property and in that capacity could not testify in our own defense – particularly if the testimony came from a freeman of colour who was falsely declared a slave and property of a white man. I thanked him kindly and he did not press it. I was sure he felt there would be another opportunity.

Our walk was pleasant enough and when we arrived at the Planet's offices he bade me a good day and continued on his way.

Work that morning consisted of helping Rufus edit the final copy for the next edition. We depended on contributors from the smaller villages around Chatham to keep us abreast of local events. The correspondents were good at this, but they could not write. Some even went so far as to attempt submissions in rhyming couplets in an effort to "improve our dry prose" as they saw it. Our job then was to translate it into an acceptable style. Even the less artful of these submissions still required careful attention to spelling and grammar.

As the midday break drew near, I was just donning my coat when one of the local boys came running into the office breathless with the news that the two Americans had tried to grab a young coloured man and force him onto the westbound train. The messenger did not know who it was, but the two slave catchers and their victim were "… holed-up" he said, "in the train station and one's got a pistol."

Both Rufus and I ran for the door. I had told him about my encounter with Livermore earlier that morning and he concurred with my assessment of the situation. He also told me that he had no intention of ever giving slavery a single column inch of favourable press.

By the time we arrived at the station on Queen Street, Livermore and Branson had forced their way aboard the westbound train with their captive in tow. People blocked the tracks and from the platform I could see the engine cab was empty so the train was going nowhere. Only a few members of the crowd were trying to board the train to take the trio off. The rest were content to block its exit until the constabulary arrived to deal with the situation. Osborne was among those who wanted to storm the carriage where the young captive was held. He picked up a chunk of aggregate used for track bedding and heaved it against the closed door to no effect.

Rufus told me to circulate among the crowd to determine who the captive was and to piece together the events up until now. He set off to find the stationmaster to discover what the official course of action was going to be.

In speaking with an older white gentleman, I discovered that the captive was a teenager named Mason who had been hired to help carry Livermore's trunk to the station, then captured at gunpoint. The gentleman who gave me this intelligence was incensed that these two foreigners would dare to attempt such an illegal act on British soil.

This was the first anyone knew the two Americans were armed although Osborne had suspected it from the outset. Now, I supposed Osborne was armed as well.

Several other people in the crowd provided bits and pieces of the story, but the din of the throng was rising as they waited for the constables to arrive. Livermore, Branson and Mason were contained in the third carriage back from the engine and I tried looking in its windows, but could see nothing of the trapped fugitives.

From the back of the crowd came shouts of "Clear the way… Out of our way…" I thought it was the constables arriving finally. Instead six young men, four blacks and two whites, came charging through the crowd with a length of rough-barked pine log about eight feet long and suspended from ropes slung over their shoulders. They charged like ancient knights with their battering ram at the closed gate of a castle keep. I could hear Osborne above the mob yelling at people to let them through.

It only took two thudding blows from the log before the door to the coach split and Osborne and his followers were into the carriage.

We could hear shouting from the car's interior. One of the voices was Osborne's, then there was a shot.

The hundred and fifty people surrounding the train grew silent, as did the voices from inside the carriage. Two men appeared helping a third. The wounded man was a local who worked with James Bell in the plastering trades and was an ardent abolitionist. His lower forearm was bleeding profusely. He was helped off to where one of the crowd sat him down and tied a clean handkerchief over the wound to staunch the flow. Then young Mason appeared in the doorway escorted by two of the firebrands who had helped to free him. A moment later, they were followed by Branson and Livermore. Behind Livermore came Osborne with a small pepperbox pistol held to the back of Livermore's head. All of this happened just as two constables arrived at the station. They took Livermore and Branson in hand and manacled them. Once safely away from Osborne, Livermore began protesting loudly that he was an American citizen and could not be treated this way. However, he grew quiet very quickly and I noticed, as they swept past me, that his manacles were applied so tightly they had already cut into his skin and a small rivulet of pinkish blood was seeping down onto the backs of his hands.

Later, when I had the chance to think about the day's events, I realized there was considerable truth in what Osborne once told me. "The difference between us and the South is that we may have a hateful bigotry sometimes and mobs sometimes, but we don't have mob rule. In the end we have the Queen's law which protects and guarantees us our freedom and we all support that – coloured and white."

It was several days before I saw Osborne to get the full story of the events inside the carriage. In the interim, I was present when the magistrate arraigned Livermore and Branson holding them over to the fall assizes. They would have to sit in gaol for at least four months before the sessions started. Once again Livermore bawled about his rights as an American. Branson looked at him with undisguised contempt and thanked the magistrate then asked the turnkey if they could be placed in separate cells.

On the following Saturday morning I was working my usual half-day when Rufus asked me to go to Mary Anne Shadd's office to pick up a docket she had been working on. At the office of the former publisher turned schoolteacher, I was pleased to see Osborne sitting with her and talking over a cup of coffee. The coffee meant they were not in rush for some important deadline and so were at leisure to speak with me.

"The engineers fled the cab as soon as they saw the crowd gathering," he eased himself back into his chair and began an almost defiant recitation of the incident. I often felt that he held me in some contempt because I was not as quick to the violence he thought necessary to overturn the laws and people who permitted slavery to exist. "One of them came back through the crowd to see what was going on. When he heard that there was a kidnapping in progress he told us he wouldn't move the train, but that the only way through that carriage door was to break it down.

"Two of the young farm lads knew where some pines had just been felled and they set off with enough men to carry one of them. The trainman looked about himself and decided that maybe he should go for the constable. 'But first' he told me, 'I think I'll look up the stationmaster to see what he says.'

"By this time the crowd had grown to seventy or eighty people and those damned slave catchers were getting nervous. One of them, that man from Louisiana, yelled out the window that he would let Mason go in Windsor if we would let the train pass. Solomon Grogan responded with a rock that almost caught the American on the head.

"When the men with the tree got there..." I told him I had arrived by that time and was caught up in the action, but was unclear about what happened in the car. There had been lots of rumors, but only a few were plausible so I would appreciate hearing the story from Anderson himself.

"It happened very fast, I tell you that. Stephen Goodson" that was the plasterer's apprentice, "was the first to confront the man from Louisiana. The Southerner held his pistol in his right hand, but pointed at the floor. Goodson reached for the American's coat and the American cocked the small cap and ball then started to bring it up so he could aim it. But Goodson had blood in his eye and continued to abuse the man. The Southerner tried to back away so he could cover us, but one of the seats stopped him from retreating any further. Goodson went to knock the pistol to the side and it went off. The bullet hit him in the left arm just above the wrist and he swung out with his right arm striking a horrendous blow. I thought the slave catcher would go down right there, but he stayed on his feet.

"It was Livermore and in a second, I had my pistol out and aimed at him because I thought he might have a second gun on him, but he wasn't that smart. The other American, the Texan, saw my pepper box and immediately put up his hands. We weren't sure whether he was armed with a pistol or not. When we searched him, all we found was his Bowie knife and a smaller pocketknife.

"The Texan turned on his friend and pushed him from the back. 'You fool. Do you want to hang? They have us. Just give it up.' And that ended it all."

When I returned to the office, I wrote an account of the incident including Anderson's story about what went on inside the train.

I still have it and have entered it into this journal in its entirety in the hope that someone will read this at a future date and understand that how we, Negroes and whites, treated each other here in Canada West in those days, was neither all one way or the other, but a careful blend.

CHAPTER FIVE

June 30, 1878

Until this past Thursday I was of the belief that Eunice did not wish to hear anything of General Sherman or Mrs. Lincoln. Then, without provocation, she asked me when we would receive our letter from the president's widow and if I was expecting another from the General. In the way she said the General's name I knew she had not softened toward him. Nothing has yet arrived from Mrs. Lincoln, but then France is very far away, and I told her so. This did not make an impression on her and she is still impatient.

Eunice and I first met when I was nine years old and she was seven. She doesn't remember our initial encounter, but I clearly do. She could be as commanding then as she is now. Albert and I were playing war in the bush lot we called Wellington's Bush and imagining the Duke of Wellington with a grand bushy beard. But we had never seen a picture of the hero who turned out to be cleanly shaven, so we did the best we could with nothing more than his name and our imaginations.

The war we were re-enacting with sticks for muskets and swords was the Mexican War. This was the most recent conflict to catch our attention and stories about it were still filtering back from the Southwestern States. Our army consisted of a dozen boys and it is peculiar I remember all their names to this day. I was General Winfield Scott and Eunice's older brother, Morgan, was Santa Anna. This had been decided democratically, or at least that was how we viewed the process because everyone agreed our method was the fairest. We drew two circles. One was about a yard across and contained the second circle in its centre. This second circle was only six inches in diameter. We all picked up a stone and, from a line drawn at a distance of about twelve feet from the perimeter of the outer rim, tossed our rock toward the smaller circle hoping it would land within that ring. When a stone landed in the inner circle, the soldier who threw it became General Scott. When more than one did, there would be a second round of stone tossing by those who landed fairly. Santa Anna was chosen according to the stone that landed furthest from the inner circle. That these conditions did not prove any suitability for the role of the heroic commander invading Mexico to set things straight with the dastardly defender, Santa Anna, cowering behind castle walls was beyond our concern. As Santa Anna was always destined to lose, he was not expected to put up much of a fight and no one really wanted to be on his side. His soldiers were neither valiant nor vigorous, but it did give the appointed Mexican troops the chance to die with a great deal of drama. Soldiers were chosen for each side by alternating selections. First, General Scott would choose his most important man. I always chose Albert when I was the general. Then Santa Anna got to select his man. This went back and forth until all were accounted for. Once our armies were established we went off into the woods to plan strategies. All except for one boy, who was chosen as timekeeper. None of us had a watch, and most of us did not even possess a pocket to keep it in if we had been so fortunate, so the timekeeper was the best number counter. This was always John Martin. He would sit apart from the warring parties, usually under an oak we had designated for the purpose, and count to three hundred. When he reached the mark, he would shout out the number "300" or something like "charge" and the Battle of Chapultepec would be on.

Chapultepec Castle had already fallen twice that morning under two other retiring Santa Anna's.

Eunice walked straight into the fray ignoring the volleys of shouted gunshots and canon bursts. High yellow, her cream-coloured skin glowed in the shade of the woods and her hair was pulled back until it was almost straight, defying the natural curl. She wore a light, white summer dress trimmed with embroidered flowers. Underneath it a snowy blouse covered her from shoulders to chin. There weren't many girls her age in Buxton at the time and she was most assuredly the prettiest.

Like a fever that quickly overtook me, my heart began banging against the walls of my chest, as if trying to escape its physical confines. I believe I may have let out an audible moan when I saw her as several of my soldiers looked at me in a distinctly disgusted way.

Morgan and Eunice had arrived in Buxton only a few weeks before and occupied a house on the southeast corner of the square just below King Street. Their father was a smith and opened a new smithy behind the square. They had come from the Queen's Bush, which was a tract of land northwest of Toronto. Land ownership in the Queen's Bush was always uncertain and Buxton offered the chance to hold property with a legal deed, so many runaways migrated there.

"Morgan" she called. "Morgan. Mama wants you. You come right now. She needs you to help fetch some flour from the mill." Morgan was sullen in response.

Magical light radiated from her face. Albert saw it too and this was the first time I became aware of a special male beauty. Later I would admire it in both coloured and white soldiers and my friend Benjamin.

Albert's face was lit from within as he watched her. When she caught sight of him, her aura grew and the shrewish sister-voice she nagged Morgan with retreated into humble shyness. Even without the instruction of a previous heartbreak, I recognized my cause was lost.

After that, our war dissolved into other endeavours. Smaller bands of soldiers set off to seek their own adventures and Albert disappeared toward home through the scrub. If I returned home, I would be put to work. For an hour I sat beneath the counting oak trying to think of something that would make Eunice see the great heart within me through my unremarkable visage. She had to choose me over my best friend.

That I failed in my desires is self-evident. Anything possible to steer her attentions toward me, I sought to accomplish: capering like a ninny, running like the wind and climbing trees to their very roofs to prove how unafraid I was. Nothing availed and yet the three of us became inseparable. My glue in this triumvirate was sickly longing. Neither Eunice nor Albert was aware of my true feelings and I buried them as deeply as I could, being content to come within her orbit every day. As for Albert, I became more and more ambivalent toward him. I tolerated him when she was around as he was often simply my vehicle to be near her. Yet, Albert was still my friend and I know now that our friendship was due to his efforts, not mine.

It is difficult to say whether this was my first encounter with lust or if I was unfortunate enough to fall into true love at such an early age. The difference between the two evades me still. Either way, from the branches of my present age I look over the different landscapes that have made up my life and realize that this was a path I never should have taken, but which has determined the direction I have so far followed.

I write this by way of explaining my need to be with Eunice and how I came to be unencumbered by matrimony when I moved to Chatham. But, when I face it on paper, I must ask for whom have I written this? As Eunice is as content in our lives as she is able to be and I will never show this journal to anyone, then I must be setting these very private words down for myself and reasons I suspect I do not yet know.

Helen came into my life in a conventional way after I began working at the Planet. She was affiliated with the First Baptist Church on King Street. I attended services there when I was in Chatham and Helen played the piano for them. She was a sturdy girl with a considerable laugh and outside of church exercised it frequently. This drew me to her immediately.

We met at social functions throughout '58 and '59. Unlike Eunice, Absolom liked Helen immensely and encouraged me to propose, which I eventually did. Now I wish I hadn't.

But this journal is becoming too morose. If I do not abandon this line of thinking then I shall be in a sour mood all evening and the weather is cool enough that Eunice is cooking a roast of pork and I would like to enjoy it.

July 10, 1878

After hoeing the fields since early this morning, I quit just before lunch. The heat was beyond my ability to endure. The difference between being free and being a slave is not necessarily the type of work, but the ability to leave it when the conditions become too brutal.

By 10:30 in the morning, I had drunk all the water I brought with me. Each time my mattock shredded the ground, the newly turned earth released its steam and the thickening leaves of the tobacco plants prevented it from rising, trapping it around my legs and waist. Twice in the course of the morning I had to seek the shade of an elm tree. Eventually, even that ceased to be a remedy and I shouldered my hoe and walked home with the sun burning through my hat and into my scalp.

For days like this, I have built a bathing platform behind the house and away from the view of anyone who might be passing. I have a zinc bathing tub set up directly below the spigot of a pump. On three sides of the platform, I have built a privacy screen, but left the fourth side open so I can sit in the tub up to my neck in cool water and look across the fields. Above the tub, to provide shade, there is a roof supported by four uprights. The pump feeds from its own well, so there is an abundance of water. Fortunately the soil here is sandy and the deepest of three wells on the farm is less than thirty feet deep. When I come home, I undress and pump a few buckets of water, which I pour over myself. This usually invigorates me enough so I have the strength to finish filling the tub. Then I sit and look at our fields.

There is always something to see in them. If I sit very still, small cottontail rabbits hop in and out of the rows of corn. Once, I watched as a hawk dropped straight down from the sky to snatch one of the unsuspecting bunnies to carry it away. I suppose it returned to its nest with the rabbit as food for its own young. Another time, I watched a roiling mass of thunderclouds advance up from the lake and out of them a funnel spun toward the ground. Before I could leap from the tub, it roared off away from me to the northeast and, as I watched from safety, it flattened crops and destroyed a small shed four farms away.

Occasionally, I am visited by wonderfully beautiful birds that I wish I knew something about. We have the usual barn swallows flitting in and out of the eaves of the barn and the house. Ten days ago, I was sitting motionless in the tub when a small bird with a yellow body and grey wings visited. I don't know why it wasn't frightened unless it was because most of my trunk was beneath the water's surface and it did not associate my head and shoulders with my being a man.

Stubbier than the bush canaries we are used to seeing around the edges of our fields, this tiny bird flitted from branch to branch. He had a short, black, needle-sharp beak and a black mask that extended from the beak around his eyes almost like a luxuriant eyelash. He was only four or five inches long and he 'tisked' at me when he finally saw me in my tub.

I cannot induce Eunice to try my bath. She wears her heavy black dresses or a gray Mother Hubbard despite the heat. Sometimes I have to suggest she bath and change her clothing as her odor is overpowering. It is like she is in her own small world where nothing of our physical realm matters.

After spending an hour refreshing myself, I dried off and put on some clean work clothes then went to my workshop in the barn to continue finishing a hallway table, which was commissioned by a woman from Chatham. This job has taken a considerable amount of time as the wood is mahogany and I have never worked with it. I ordered it from New York and that took six weeks for it to come by train. Working slowly, I carved two ball-and-claw feet on the front legs with a chisel and inlaid a floral design in maple across the front of the silverware drawer where the pull would be attached. I am very pleased with the work and would like to work in mahogany again as it is extremely handsome.

I began applying a French polish finish early last week and am on my fifth coating. This is a time consuming process requiring the build-up of layers of shellac. The shellac is mixed with walnut oil then applied to the wood using a clean piece of cotton rag wadded into a pad. Then it is rubbed into the wood in a circular motion until the wood glistens. By far, this is the most beautiful finish I have ever seen except for japanned lacquering. Because of the richness of the mahogany, I did not want to use the coloured lacquer and so have decided to undergo this laborious process.

Today was a good day to add another coat. Our workshop is beside the stable so the main floor where we store our equipment and the loft provide a barrier to the heat. The barn's foundation, which makes up the walls of the workshop, is composed of stones and mortar with dirt banked against its outsides. Because of this, my small factory is a cool and pleasant place to spend hot days and warms up quickly in the winter when I light the wood stove I use for heating.

Once everything was prepared, I began applying the thickened paste in expanding circles. The motion is mesmeric and eventually I stopped thinking about the manner in which my life has progressed. It is like being asleep yet conscious of the things going on around me. Flies hurled themselves against the glass panes in the windows set into the stonework without disturbing my concentration. Next door in the stable, the hoof-clops of either Sam or Billy, our two mules, sounded dully as they entered the barn to escape the afternoon sun. When this coat of polish was finished, I decided I would pump some cool water and splash a bucket or two over them to provide them relief. They are good animals and deserve the best treatment. Neither complains when I ask it to give its strength. Sometimes it seems that when they see me working to my maximum, they pit their muscles along with mine in a joint operation against whatever task is in front of us. Round and round I rubbed making sure the polish flowed evenly into the wood and that there were no patches darker than any other. It does not require any strength to apply this finish and the job takes on its own rhythm. If I could sing, I would. Instead, I hum and it must sound strangely demented.

There was still a considerable amount of day left after I watered Sam and Billy so I decided to go into town. It was too hot to return to hoeing the field and I wanted to pick up some replacement hinges for the barn door that I ordered from Morgan three weeks ago. He took over the smithy from his father who died a few years ago. Stopping by the house, I told her where I was going and asked Eunice if she would like to come with me. I harnessed one of the mules to the democrat so she could ride comfortably and pick up anything she needed while I collected the hinges and the mail. I was also becoming anxious to hear from the General and did not like the thought of a letter sitting there all week. As Eunice was busy with her own work she declined the invitation.

Sam drew our wagon along at just enough speed to create a breeze making the ride very pleasant. The earth beneath us was hard-packed and baked so Sam's hooves did not raise any dust.

Morgan was not in his shop. I headed to John Edward's store and post office. Morgan was there talking to Edwards. Morgan is a good blacksmith and I was pleased when he told me the hinges were ready and made to leave so he could be in his shop when I went back to pick them up.

"You got another letter from the Office of the Commanding General."

I asked when it arrived. This was Wednesday and we had picked up the mail on Saturday as was our custom.

"Come on the train Monday morning."

"If another comes for me would you send Lincoln with it?"

"We don't normally do that. But if you pay a little something, I'll send it right along."

I was tempted to say that he didn't normally do anything, but held my tongue. My mail could very easily be delayed on its arrival or the letters I sent could go astray. We negotiated a price and it was little enough that I decided to give Lincoln something extra that his father would never know about.

After picking up the hinges I untied Sam from the public trough and we headed back the way we came. Sam was a smart mule and did not need steering. He knew the way home and set off at the same pace we had come into the village at. I held the reins loosely across my lap while I opened the letter and started to read. Occasionally I looked up to find Sam on a true course.

To my astonishment the letter was set in type. I knew a typist had created it but I was only familiar with the new typing machines that it had been written upon from newspaper reports.

Gen. W. T. Sherman,
Commanding General,
United States Army,
Washington, D. C.

Mr. Frederick Douglass Macdonald,
Buxton, Ontario
Canada

Thursday, June 20, 1878

Dear Sergeant Macdonald,
Once again it is with pleasure I address you. I received your first response on Friday, June 14 and your second letter on Tuesday, June 18. It is gratifying to know that you will endeavor to answer Mrs. Lincoln's questions. I now believe I know why Mrs. Lincoln is interested in the private colored soldier's point of view. During her tenure in the White House, Mrs. Lincoln had a colored personal modiste of some repute. If the president's widow lived up to the character she showed General Grant, Admiral Porter and myself she most likely discouraged the society of the women of Washington and found herself with only her family and servants, including the seamstress, as friends and confidants. The seamstress' name was Elizabeth Keckley and, as you are undoubtedly aware, was the author of that questionable book "Behind The Scenes". I am quite sure it is Keckley who has influenced the late president's widow in this quest, but of motive I am not certain.

Your descriptions of the settlements of Buxton and Chatham were both entertaining and informative. I knew large numbers of slaves had escaped north to Canada West, but their situation, once they arrived there, was never described to me nor, I believe, generally made public. It is gratifying to know that they were capable of becoming good citizens and I think Queen Victoria's governors should consider themselves fortunate. Of my personal experience, I know black men made good and some even excellent soldiers. You are as good a case in point as I can think of. So it is not surprising that they profited. I only wish our own country had not gone to the expense of so much blood to discover this fact, which it still has not.

I should inform you at the outset of this letter, that I knew you were a reporter once and that you continued to report on the war. You were so different from the other Contrabands that I had Dodge look into your history. His agents informed me you were still sending back reports to your newspaper in Chatham, but what I read from them was only fact and reported after any actions had occurred so I did not mind.

Now I will tell you what I told Thomas Knox, the scribbler for the New York Herald. "Come with a sword or musket in your hand, prepared to share with us our fate in sunshine and storm, in prosperity and adversity, in plenty and scarcity, and I will welcome you as a brother and associate; but come as you do now, expecting me to ally the reputation and honor of my country and my fellow soldiers with you as the representative of the press which you yourself say makes so slight a difference between truth and falsehood and my answer is Never!"

Frederick, you came and bore the musket and sword. My only question has ever been whether you came as a soldier first or a reporter seeking stories and adventure and posing as a soldier to attain such. Your following behavior convinced me you were always the soldier first.

If it lets you rest easy in my company, I allowed the fiction that I did not know your history. Those scribblers whom I hated were the ones who would have gleefully published battle plans on the eve of a fight simply to sell newspapers all the while ignoring the carnage they created in the name of a free press. I can still think of several of these vermin whom I would cheerfully have shot were I not afraid it would have raised a self-righteous howl from their surviving brethren.

Regardless, you need not fear my condemnation. The people whom we represented had a right to know the truth of the matters at hand.

In your second letter you began to tell me the story of your meeting with John Brown. I am fascinated with the man. I have heard many stories about him over the course of the ensuing years, but have not yet formed a true opinion of him. The only other man I have met who was personally familiar with him was General Lee. Lee's familiarity was simply based on capturing him at Harper's Ferry. What was Brown like? Was he as fiery as the illustrateds made him out to be? Many, including me, believe that his execution was one of the primary causes of the Insurrection and was criminal in itself. I have confidence that you will include as much intelligence about Brown's time in Canada as possible.

As for me, my career in service has taken me down a series of strange roads, but I have managed to maintain my independence from the requirements of the country as the politicians see them.

Right now I am attempting to have our western troops return the Cheyenne, Bannock and Shoshone back onto their reservations. This is like joining combat with General Forrest. The Indians conduct a mobile, cavalry war attacking individual homesteads and wagons heading overland to California. It would be much simpler if they built forts and defended them. The situation, which is now rearing its head, is that of the Bannock and Shoshone. White settlers have let their hogs run wild on the plains belonging to the Indians and these pigs have destroyed much of the root crop the Bannock and Shoshone depend on for winter survival. It looks bleak for the next few years, as sympathetic as I am to the Indians' situation eventually we will prevail.

Much of the past thirteen years have been spent in restructuring our force to accommodate the former rebels. It was President Lincoln's wish that the members of the Confederacy be welcomed back into the Union and that we help them become good citizens. A large part of this has been to integrate their former professional forces with ours. This was much easier than I expected because many of the Confederacy's officers were trained at West Point and had close ties with our Union men.

My real work has come in ensuring that a junction of all offices pertaining to the command of the army be established under the authority of the Commanding General who is responsible only to the Secretary of War and President. President Grant was kind enough to make this official two years ago and things have moved along at a better pace. I sincerely hope President Hayes maintains this stance.

Washington has changed favorably since we first knew it. I do not remember if you ever served there, so I may jump to a conclusion in addressing your familiarity with the city.

The mud-caked streets of the war years have been cleaned and paved over. Substantial buildings have been erected and the city has become a capital worthy of inclusion with the great European cites like London and Paris. This was largely due to the efforts of Alexander R. Shepard who was its second governor.

By bringing the federal politicians to heel on the matter of payment for the city's maintenance, Shepard created a new Washington that encouraged refinement. Social advantages were among the benefits of this new city. Libraries and great collections, with millions of books and artifacts, are starting to rise where students and teachers alike can plough with their eyes and brains. Intellectual conversation and wit now rivals the salons of London. It is fair to say that Washington is taking its rightful place and is a delight to live in. It often saddens me now, to think of how close this great city came to falling into the hands of the Confederacy.

On another subject, as of this writing I have not received any communication from Mrs. Lincoln.

With business pressing, I have not the luxury of writing a broader letter. Before I relinquish this note to the mailbag, Mrs. Sherman, who remembers your name from my letters home during the war, wishes me bid you and your family well.

I look forward to your next letter.

Your old friend,
W.T. Sherman

I looked at the letter once again. Although the text had been created by a typist's machine and the formal signature line read W. T. Sherman, below it, scrawled in ink was the word "Cump" the name by which only his closest friends addressed him.

CHAPTER SIX

July 14, 1878
When I arrived home on Wednesday, Eunice grabbed the letter out of my hands. She wanted to see for herself what the General was writing to me about. We were in the kitchen, she stopped slicing the cucumbers she was preparing for supper and wiped her hands on her Mother Hubbard before she pulled the letter from its envelope. Her face became placid as she read. I could see her eyes working and lips moving, but could not discern what she was thinking. Then after almost five minutes she broke her silence.

"He sends his letters to the printer now?"

"It was written on a typing machine. I've been reading about them in the newspapers. Someone invented a machine that lets you set type directly onto the page without a press. It was introduced in Philadelphia at the Centennial Exposition two years ago."

The Exposition was the first real sign that America was recovering from the Civil War. Dozens of inventions were introduced and it has been inspiring a mood of intellectual adventure in the field of commerce that I think will last into the next century.

"How come it's all written in capital letters?"

"I don't think these machines have small letters. I think you might have to change the type faces on the keys to get a small letter."

"How will children learn to read and write properly if this is all they see?"

Eunice was always looking at the bad side of things. She could always find a reason not to agree with something. I don't remember her being so dismal when we were younger. It's only since the war that she has become like this.

"He doesn't like Elizabeth Keckley because she's a Negro."

"I don't think it's because of that. Look what he has to say about the coloured troops who served in the army and are still serving. He even..."

"What else is he going to say? He wants something from you. That old general is as white as white can be and smart as a fox. He doesn't care about what we did here in Buxton. He doesn't care about what we did during the war. Sherman is just like Grant – a killing machine. Does he even have a family outside a wife?" I know the General has six living children, four daughters and two sons, which he holds in extreme delight.

"Of course..." She was like a locomotive with a full head of steam and a broken relief valve allowing no safe way to let it out except to run at full speed toward its intended destination. And she could not yield the track to me.

"Look what he says about the Indians out west. He intends to kill them. These men are murderers and he is the coldest of the cold. I don't have any particular love for Southerners, but what he did to Atlanta was crueler than anything any overseer could think of. At least slaves were good property to own and a lot of slave holders did not treat their slaves in such a bitter way."

Having served with the General and become close to him in the final days of the war, I could not agree with my wife. I suspected her own history as the cause for her hatred of General Sherman and any lingering memory of the Civil War.

Eunice has not been further south than Boston and does not have a history in the slave world. Before their incumbency in Toronto and the Queen's Bush, her father had been a house slave on a Virginia plantation. When I first met him I could not equate him with the fugitive slaves like our neighbours or my father. Clarence Jordan was a man of manners and pleasingly spoken. How he learned the trade of smithing was a mystery to me until I asked Morgan about it. The transition from refined gentleman's valet to a brawny-armed blacksmith was simple. He had to earn a living and there was little call for servants in the wilderness. Fortunately for him, and the rest of the Jordan family, an elderly smith understanding his plight took him on as an apprentice. Eunice was clearly embarrassed by what she took to be her father's decline in society. That her elder brother learned this trade and inherited the smithy from their father was an additional slander that was difficult for her to overlook at times, but did not come between them.

It wasn't until the war years that Eunice saw and learned what hardship was. Once she graduated from that education, she could never forgive those who inflicted suffering in such a scientific way. She hated white people and it mattered not that they were from Canada, the Union States or the Confederacy. In her view all were responsible for the suffering of slavery and the further suffering brought about by the war. Foremost in this hatred were Generals Grant and Sherman.

"None of those men are any good. All they know how to do is destroy. Look at all the men like Albert who should be home with children and grandchildren instead of rotting in far away ground. Can you tell me why? I can tell you. It's because generals tell them to go out and get themselves killed. You never seen generals getting killed…"

This wasn't true. Generals died everyday in battle. Some by shear bad luck and others from their own hubris. The Confederate generals Stonewall Jackson and Jeb Stuart were two good examples as was McPherson. I saw first hand what a general's employ could be and I believe this was as man-killing a job as any could be, it was just that the time it took to bring on their demise was much longer and more painful than a sudden ball through the brain, but I kept my opinions to myself.

"The only good thing that man is doing is helping Mrs. Lincoln. She needs to know what her husband died for and how he helped us. When she writes to you. I'm going to send her a letter too. That war cost me just as much as it cost you and I have a right to."

Sweat beaded her forehead. The heat of the day had not been lessened by the coming of evening. It was evident that she would not relent and her invective would continue into the night, so I shut myself into my office and attempted to block her rancor from the kitchen by writing in my journal.

During our meal she ceased cursing the General long enough to eat, but started immediately again whilst she washed the dishes. Later that night, I closed the door to my bedroom. I could hear her through the door to hers.

Eunice and I have not been a proper man and wife since the year after our marriage. When no children arrived, she had ceased to share my bed and when I asked her what was wrong, she told me it was not proper to do such things and threatened to 'geld me like a young colt if I approached her again.' Since that time, I have tried to be as good a husband as possible in all other aspects. When it comes to running the farm, the furniture manufactory or the boarding house, we are in accord and have no problems. But in the case of our private pleasures and my husband's rights, there is no accord. If we belonged to another church or lived in another country, divorce might be a solution. Dalton Walker, who served with our armies in India once told me the Mohammedan could sever himself from his wife by proclaiming loudly 'I divorce thee, I divorce thee, I divorce thee' and it would be done. It is not that I wish to divorce Eunice; I have loved her too long. It is just that I miss the warmth of another in my bed and the spectacular intimacy of being the centre of another person's life. I understand now that I was the center of Helen's life and that was the great pleasure of our brief time together. Today, I am sure that feeling was what I have been seeking all along. But, it was spoiled by my adoration of Eunice and I have dreamt of becoming the same thing to Eunice, but that has never come to pass.

I spent the rest of the week working in the tobacco. The heat was killing and usually, I would quit by eleven a.m., then after a soak in the outside tub I would work at the mahogany table until suppertime. I did my best to stay out of Eunice's way, so in the evenings I wrote a long letter to the General telling him what I knew about Brown's time here and where he went from Chatham.

CHAPTER SEVEN

Mr. Frederick Douglass Macdonald,
C/O General Delivery
Buxton, Ontario
Canada

Gen. Wm. T. Sherman,
Commanding General
United States Army
Washington, D.C.   Sunday, July 21, 1878

Dear General Sherman,
I am much relieved to find that our friendship will weather my deceit. I still reel from the audacity of it and can only apologize once again. However, you have set my mind at ease and given me the task of finishing Brown's story, so I shall do my best to accomplish this in a satisfactory manner.

Let me begin by describing Brown as I saw him on that first day. He was about two inches taller than I, making him around six feet tall although he stooped slightly so his true height was hard to judge from a cursory glance. He was also slight of build but strong and with the leathery complexion of a man used to living out of doors. His hair was still a rich chestnut, but with grey invading it while his full beard had already turned snowy. Because of this, I believe the later engravings of him at Harpers Ferry and his trial were accurate. He did indeed have the look and air of a warrior patriarch about him with his sharp nose and dark, searching eyes. Everything about his face was angular. When I looked into his face I registered a physical reaction in my stomach, but a more important testimony to character was that I felt I had opened a gateway into my own soul, which invited him in. For all his hawkish features, his greatest strength was his kindness and civility. To reconcile the Brown I knew with the stories of murder coming out of Kansas and Missouri has been impossible for me. I have no problem in believing that he carried on as a soldier and may have done things in the line of duty that we all have, but this does not make him the evil presence Southerners would have us believe he was. That he was capable of serious martial efforts there can be no doubt and yet he did not wear a dangerous air as a badge like other men of our acquaintance.

The little I know of Harpers Ferry, beyond what was reported in the day's journals, comes from my friend Osborne Anderson who has already been noted in an earlier letter. Osborne was a survivor of that doomed expedition and wrote a detailed pamphlet immediately after his escape describing the events of Oct. 16 and 17th, 1859, and the aftermath. I do not believe this publication was circulated widely in the Republic before the Civil War and it was certainly overshadowed by the events of 1861. In this tract, he denies many of the slanders against the brigade of soldiers under Captain Brown and the coloured population of Harper's Ferry and he contests the belief that the slaveholders were courageous in their defiance of this rebel group.

To the best of my knowledge, Anderson survived not only Harper's Ferry, but the war itself and has been active in advocating for the rights of the freed Contrabands. I have not heard from or seen him since the day he left here in 1859 to join Brown.

From conversations shared by you and I while on campaign and your request for more intelligence I assume you, like me, are becoming more than just one who merely survived these days. I find myself with a need to indenture these small bits of knowledge to the greater events that involved us. Maybe we are still too close to the battlefield or perhaps there are circumstances yet unrevealed that confound me, but I am in no little way becoming a student of all that transpired so I may yet understand the import of what we accomplished. I would not like to see the Union return to a condition of perpetual hate for its black population: yet I fear this shift; especially with the adoption of popular, but ill-informed, versions of the actual events.

One such pernicious challenge to the truth came even before Harper's Ferry. In a subsequent conversation with Dr. Delany, he warned me that Brown was 'unstable' and 'dangerous' to the cause of coloured people: "Have nothing to do with him if you can help it Frederick. I know many of our people are smitten with him, but he will drag us down and he will give ammunition to our enemies who wish to keep us here in bondage upon this continent."

My experience of Brown up to this point did not indicate him to be detrimental to anything but Dr. Delany's reputation. Many people, whom I admired and loved, including my father and Mary Ann Shadd, were ardent supporters of Brown and went out of their way to aid him.

I will return to Harper's Ferry later for it truly was the slow match touched to the powder magazine.

My next encounter with Brown was at the Planet's office. Mary Ann had recommended he seek me out for some business he had in mind. When I arrived one morning in the final weeks of April that year, Brown was in situ waiting for me. He was chatting with Rufus in a cheerful manner and answering questions without dissemblance. Rufus was enjoying Brown's company as much as Brown was enjoying his. They were similar men, both had a true understanding of whom they were and what God had destined them to achieve. Brown and Stephenson were dedicated to improving the future of coloured people and striking down that Southern institution. A pot of tea sat on the corner of Rufus' desk and both men were drinking from flower-decorated, china cups and saucers. It had all the appearances and gentle nature of a garden party. Brown was talking about some cattle he once owned.

"I had been to England on other business and had the opportunity to inspect their stock. They have very good cattle and their breeds are particularly well adapted to the English climes. However, I always felt they were too delicate for northern New York where I lived at the time. At my home in Essex County, I had already endeavored to breed Devon cattle with some hardier stock from Connecticut. The result, by God's good grace, was a herd of prime animals that attracted the attention of buyers from across the entire range of New York, Pennsylvania and Ohio and in 1850 was the talk of the Essex County Fair." Although a modest man, his one vanity seemed to be his ability to work with and judge livestock.

"You won't find exotic stock like that around here,' Rufus said. 'Most of our farms are crop-based and the cattle raised on them are usually Herefords for meat and Jerseys for milking. The British here-abouts are very particular to breeds from the old country."

"They would do well to look at the... Ah! Here he is" Brown turned to address me as I entered the area where Rufus and I, along with several other reporters, kept our desks. It had been a blustery day with a return to colder weather so I still wore my winter coat. I was in the process of doffing it when Brown suggested we stroll to Tecumseh Park.

Rain squalls scudded by as we covered the distance from the office to the park. I was dressed for it as my coat was also a waterproof, but Brown had only a tweed overcoat to protect him. Despite the soaking I could see he refused to let it bother him. In the park we encountered a mixed group of men numbering thirteen. All were aged between twenty and mid-thirty. They were exercising by running. Sudden sprints carried them over the damp lawn singly and, at other times, in groups of twos and fours. One skidded onto his hands and knees after slipping on a residual leaf from the previous autumn. I expected them to break out into laughter, but the potential comedian simply got up, went back to the start and made his run again. A man with a Virginia accent, whom I was introduced to as John Kagi, was ordering and encouraging the group to exert themselves. The Virginian's voice rang across the park and it seemed more of a military rehearsal than a group committed to "... organizing a new Masonic Lodge for coloured men," as Brown put it.

Given Brown's history over the past three years, I accepted this fiction and did not question it because sometimes the further attainment of truth requires discretion of the instant. These men looked no more like prospective Masons than I looked like an Irish priest.

Their activities excited me. I could see earnest purpose in what they were doing and I felt a strong desire to join them. What exactly they were training for, I could not tell, but I knew that whatever it was would be a blow against slavery.

'How strong, Mr. Macdonald, is your belief that slavery is against the laws of God and the natural order of mankind?'

His question caught me by surprise and although he must have had an answer in mind, I was not sure how to respond correctly. Fumbling with my words, I assured him I was '... of the opinion that God could not condone such unjust and inhuman behavior. Although I have never been enslaved, my father was and by a miracle escaped to freedom here in British Canada.'

'Your father is a good man and Mary Ann Shadd thinks you are carved from the same marble. So I am inclined to give you my confidence and ask a favor of you.'

My heart rolled over in my chest and I wanted to agree right away, but one of Absolom's teachings was "... never to agree to something before you know what it is. Only fools make that kind of promise out of love or loyalty. What they don't understand is that the person beseeching the favor does not truly love them and is always seeking an advantage."

Before I could ask the Captain what the favor was, he addressed it. 'You will understand this is in confidence?'

I agreed.

"Before many months pass, I intend to carry our operations from Kansas and Missouri to the rest of the South. Those men you see training have been my most generous supporters. They readily invest and risk their lives to drive Satan's curse from the world. Each one has been wounded or lost a loved one in recent conflicts."

Evidently he did not recall that I was present when he solicited Dr. Delany's support.

"This is nothing new. You have heard this before. But, the action I propose now is to hold a conference here in Chatham or Buxton to garner support and move us beyond idle talk and on to the crusade God has destined us for.

"What I would like you to do, is attend the conference and prepare an independent record of what is said and done by the various members. This corps of men will be the core of God's army,' and he smiled at his play on words. 'I am hoping He will provide me with more men willing to risk the initiative by force of arms. If we have sufficient force, then the local slaves will rise up and join us.

"Dr. Delany has been appointed recording secretary for the conference, but I fear it is possible the minutes may not accurately reflect what is said, particularly if the statements do not concur with beliefs held by a number of local individuals, so a second history will serve us well.

"We will carry our Kansas work to the east before the next election. Nothing is visible in the future to change conditions in the Southern states. President Buchanan has proved he is of little worth and there is no real opposition from the Republican Party. A few men have offered to stand for election, but none of them are inspiring.

"There are several dictates which will determine where we strike. Probably the most important will be the availability of arms for the freed slaves and freemen who join us. Certain parties in the North have offered me a number of Sharps rifles, but there are not enough to arm everyone. We have one thousand pikes being fashioned and they will be ready shortly. But pikes are of limited use against grouped musketry, so we will need to find an arsenal containing rifles, powder and ball. With a reasonable number of arms and divine guidance, I prophesy that we will be able to sweep through the slave states close to the border with the free states and down as far south as South Carolina. Perhaps even Georgia and Alabama. If God grants us success like that, then influencing other slave states to abandon their evil condition will be that much easier.

"We also have a number of confederates who are willing to join us from Pennsylvania, Massachusetts and New York, but our operations must be close enough to the line dividing Slave from Free so they can reach us before the government blocks their entry into the fray by sealing the roads leading south."

Captain Brown was talking about revolution. The action every young man of my acquaintance dreamt of. His words were exciting me and I could not refuse his request to become his historical voice, but I wanted more. I wanted to join Kagi and Brown's sons in battle. My longing to carry a musket extended beyond simply marching with this happy band. For if blood was to be shed in our righteous cause, I wanted mine to mingle with theirs. I told him so.

"Son, a divine vision has come to me in the night in which I saw John Kagi under the water. I do not know what it means, but maybe God has a different purpose for me and my troops. There is every chance our adventure will not succeed and it is best if you are not with us if it does fail. You are still young enough that you would be able to fight again later. For the moment, you will serve me far better by ensuring what was said in these next few weeks is reported accurately and handed over to people who know what to do with it like Rufus or George Brown."

I felt, for a moment, like I was receiving Absolom's kindly counsel.

"If we should survive this effort, I will send you the details and would like you to append them to what you are about to record here as a celebration of God's will and so the world can see how determination can make right prevail.

"Mrs. Shadd and Mr. Stephenson think you are the man to accomplish this. Mr. Stephenson has even offered to house the archive you create. Will you give me your hand on it?"

I could not refuse Old Man Brown anything. General, when I tell you he was the most personable man I had ever met up until that point, it is no exaggeration.

The next few weeks were busy. It was decided that the conference should be held in Chatham so the influx of people would not excite attention. Brown wrote more than one hundred letters to those involved in the movement who might support his methods asking them to make the journey for May eighth. Many responded favourably, but curiously, some declined the summons.

The cold, wet weather persisted through the start of May and a lot of people grumbled about it. I took the opportunity to go to Buxton for a day and looked forward, with a great deal of pleasure, to seeing my parents again. Absolom picked me up at the station and took me home so we could have lunch and visit with my mother. Protected from the weather by the cabin of our buggy, I asked him if he was going to attend the conference. He acknowledged receiving Brown's letter and said he would be there.

Knowing roughly what Brown had in mind, I wondered what my father would make of it. "Brown is proposing a Kansas-style raid into one of the northernmost of the slave-holding states."

"I thought as much."

"Are you in favour?"

"Yes, I am. If I were unencumbered... without a wife and children who still needed me from time-to-time, I would go with him."

"I want to join him, but he won't let me."

"I'm glad he won't."

"But I want to go with him." After a pause to catch my courage, "I'd like you to speak with Captain Brown. I don't need a commission. Becoming a private soldier would be fine with me."

"Frederick, it's not a good idea. There will be shooting and people will be hurt. Anyone with Brown who's wounded will be beyond help and may be abandoned. There will be no mercy shown by the Southerners to those left behind. I'm an old man and if I get killed, then the world isn't losing much. But, you're young and among the first of our people to be educated and have a chance to change the future. You're our new sword and you and the others who have come out of our school here in Buxton will change the world in ways that will take a real hold. It's no good to have you dead in a field or on the end of a rope when there is so much that is more important."

"But why is a white man like Brown battling for us? How does it look if we shirk God's call and skedaddle out of harm's way? How does it look for the whole Negro race? I'd be happy doing whatever is needed and fighting alongside of Brown. If I am shot, then that's God's will. There's so much I can do and my soul hurts from the knowledge that all I do is sit here scribbling..."

"He won't be coming back."

"That's not true." I interrupted. "We don't know that for sure."

"If I am sure of anything, it is that John Brown won't be coming back from wherever he is planning to strike. Frederick, he is setting out to become a martyr. Martha and your godfather feel the same way. I've talked to mother about it and had her write letters to Douglass for me. John Kagi and the others know what will happen on this raid and they have accepted it..."

"As will I," I interrupted.

"But they know the pain and agony that awaits them. They have dispensed this fatal medicine to others in Kansas so they know what it will be like and are willing to die like that. You only dream of what is ahead and cannot see the horrible reality of such miserable death because you've never seen the misery one man can heap on another. Those men will die slowly and without the grand dignity you see in that head of yours. This isn't Wellington's Bush."

"I know all this," but I really did not, "and I will still go."

Absolom's face had kept his own pain at bay from the moment I entered our cart at the station in North Buxton, but now it began to seep into his expression from around the corners of his eyes. It was so much like him to want to bring me home himself. We loved each other with the truthful devotion that exists between a good father and his son. While we spoke, his pain rose like a blush, troubling his features, which wrinkled more with each wave. Then his voice increased in pitch and became more urgent than I had ever heard before.

"You will not go. Haven't I lost enough to that goddamned slave trade?"

He had. An entire family. But I remained insistent and rancorous despite the tortured sweat that broke out on his brow. Looking back now General, I can only hate the pitiless arrogance of youth.

"I will speak to him again... and again... and again, until he accepts me."

Luncheon was ruined by my churlishness. Like a spiritualist, my mother sensed the foul imp that had come between my father and me. She carried on with laying the table and serving the meal, all the while keeping up a cheerful discourse in an effort to bring us back to a happier perspective.

After our meal Absolom excused himself and retired to their bedroom. Once his door had closed, my mother told me that the doctor wanted to admit Absolom to the sanatorium. The pain in his stomach was so bad at times, she told me, that he would cry out. I could not imagine my father so sick. Yet, I had witnessed how completely this illness had overtaken him in the cart. I now felt it had been me who brought his attack on and it hurt to realize that I had been so selfish.

Absolom did not leave the bedroom for the rest of the day. Before I left to return to Chatham, he called for me.

"Please don't go with Brown. Frederick, he is a very good man, but because he is so good he is extremely dangerous. He sees nothing but his own vision and that's why he will create great grief. There will come a time when England and France will influence the South and the Southerners will see the error of their way. Or it may be that, after a time, slavery will no longer be profitable and the plantation owners will abandon it. We may even have to embrace arms to kill them. Whatever happens, something will occur soon and slavery will be gone.

"If it does come to a fight, you must fight, but you must wear the uniform of a regular army. What Brown will propose next week is to enter battle under a black flag with no nation or people behind him. His sentiment is admirable, and he may even be directed by God, but that I doubt. God has not concerned Himself with slavery for nearly four hundred years, why would He suddenly be interested now? Brown has worked himself into a state and the way he sees it, he must now die to give us all absolution. There is no way out for him. Please don't go with him."

I did not answer him. I could not answer him because I could not believe Brown was so destined and I was still determined to go.

As my departure for the train back to Chatham neared, I kissed my mother goodbye and drove our wagon over to Albert's farm and asked him to carry me up to the station then return the democrat to my parents.

A week later fifty men gathered in the First Baptist Church in Chatham. They were a mixture of Negroes and whites, but all were committed to the eradication of slavery. Absolom was among them. The doctor had given him a bottle of laudanum pain killing medicine. Increasingly, over the course of the day, he would excuse himself from the aggregation to seek the privacy of the church's vestibule where he would drink directly from the bottle. When his eyes became luminous with relief, he would return to the assembly and listen intently to the arguments. A healthy Absolom

64

would not have sat back, but would have stated his own convictions and beliefs as to the efficacy of Brown's plans.

Sadly, neither Frederick Douglass nor Harriet Tubman chose to attend. Douglass' later behaviour in the days and hours leading up to the failed insurrection caused me shame, which I would get over. Of Harriet Tubman's courage and spirit I had no doubt and it was her absence that caused the first cracks in my unwavering belief in Brown's ultimate success.

The convention was governed by Jeffersonian principles. After Brown outlined his plans to create a new country by insurgency, where freed slaves and men of good will could live together in democratic and religious harmony, a quiet dropped onto the hall. What remained unspoken, but known to all were his specific plans to invade some locale in a slave state hoping to inspire a rebellion. All around faces registered different emotions, but the two most prevalent were disbelief and fear, and fear far outweighed the disbelief. These men, whom I had admired since birth, were now a bas-relief, stunned into a black tableau marbled by motionless white faces. Aside from Brown's soldiers, fewer than ten showed their support for the idea with gleaming eyes. It was a call they had been waiting for. Among them was Osborne Anderson. My heart would have congealed with disappointment had he not been in favour of such an expedition.

Debate was encouraged. That was one thing General, Captain Brown would listen to what others had to say and if a suggestion was deemed beneficial to the overall plan, it would be adopted no matter who proposed it. Indeed, several amendments to his strategy were created this way.

As Brown spoke and answered questions, I saw Dr. Delany had ceased taking notes. He stared at Brown with unrelieved malevolence but did not speak. Perhaps it was because some gave their tacit approval to the scheme or because, as I suspected then, and still hold the conviction now, Dr. Delany was simply a coward bringing straw arguments to the debate to forestall making a commitment one way or the other. A commitment would require he either reveal or suborn himself to Brown. Either way Delany would lose the prominence he had attained with all of his fanciful schemes. Brown had taken his measure and was correct in asking me to act as a supplementary recorder.

With the basic structure of the plan in place and adopted by the general group of delegates. Brown moved the conference into its second phase. As much as he needed money, he needed men. He told me once that after having been through the bankruptcy courts, "… money no longer holds an allure nor presents a fearful face to me. It is simply a river that flows from one hand to another. Sometimes it dries up and at others it runs in full flood. God controls its ultimate flow and when His plans need irrigation,

He opens the gates and fills the flume."

Brown begged for any young man from either the Negro or white community to join him. At least three fellows I attended school with felt the same way I did. Isaiah Matthew, Edward Nolan and Aaron Highgate all went to Detroit on their way to join Brown's army, but returned to Buxton when they heard he had been captured.

Once the first day of the conference was finished, I asked Brown how long he would stay in Chatham. Kagi and his men would depart later in the week on one of the afternoon trains to Windsor and thence to the United States. Brown had more business to conduct in Ohio and Illinois and would likely be back and forth as time permitted. However, before leaving for America he wanted to see Absolom home and to pay his respects to my mother.

Already there was a change in the air around Chatham. The Negro community had been electrified but divided itself into separate camps over the news. Those who embraced Brown's philosophy: that slavery itself was a war on the slave, and that making war on the slaveholder was not only acceptable, but necessary, were relieved there now seemed to be some forward motion. Dr. Delany's adherents appeared frightened of the prospect of another slave rebellion led, this time, by a white man. After Brown departed for the Michigan border, several people from our church who were friendly toward Helen and I suggested that Dr. Delany could not be trusted to keep the secret of Brown's plans.

In his oratory Captain Brown had described a town much like Harpers Ferry in Virginia. I believe he had already chosen it as an ideal location to carry out his strategy. It answered all the requirements to give the plan its greatest chance of success. The only things he did not reveal were the town's name and when he would carry out his operations. Without this information, Dr. Delany could do very little except raise a general alarm which would then see Brown change his plans.

The following morning was Sunday and we attended services, then departed by train for Buxton. Because Absolom rarely ate anything before noon, his stomach pain did not bother him in the mornings. It seemed only to set in once he ate his noonday meal and grew throughout the remainder of the afternoon. He and Brown sat together and talked about people they knew and what the future would hold if slavery were ever abolished. Brown paid careful attention to Absolom's advice and asked him a great many questions.

Albert met us at the station in North Buxton and it was evident that he was in awe of Captain Brown. He was all, "Yes sir captain. No sir captain." To which Brown answered quickly and positively.

When Brown leaned over and whispered something in Absolom's ear, I saw a small shake of Absolom's head in response. After that Brown was less attentive although he did not ignore Albert completely.

While I helped Albert take the tackle off of our mule in the barn, Absolom and Brown went into the house to warm up. My mother had laid out a massive luncheon on the parlour table. There was roast pork and boiled cabbage, sausages, potatoes, turnip greens, a young tom turkey, gravy, bread, butter, pickles and relishes as well as milk, cold water, coffee, tea and preserved fruit. Before Albert and I were allowed to attack this feast, Brown bade us sit down and bow our heads.

"Heavenly father," he intoned. "We thank thee for our bread this day and we beg that you end the misery so many of our brothers and sisters live in. We also ask that you shine the light of your wisdom on our Southern brethren and open their eyes to their own falsehoods and misdeeds. Recognize, oh Lord, that the warmth and hospitality of this family gives truth to our belief that those of the sable race are no less men than are we who presume to preside over them. Amen."

In the blink of an eye, Brown changed from his role as a man of God to a devout trencherman. He chatted and even flirted childishly with my mother while loading and devouring his plate not once, but twice. Absolom enjoyed watching him eat but picked lightly at his own food. Albert and I hung on his every word and suffered from his teasing. Brown kept feeling the muscle in Albert's arm and telling him that "… now there's an arm to smite down evil doers," which pleased Albert beyond words.

The return train to Chatham that Brown planned to catch did not pass through Buxton until almost ten o'clock in the evening so lunch lasted a long time. After which, he inspected our barn while he and Absolom discussed the coming year's crop, the quality of the ground, the lateness of spring's arrival and cattle. When Absolom took Brown into the village to show him our furniture manufactory, I could tell Absolom was beginning to suffer from his stomach complaint, but his pride still shone through as he showed Brown the furniture he was assembling and the finished work awaiting delivery.

Word flew around the square that Osawatomie Brown was at the factory and soon people who never had occasion to walk through our doors were flooding the workshop, all eager for the chance to shake his hand. Even Eunice stood shyly in the corner trying to hear every sound he uttered. Over an hour passed before we could extricate ourselves from the dozens of area residents who came to our shop.

Albert drove us home again. Even though it was our carriage, he would not surrender the reins to me while Brown was in the car. But at home, Brown asked the Mighty Arm, as Brown now referred to Albert, for some privacy with our family. Albert was crestfallen. Seeing the collapse of his young friend's aspiration to stay as close as possible for as long as possible, Brown suggested that Albert return in two hours so they could visit before Brown needed to be driven to the station. "It will be late when I leave to catch my train Albert, but I would appreciate it if you would drive me. You know the way and are one of the best pilots I have ever had the pleasure of riding with."

Albert almost skipped home through the rainy afternoon.

In the house my mother fretted over Absolom. He was evidently in a great deal of pain, but tried hard not to show it. She made him lie down then placed a pot of tea on the table with three cups and saucers.

"Did the conference go as well as you expected?" Martha began.

"In some ways better and in some ways it did not live up to expectations. We received the support of the delegates, but not as many men volunteered to serve in our expedition as I had hoped."

"It will be difficult to find men who are willing to go against two governments..."

"Two governments?"

"It is bad enough that the South is against emancipation, but the federal government in Washington does not wish to antagonize the South so it is against it as well."

"I never thought of it that way Martha," Brown admitted and urged her to say more.

"You might have a chance if you had the federal government on your side, but they will not choose you. And all those States that prattle on about their God-given state's rights will only ever come together for one thing and that is to defeat you John."

Normally, my mother remained close to her stove and to Absolom supporting him physically and spiritually. I knew she was a staunch abolitionist, but perhaps because of my love and admiration for my father, I could not see that Martha thought long and deep about these things, nor that she had opinions that were her own which she contributed to reinforce or illuminate Absolom's opinions. So her words were a surprise.

Brown listened placidly to her and considered her every point. "When you strike, you will find yourself faced with a new enemy every day until you are defeated and I fear for your safety in your defeat. Each state will declare war on you and put all their treasure into defeating you. Once they do, John, they will not be inclined to show the slightest mercy to you or anyone captured with you."

"Martha, I know this and it does not frighten me. God has a plan for me and He will do as He wishes with me. There is little I can do about this or want to do."

"Then I forbid you to take my son. He is only seventeen and he deserves a chance at life.'" Martha had never forbidden anything that I could remember. All things were negotiable and she usually offered compromise, but not this time.

"I know. Absolom and I have already discussed it.' Absolom and Captain Brown had been so busy forgetting the South and slavery for a few moments that day, that neither had addressed Martha on the subject. I was heartbroken to hear Brown say '... No Martha, I promise he will not join the ranks of my men on this raid."

With that Martha poured more tea and asked about Brown's wife Mary, but I could no longer stand my fate being decided by others. I felt that because I was working and behaving in the manner of a man, I had the right to make my own decisions and said so.

"Please, Captain Brown hear me out. My mother and father worry like all good parents and I would not normally go against their counsel but you can appreciate the condition of the South and how men like you and me must destroy it. I can fire a musket as well as John Kagi and I'm nearly as strong as Albert. If you don't want me to fight, then I can send reports back to Rufus who will distribute them for us. You will need someone whose sole job is to record what we see and do then report on our success. Even if I perform this small thing I will make a difference by taking that job from your hands so they are free to fight."

"Frederick, I will not take you. But I do have other orders for you, which I hope you will accomplish without further discussion. Tomorrow, we are meeting again. Dr. Delany has proven his worth and I need a reliable reporter to write the minutes. I am also going to need someone here in Buxton to continue recruiting for our expedition. I was going to ask Absolom, but you know yourself he is too sick and needs rest. Your father has served God in this and now he must recover. He has asked me to refuse you because he and your mother need you by his side in his illness.

"This I say to you as kindly as possible, you cannot come with us. Kagi and Osborne and I will probably not outlive this raid. We know that. But what we are determined to do is ignite the powder that will start the war to end slavery and you and your friend Albert need to be part of that war and not this pitiful little skirmish. The men who are with me now have seen a great deal and can die happily. Some even wish to die in His service. God grant that we aren't so desperately foolish that we would share our graves with two fine young men like you. For the grave is a lonely place where we all await the redemption and there will be no comfort in the dark of death until that day."

General, Brown's words fell on ears that were deaf, but are now grateful. We know that betrayal began taking place before the conference even convened. I will not accuse Dr. Delany of this. Another named Forbes who purported to support Capt. Brown, and indeed won his confidence, began his campaign to disparage Captain Brown with the so-called Secret Six almost immediately although still pledged to Brown. Fortunately, not much credence was given to Hugh Forbes, and Captain Brown along with his party of men were able to journey to their base on the Kennedy farm with relative ease and safety.

Needless to say General, I was not with them.

I recently had occasion to read General Thomas Jackson's report on the execution of Captain Brown. From the late general's account, Brown's executioners obviously set out to punish him. Southern vindictiveness was not mirrored by the Union in the execution of Mr. Lincoln's murderers. The photographs by Mr. Alexander Gardner show that they were given enough drop to ensure their necks broke cleanly and most likely they felt nothing except the trap falling out from under them. General Jackson's record of Captain Brown's death makes it plain he dropped less than two feet. As we both know, this was not even enough to render the old man unconscious. He must have endured unimaginable agony as the noose slowly did its work. Those who oversaw Brown's murder allowed him to strangle at the end of his rope. Had he known this would be the case, he may not have met death so cheerfully.

John Kagi, as you know, was shot down in the river and his body slid beneath the waves.

There is little more I can tell you. I will now finish this letter and take it to post tomorrow after I finish my work. I hope this finds you and your family well. I was pleased to hear that Mrs. Sherman remembered my name and I would ask that you pass on the best regards of my wife and I.

Your friend and former brother-in-arms,
Frederick

CHAPTER EIGHT

August 2, 1878
Absolom died on the same morning they hanged John Brown. In one stroke I lost the two most profound heroes any man could wish to pattern himself after. Captain Brown was executed in carpet slippers, as though his enemies were simply putting him to bed and did not see the necessity, or dignity of proper shoes. They added a further insult by not removing the rope from around his neck before handing his body over to his wife Mary. This was something I did not know at the time. I learned it later from General Jackson's and other accounts of the execution.

While John Brown was strangling on the gibbet, Absolom died in a dreamlike state of happiness. He had been delirious for six days and all the while his lovely brown eyes beheld some private joy I would never be privy to. I did not know that people who were delirious had moments when they slept and periods when their mind was awake. The physician who attended my dad explained all of this to me by way of preparing me for Absolom's passing. Whenever he was awake Absolom's face lit up with the innocent smile of a child expecting some treat. When the end came, it happened so quietly I was not even aware he had gone. My mother, Martha, had to tell me and I could not bring myself to close his eyes. She did it.

While he held to life, I hoped something divine might happen and my father would recover even though I knew rationally what the end would always be. The moment he died, the defeat of that hope was so certain, it opened a hole in my soul, which has never healed.

Before drifting away, Absolom was wracked by excruciating pain. His agony was only slightly controlled by regular ingestions of laudanum. His clothing was constantly in need of changing because of the sweat pouring off him and his voice had subsided into a croaking whisper.

Helen and I came home to help my mother. We decided to get married the following spring and wanted Absolom to give us his blessing. We accepted that he would not make it through to our wedding and so wanted to share our contentment with him as a parting gift. My romance with Helen eased my sense of unworthiness and disappointment in not being accepted by Brown. But when the news came to Chatham that Brown was to hang, I was the first to see it and am, ashamed to say, relieved at being talked out of going to Harper's Ferry.

Three days after we arrived, Harriet came from Dresden, where she lived with her husband and two children. Two months had passed since she had last seen Absolom and was horrified at how the disease had destroyed his body. He was so emaciated the tips of his hip bones threatened to break through his crepe-like skin. Food only sickened him and I am of the opinion he starved to death.

The four of us took turns bathing and watching over him and providing what little comfort we could. In the mornings before his condition worsened, he would be talkative and told me about his escape from Kentucky. He wanted it written down to make sure his grandchildren and great grandchildren would know what he endured to bring them to Canada. He would have penned it himself, he was well spoken, but he had never learned to write more than his name or use numbers in his carpentry calculations. Nothing pleased me more than taking his dictation.

"Frederick, always remember freedom is the certainty that you and your family have a future and that you have a place in the line of all the generations in your family. Slavery took that away from us and made us niggers. I don't know where in Africa we came from and I don't know how many aunts and uncles or grandparents and great grandparents I have. But from the day I set foot on the deck of the Scone you, your children, Harriet's children and all of our descendents will know absolutely who we are and who they are."

On a sunlit autumn afternoon of the kind we cherish for hunting, ten days before he died, Absolom waited until mother left his bedside then motioned me closer.

"Kill me," he whispered almost unintelligibly.

"I couldn't hear you dad."

"Kill me," forcing it as a whispered exhalation, the words coming with short pauses between them. "Please stop the pain. I can't stand the pain anymore."

Even now my feelings as to why I did not do as he wished drift from reason to reason like a fall leaf caught in a spring freshet. I worried about my soul and how an act of kindness would go against the most important commandment. Now that matters little. Out of true kindness, I did much worse in the war. But the real reason was that Absolom was my anchor in this world. He was the one who kept me from despairing over the lives of the slaves: certainly some of whom were my cousins. Absolom had been my protector from the evil of the world and I was terrified I was not capable of defending myself even though I had personated as a fully-grown man in order to join Brown. I did not want him to go because when he was gone, he would have taken the final days of my childhood with him. My golden memories of childhood, where the world could not and would not harm me, would wash away like that leaf.

And, if it ever came to light that I had somehow been the author of Absolom's passing my mother would exclude me from her life. Her love for the man was predicated on an all-consuming admiration and compassion.

Before marrying Martha, Absolom had been married to Harriet Butler, another slave on the plantation where he was born.

Henry Masterson owned both of them and thought so little of his human stock that when he named Absolom, he chose the wrong name. Only later, when he was speaking with the Reverend Trask from his church, did he realize that he had even named the slave child after the wrong biblical figure. He had confused the prophet Amos with Absalom and Absalom with Absolom.

Masterson's confusion with the bible and its characters beggared his understanding of the ill omen he had bequeathed to his son. The name of the star-crossed third son of David was not viewed favourably among the residents of the slave cabins who knew their bible better than he. Until my dad endeared himself to the main body of the slave population by his sunny disposition and the thoughtful manner most people avoided him. Further south, they would have said he had a gris-gris on him, but there was no equivalent superstition that I know of on the plantations around Louisville.

My white grandfather saw it as his right to use the female slaves on the plantation and never acknowledged the product of these liaisons as his children. I cannot imagine how one could do this, but my grandfather even sold several of my aunts and uncles to other farms in the area and to slave traders. One of these traders, I believe, was General Forrest. If I could have trained my sights on General Forrest, I would have killed him for this and the only pity in it would be that he would never discern the author of his death. In truth, I do not know how many brothers and sisters or half brothers and sisters Absolom had.

The only generous act my grandfather performed for Absolom was training him as a cabinet and fine furniture maker. And this was unintentional. When Absolom was nine years old, grandfather's banker delivered the news that Louisville was suffering a shortage of craftsmen. The banker knew a freed man who, for a fee, would apprentice Absolom. That my father and grandmother would be separated while Absolom was still such an early age was not a consideration. My grandfather only saw the potential of good wages at a time when the farm was failing. Eventually, the benefit of this accidental kindness was passed down to me when Absolom instructed me in the craft.

Although it should be impossible for me not to, I do not hate my grandfather. His attitudes regarding the human beasts supplying his fortunes were not solely his; they were the climate of that day and that society. As greed has forever been the way of the world so I am at my most charitable when I say that all I feel toward him is a desert drained of emotion by the searing sun of the slave years. He was simply one lone man whom I have never met and whose surname is not mine and whose first name I struggle to remember.

That Absolom should choose to abandon his father's name is not surprising. Many fugitives abandoned their slave names once they made it to Canada West. Yet it had nothing to do with being African as Dr. Delany asserted. I doubted if there was one drop of pure African blood in Buxton and by 1860, I believe, it would have been extremely difficult to find a pure African except along the Gulf of Mexico where it was rumored they were still smuggled in. So most of us had white family somewhere.

To celebrate his freedom Absolom chose the clan name of those who helped him. Once he told me he also chose it to recognize that it was not only Africans who had been conquered and he hoped we could succeed in the same way the Macdonalds had when the Highlanders were cleared out of their traditional lands a century before. Eventually he hoped we would be recognized as equals to our white neighbours, but that was going to take hard work and quick intelligence.

Because of his skill as a furniture maker, Absolom's product was in increasing demand around Louisville. Several businessmen who used him to provide elegant finishing in their homes and offices tried to purchase him. One even promised that after ten years in his service Absolom could purchase his freedom as well as that of any of his family. Absolom's father would not hear of it and Absolom continued to embellish the grander houses of Louisville six days out of the week for no recompense except the gratuities happy clients slipped to him without grandfather's knowing. This left little opportunity to meet and court a prospective wife, but somehow he caught the eye of Harriet, for whom my sister is named, and they fell in love.

Harriet was a handsome Christian woman who laughed at his stories and desired the same things he did. Foremost were freedom and the money to purchase it honestly.

With the permission of his father, Absolom and Harriet spoke the vows that would bind them together until '... death or sale' would force them apart. It was safe to conclude Absolom would not be sold off the plantation except in a deep financial crisis when it came down to a choice between keeping the land or the slaves. The true terror was the sale of Harriet. Her value was nowhere near Absolom's and if slaves had to be sold, she would most likely be among the first.

Harriet proved to be extremely fecund and within weeks of their marriage she was pregnant with my half-brother Rueben, who was quickly followed by a sister. Life in the slave quarters was hard at the best of times and many children did not attain the age of one year. The couple's second child died within hours of her birth. Less than a year later Harriet bore another girl, to be named Sally, who was stronger and survived her first ordeals.

The overseer on my grandfather's plantation was responsible for the daily lives and work of the slaves. Among his responsibilities, he was accountable to the "Massah" for the balance of male to female slaves. Robert Butler could count and write a fair hand. The sums he did, he read out loud as he did them. When he tallied the number of men against the women, he did so in one of the slave cabins arrogantly presuming the slaves would either not know what he was up to or that they were so docile they did not care.

Absolom's mother was doing the wash because it was raining outside and listened carefully. She knew what was coming and on the following Sunday told my father.

Every Sunday after that Absolom slipped away into the underbrush on the banks of the Ohio River taking his tools with him. For months he had over-ordered enough cut lumber, when giving his weekly construction requirements to Butler, to build a small rowboat. Butler did not notice anything unusual. Over four successive weeks Absolom secretly built his boat. On the eve of the fifth Sunday when all the other slaves were preparing to enjoy their one day off, Absolom and Harriet took Rueben and Sally and snuck off into the night.

The product of his four weeks work was only in use for an hour, for that was how long it took to row across the river, then it was abandoned. Harriet had sewn a knapsack from scraps of cloth she and my grandmother had horded with which to repair their winter clothes. Into the knapsack Absolom placed Rueben, now four, and Sally who was almost three. They were told it was important to stay quiet and not to cry if they heard any dogs nearby. Absolom rubbed raw, red onion onto their feet and the soles of their shoes then slipped some into their pockets to eliminate their human scent in case hounds were unleashed to track them. Then the family set off, heading upstream, along the bank of the river toward Cincinnati. It was farming country all the way and the moon was nearing its full stage so they could see anyone approaching from as much as a mile away. Twice they scuttled into the brush on the bank of a ditch as mounted horsemen approached. The children followed their instructions perfectly and the danger passed.

August 3, 1878
They travelled north being passed from hand to hand, for nine days until they came to the General Hull Road that traversed the wilderness to a point just west of Sandusky on the Lake Erie shore. There were Indians and

wild animals, swamps and rivers to cross and the night airs associated with low wetlands.

Four nights into the journey, the weather turned unseasonably cold. Absolom dared not risk a fire. He bundled the children up in two of the family's four blankets, then placing Sally and Rueben between he and Harriet, drew the remaining two blankets over top of them. By morning Sally was shaking from the night's cold and Rueben was feverish to the touch. Harriet gave them powdered willow bark she brought from the plantation. It was good for lowering fevers and reducing aches and pains. The medicine worked for Rueben and by noon he was starting to brighten up, but Sally remained quiet all day long. The family settled in for another night. Before going to sleep, Harriet gave Sally another willow bark treatment. The small girl could not stop shivering so Harriet opened her dress and pulled Sally against her breasts and stomach hoping to warm her that way. But, by morning, Sally was no longer breathing and had grown cold.

Tearfully, Harriet whispered that Sally was dead. Crying silently, Absolom cuddled the infant to his chest, kissing her cheeks and forehead. He had no shovel with which to dig the grave, so he scraped out a foot-deep trench with his prized wood slick: a big chisel for shaping joints in barn and house beams.

Indian summer's heat returned and with it so did the mosquitoes. They hovered in cloud-like swarms darting in groups to draw blood from the travellers. Unrelenting, the Ohio forests stretched on and so did the insects and creeks. At a few places where the creeks were too deep, the family deviated from their northward progress until they encountered a ford. As they emerged from one of these crossings, Harriet said she was feeling unwell '... a headache and a small chill.'

By evening of the following day Harriet was suffering from chills so severe they caused her body to arch and buck. Sweat poured off her. When Absolom touched her forehead he knew she was seriously ill and decided to camp to give his wife a chance to recover. Two nights later Harriet joined Sally. Absolom had seen malaria before and knew it was this disease, caused by bad night airs, which claimed Harriet.

Father and son continued another three weeks, often traveling all night and hiding in the underbrush during the day. Absolom carried Rueben most of the way until the pair reached the shore of the biggest lake Absolom had ever seen. He had heard about Lake Erie from white farmers who helped him. When he asked how he would know if his family arrived at the right lake they told him, good naturedly, he '...would know it without doubt.'

Before arriving on the lake's shore in the early morning of the forty-third day of their escape, Absolom noticed the soil becoming sandy and trees becoming scrubbier. The ground cover itself was now comprised of coarser grasses and weeds. The wind carried a deep-throated hiss from beyond a small bluff of dunes directly in the fugitives' path and the bright breeze blew the sand off the top of the dune and into their faces. Holding Rueben's hand, Absolom struggled up the near side of the sand hill with his feet sinking at each step. He lowered his face to keep the flying grit out of his eyes and instructed Rueben to do so as well. Then they were on top of the dune and the white-capped lake stretched out as far as the eye could see. Two schooners were running before the wind as they made their way into a port a few miles to the east of where the pair emerged.

Absolom wished Harriet and Sally had survived the trip, but could not express this aloud. Rueben still did not understand that his mother and sister were lost to him forever and Absolom had no wish to broach the subject until they were absolutely safe.

August 5, 1878

Father and son camped in the dunes inland from the lake. Absolom reasoned that a gentle shoreline with hard-packed sand like the one he saw would be a byway for foot and horse traffic heading to the port. At one point the jingle of an animal's harness woke my father, but it passed by quickly and he was asleep before it was completely out of range.

With morning's first light, Absolom picked up the still sleeping Rueben and trudged toward the port. They had finally run out of food and Absolom hoped he might be able to find some work he could do for food. It was for just this purpose that he had carried his tools with him. They had replaced Rueben and Sally in the knapsack making it easier for Absolom to carry Rueben in his arms.

Sandusky had an air of prosperous commerce about it. There were shops and stores lining the road leading down to the harbour and many of these were freshly painted. Along the harbour there were storage elevators for grain. Seven large ships were tied to the quay in front of them. They were all sailing vessels and two were being loaded. A Negro was wheeling sacks of grain from one of the silos to a ship with three masts. Three other men followed him, each with his own truck and bags. Absolom and Rueben walked back and forth along the dock watching and waiting and hoping not to attract attention. Even though Rueben had lost a considerable amount of weight, Absolom was so starved himself he had a difficult time holding Rueben in his arms so the boy would not wander away.

Absolom recognized this as a place of great danger and all their efforts could end in disaster. Handbills offering rewards for runaway slaves were prominently posted on the walls of some of the stores they passed. Absolom had not seen his own picture, but knew it was advisable not to tarry.

When the Negro loading the ship made his third trip back to the storage elevator he had to stand in line to wait his turn while two other labourers acquired their loads. Absolom, with Rueben cradled sleepily in his arm approached him quietly.

"Can anyone get a job loading ships?"

"You have free man papers?"

"D'you need 'em?"

"Yes suh. Don' even think of talkin' to the boss wit' out 'em"

"I need to get some work. My boy's pretty hungry an' we ain't eaten for two days. I'm a good finish carpenter, but I'll do anythin'."

"No papers, no work." Then very quietly "You a fugitive?"

At the end of his strength and stretched to the limit mentally, Absolom looked the man in the eye then lowered his head and admitted he was. The man reached in his pocket and took out a twenty-five cent piece and gave it to him.

"Go get something to eat. You trying to get to Canada?" Absolom nodded. "Come back in one hour. That's all the loading we got left. I'll talk to the captain an' see if there's anything we can do."

An hour later Absolom placed his son in a small chest provided by the ship's captain. His newfound friend eased the chest onto his barrow and told Absolom to shoulder his tools and follow him.

There was nothing that Absolom could see to indicate the ship was of British registry. He couldn't read the name painted in gold lettering on the black stern. If he could he would have known the ship was *The Stone of Scone* and her homeport was Amherstburg, Canada West. The Stone sat awaiting customs clearance before sailing.

Captain Bruce Macdonald knew the risks he took in bringing Absolom and Rueben aboard, but being a dedicated Presbyterian and a Scot, he was an Abolitionist of the first rank. A struggle with his conscious over duty to the ship's owner and his duty to God might have ensued had he not owned the *Scone* outright. God would have won anyway.

The customs agent was a familiar old face who never looked at anything too closely. On most trips, he did not ask to see the crews' papers and even nodded cordially to Robert Searle, the black deckhand who was author of this conspiracy. Capt. Macdonald placed Absolom and Rueben in the mate's cabin and pre-empted a trip below decks by greeting the customs agent from the wheelhouse with a glass of whiskey. The conversation was cordial and finished quickly. The agent stamped the clearance papers with his seal and bade the captain and his crew a good trip saying that he would see them again in a few weeks.

Once in the broader seaway the ship took the breeze tacking back and forth between two sandy points before rushing into the open lake.

The port lights on the mate's cabin were open and the lake's scent filled the small space. Unlike anything Absolom had ever smelled, it was all at once cool and fresh with a vague, savory perfume that was more herbal than salty. Responding to its call, Absolom stood back from the open porthole and watched as the last of the United States streamed past his view. Before he died he told me he loved his country, but was not sorry to leave it.

Once they were several miles from the Ohio shore, Captain Macdonald sent for Absolom. On entering the tiny wheelhouse Absolom was so overcome that he dropped to his knees and took the captain's hand then pressed it to his face.

"Captain thank you, thank you, thank you. I can't be thankin' you 'nough. My boy and I thanks you with all our hearts."

Embarrassed, Macdonald raised my father from his knees to a bench and, using his own pocket-handkerchief, dried Absolom's tears. "It will be fine. You are safe now friend. Just take a moment and we'll talk."

"It took me longer than a moment," dad told me. For nearly half-an-hour he rested his head on his hands and wept. In the meantime, Captain Macdonald had Searle, who doubled as the ship's cook; prepare a meal for the two refugees. Searle cooked, not because he was a Negro, but because the other sailors had tried their hands and came nigh to poisoning the crew.

When he recovered enough to speak, Absolom stood and looked about him. The shore was now a thin line of green separating the lake from the sky. With the wind out of the north-northwest, the *Scone* tacked, fell off onto a broader reach and loped easily over the five-foot waves heading for the lake's eastern end.

"Are you alright now?"

"Yes suh."

"Robbie will have some food ready shortly. You and your son need to eat."

"Again, thank you suh. I don't know what would've become of us if you didn't help us."

"It's a privilege God has granted the crew of the *Scone*." The captain stopped just long enough to look at the heading the wheelsman was steering. "Do you know anything about Canada?"

"No sir, just that it be free."

"Well, I will take you to Toronto. It's about five days sailing from here if the wind holds. Longer if the wind goes flat. But don't worry we have enough food. To get there we will have to go through the Welland Canal, but that is all located within British territory so you needn't worry.

"Toronto is the biggest city in Upper Canada. There are a goodly number of fugitives and freed men there to help you. Robbie says you are a carpenter?"

"Yes suh. I be a finished carpenter and cabinet maker."

"Good. I can use you, if you don't mind working, and I will pay you for what you do."

For the first time since escaping Kentucky, Absolom and Rueben slept in a bed, free from concern. They slept snuggled like spoons for a full day. Captain Macdonald gave Absolom clothes from the ship's stores, and Searle stitched a rough suit for Rueben from cut-down pants and shirts. The collar was the only thing that did not fit properly and after howling with laughter, Searle removed the offending cloth and fashioned a new cuff for the neck. Within two days, Rueben had developed the roll of a sailor as he walked the deck from bow to stern stopping to watch as the deckhands adjusted the outhauls on the heavy booms or heaved on the throat halyard of the big mainsail's gaff to put more tension into its leading edge. As often as not, they would interrupt their task to ruffle his hair or let him try his hand at some minor job.

August 6, 1878

As the ship steered its course taking it south of Long Point the faithful wind disappeared. Midway through the afternoon and the sky was high and blue. Nothing showed the promise of any breeze despite the fact that Captain Macdonald surveyed the lake in all directions. Absolom continued planning the piece of ash he was shaping as a new tiller for the ship's boat. The old tiller was rotted at its base and any pressure from wind or waves in an emergency would see it split into useless kindling. As he rhythmically followed the wood's grain with his block plane the ship rocked slowly from side-to-side on the lake's oily surface. The sails flapped hungrily without wind to hold them in place. Within minutes Absolom felt his stomach thicken, then convulse and he rushed to the rail. Rueben watched his father, terrified some sickness had come over him and that Absolom would die.

The crew laughed, not unkindly, at Absolom's discomfort. It was a common ailment sailors saw nearly everyday when their vessel had passengers on board. When my dad finished being sick, Sandy Macdonald used a bucket on a rope to haul clean water over the ship's rail so the stricken carpenter could wash his face. My father tried to grin. Captain Macdonald had warned him this might happen, but that it would more likely occur when the weather closed in and the seas rose. Absolom said he wanted to throw himself into the lake just to end the illness.

It took several hours for the queasiness to subside. Meanwhile the Scone continued to bob on the calm lake's surface.

When the sun dropped toward the horizon, it became a huge orange lantern and the crew brought their suppers out on deck to enjoy the beautiful evening. Capt. Macdonald and his Mate sat on a hatch cover chatting with the deckhands. Unlike the navy, it was informal and the men respected each other. They shared stories and recent news from home that arrived in the mail they picked up in Sandusky. Absolom listened without contributing anything until a sailor named Burke asked him to tell his story.

My father was embarrassed by his plantation speech, but he told his tale of the terrible journey as best he could without further dissolving into tears. When he finished, the seven sailors crowded near him on the cargo hatch he and Rueben were sitting on. Some touched him on the back in the way one man will do to another when he wants to share comfort.

"You'll have another family and you've got a strong lad there to take pleasure from for now. Once you get your feet set on the path you'll prosper in ways you never imagined," Sandy said to him.

"You and your brothers are all very kind."

"My brothers? Oh no. These are not my brothers, we're clansmen. We share the same name because we're from the clan Macdonald."

Five of the seven men bore the name Macdonald, and were in fact loosely related, so my father assumed they were born of the same mother. Burke and Searle were the only unrelated crew and Searle often joked about being the black sheep of the clan. 'We've known our share of sorrow too. Nothing like being a slave, but it was hard enough on our grandparents.'

Absolom was not sure he heard the captain correctly. He had heard older slaves, some of those whose parents had been captured in Africa, talking about their tribes and clans. They believed, nay, prayed some mighty clansmen would arrive from Africa to set them free and smite the slaveholders. Mostly, it was the same wishful thinking boys indulge in when they call down the curse of an older brother upon a foe. But now, here was a white man who also claimed to have a clan.

"What is clan Macdonald?"

"Oh. It was the biggest clan in Scotland, but now it seems like most of us are over here. The English kicked us out and took our lands…" offered the captain.

"Aye. The English and their damnable lairds," added his mate. "We fought them with all our might and showed them a thing or two…"

"True enough, but we still lost and here we are now."

Absolom was confused. He did not know the difference between a Scotsman and an Englishman and had never heard a white man talk about defeat either. He didn't think it was possible. White men were powerful and stuck together.

"Were the English clans bigger?"

"Nay." Frowned Sandy. "The English dinna have clans. They were all loyal to their king and fight as one giant army. We were too divided. There were the Lowland Scots and Highland Scots. Then there were all the different clans and they spent their time bickering while some collaborated openly with the English.

"Aye. And before you could ken what was happening, they were on us and made the clearances." It was rare, but Captain Macdonald still had a Jacobite fire burning in his heart. Most Scots in the new world had quietly resigned themselves to making their way in their new life and swearing loyalty to the British crown.

"You see the way a clan is, it's mainly a defensive group of related families. There was no military training for anyone except what they learned at their da's knee. The English all work together and they want one thing: to be the most powerful nation on earth, which they are. The only way they could do that was to get rid of their clans and that they did a thousand years ago." Macdonald wasn't sure if he was right, but it sounded about right and no one here was going to contradict him. The theory fit nicely with how they all felt.

"Once defeated, our parents and grandparents were forced onto coffin ships and sent to Cape Breton and Upper Canada. Great numbers died on the way here. These ships were less crowded, but they weren't much different than the slave ships your people came on."

All of this new information served to confuse my father at first, but he was not as ignorant as the slaveholders thought him to be. Gradually, as he listened to Captain Macdonald, Sandy and the others tell the tales of how their destitute families arrived less than a century before, Absolom began to understand that the white world was not all- powerful and all whites were not treated equally. This new intelligence came as a shock and dad spent a great deal of time on the remainder of the voyage mulling it over and asking questions on points that needed illumination.

The *Scone* lolled for two days before Captain Macdonald saw a roll in the lake from the south foretelling wind that would come from the American shore. For the duration of the calm, Absolom was always on the verge of being sick, but never repeated his visit to the rail. At sunset on the second day, the wind picked up and the crew trimmed the sails to drive the schooner toward the mouth of the Welland Canal at Chippewa on the Niagara River.

Two days after entering the Canal, the *Scone* came to rest in Toronto's

Harbour. In the close confines of Humber Bay, the wind died and a small, wood-fired, steam tug raced up to the ship's side, where money exchanged hands. Then, puffing a mixture of white smoke and condensation, it picked up the towline. The tug, *Alice*, pulled the *Scone* through the Western Gap and into the inner basin of Toronto Harbour. Once the *Scone* was fully into the bay, the *Alice* eased the schooner's bow around in a tight circle so the ship was pointing windward and waited for the *Scone* to set her anchor in the mud. Then the *Alice* scurried off to take another windjammer in tow.

Captain Macdonald sent Absolom and Rueben ashore in the ship's boat with Sandy and Robbie Searle. The quartet walked the two miles to the door of Thornton and Lucy Blackburn where the sailors handed my father and half brother over to the couple who had escaped earlier that year from a plantation only fifteen miles distant from the Masterson estate.

Before leaving the ship, Absolom requested an audience with Captain Macdonald.

"Suh. I cannot tell you what your kindness means to me. I be afraid to ask you this, but you are as good a man as I ever met. Rueben and me will do well if all is as you said, but I do not want to bear the name of my father into this new life. I would like to give my son a name he can be proud of and I can think of no better name than Macdonald. But I don't want to insult you. If you don't want a black man to bear your name I understand..."

"Don't worry. I would be proud to share our name with you and have you and your family as clansmen. All I ask is that you tell me where you are and what you are doing when you can. And, if you need anything I will always be there to help."

The tears welled up in my dad's eyes once again and he took Captain Macdonald's hand and pressed it to his cheek.

Absolom did stay in touch as he made his way through Toronto to the Queen's Bush, then Amherstburg and finally Buxton. As his new life developed, he bore the name Macdonald with pride. His friend and clansman inducted him into the organization that helped fugitives and which we now call the Underground Railroad openly.

Captain Macdonald sent a telegram that he will come to Buxton for my father's funeral and he will bring a piper.

CHAPTER NINE

August 22, 1878

"You've got another letter. This time from Mrs. A. Lincoln. Is that "the",
John Edwards pronounced the article as though it were spelled 'thee',
"Mrs. Lincoln? Abraham Lincoln's widow?" My importance was growing
and in Edwards' estimation it might be worthwhile spending time with me.
Even in our adolescent days we had never been friends. It had occurred to
me more than once that he thought me a fool for enlisting. By his reasoning, slavery and a state's rights to decide on slavery, were of another world
and none of our business in Buxton.

"Probably." And I held out my hand for the letter. He had driven it out
to our farm to deliver it personally instead of sending his son with it. But
more than the money we had agreed upon was involved, he wanted personal confirmation and he wanted to be there when I opened it. He never
took his eyes off of the wax-sealed sheet and his breath grew louder as
though he was having a hard time catching it.

"Thank you," I said as I turned to enter the back door of the house.

"Uh, Frederick, you forgetting the money?"

"Oh. Right. I'll get my purse." I went inside and returned with an old
leather billfold and counted out two of the twenty-five cent shinplasters.

"Thanks." It was not heartfelt.

"I suppose you want to know what was in the letter." Edwards' face shone
with appreciation. This was as close as he was ever likely to get to someone
of import and I felt small denying him this dalliance. I opened the letter
and scanned it quickly.

"She doesn't say much. She just wants to correspond with me about the
coloured troops that fought in the war. She was a supporter of them."

"Does she say how she's doing since the president was murdered?"

"No I'm afraid not. All she wants is a letter from me telling her about my
experiences during the war."

"You going to write to her?"

"Of course I am. It would be impolite not to."

"Well, say hello to her for me..."

"I'll do that." I watched him ride away a happy man.

I peeled the letter open and started to read it again.

From where I stood, I could see Eunice watching me from the corner
of the hen house. She didn't like Edwards and as long as he was here, she
would not venture out. As soon as he had driven back down the lane and
turned out of it onto Wellington Street she emerged from her hiding place.

Mrs. Abraham Lincoln,
Pau, France

Master Sergeant Frederick Douglass Macdonald,
C/O General Delivery
Buxton, Ontario
Canada

Monday, July 1, 1878

Mr. Macdonald,

General Sherman has kindly forwarded your address and assures me you are aware of my needs in attaining more knowledge regarding life in the ranks of our United States Colored Troops during the latter portion of the Civil War.

It is very gracious of you to consent to correspond with me on this subject. So rarely do we cross the stringent lines of our society. If people of my station did this more often, we might find this world to be a kindlier place than we imagine.

Despite this and the General's assurances, I do feel it is important to explain why I have undertaken this quest for understanding when most of my contemporaries would prefer to ignore the existence of any race or position in society other than their own.

Three days hence shall be the Fourth of July. It is not celebrated here in France, but then we do not rejoice in Bastille Day at home and both occasions mark freedom from monarchy. This should be a day of universal celebration and fraternity. I fear this is not the case. From correspondents throughout the heartland of America and reports from my dear country's major cities I discern an escalating amount of hate and disquiet in the South and among the working classes of the North toward those colored people who so recently gave their lives for the preservation of our Union. I have heard, but cannot confirm, that rascal Nathan Bedford Forrest is in his own way fomenting some of this mischief although he denies it in the press. This hate is now directed toward your race but I see it as growing to include Israelites and Catholics. In fact, as some would have it, the valued freedom of the United States is only expressed for those who qualify.

My late husband did not become the president to represent a minority. He did so because he believed in a republic that represents all, and I supported him in this.

I do not know whether you are familiar with my personal story and family background. My birthplace was Lexington, Kentucky, and yes, my family was well off enough to own a number of Negroes. But, I have never personally owned another person, nor have I condoned such possession. Please set your mind at ease that I do not have some purpose reflecting the

Southern view.

Perhaps we should correspond in Latin or Greek. We could even write to each other in French, which I am becoming quite good at. Do you speak and write French Mr. Macdonald? General Sherman assures me you are capable in both classical languages. I am well educated, having attended the Shelby Academy and Madame Mentelle's Boarding School.

The president valued education, as he did not have a surfeit of it himself. He was a dear man and highly, highly intelligent, but sadly undereducated and self-taught. This lack became apparent during his tenure as president and I was oft times his sole trustworthy advisor in matters of policy. Many members of his cabinet were openly antagonistic at best and could be downright treacherous when their personal interests were in conflict with policies that would benefit the country.

In fact, I was the unheralded author of much of the legislation Mr. Lincoln passed to free your people. My dear friends Elizabeth Keckley and Senator Sumner were my own inspirations and counselors in this. Together we guided my husband's hand when he was uncertain of the course he should take.

This may seem strange to you. As a woman born of the Southern elite, one would presume a natural prejudice in these matters. I can assure you that even the loss of members of my family on the side of the Southern Confederacy has not altered my conviction that the Union cause was right and just. For that matter, those who fought for the South under the guise of chivalric obligation may have justly reaped the reward of that style of life and its peculiar institution. I can only agree with dear Elizabeth's thesis that the former slave and dissatisfied freed Negro has value to add to our understanding of the current situation and I find such a premise sufficiently intriguing to investigate it further.

In this way, perhaps we may avoid entirely, or stave off until a solution can be found; the desperate times I fear are coming for your people and my country.

The first of the colored troops I tried to speak with were almost incapable of speaking English and I did not understand them. Colonel Higginson, who was their commander, urged me to listen attentively. Even then I could not understand them. This is how I came to ask our mutual friend General Sherman to find me a capable Negro with true field experience of whom I could ask questions. He speaks very highly of you. You hold a special place in his heart that I have not seen before. The General tells me you live half way between the world of respectable whites and former slaves so you must have some insight into their existence and will be able to frame it properly for me.

I would be grateful if you were to pen a few lines to help me understand why this animus exists.

In my own heart of hearts, I believe it was Stanton and the others who erected the barricade to the rightful evolution of your race by placing their desire to hold power ahead of the needs of the country.

In recent years I have been troubled with aspersion from my own son and others who do not like my opinions or the manner in which I voice them. Because of this, I must be very careful in anything I say until I am absolutely sure of the truth of it.

May God bless and preserve you and your family.

Sincerely
Mrs. Abraham Lincoln

ALL HELL
Book Two

CHAPTER ONE

August 23, 1878

I wrote a brief communication to the General last night informing him a letter from Mrs. Lincoln finally arrived. I sent my note and a copy of her letter earlier today when I arrived in Chatham.

At the same moment I received the letter from Mrs. Lincoln, a telegram arrived from Mrs. Bell about one of our tenants in the boarding house.

Against her recommendation, I asked her to let a room to Josiah Smith, a veteran of the 102nd Michigan who was wounded at Honey Hill. She reported trouble with Smith from the outset and it worsened over the past weeks. I was forced to go to Chatham to deal with the situation.

I caught the morning train and what is normally a short trip, taking no more than one hour, seemed interminable. As usual Eunice was angry. She wanted me to evict Smith saying "He's too much trouble for the money. That boarding house is for us to have the money to enjoy our old age not for him to milk it out of us." By the time she finished, her voice had risen to a near scream and I was glad to get away from her.

He had served our cause and been a good soldier, so I was reluctant to put him out on the street. Life had dealt him a series of hard blows and I felt that if I could do something for him to make his life easier, I would.

The journey was made the more difficult by moving expediently in the heat of the dog days, which are once again upon us. It has been hotter than normal all summer and the weather lies like a heavy woolen blanket across the town. Even the maple leaves look tired, like they are waiting for the first temperate autumn breezes although it means they will die. Neither does the Thames River do much good. It boils along and you can see heat shimmering just above it. When I asked three boys who were swimming if it helped, they said "Not much, but it's the only way to cool off."

Before going to see Mrs. Bell, I stopped by Rufus' office and made arrangements to have lunch with him. He is now the provincial Member of Parliament, spending most of his time in Toronto, but the house is off for the summer and he is in town. I wanted to take the opportunity to discuss the correspondence I was being asked to undertake.

When I arrived at the boarding house, Mrs. Bell met me in the side yard. She is an older woman who, along with her husband, simply walked away from their Maryland master one morning. He was not expecting it and had treated the couple like they were part of the family. Still they wanted control of their own lives.

Richard, Mrs. Bell's husband, tried farming near Buxton but a falling tree in the first season of land clearing pinned him to the ground breaking his left leg and leaving him unable to do heavy farm work. As members of Martha's church, she felt obliged to help and asked me if there was anything I could do to ease their worries. At the time, my pay from the army was lodged in the Canadian Bank of Commerce. I did not want to spend it frivolously as many other former soldiers had, but I had not made up my mind as to where it would be best invested. My banker, Mr. Raymore, advised me to place the funds in real estate saying "Chatham is a concern destined to grow because of its position on the Grand Trunk and the Thames River. We'll be the center from which grain and produce is shipped to Toronto and Windsor. And, I expect that someday a port will be opened at the mouth of the river so we'll have barges loaded here and towed down to the lake to be shipped on to Chicago and New York."

His arguments were plausible and I asked him to undertake a search for a property that would not only grow in value, but would generate enough income to maintain itself and pay the small mortgage I needed to buy it. Ten days after our discussion I received a short note saying he had found a brick boardinghouse on Grand Avenue that would suit my needs. It was more than I thought I could afford, but I decided to discuss it with my mother.

More and more, I was coming to rely upon Martha for advice on financial matters. I was seeing what Absolom had seen in her and it was very strange to go from thinking she was simply the woman who nursed my hurts to someone who had a good sense of business and the tough-mindedness to adhere to the decisions she knew to be right. She cautioned me that I still had an obligation to the farm and the furniture manufactory. "If you are going to undertake this, I think it would be a wise idea to have a dependable agent living on the property to deal with the daily problems that will arise." I believe she already had Mr. and Mrs. Bell in mind when she spoke.

In a fortnight the decision was made and the plan put into action. Mr. and Mrs. Bell were very glad to be offered the post. Mr. Bell was also accepted as a clerk in the town's general store. With the small return from selling their farm, his wages and their share of the boardinghouse income they could live comfortably.

At first they resided in the back of the house occupying a small apartment beside the kitchen, but this proved less than accommodating. Mr. Bell approached me with a plan to add a second story onto the carriage house where we could install an apartment for them. It would not need to be brick like the main and carriage house, but could be frame and hidden under the eaves of the new roof. It was an opportune suggestion because Mr. Raymore had already made it known that a new roof was required for the carriage house. Mr. Bell's perception was very welcome and I knew my investment was in good hands.

Josiah Smith was a tiny gnat of a man. It is hard to believe he had been a soldier unless the observer had been a soldier himself and lived among the stunted coloured men who rushed to arms. Although not tall, I towered over many of the former slaves who had been poorly fed for generations. Lacking good meat, they could not reach their full height. Yet, when you look at the children of Chatham and Buxton, in many cases just one generation removed from bondage, they grow tall and strong and handsome. Smith was a former slave who escaped to the 102nd then chose to come north to Canada.

Today, there is little of the soldier to recommend him. The hair, which has not fallen out, is grey and his bare scalp mottled. His eyes are constantly rheumy and often seep from the corners giving a mournful, sickly look to his lower face that is reinforced by a mouth devoid of all but one tooth. His arrival in Chatham was unannounced. I had no idea he was coming, not having seen him in nearly a dozen years and only having met him briefly when we entered Savannah in the final days of our march to the sea. After he applied for a room I used to seek him out on occasion to ensure he was fairing well. At first, when he arrived, he was employed by the Grand Trunk Railroad to work in their freight warehouses.

This occupation lasted several years, but a fondness for alcohol developed in the army, returned. Smith next labored as the shoeshine man at the Villa Mansion Hotel. He still attended church on Sundays and was reasonably respectable in doing so. Most recently, Smith ceased attending divine services, paying rent and bathing. The drinking had become all consuming and when he could accrue enough alcohol, stayed locked in his room. Mrs. Bell made particular comment on the odor emanating from behind his door, complaining that he had not let her in to change the linen in more than three weeks.

Mrs. Bell was hanging wash on the line when I arrived. Her pride in keeping a clean house was also mine. I was proud our boarders felt they were treated fairly and with courtesy. As a result, there was rarely a vacant room and usually there was a list of young men who desired to live there.

"Mr. Macdonald, something has to be done. The other boarders are starting to complain and Mr. Smith will not come out of his room for any reason."

"When is the last time you spoke with him?"

"Two days ago."

"Are you sure he's alright?"

"I hear him moving behind his door and sometimes talking to himself. Once in a while he yells and curses. It sounds like he's speaking to soldiers."

She finished pegging the last of the white sheets to the line and stooped to pick up her basket.

We entered through the back porch and went into the kitchen. The noon meal for those who took lunch instead of supper, because of their work, was laid out on serving trays. With only a few boarders home during the day the house was churchlike in its quiet. I asked Mrs. Bell to wait in the kitchen while I went up to Smith's room on the third floor. The stairs rumbled as I ascended, echoing in the silence and sounding like an assault rather than a transit from one floor to the next. Each landing giving off the leathery smell of wood soap and wax.

Tapping on Smith's door I wasn't sure what to expect, but I balled my fist without thinking. "Get the hell away from here."

"Joe, it's Fred Macdonald. I need to see you."

"Get the hell out of here. I know you. You goddamned rebel." His voice was thick with shouting.

"Joe. Please. I need to speak with you. Open the door." There was a heavy bang against the door from the inside of the room that caused me to step away from the threshold.

"Get the hell out of here ye Secesh bastard. I'll kill you, you come any closer. Goddamn you." Then, "Musket's loaded and they's four of us here. Come any closer and I blow yer brains out."

I paused momentarily to consider whether he did have a rifle, but decided it was as likely as there being three others in the room with him. I could hear him giving directions to someone, but no responses. That he imagined the company of others worried me. After the crash against the door, there was an icy stream of silence so I tried my master key. An ocean of stench washed over me. Mixed with rotting food and decomposing human sweat was the overriding stink of human excrement. The heat of the day was baking the smell permanently into the walls. The towels from the washstand were smeared in the drying waste from his bowels and were piled in the bowl. Its pitcher was smashed on the floor and the larger shards had just been kicked aside. I built that washstand in our shop as one of five to furnish the rooms in the boardinghouse. Now it was covered in scrapes and burns and pushed half way across the room. I could just see the balding top of Joe's head above it. The left side of the washstand was pushed against the bed and the room's one chair was tight to the right side forming a sort of lunette like the ones we quickly constructed before a battle. As in entrenched positions, the troop's garbage was thrown out in front of the washstand. Among the detritus were empty liquor and Imperial Cough Medicine bottles. The cough medicine was infamous for containing a large volume of alcohol and was a favourite among the town's drinking men when they could not afford proper liquor. The sheets on the bed were wrapped into a stained rat's nest and the mattress was covered in more excrement. Hidden behind one of the towel rack's uprights, taking cover from me as if I had a gun, Smith peered out.

"Y'all get the hell out of here you goddamned rebel. We don' want no truck with ye." And with that he aimed his imaginary gun at me working his finger on the hammer to cock it in preparation to shoot. Then he yelled at the far side of the room. "Enfilade fire" and he flexed his own trigger finger. But there was no report and I did not fall down. Instead, I retreated out the door and down three floors to the kitchen where I sent Mrs. Bell to bring Dr. Abbott.

When he arrived we shook hands in the kitchen and I gave him a brief account of what I had seen so far. Here was the man who had been a personal friend of President Lincoln. He was one of the first Negro doctors ever to graduate on this continent and he distinguished himself throughout the war by running hospitals for both the soldiers and Contrabands. Now, he was here at my bidding to treat one more wounded soldier.

I am the reason Joe came north. When we first met I answered all his questions about Canada that I could and maybe painted a little brighter picture than I should have. Until he met me, the country where Negroes were free was a story whispered only in the darkest corners of slave cabins. It was something to hold on to even if no one knew it existed for sure. Joe couldn't ask enough questions. He had never seen snow and talked about it over and over. I believe he thought snow would be the cleanser to scrub away all the foul oils of the civilization he knew. Joe's questions often concerned themselves with the amount of food you could eat here and how much a man could earn. In exchange, he told me about life on the plantation where he worked. He did not know his parents and he did not know which of the other children he was penned with in his earliest memories were his brothers and sisters. He was not even sure Smith should be his name. I am afraid my prejudices of the time against the white Southerners were all too evident. Joe seized upon these and I believe my views caused him to come north.

"Joe. My name is Dr. Abbott. Are you not feeling well?"

"Get 'way from me goddamn you. I will fire." Joe made another futile attempt to fire his musket. Dr. Abbott, not having seen the heat of battle, was unfamiliar with what Joe was doing when he pumped his ramrod home and worked his thumb and forefinger.

"You need my help Joe. I can make you feel better." With this, Joe started scratching the skin on the side of his face continuing until blood dribbled along the line of his jawbone, all the while cursing us in a scream. In a little while he began brushing at his clothing as if to knock something off.

In a quiet voice, Dr. Abbott suggested I go for help from the Constable. "He's suffering from delirium tremens and could be dangerous to himself or us. Ask the Constable to bring two strong warders from the hospital." But before I made the descent to the first landing in the stairway, I heard Dr. Abbott shouting for me to come back.

Joe was lying sprawled across the dresser he had just knocked over. He was not moving and could have been dead except for a small flutter of his partly opened eyelids. The rest of his eyes had rolled back in his head so only the whites showed and colour was already draining from his flesh. At first I suspected he hit his head on the bed or dresser, but Dr. Abbott disabused me of that notion. "He leapt up and charged at me like he was topping a rampart, then just collapsed. He's in very bad condition. Run for an ambulance and I'll see what I can do while you're gone."

I was away less than half an hour, but when I returned, Dr. Abbott looked at me and shook his head. Joe died ten minutes after I left. Dr. Abbott thought it was a massive stroke.

"Was he like this, even in the army?'

Joe had been a good soldier. Not an exceptional infantryman, but one who could take an order and carry it out. It was only after the war was long finished and he moved away from the United States that he started to display bothersome signs. I thought about this as we waited for the ambulance attendants to wrap his body in a shroud and carry him down the three flights of stairs. On dying, his bowel let go and the fresh smell added to the already horrendous odor of the room. It drove Dr. Abbott and I down the stairs.

Once we entered the kitchen to wait for the stretcher-bearers, Dr. Abbott asked Mrs. Bell to make some tea. He fussed for a moment with his black leather Gladstone then looked at me and said "I'm seeing too many men who endured the war only to break up this late in the day. Friends send me reports from their practices in New York, Baltimore and Boston detailing the same symptoms and sometimes the same results. I am not surprised he died…"

"But what causes it? Surely not the war, not after this long?"

Turning away from me for a moment he oversaw the process of brewing tea after shooing Mrs. Bell out of her own kitchen. "We're not sure. It might have something to do with terror brought on by the artillery fire in some of the big battles or just a build-up of fear finally emerging, but I think not. It's something vastly different, but it does seem to be tied by the war and a man's experiences of it."

"But we know he has been drinking heavily for a while now…"

"Try to think of that as a symptom itself. There are those in the medical profession who believe drunkenness is treatable like a disease and I'm one of them. I just wish I had known Smith was in trouble earlier."

Drinking was a problem during the war, particularly when we were in winter quarters. Once on the move or committed to battle drunkenness quickly abated. No one wanted an inebriate next to him in the line. It was more a problem among the white soldiers. Our coloured troops were committed to the cause because most of them had seen the worst side of humanity and were dedicated to eradicating it. Still it happened. Once I was asked by Colonel Higginson to advise him on the punishment for a Dresden man who was found guilty of being drunk on picket duty. I told the Colonel to '… treat him just like any other soldier. Just because he's black it's no license to behave like a low cur.' He was tied to a tree for a day and a night.

We sat drinking our tea as the ambulance men brought Joe's body down the stairs. Neither Dr. Abbott nor I watched, looking away instead, as they carried him out the front door and down the steps to their waiting trap.

"This happens a lot."

"Is it just to veterans?" He mumbled assent.

"And we don't know what causes it?"

"No. It's a mystery. We're not even sure it's because of the war. A lot of men were affected in the head by what they saw and had to do. Those we understand. But there's an entire group who started reacting after they returned home and are still reacting to their experiences. It seems almost as if it is a delayed case of Soldier's Heart. Sometimes it is not so evident, making life a veritable hell on the person's insides, until, like your friend, it all boils over. We don't know how long it will keep appearing in veterans."

The shock of Joe's sudden death knocked all the questions out of me and I could think of nothing more to ask, but I also suspected he did not have more answers. Dr. Abbott is an honest and thoughtful man as well as being straightforward. After the removal of Smith's body, Dr. Abbott left me sitting alone with the remainder of my tea and my thoughts. He went on to the hospital and I sat there wondering whom I could tell in the United States that Joe had died. There were probably a few former privates who might care that an old friend was gone, but I could not think of any names for them.

Turning this question over in my mind, I sat at the kitchen table until I looked up at the kitchen clock and realized I had missed lunch with Rufus.

I spent a good part of the remaining day arranging to have Joe buried. After that, Mrs. Bell and I stripped his bedding and threw it out. Then, with the aid of a hired girl, slid the mattress down to the ground floor and out into the side yard to await Richard Bell's arrival from work. He would haul it away so it would no longer offend the very air that surrounded it.

Mrs. Bell and I set to work stripping the rest of the room. In an effort to purify it I had the hired girl bring a solution of lye soap and hot water to start washing the walls.

I suppose I should have waited upon some official order to do so before we set about emptying Joe's room. It was not that I wanted to remove him from our lives so quickly, but the stench made cleansing urgent and a kindness to the other boarders. In any case, Joe had not accumulated much. We found no savings or any will to indicate what to do with his few belongings. In the end, we wrapped them up and I took them to the church so they could be distributed to needy members of the congregation.

Once we finished, I stopped by the bank and made arrangements with Mr. Raymore to honour any reasonable bill from the undertaker for Joe's funeral. From there I went to the Planet's offices seeking Rufus, but he had left for another appointment. After quickly penning a note explaining my rude behaviour, I departed to catch the early train knowing that I would return in two days for a funeral at which I was likely to be the only mourner.

Today has been one, which I will not remember fondly. I alighted from the train thinking that it was over and a pleasant walk in the cooler evening air would help to purge it. But it was not to be so. Waiting in the road at the end of the platform was Benjamin with my buggy.

"Climb up and I'll drive you home. There's been some trouble with Eunice."

"What kind of trouble?" He told me how our neighbour, Tom Knox, found her wandering along the concession road in her nightdress. She didn't seem to know where she was or how she got there. Her bare feet were cut from the rough ground. Tom and his wife Bess brought her home and were now waiting there for me.

"She knows where she is now, but she's still confused about things. Bess thinks it might be that she's going through the change. But I don't know about that. Mary is going through it and she gets upset sometimes or she gets really hot at night, but she never forgets nothing."

"Did she look sick any other way?"

"No." Then we fell silent for the rest of the trip.

CHAPTER TWO

August 24, 1878

When I arrived home last night, Tom and Bess were sitting at Absolom's table. They had made a pot of tea and placed a doily under it so the heat would not damage the table's finish. It was an act I appreciated. Two good china teacups and saucers with Eunice's delicate, silver sugar spoons resting alongside accompanied the teapot. The matching creamer and sugar bowl were sitting on a separate doily. Tom rose from his chair and Bess looked up when I entered the kitchen from the mudroom. Tom is five years older than me and already his hair is starting to turn grey. He was wearing a clean shirt with the sleeves rolled up. Below the folds of cloth his bare arms revealed the muscle that is our basic tool as farmers. His hand was outstretched. The severity of the situation demanded more than a casual greeting and he took my hand in a tight grip and shook it up and down twice.

"Benjamin told you?"

"Yes…"

"She's sleeping quietly now," Bess said as I sat down. A substantial woman, Bess had mothered six children and all of them had survived and were attending school. The oldest was almost finished and was planning to be a teacher. The rest were still a ways from graduating. Tom and Bess were prouder of them than they were of the fine farm Tom had chopped out of the hardwood bush just north of town. They were among the most respected families in the community. "She was very upset and it took a long time to get her to sleep."

"What happened?"

"Bess and I were coming up from the lake where we were fishing for yellow perch. From the wagon I saw her squatting in the grass along side the road. Didn't recognize her at first. It was the light colour of her nightgown that caught my eye. It stood out in the dark. She didn't know her name when I called to her. She heard me, but didn't recognize us. Eunice wasn't frightened at first. She came up to the wagon like a child does when they're ready to go home. I wrapped an old lap rug around her and she just sat there quietly.

"Halfway back to the farm here, she asked me what she was doing in my wagon and I knew she was coming out of it.

"When we got here, I sent Bess to get Benjamin to pick you up at the train. We've been here ever since. Eunice seems to be alright now, but I'd get her to Dr. Abbott."

Tom was a good friend and I told him I would take his advice although

I had already made the decision to take her to the doctor as soon as possible. Bess lifted herself off of the chair and brought another teacup from the sideboard for me. We talked quietly for three quarters of an hour before they left for home.

There was a sadness throughout the house, as if someone was about to die and the house knew it. The slow ticking of the clock penetrated the silence reminding me that I needed to go to my room.

Of the six coal oil lamps that normally illuminated the kitchen when Eunice wasn't present, only two had been lit. I blew one out, but bypassed the other because I wanted to look in on Eunice and did not want to stumble against a chair or any other furniture. Like everyone faced with someone sick I believe that uninterrupted sleep and time are the best doctors. When I opened the door to her room Eunice called to me in a weak voice. "Frederick?"

I leaned into the room without actually entering it.

"Oh Frederick. I'm so frightened."

Opening the door fully, I crossed to her bed and put my arms around her. "You're safe now. I'll take you to see Dr. Abbott tomorrow and everything will be alright."

I did not know that everything would be "alright", but I had to say something. When I looked at her face in the gentle light that drifted through the open door, I almost cried. The beautiful eyes of our childhood were puffy and worn from fretting. They roved the room wildly pausing only to stop and stare into my face every so often. I could feel the fear shaking her as I held her close to me. It was like a marrow-penetrating cold. For a second, I wondered if there is an emotional form of consumption, then put the thought out of my head. For a woman who was so strong this was tragic.

We rocked back and forth on the bed for a long time. She would stop every ten or fifteen minutes and push herself away from me. Then she would stare into my eyes and beg me to help her.

"Please don't let me go crazy. I could not stand it... You mustn't leave again. If you do, I don't know what will happen."

Stroking her hair, I assured her I would be there all the time for her. I meant it too. I still loved her with the same heat as when I secretly coveted the attachment she had with Albert. I kissed her face and eyes and was surprised to find her cheeks wet, not from her tears, but from mine.

Eunice looked into my eyes with wonder then put her hand up and brushed the tears from my face. With that she calmed down and her trembling ceased.

I don't know if it was this brief display of affection that brought about the change which allowed her to sleep, but within a few minutes her breathing went from sharp sobs to a slow rhythmic pattern and before long she was slumbering in my arms.

Thus it was that I was able to carefully lay her back onto her pillows and pull the bedclothes over her shoulders. I kissed her goodnight lightly on the forehead.

Had it been any other season, I would have stayed in bed this morning. Instead, I was up before five to continue with the harvest. My day in Chatham yesterday had put us behind and there was still a lot of tobacco to take off. I could see lamplight coming from the spare room in the barn where the two hired men were up and about. They would come to the house for breakfast in a few minutes. Eunice normally cooked it for us, but I let her sleep. After I getting myself dressed, I set about frying meat, cutting up bread and filling the big two-quart coffee pot with water and grounds. I added some egg shells to the coffee because I liked the way the coffee tastes when I do that. Eunice always claimed there was no difference in taste and refused to waste the time.

After limbering the mules to the farm wagon the three of us walked out in the graying light and headed into the east field where the sand priming was almost complete.

By nine-thirty we had half a kiln worth of leaves bundled and stacked on the wagon. Temperatures had broken overnight and, although it was still warm, it wasn't that bitter heat that draws the life out of you. When we took a short break for water and a slice of bread, I left the two men alone to continue their job and headed back to the house to check on Eunice.

At first I could hear only the normal noises of the house. Flies buzzed in the kitchen. The roof grunted rudely as it heated under the ascending sun, but the floor was polite and the only hiccoughs the maple planks made were soft footfalls from my stocking'd feet. Then, like one would sense a ghost who really isn't there, I became aware of Eunice. The door to her room was half-opened like I left it earlier. Looking in on her, I was satisfied she was accumulating the sleep she needed to mend. She lay propped upon her pillows and an old copy of the London Illustrated News had fallen from her hands onto her lap. Her hands were curled slightly inward and the fingers of her right hand wrapped themselves loosely around her thumb in the same way a child would make a fist.

Pulling the door almost closed, I went to the cupboard and took out what was left of a cooked ham and a cucumber. On the cutting board near the sink, I started slicing the cucumbers and putting them on a plate. From the window above our drain board, I could see more than a mile up the road and I watched as an animal carrying a rider turned off the Central Road and onto Wellington heading in our direction.

Ten minutes later, I could make out John Edwards in his dark suit as he joggled about on the back of his mule. I have never seen a more unsuitable horseman than Edwards. My guess is that he has no love for animals and they return the same affection.

There was only one reason Edwards would leave his store to come all the way out here. He carried a letter. The only person it could be from was the General, as my response to Mrs. Lincoln has not had time to reach France. As well as getting paid, I knew Edwards would want to know what the letter said and I supposed a little of its content might be fair currency for his efforts and it will keep him working for, instead of against me.

> W.T. Sherman
> 817-15th St.
> Washington, D.C.

Mr. Frederick Douglass Macdonald,
Buxton, Ontario
Canada

Sunday, 10 August, 1878

Dear Frederick,

Thank you for your last letter. I hope this finds you well. We are all healthy and happy here in Washington. My wife sends you and your wife her best regards and has expressed her interest in meeting your family someday. Hopefully, we will be able to arrange this in the near future.

Mrs. Sherman often complains, and not without cause, that I keep too much to myself and have no confidant, other than her, to express my concerns to. She often suggests I seek out someone who understands the army and role of the soldier. I speak to her about it, but try as she may, she has not the experience or training to comprehend all this entails. Nor do my children. My son Tom knows the army, but he is moving away from it and toward the religious life. As many of my surviving contemporaries in the service have now accepted positions outside of the army and with Grant overseas I have few I can trust to speak to in confidence. Mrs. Sherman tells me, nay commands me, to tell you that she is happy you and I have re-united and she is very correct in this.

Washington has become a snake pit of politicians and would-be politicians masquerading in soldiers' uniforms. There are many who walk the precincts of this department who would make a federal case if they knew I were confiding in a former private soldier and worse, a Negro. I must confess, that with some of the things I have said about your people in the past

I wonder if you even see me as suitable to be your friend.

To avoid being accused of going crazy again, I believe it best that we keep further letters in this correspondence private and in doing so, I will suggest that future letters be directed to my home. Mrs. Sherman has been forewarned to be on picket duty and will advise me of mail from you.

The business of running an army goes on as regular as clockwork. Right now, my most pressing concern is the Western situation. It is a difficult moral problem. When we prosecuted our war with the Confederate States, we were dealing with a heinous group of traitors who put their own profits and property above the good of the Constitution. I can see no wrong in the way I treated Georgia and the Carolinas. For this Lincoln, Grant and I are the most hated men in the South. I am sure that somewhere in a reconstructed city or on a plantation, some mother uses me to frighten her children into behaving. Even this does not bother me, because I did not choose to go to war. It was forced upon me. My only choice in this was how to end it. I simply fired the last shot.

Now, these venal Washington rattlesnakes force me into acts I do not condone in order to keep the hollow promises they make to anyone with as little as an uncommitted vote.

I understand and support the need for the transcontinental rail line. Undoubtedly this is the most important ambition since the ending of the Insurrection. It is with this one thread of steel that we will bind the country together once again and shift the way we view ourselves. Instead of the tired old north and south inclination, we will see ourselves with the east and west being the most important of our perimeters and this will leave us so much the better. It will help in pushing that awful war further into the background of history.

The problem, as I see it, is that there is too much of what the politicians view as empty land between Missouri and California and they want it. In truth, this is not empty. I have ridden through large portions of it and seen who the Indians are and how they have made themselves subjects of the land. I cannot count them as a culture nor their interests more important than our ultimate destiny, but we are not wholly without sin. We believe the land should be suborned to us and we waste great energy in trying to make it so. But, if we were to cease our efforts, the land would revert to its original state in a very short time. The Indians prefer to live off the land without improving it and this drives the politicians crazy and I am an expert on being crazy.

Whenever I speak with them, I can feel their frustration and greed for the land and a growing population. They believe there is security and eventual dominance in numbers. Their idea is to flood the plains with settlers, new immigrants, who are so starved for land they are willing to fight and kill anyone who gets in their way.

I think if we offered a fair deal and stuck to our promises, we would find that in generations, the Cheyenne and Sioux would become as good citizens as many of the Negroes have shown the potential to be. We do not want to see them as future citizens because in doing so, it would deny the myth of empty spaces and uncaring savages that we have cloaked ourselves with.

It has grieved me that I must now encourage the killing off of the Indian's food sources to bring them to heel. By depriving them of their living, I think we can bring them to an accord without coming to complete war.

Phil Sheridan is treating this like a sport. He has been a good soldier and friend. I depend on him, but I see too much enjoyment in his dispatches. He may have become tainted from nearly two decades of continual fighting. Do you remember the respect we had for General Johnson? If you do not respect your enemy, then you cannot make peace with him and often, like in the Custer debacle, this can lead to disastrous results. Custer did not respect Sitting Bull when he should have. We are still filtering through the reports here and all evidence shows that the massacre could have been avoided had Custer shown the respect due to Sitting Bull. It may be the same respect you show a rattlesnake or a grizzly bear, but it is respect nonetheless.

Sitting Bull has become a national villain, yet my own opinion is that his generalship was sound and his duty to his people faultless. I cannot say this in public, but I am glad Sitting Bull has escaped to your country and I may yet greet him warmly one day. For now, my masters dictate that, if I can, I should pursue and kill him. Still, I would like to sit down and talk with him before this happens.

To change topics, have you heard from Mrs. Lincoln? To the best of my knowledge, she is still in France at the address I provided. This need to find out about the colored troops, however, may have been a whim that has since been forgotten. But it at least has been a fortunate whim for the pair of us.

Mrs. Sherman is making noises from the kitchen for our Sunday dinner, so I will bid you a fond goodbye and say only that I look forward to hearing from you.

Best regards
W.T. Sherman
(Signed Cump below)

CHAPTER THREE

August 25, 1878
Seeing General Sherman for the first time it was hard not think of he and McPherson as a modern Achilles and Patroclus. While General Sherman admired and tutored the younger officer, he also cared for him deeply as a friend. After McPherson's death, whenever his name came up, which was rarely because of the sagacity of Sherman's staff officers, it was apparent the General loved this fellow Ohioan very much. I only saw McPherson once, and noted he was a comely man well above six feet by my judgment and with a face lighted by good humour. He was, perhaps, twelve to fifteen years my senior. That's all I can comment on the young general and my observations were made in a moment and before I met General Sherman for the first time. When I met the General he was deep in grief.

For days before I actually arrived, my coming to General Sherman's headquarters was heralded by exchanges of telegraph signals between Generals Dodge, McPherson and Sherman. It was these, the General told me later that caused him to wonder about the "curious nigger" from British Canada.

The summons to meet the General came early on the morning of July 22. I was to attend his headquarters at 10 p.m. At first I thought it was because he did not want to be seen with a nigger that he chose that hour. Only after meeting him several times did I come to understand that Sherman treated with people at all hours of the day and night.

General Dodge sent for me just before eight o'clock that day and personally gave me the order to see the General. It was at that time I had my one glimpse of General McPherson. He was visiting General Dodge to impart orders that directed us to destroy a railway line to our north. By doing so we would deny re-provisioning and reinforcements to the Secessionists defending Atlanta.

The sun was warm and there was no breeze, but it was still not so hot as to make rest uncomfortable. I sought out an oak tree to cook my lunch under. Many of my fellow soldiers resented my presence and more than once I heard the murmured comment that "Niggers were the cause of the war…" and "…there would be no fight if all the niggers got on a boat back to Africa." Still there were a number of men for whom my race did not matter or who were admitted Abolitionists. They shared the dappled shade and my small fire in cheery comradeship.

As with all easy days when there is little but camp duty to attend to, rumors occupied our time. Rumours often proved to be true. The most prominent tale flying around our encampment was that we were no longer fighting General Joseph Johnston, but that we were now facing a determined and ambitious commander named Hood.

General Hood had a fearsome reputation. He, it was said, could not wait to get at us. Those who seemed to know everything before it happened said Hood would attempt to drive us away from Atlanta and back toward Kennesaw then down the slope we fought so hard to conquer. And we would be forced, once again, to fight against the mountain.

Sergeant Albion Chatterton, a native of Dayton, Ohio, and three others shared the fire with me. Albie was neither a religionist abolition man nor one of ardent political fervor. He was the simplest and best of patriots. Hating the Rebels for what they were doing to his country, he gave them no quarter on the battlefield and hoped to give them none at the surrender table. That I was willing to fight for his cause made me his friend. He had also been to Niagara Falls once and crossed the border to take the view from the Canadian side – making him, in his light, an expert on my country.

"If we really are fighting Hood, then look out. He fought at Gettysburg and Chickamauga and was shot up so badly he has to be strapped to his horse every morning and fights all day that way."

There was a round of agreement to this pronouncement. We were ready for a great fight and felt if we could but join the enemy on fair ground we would be in possession of Atlanta in a few days.

Gradually our conversation drifted to the election. Many of the men voiced their approval of the Democratic candidate General McClellan feeling he would treat them as well as he had when he was in charge of the army and that any peace he made with the Rebels would be one that brought honour to the living and fallen alike. Mr. Lincoln receiving the nomination of his party was not unexpected. However, we did not think he stood very much of a chance.

Some men were still cooking their meals when Hood's men made themselves known. At first there was a simple scattering of musket fire to the east of where we sat and we rushed to pick up our guns and battle harness. I was running toward the firing, trying to buckle the straps that held my cartridge box and bayonet. There would be time to attach the long sword to the end of my musket if the situation became so critical that we needed to grapple with the enemy.

As I raced to the entrenchments we had spent the morning digging, the air shrieked with canon fire. Shells tore by overhead to explode near the wagons behind McPherson's camp. By this point we knew the attack was not a demonstration, but in earnest. Within minutes of the artillery opening, we saw emerging from the dense trees a butternut line of battle fronted by color bearers and mounted officers. The line stretched away into the smoke.

Changing my direction I turned toward the works that had recently been abandoned by the enemy. Calling to several privates who looked confused, but were armed, I ordered them to follow and we settled on the near side of the big mounds of dirt and began returning fire.

These works had been prepared by the Confederates before they fled our advance so the slope leading to the crest of the berm from our side was steep and difficult to climb. The other side, which was actually meant to offer protection to the troops using this defensive position, had protected slits through the logs where a sharpshooter could position himself and fire wantonly at the advancing enemy. It had been presumed we would be that enemy. When we first came upon these abandoned fortifications, we intended to reverse the slopes. A company of infantry had been ordered to do this, but Hood's men attacked before it could be accomplished.

Within minutes, more and more of our men joined us on the earthworks. We could not let the enemy develop an envelopment. I noted that a number of soldiers who were now joining me had new Henry repeating rifles and so I sent ten of them to the eastern end of our fort where I feared attack the most and told four to attend the western end. After half an hour I had nearly a full company with me, but no officers. There were two corporals who were not pleased to be taking orders from me.

When one of them refused to answer a command, I pulled two privates aside.

"I have given you a lawful order to take three men to act as sharpshooters and move to the top of our works from where you can best pick out targets. Will you do this?"

"I don't answer to no nigger. Don't care if you got stripes or not. You're nothing but a trained monkey. So go to hell. I'll wait for an officer to take orders from."

"If you do not do this at this moment, I will instruct these men to shoot you."

"You can't..."

I ordered the two privates to train their guns on the corporal. "You have ten seconds to follow my order."

The two privates looked frightened. I unholstered my pistol and pointed it at them. Both knew and I knew, and the corporal knew the outcome would be unpleasant for me if I ordered them to shoot. Still, if I did, the corporal would be dead and not know the difference, so he called to several men and moved to the high point of the works.

What caused me to think of this engagement and meeting that evening with General Sherman was a tintype I received from my sister this week that reminded me of when Helen and the baby died and how those two small deaths changed my life from the course I finally thought it would take.

Harriet sent it to us. The child, maybe eighteen months in age, was the baby girl of Harriet's sister-in-law. Perhaps Harriet just needed someone with whom to share her grief.

I think it is her way of trying to keep Absolom's family together. A daguerreotypist from Petrolia made the picture. His studio name is stamped on the lower right hand corner of the brown leather folder holding the picture. The image shows an infant in sleeping repose. The child is dressed in a white lace gown with flowers surrounding her. The tiny corpse appears so restful that a person unacquainted with the circumstances of her typhoid fever would simply assume she could awaken momentarily to ask mama for a biscuit.

That she sent it to me was unthinkingly cruel. I have never spoken with Harriet about Helen and my son. For a long time I did not know what to say, nor even how I should feel. Helen and the infant, whom I named Absolom, died almost three years to the day after my father. I buried them together next to Absolom in the graveyard near the school.

Taking pictures of the dead is not common practice in our village and I find the procedure inhumane. But, there are those who do find it consoling to be able to look through the window of a gilt frame and see the face of a departed child or wife.

Helen followed our stillborn son's passing within the day from an ailment the doctor could not explain. Burning with fever, she cried in pain throughout the night, but her groans lessened as morning came on until finally they ceased to trouble her altogether.

Martha acted as midwife until the trouble began. My mother stayed by her side trying to ease Helen's pain with every remedy she knew until the doctor she had sent for arrived. Then with nothing left for her to do, she expended her efforts in trying to comfort me.

Death, when it comes within the family is best left to the women. Like most other men I had no skill at that time which would allow me to treat or even comfort a dying family member, but death is no longer a stranger to me because of the war. When Absolom died I sat by the bedside holding his hand and talking to him hoping he could hear me. I watched his eyes become dreamier with each passing moment and I knew that he was loosing the last cords binding him to this world, but I did not want to admit it. As Helen died, I sat in the kitchen of our house drinking tea and waiting for the end while secretly drawing comfort by stroking the top of my father's table.

In the weeks preceding the infant Absolom's arrival, I was excited in ways

I was not prepared for. My pride in siring a child over-rode all other events in my life. Suddenly I felt closer to Harriet than I had since she left home. We were now both adults responsible for families who depended upon us. Of more importance, the coming of my son gave me a fixed place in the line of my family. I would come after Henry Masterson and Absolom Macdonald, but ahead of the new Absolom and those faces yet unknown. How many generations of my clan could not claim as much, I do not know.

I vaguely remember sitting in our kitchen with Mother until Nanny Roberts, who often helped my mother and now assisted the doctor, came out and told me I should go in to be with Helen.

It was somewhere near eight o'clock in the morning when she gently laid her hand on my shoulder.

"There's not much time" Dr. Morton said as we edged past each other in the doorway of the bedroom. "It's best to say goodbye now Frederick."

In the sickroom light filtered through the fine lace curtains my mother kept drawn.

Like the uncertainty of how we will act under fire, we never know how we will react to a dying loved one until we have to sit with them. I sat beside Helen and, placing my hand on hers, told her very softly that the young Absolom was "… as beautiful a boy as she would ever want." And, that she "… would hold him soon."

I could not tell if she heard me, her face was tight and awash in sweat. She made a slight coughing sound and the next moment the strain began to leave. Her face grew calm and the sweat began to dry almost immediately.

There was no measured beat of a clock or other sound in the room to judge the passage of the day. I sat, softly weeping. Whether for ten minutes or an hour, I do not comprehend. I have no memory of again looking into Helen's face until I looked up and saw her now dull eyes partly opened. They startled me at first until I divined it was her death stare. As gently as I could, I lay my fingers upon the lids and eased them down. It was this action that opened the dam I had built to contain my emotions. I cried copiously. I wept for Absolom and for Brown and for Helen and the baby, but I wept most for the emptiness in my soul and was fearful that it would remain that way forever.

With the loss of Helen and the baby, life ground to a halt on the farm. I fed the animals and tended to the simplest chores, but it remained for Albert and Benjamin to rescue me by tilling the stubble under in the fields so they would be ready for the spring planting.

From the start of November until Christmas I read a great deal and visited Rufus in Chatham. On one occasion, at the start of December, I accompanied him to Toronto where we had supper with George Brown. All our talk was about the Civil War in the United States. Brown was of the opinion the northern states would quickly overcome their southern counterparts. But Rufus, an American by birth, felt there would be great bloodshed before Mr. Lincoln could bring it to a conclusion. Not having the same access to informed people as Misters Brown and Stephenson I kept my views to myself.

Privately, I thought the South was a bitter enemy fighting for the thing they prized the most which was their human property. Without it they could not work the fields or transport the cotton to the wharves for shipment. The grand homes and great estates would whither quickly if denied slaves and this was something I could not see the Southerners giving up easily.

What chagrined me most was the determination to keep men of colour out of the Union ranks. If Mr. Lincoln would only allow us to fight, we could provide such overwhelming force that Jefferson Davis and his Confederates would never think about secession again. But I was not that naive. I well recognized the prejudice Americans in the North held against their Negroes. It is safe to say this now with the benefit of history already written, but I felt at the time that with luck there might come a series of setbacks or even disasters at the hands of the Secesh that would cause a great reversal of Northern opinion.

Aboard the train home to Chatham, Rufus and I continued our conversation about the war. He was my best source of intelligence about the Negro situation in the South.

"This is a white man's war," he cautioned me. "Many believe it should be fought exclusively between white men and that emancipation for the slaves will only be a by-product if all else is accomplished first. Even the Abolitionists are fearful of arming the slaves. Vesey and Turner are still fresh in the memories of many people. It will take a dozen more Antietam's and Shiloh's before enough white blood is poured onto the battlefield and the administration comes to its senses. When that happens you will see an outpouring of African manhood the like of which the world has never imagined. And with it will come the demand for rights. The right to be treated as equal; the right to own property; the right to have a voice; and the right to learn to read and write. Those rights frighten white men to the soles their boots. You may want to fight, but I do not believe that the North will allow it. Even if it means losing the entire war."

Mother and I had discussed this eventuality many times since the start of the war. It frightened Helen when we did. She was glad we lived in Canada West where American law held no sway and the opinion of the Crown was of far more importance than a bumpkin's in Washington.

Now the poor girl was gone and I was free to do as I pleased, including going to war.

"This is the time you should go and fight if you still want to and they'll have you. Maybe your name would have been remembered in a poem or song, but it would have been foolish to hang with John Brown. He did not have an army and there was no respect for his men as soldiers. They put ropes around their necks as though they were common murderers. Soon you will be able to wear a uniform and carry a rifle issued to you by a lawful government. Your father would allow it. I would even have trouble stopping him from going himself if he were still alive."

That and Rufus' information settled the question for me.

When we arrived in Chatham on our return from Toronto, I stopped long enough to book passage on a train for Detroit, then went home to make arrangements for my continuing absence. It was my intention to seek information about enlistment in other endeavours so I might be on hand when the Union came to its senses and began recruiting coloured men.

The trip to Detroit was accomplished in less than three days. Try as I might, the only position I could be engaged in was as an officer's body servant. With my colour being pronounced, I could not pass as a white man or even an Indian. I stayed in a black-only boarding house near the river, taking my meals there and growing more frustrated with each passing hour.

One of the men staying at the boarding house, Robert Jerome, told me about a notice he read in the "Weekly Anglo-African" that teachers were being recruited to instruct freed slaves on the Sea Islands along the coast of South Carolina. I had no idea where or what the Sea Islands were, but I was going to make it my business to find out.

Returning to Chatham, I stopped to see Rufus at the Planet's offices. We took down his big gazetteer of maps and scoured the coastline for the Sea Islands. All we could find were Hilton Head, Paris, San Simon and Jekyll Islands along with what appeared to be a host of smaller sandbars pretending to be islands. These barrier islands turned out to be those I was looking for.

Early in the war, thousands of freed slaves made their way to the headquarters of the occupying troops along the coasts of Georgia and South Carolina. They had no means of making a living, nor any hope of an eventual livelihood. They could not read or do sums. Most worked in the rice fields on big plantations that lined the coast. They were in need of teachers who could teach them how to read and write enough to make their way in the new world they were facing. It was already assumed none were going back to their former lives.

"You have every quality they wish for," was Rufus' comment. "You should go. I have a friend who may be able to help."

"I was going to speak with Mary Ann."

"This man can help you much more. He is already in the army and is in great sympathy with the freedman's cause. He's enlisted in the 51st Massachusetts regiment, but he craves more. Already he is lobbying for the commissioning of regiments comprised of freed slaves. And if you doubt his sincerity, I have been acquainted with Thomas Higginson for several years and know for a fact that he is one of the Secret Six who financed John Brown out of his own pocket. If there was ever a man who knows what the pulse is, and should be, it is Higginson."

Rufus left his chair and went to the work desk that had six rows of pigeonholes above it. These contained documents and copy we used to create the newspaper. From four alcoves in the centre of the cabinet he began pulling papers and laying them down, in order, on the writing portion of this desk. Then I saw him do something I had never seen before. He reached into one of the pigeonholes and pressed upon the back panel, whereupon the panel dropped backwards to reveal an opening the width of the four sections. Into this opening his hand disappeared then reappeared holding a bundle of letters.

"You understand that you have not seen these. Their very existence could mean my life if the wrong person was to hear of them. I am watched already by Secessionist agents. They do not dog my every step, but they know who I am and where I go." Then he handed the letters to me and bade me read several. "Start with the last one. That will paint a clear picture of what is happening."

The communications were from several people whose names I did not recognize and at least two that I did. Frederick Douglass and Rufus were in regular correspondence as was Thomas Higginson. It was a Higginson letter that my friend recommended I peruse initially.

I do not remember exactly what it said so I make no attempt to report it verbatim here. The content, however, was fiery. In essence it expressed the theory that elements in the government were attempting to block the recruitment of Negro soldiers because Mr. Lincoln was prepared to sacrifice the freedom and rights of his country's Negroes if he could mend the schism with the South.

This, I think more than anything else, determined me to go south, if not to fight right now, to at least provide the education that was stolen from the slaves. With education, they could never be made slaves again.

It is funny how the mind travels its own road. At the outset of this entry, I wished to describe my first meeting with the General. Now I have found I have written about some of the events that led up to that first meeting, but not the meeting. So like the child's prayer asking the Lord "… if I should die before I wake, I pray the Lord my soul to take," if I should die before I wake, I would like to at least have reported my impression of my General and friend.

On the first day of the fight on the Georgia Railroad line we fought until dark. By mid-afternoon, it was apparent that we had driven the Rebels off although there was still shooting from the line of oaks in front of us. It wasn't safe to raise your head above the top of the earthwork, but at least we did not fear being overrun.

Around two o'clock we were finally joined by Lieutenant Carson. There had been trouble down the line when several companies of Hood's men under Gen. Hardee broke through our lines, but in our position we were well protected and had sufficient men to deter even the most determined attack.

Lieutenant Carson was addressed by the corporal whom I threatened to shoot.

"Lieutenant. That goddamned nigger threatened to shoot me and threatened the two privates who he told to shoot me."

"Why did he do that corporal?"

"I tol' him I weren't goin' to take orders from no nigger."

Turning to me the Lieutenant grinned slightly and asked "Why is this man still alive?"

Dumbfounded I could not say anything. I had not expected support from this quarter.

"Sergeant," he continued. "If I ever hear of you shirking your duty like that again, I will personally tear your chevrons off." Then to the corporal, "This man is your superior. You will treat him as such any time he speaks to you. You should consider yourself lucky I was not here to see the incident. You are going on report and I am recommending that you lose your rank and the privileges which come with it."

All of this was done under the protection of the works.

This was called the Battle of Atlanta. For us it had been hot work, but for others it was much more catastrophic. Sometime shortly after two, rebel pickets shot and killed General McPherson. Most of the men at our position did not hear about it until after six-thirty. By that time I had returned to our bivouac area to prepare for my meeting with General Sherman, although because of the day's fighting I did not expect him to want to see me.

Making my way through the blackness, it took some time to find the General's headquarters. I was afraid I might encounter a stray rebel or worse, meet up with one of our sentries who was nervous enough to shoot first and challenge afterward. This had happened more than once and I anticipated the real possibility of it happening to me.

Reckoning that the safest approach would be the most visible, I reached headquarters by following a road for the last quarter of a mile making no attempts to hide myself or otherwise look suspicious. At the perimeter of the camp a sentry challenged me. When I told him my name and business, he turned slightly and called for his sergeant.

"You're early. Uncle Billy didn't want you here until ten." It was just after nine by my watch. "It hasn't been a good day and you might have to come back tomorrow. Come with me," and he led me into an area bounded by tents and trees.

Pointing at a bench away from the main cluster of tents he told me to sit. "What happened today?" I ventured.

"Didn't you hear? Sharpshooters killed McPherson. Gunned down without warning." This was proved wrong, as details became known. It was eventually discovered that a young rebel named Coleman killed our general. "They brought his body back a few hours ago and Uncle Billy is beside himself."

"Maybe I'd better come back tomorrow?"

"He ordered you here for ten o'clock. He'll see you at ten o'clock. Uncle Billy will tell you if he wants you to come back."

The intelligence that McPherson was killed was like a blow from some strong man. As I recovered from it, I perceived that the camp was quieter than most bivouacs. There were low voices going on all about me, but they were between two or three men at most. Not like the usual camp chatter.

About five minutes to ten, I had just looked at my watch, the sergeant appeared out of the gloom and told me to follow him toward the Howard House where the General's headquarters were established.

At first I did not recognize him. He looked like an older private soldier. He was hatless and dressed in a plaid shirt with a sweater of some sort to protect him from the night air. In his right hand he carried a coffee cup and was accompanied by an officer whom I would come to know as Captain Nichols. As they spoke in voices so low I could not make them out, he kept looking toward one of the tents surrounding the house and which had two sentries mounted at its entrance. When General Sherman drew near unto me I saw his honest face plainly. His red hair did not quite hide a thin patch and it badly needed combing. Unlike many of the other staff officers who hid their faces in masses of manly whiskers, he wore his beard short and it may have been the neatest thing about him. It was wet and I could see that his eyes were abused from crying.

"Thank you, captain. We will speak more about this later." Then to me… "Come and sit with me sergeant. I've been expecting you."

CHAPTER FOUR

September 9, 1878
We finished getting the tobacco off the fields well before the start of the month and I took in some three-dozen melons this morning. With the tobacco in the barn I am no longer anxious about a sudden frost snap running the entire tobacco crop. I still have some greens in the kitchen garden, but if we get a frost it will be no great loss. There are already signs of autumn in the trees with the first spots of colour starting to appear. It will not be long before God applies his paintbrush to our landscape.

This year tobacco is going to be our most profitable crop and I thank the good Lord that ours has been safely in the storage barns for three weeks now. A buyer from Montreal is coming at the end of next week and "The Daily Globe" predicts a good price.

Many people here in the village don't agree with my growing tobacco because smoking or chewing is viewed as a sin. The new Women's Christian Temperance Union can claim most of the village women as members; including Eunice, my mother and sister. I find myself divided on the subject too. I do find that here in Kent County it is mostly the lower classes who use tobacco in public and those are the same people who cannot control themselves in their use of spirits.

During my time in the army, I saw enough drunkenness to last me to the end of my days. Men, who would normally lead a sober, Christian life, debauched themselves in places like Milledgeville and Columbia. Young soldiers who had never been anywhere other than their farms, were on campaign with rougher, older men who gave not a thought to drinking from a whiskey bucket until they could no longer stand. Many women were affronted by these men and those of us who preferred sobriety were virtually powerless to stop these vandals except by drastic means.

During the burning of Columbia, I interrupted two private soldiers from an Indiana regiment who were accosting a young woman in the middle of a street. Fire was raging all about us and I had just left General Sherman who was trying to direct the efforts of officers and enlisted men in their attempts to subdue the conflagration.

Fiddles and accordions were playing drunken airs as men rushed from house to house setting blazes despite the General's orders that only public buildings, cotton and war materials should be ignited. One private was holding the woman while the other was trying to lift her skirts. She was struggling against hands, which had choked the life out of strong soldiers scant months before on the slopes of Kennesaw Mountain and on the road from Atlanta itself. Knocking the attacking private down, I commanded the other to release the girl, but he snarled calling me a "dirty nigger". The soldier whom had momentarily been forced to one knee by my blow was coming up with a dagger in his hand. I drew my pistol and fired it into his face killing him instantly. This caused the other to let the woman go and he ran off down the street. I escorted their distraught victim to what had been her home. It was, by then, a blazing ruin.

She told me she had an aunt outside the town who would take her in, but had no way of reaching her. Realizing it was unsafe for the young woman to remain within the city, I escorted her toward the town borders, but stopped when I discovered an Ursuline convent and left her with the sisters there.

Later, I reported my actions to General Sherman.

"This man was serious in harming the woman?" I confirmed he was. "And you shot him?"

"I did General."

"Good. Very good," was all he had to say.

I have to admit that I have never seen tobacco cause such a strong reaction. If anything, men who smoked a pipe in the evening seemed calmer and less bothered by events. I can see good in that despite what Temperance people claim. This memory, even though I do not indulge in any form of tobacco use, allows me to grow it as a crop.

Tobacco is also extremely profitable and it gives us the money to undertake other adventures. From the profits of the past seasons, I have added a new lumber dry to our barn and been able to invest, as a partner with Benjamin, in a steam-powered, sawmill.

With the bundles of leaves awaiting sale, I now have nothing to worry about except Eunice and she shows good signs that her illness is passing. It took nearly a week for her to recover enough so she could perform her duties around the house.

On Saturday night last, Harriet and her children along with Mother came to visit. So did Morgan. Morgan has the ability to arrive in conjunction with Harriet's appearances causing me to think that maybe my shy brother-in-law is mooning after my sister. Nothing will ever come of it because she is happily married to William and Morgan would never interfere with that. Were she a widow, I would even encourage him, as he is a very good and pleasant man. Still, he likes to be close by her and thinks that we do not notice this schoolboy attention.

The company of so much family was good for Eunice. She brightened up and happily visited with everyone well into the evening. The gathering was so enjoyable that at one point Mother began singing "Oh Come Loud Anthems Let Us Sing" and Eunice feeling more mischievous and spritely replied with "The Banks of the Nile".

I don't know when it was written or who the poet was, but this is an exceptionally beautiful piece of music and it makes me wish I could sing instead of croak. It is a lovely ballad about a girl who dresses as a boy to join her lover in the King's army in Egypt. Eunice's voice rang high and true with the clarity of a perfectly cast bell. As she sang, she drifted and I was gratified to see that she seemed at peace.

When she finished, Morgan added his party piece. It was another ballad that I am partial too. Despite his brawny arms and thick chest, Morgan's voice is more tenor than baritone and his enunciation pure. One of the things I liked about his rendition of "The Scarborough Settler's Lament" was his ability to perfectly mimic the Scots accent. If you closed your eyes, you would mistake him for Captain Macdonald.

Encouraged, but lacking faith in my ability, I rendered our old marching song "John Brown's Body". Smiles broke out and biscuits and tea were offered all around to prevent me from singing more.

Earlier in the week Rev. King commissioned a set of bookcases for his house and another for the school. We met on Tuesday to discuss the project and settled on white oak as a good wood for his personal shelves. It is lovely and formal and not so expensive that it will stress his finances. The shelving for the school required a little more consideration. Oak will stand up to generations of punishment, but it is more expensive than the pine I first suggested. When we considered the cost over the years and the longevity of the oak it seemed only sensible to invest in the better lumber.

Our conversation lasted through the gloaming. At one point, as I walked him to his buggy, he complimented me on the rich smell of the cured tobacco that hangs about our farm at the moment. I believe he might have liked to smoke a pipe in the evening but he could not stand against it and indulge in it at the same time. Tobacco imported from the United States was also expensive, so I ventured the offer of a pound of cured leaf. He declined my gift but I could see it caused him to struggle with his conscious.

'That would be most welcome Frederick, but I'm afraid I must abstain. Still, is there anything I can do in return?'

There was, but I wasn't sure how to ask. Curiosity about Rufus and his part in the War was now consuming me. His mysterious correspondence had been driven from my mind by the grander drama of the war, but since writing about it in this diary, my curiosity has returned and now it consumes me.

Before I inscribe the Reverend's version of Rufus' tale here, I must report receiving three letters in one day this week. One was from General Sherman explaining that he wants me to know about actions occurring at higher levels during the war. These do not come as a surprise given the occasions I was privy too. General Sherman's letter also contained a copy of a letter he received from Mrs. Lincoln. She was very frank. I also received a letter directly from her.

On Thursday morning, I needed a new scythe blade. One of my two hired men struck a rock and broke a blade midway along its length. And so, I saddled Sam and rode into town to Edward's store. My two men were still in the field with one cutting and the other bundling. But that was a poor economy as I should be cutting too and if I did not go quickly I would be paying one of them to be half idle.

After stopping at Morgan's forge where I bought the new blade, I walked over to Edwards' to pick up any mail. Edwards was in a big mood.

"I was just going to come out to see you as soon as I finished sorting the mail," he bellowed happily. "You've got two letters: One from General Sherman and one from Mrs. Lincoln. You must be some important."

All I could say without making myself seem truly self-important was "Not really important John. Mrs. Lincoln is just curious about how black soldiers felt and the General remembered me because I can write a legible hand."

"It must be more than that…"

But I cut him off. "That's all. I swear." Then, I told him a small, white lie, that wasn't quite a lie, about being a writer for the General and being able to remember many of the details of our campaigns.

I opened the letter from Mrs. Lincoln in front of the postmaster and slipped the General's into my shirt pocket.

"Not much here John. She thinks I should make the acquaintance of a Dr. Abbott whom she believes is living in Chatham."

"Our Dr. Abbott? She knows him too? How did she get to know so many coloured people? I mean she was Mr. Lincoln's wife and they were not the kind to keep company with slaves and coloured people."

"I think Mr. Lincoln did. Dr. Abbott told me once that he used to slip away from the president's mansion late at night to go down to the camp at Iowa Circle where the freed men stayed and Mr. Lincoln would talk to them and listen to them sing. Sometimes, he would even join in the singing. There never was and never again will be a president like him."

"They must have been good friends for Mr. Lincoln to let him find that out."

"I believe they were. After the president was slain, Mrs. Lincoln gave Dr. Abbott a shawl that Mr. Lincoln wore when he was inaugurated. Something like that is pretty important. You do not give it to a passerby. I think Dr. Abbott must have done something special for the president to have received such a generous gift."

"Do you think Dr. Abbott was the president's doctor?"

"No. As much as he liked coloured people, Mr. Lincoln was not a fool. He knew the voters would not stand for a Negro doctor treating him. Dr. Abbott would have cost the president the election in 1864 and may even have got him assassinated earlier."

"I would like to know what that is all about. It seems there was a lot more going on around here than any of us ever heard about. Hey… you haven't even told me what you did in the war."

"There is not much to tell." Then I added, "honestly John. I joined the First Carolina Volunteers under Colonel Higginson then was sent to serve under General Sherman because he needed a coloured man who could write and had enough education to deal with the thousands of slaves who were running away from their plantations."

"If that is all, how did you get that scar on your face?"

"I did not say I did not fight. This came from the Kennesaw Mountain battle. A Secesh hit me in the face with the butt of his gun just as a canon shell exploded near me and a piece of it cut my cheek. I was knocked down and lay insensible for the duration of the battle. When I recovered, I discovered my friend, Albie Chatterton, killed the man who struck me before he could bayonet me.

"That is about the most exciting thing that happened to me during the entire war. Our march on Georgia was like a quiet stroll by comparison."

Edwards was satisfied with my explanation. It obviously gave him great pleasure that I shared this correspondence with him. The suggestion that I find Dr. Abbott and my views on Mr. Lincoln's friendship with coloured people would quickly fly around the village and I would not be surprised to find it known in Chatham after a day or two.

Leaving the store with my new scythe blade, I mounted Sam and turned him toward home. While he shuffled through the dust, I opened the General's letter. Sharing Mrs. Lincoln with Edwards does not bother me, but I like to keep the General's correspondence to myself, savouring our friendship for several days before sharing it with anyone else.

W. T. Sherman,
817-15th St.
Washington, D. C.

Mr. Frederick Douglass Macdonald,
C/O General Delivery,
Buxton, Ontario
Canada

August 24, 1878

Dear Frederick,

This will, of necessity, be a short note. I received the following letter from Mrs. Lincoln this morning and thought you should be apprised of its content.

It is very difficult for men in the ranks to know all that affects them. As leaders, we are often forced to keep intelligence confidential. With the war firmly resolved these things are part of its general history and I see no reason to keep them from you any longer.

Even though you were attached to my headquarters throughout the Georgia and Carolinas campaigns, there was information I kept strictly to myself. Some of it, you may already have apprehended. Much should have become evident to you on the night the courier found us after our departure from Savannah.

Mrs. Lincoln never disclosed her feelings and knowledge to me before. Its content convinces me she was more than merely the late president's wife and I hope to encourage her to impart those things she was privy to whilst a resident of the presidential mansion.

I will be away on an inspection trip for ten days beginning tomorrow morning and hope to write to both you and Mrs. Lincoln in more detail upon my return. General Dodge will be accompanying me and he was delighted to hear you and I had renewed our friendship. He sends his fondest regards, as do I.

Your friend,
W.T. Sherman
(Also signed Cump by his hand)

Mrs. Abraham Lincoln,
Pau, France

W. T. Sherman,
817-15th St.
Washington, D.C.

July 25, 1878

Dearest General Sherman,

I have received the correspondence of our friend Macdonald. His letter was well stated and his cursive hand beautiful. I believe he could be the man who finally sheds some light for me on the unrecorded of the Freedmen's army.

There is little time left, my dear General, for us who were present to confess all that we know and to let history make its own judgments.

Before I can no longer offer my heartfelt thanks for your services to my husband and our country, I will do so now.

You were one of the few who supported my husband in the dark days of loss. And, I lay all glory at your feet for turning the tide of that terrible conflict. I know from reading various accounts of your battles after Chattanooga that you attempted to conduct your campaigns with as little loss of life as possible. Still, there was a great waste of men in the war, particularly in the Army of the Potomac, and I cannot forgive McClellan, Burnside, Hooker or Grant for their arrogant incompetence.

General Lee must share in that blame. Had he not been so competent at destroying our armies, the insurrection would never have reached as far, nor as profoundly, as it did.

I consider these men legion with the traitors within the Union Party. However, those generals pale in comparison to those Republicans who sought to undermine and defeat Mr. Lincoln. Of these that humbug Stanton was the worst.

Stanton actively plotted against my husband all the while he pretended to be his friend. I cannot account for the nights that Stanton and my husband spent in close conversation at the Soldiers' Home or in the telegraph room of the War Office at the White House. And all the time Stanton was secretly looking for a candidate to run against us at the Baltimore convention.

I know Stanton attempted to steal you away from Mr. Lincoln's cause. But as it turned out, we had well-found faith in our general.

At least Stanton stood for the war and he was not as perfidious as the Democrats and that rank traitor Vallandigham. He should have been hung the moment he left his refuge in British Canada and returned to the United States. Simply the act of referring to Mr. Lincoln as 'King Lincoln' should have been enough to convict him of treason. Luckily for Mr. Vallandigham, my husband's murder overshadowed all other concerns and he slunk off into the night and avoided the justice due to him.

Canada was a haven for those scurrilous Copperheads not to mention Confederate agents. Is there nothing we can do to pay that upstart country back?

I am afraid General, that if I continue in this vein and do not close off, I will have some form of fit.

As, and if, my correspondence develops with Sergeant Macdonald I will keep you informed of its progress. Please accept again my gratitude for the introduction to Sergeant Macdonald and for your services to our country.

With appreciation
Mrs. Abraham Lincoln

The second letter came as a slight surprise.

Mrs. Abraham Lincoln,
Pau, France

Mr. Frederick D. Macdonald
C/O General Delivery
Buxton, Ontario
Canada

August 2, 1878

Dear Sergeant Macdonald,

Forgive the abruptness of this letter, but it has just occurred to me that you should make the acquaintance of another Negro from Canada. Dr. Anderson Abbott was a friend of my husband.

We first met Dr. Abbott in the early stages of the Insurrection. He volunteered to treat our wounded troops, but was rebuffed because he was colored and it was felt that many white soldiers would refuse his care. He told Senator Sumner that as a surgeon he was qualified to cut into any man who needed his help.

I immediately liked Dr. Abbott and so did my husband. He is intelligent and a very handsome man. When he visited us at the White House and Soldier's Home, he cut a very dashing figure having the perfect silhouette for well-tailored clothes. I believe Elizabeth Keckley may have been willing to engage with him had she not already been married. Fortunately her excellent sense of propriety stood her in good stead and nothing untoward ever occurred despite the fact that she had not seen Mr. Keckley in nearly ten years.

A compromise was eventually found for Dr. Abbott although I presume his pride was hurt by it. He was employed in the Contraband Hospital at Camp Baker, then with the Freedman's Hospital. He proved so adept that he was placed in charge of a hospital in Arlington until the end of the war. He treated both the poor souls who shirked off the chains of bondage as soon as our troops drew near to their plantations and was also responsible for saving the lives of many of our fine colored soldiers who suffered misfortune in battle.

I saw him once after the president died, but several years afterward I had the pleasure of presenting him with the shawl Mr. Lincoln wore to his first inauguration. My gratitude for his kindness to me, and my family, is overwhelming. If you do meet him, please give him my respects and ask that he write me at this address.

He was originally from the Toronto area, but may have moved to your community to be closer to the border.

The services he performed for Mr. Lincoln were extensive. The main thing was that he provided my husband with intelligence he discerned while treating the Freedmen. They were more aware of the plans of their masters than their masters chose to give them credit for and they were far superior to our white agents although I don't mean that to take away from their bravery. Too many met unfortunate ends in the service of the North.

In those dark hours and days after the president was killed emotion swept constantly over me. Yet, Dr. Abbott paid particular attention to visit me and, with Mrs. Keckley, helped me organize my departure from the presidential home. I was conscious of the kindly Dr. Abbott quietly doing his job for me and my family. I have come to believe he even slowed Stanton's plans to rid Washington of me.

He is a very good and kind man. Please inform me if you encounter Dr. Abbott.

Sincerely
Mrs. A. Lincoln

CHAPTER FIVE

September 15, 1878
I was vaguely aware Rufus immigrated to Canada West from somewhere in the northern States in the late 1840s or early 1850s. He only recently told me he arrived in St. Catharines as a child and a decade later, at the start of the 1850s began work as a printer.

A fortnight ago, Rev. King told me what he knew of Rufus' activities during the War. It was not the complete story.

Although the official act of war took place in the dim April hours of 1861, war truly began with John Brown two years before. When Mr. Lincoln was elected in the fall 1860 South Carolina military cadets wasted no time in firing shells on Union ships passing up the harbour leading to Charleston. On January 9 of the New Year, they fired their artillery at the Star of the West. Father Abraham must have been very willing to give the South an ear, as most of the men I served with and fought against would not have been so lenient had a battery opened on us. It seemed to me the Secesh were taunting the North. And as Christmas of 1860 approached, the bell they came to call Secessia began to toll the list of those States who so chose to depart. For South Carolina, that first state alone, we would have laid siege to Hell. But little did anyone realize during the holiday season the opening month of 1861 would herald the coming bitterness with Alabama, Florida, Georgia, Louisiana and Mississippi choosing to depart.

The news came to us in Buxton, as it did to all the continent, arriving at first by railroad dispatch and then with more information offered in the newspapers that followed. I could see fear in Helen's eyes at supper on that first night of the war. She knew there was an ache in my heart to join the fight. What she did not comprehend was that I was torn by my responsibility to she and the child we expected and the fight against slavery.

From the moment I began my employment with Rufus, he made it plain he was my friend. My race was no barrier for him. Many of the American Abolitionists did not care for the Negro as an individual or even the race; they simply abhorred slavery as an institution. This caused me to think initially that he was born Canadian or in the home country and not, as rumor had it, in the American colonies.

Rufus took the knowledge I gained through my apprenticeship at the Provincial Freeman with Mary Ann and sharpened it until I became an effective reporter. His manner of doing so was efficient. If my mistakes required strong chastisement, Rufus was capable of it. But this was rare. Most of the time he was patient, showing me new approaches and ways to consider things. He introduced me to books beyond "The Bible" and "The

Pilgrim's Progress From This World To That Which Is To Come". He gave me Longfellow's "Evangeline" and those works of Mr. Charles Dickens that had been converted from monthly serializations into bound books. I particularly liked "Little Dorrit" because it did not quail with politeness and it attacked the debtors' prison system, which in all views, was another form of slavery.

I devoured these books and borrowed more from him or ordered my own copies from Toronto and Montreal. Montreal, being more established, had better booksellers. Rufus was correct in thinking they would improve my skills as a writer. I began to enjoy using the language and learned to look upon it as a tool in the same way a mechanic or blacksmith would his array of wrenches and hammers. They also changed my views of the world. Despite having grown up a strong monarchist, I saw beyond my loyalty to our Queen and into the workings of Parliament. We maintained a subscription to "The Times of London" and once or twice a month, bundles of this wonderful newspaper would arrive by train after crossing the Atlantic. Then Rufus and I would read each broadsheet, scouring it carefully for words from Palmerston and news from other points in the Empire and the broader world not under the Crown.

"There were rumors about Mr. Stephenson almost from the time he arrived here to take over the Planet." Rev. King eased into the meat of what he knew. "They were not harmful in anyway, but they did make it clear on what side of the slavery argument he stood. We would have liked to know more, but Mr. Stephenson is a very private man."

I had not found him so. He was highly intelligent and spoke with me at great lengths about any topic that caught his interest.

"His son Sydney is much more open about matters, but then the issue of slavery has been settled and many people no longer wish to discuss it," was Reverend King's opinion.

Sydney Stephenson, who is younger than I by fourteen years, has recently stepped into his father's shoes to take over the Chatham Weekly Planet. He has printer's ink in his veins and I think he will steer the ship on a safe course.

This is a year of change, we have a new Governor General and it looks like Sir John will return for another term as Prime Minister. Rufus and Sydney are Conservatives and both have been publicly campaigning for Macdonald in the press and on the speaking circuit throughout Raleigh Township and Kent County. People are mad for the transcontinental railway and Sir John has promised them a railroad to unite the Dominion from the Atlantic all the way to the Pacific.

Rufus has been made the Party Whip and represents us well in Ottawa.

Because of his father's political connections Sydney will find no opposition to any business plans he has. As much as I like his father, I find Sydney coldly aggressive in his ambitions.

"There is a story that circulated while you were away in the war. If it is to be believed, Mr. Stephenson operated some sort of spy operation against the Secessionists and Democrats operating in Windsor and St. Catharines.

"They say he was the agent that foiled the Philo Parsons pirates and was Lincoln's eye on Vallandigham. He has never said as much to me, but I suspect there is some truth in it."

I had only heard of the Philo Parsons incident during the war through a letter written by Mother. It was the first letter I received from her since leaving Port Royal and it was franked in Detroit, which probably accounts for my receiving it less than two weeks after it was posted. In it she outlined the bare bones of the event.

While we were resting at East Point following the taking of Atlanta, Secesh agents at Malden on the British side of the Detroit River were performing unscrupulous deeds.

On the morning of September 19, a signal was put up at Malden for the ferry that runs between Detroit and Sandusky to stop for passengers. This is not an unusual occurrence even today because of the amount of commerce between our two countries. The side-wheel Philo Parsons stopped and picked up an unusual looking group of men who came aboard with a trunk so heavy it took two of them to carry it.

As the steamer passed into Lake Erie, the men opened their trunk, which was their armory, and seized the ship locking almost everyone except the engineer and the wheelsman below. Then they made for Sandusky.

Their plan was to seize the armed steamer, U.S.S. Michigan, and afterward free as many Confederates imprisoned on Johnston Island in Sandusky Bay as they could carry.

One Secesh spy was known to the captain and officers of the Michigan by another name and another trade and was invited to dine aboard. The plan was to drug the wine supplied to the ship's officers so the spy's crew could seize the Michigan without resistance. According to Mother, the spy was made known somehow and the plan failed.

Perceiving this, the rebels turned tail and fled back across the lake. Upon their approach to Malden, they launched the ship's boat after attempting to scuttle the Parsons.

The agent who tried to poison the Michigan's officers was captured and sentenced to hang, but a last moment reprieve saved him. Another of his friends was not so fortunate. The man was hanged because he shot and wounded a passenger on another ship the gang seized to help carry greater numbers of the prisoners.

Reverend King said there were rumors that it was Rufus who in some way revealed the intent of the spy aboard the Michigan, but could not verify this, nor could he tell me any more. However, he was pleased with himself for being so worldly and it showed on his face.

More than once since returning I have been told about spies and provocateurs based in Windsor and Toronto. But it is a strange feeling to hear such things about someone you think you know most intimately.

The surprise of seeing his secret cache of letters has not left me.

Rufus encouraged me to join the fighting when the Union came to its senses and allowed coloured soldiers. Mother was also of this opinion. That is how I came to set off for Washington and the Sea Islands before such questions as a Negro's ability to fight were settled once and for all.

"I have written a letter to Higginson telling him about you and urging him to employ you in the capacity of a teacher, but not to let you languish there any longer than is necessary. I have insisted you would be a very good officer if a Negro corps develops." This came as a surprise. I had not asked him to write such a letter, but had considered doing so.

"Your mother and I spoke about this last week when she came to town for shopping. She is in favor and knows you ache to go. Since losing Helen there is nothing to stop you. If you need money, I will advance you a salary based on the articles you will write for the paper. Higginson will soon be expecting you." We had not discussed writing anything of my coming adventures; Rufus took it upon himself to assume I would do so.

After that, everything moved so quickly that I was only partly aware of what was going on around me. Mother produced Absolom's old carpetbag and packed it for me and I was thankful she did. Were it left to me, I would have carried books and writing materials but no clothes. She even packed cold weather clothing because she was unsure of how cold the Sea Islands were in winter. I was gratified to learn that in comparison to a Canadian winter, they were summery.

It took me several days to close up my house. I was sure I would be returning as soon as we defeated the Southerners. For all their bragging, I could not see them putting up much fight. In the naiveté of youth, I saw these as a people who could not even run their homes without a house nigger. How could they fight a war? This war would not take long. Six months, I thought, once the North started moving.

I spoke to Albert about looking after the animals until I returned. We walked along the fence line of my property. Eunice stayed home, so we were alone in our exercise.

"You know I would, but as soon as they start forming regiments from the freed slaves, I intend to join them."

"Does Eunice know?"

"No. I won't tell her anything until I am ready to go. You know what she is like. She will cry and wail for a month until I agree not to go."

Albert's own plans were something I had not considered. His face was lit with pleasure as he outlined his idea to go south if and when the time arrived. As we turned at the end of my property to walk its width, the sun fell full on his face and its shadow lay across my own face denying me the little warmth of that weakened orb. For a moment, I pictured Eunice a war widow and me her new husband. Before I could shut out this thought, I hurt that I would seek happiness at the expense of my best friend. Very briefly I put my arm up and around his shoulders as we walked.

We returned to my house after an hour of speculation. Albert suggested I approach Thomas Knox to look after my animals. He had room in his barn, and if the war dragged on for some reason, Thomas could be trusted to sell the mules and milch cow at a good price. Also, Thomas made it known that the problems of the United States were their own. He had no wish to fight or even return to that country as a visitor. He had been a guest of the slave pens in Virginia.

With everything settled on the farm, I kissed Mother goodbye and she bade me 'take care,' and Albert drove me to the depot.

After crossing from Windsor to Detroit I was able to catch a train to Buffalo whence I travelled to Baltimore and Washington. I accomplished all of this without stopping more than three hours. Instead, I slept on the train.

Baltimore was my destination, but Mother had arranged a special appointment for me in the capital. I was finally going to meet the man I was named for. This is not properly true. Frederick Douglass once held me on his chest shortly after I was born, but I have no memory of that.

On the platform of the depot, a young man inspected me briefly then approached. "Are you Mr. Macdonald?" When I admitted my identity he continued, "Mr. Douglass is expecting you and sent me to guide you to his lodgings." Then he took my bag out of my hand, wrenching it unexpectedly, and told me to follow him to a cab. The cab was for Negroes only.

Douglass was staying with a coloured family near Iowa Circle. As the cab's horse clip-clopped its way along the muddy street I had my first view of a Contraband camp. It was filthy and crowded with dozens of young coloured men loafing about its edges. A few women were washing clothes, but little else in the way of profitable activity was taking place.

In contrast, the Ellis family home was a substantial brick structure that bespoke hard work and success. A coloured maid answered the door and led us down a hallway lined with pictures of different pastoral scenes. Mr.

Ellis was dressed in an expensive suit with a cravat tied four-in-hand. I knew who Mr. Ellis was because I recognized Frederick Douglass as he rose from his chair to greet me.

At home, in Mother's house, we had an etching of Douglass. Absolom made the frame and purchased the glass for the picture and it was revered as much as any holy item.

This was the period when Douglass had started wearing a beard. His head appeared larger than a normal man's and the whiskers that adorned his chin made it seem longer. In a word, he was leonine.

Douglass shook my hand warmly then looked me up and down for a moment before he spoke.

"If your heart is as strong as your person appears to be, I will be more than content with my namesake. But come and sit. I want to hear about your mother and your life in Buxton." We passed an hour in pleasant conversation before Mrs. Ellis announced that supper was ready and we went into the dining room to eat. Mrs. Ellis and her two daughters joined us. The young man who had taken my grip was Douglass' son Lewis, who would later fight with the 54th Massachusetts.

Conversation of the evening revealed that Lewis was of the same cut as I, a man waiting for greater powers to move in his direction. The main difference was he had his father at his side to advise him and I only had the memory of mine.

With coffee, the conversation turned to Absolom himself. I knew there was a friendship between the two men, but I assumed it was a letter-friendship interrupted by occasions when one or the other was too busy to write. Douglass began a series of stories that convinced me it was more.

As children, Harriet and I were aware that our father sometimes undertook journeys that we assumed had to do with the workings of our farm or his cabinet-making business.

"Your dad was one of the most important conductors on the railroad. He would venture into the border states and bring fugitives out with him. With each trip he made his way further south and more than once he came close to being captured. He worked closely with Harriet Tubman. Did you know your sister was named for her?" It was nice to think so, but I knew otherwise and did not disabuse him. "But I think his biggest victory was in helping Brown bring nineteen runaways up from Kansas.

"He refused to carry a gun on most of his trips. It was not that he objected to the use of weapons. Instead, he reasoned that a gun would give him away if he was ever searched.

"Captain Brown had no such apprehension. His face was already too well known and there was an unwritten death warrant upon him. When your father joined the Brown family in Kansas, he asked for and was given a pistol.

"As they were putting together the outfit they needed to make the journey northward, a bushwhacker approached Brown in a general store by sneaking up behind our great friend. The bushwhacker's movements advertised his intentions and your father came up behind even more quietly than the assassin. As the man began to draw his revolver from his pocket your father took his out from underneath his coat and calmly shot the man dead. Then he announced any other person attempting to interfere with Brown would meet the same fate."

From there the stories about Absolom tumbled out and for the first time I knew what it was to be a part of a line of respected men although my line only stretched back one generation. I resolved to make it a line any child in my family would be proud of by my actions, if allowed to fight in this war.

CHAPTER SIX

September 22, 1878
Colonel Thomas Higginson is the most Christian man I have ever met. He lives by the principles of Christ whether they cost him treasure or prestige. I am sure he would have welcomed a martyr's death during the war, but a serious wound denied him this end and he was mustered out of the Southern Department toward October in 1864.

From my reading of late, he has been spared for higher purposes. I have seen his name in the Atlantic Monthly Magazine and was overjoyed to obtain a copy of his book: "Army Life In A Black Regiment", and I am mentioned in it.

To say that I was delighted someone has told the story of black soldiers: not as an addendum, but as the main subject, would be sublime understatement. He not only recorded our initial actions, but of equal distinction, the voice of the Negro freed and armed for the first time. He also undertook the transcription of their spoken word and hymns they sang, which was the true speech of the slave. This he did before the voice of the slave disappears in due course through education and citizenship.

From the moment we met, I could tell he was not a Sunday Abolitionist. He seemed to genuinely care for Negroes and did not treat them with disdain. Where others accused the Negro of starting the war, he celebrated the fact that the Union was fighting for their freedom.

The Colonel did not look like a fighting man. His frame was slight with a finely formed face and poet's eyes. He looked more like the man of letters he has since become. His hair was not thin, but it was not a thicket either. When I was introduced to him, he wore it closely cut in military style and he had the beginnings of a campaign beard. Many of us did not shave when we could avoid it and we looked like great and terrifying warriors with hair sprouting all over. On the march this had a practical purpose as it saved us time, but in our regular encampments where we had access to barbers we avoided shaving. It was an affectation we enjoyed.

After my evening with Douglass, I returned to Baltimore where I had booked passage on a southbound steamer. Douglass made me feel that this war and whatever contribution I made to it, even if it claimed my life, was ordained by God.

Oddly, I do not remember the name of the ship that carried me to Port Royal, but the trip took us far from land for nearly four days. All that time I was segregated, with the other Negro passengers, from the whites. It bothered me, as I was still unused to it, but I accepted it because I knew that everything would change once we won the war. Sadly today, it still has not changed and there is no sign it will in the future.

Port Royal is on a low, scrubby point jutting out into Port Royal Sound almost due South of Beaufort in South Carolina. It is surrounded by islands and other parts of the mainland and is similar to a river's delta, which I suppose it is.

The weather was pleasantly warm and the palm trees keep their fronds year round. There are a great number of plants and trees there, which I did not recognize. The birds and animals are also different. But, what confronted me most amazingly was the difference between my world, as a free and educated man, and the local Negroes as slaves only recently liberated.

Many of these people from the region around Port Royal and Beaufort refer to themselves as Geechee or Gullah. I did not know if this was a type of people or if it identified their language. The language they spoke was certainly a dialect I had never encountered up until that time or since.

One practitioner, Robert Smith, told me he thought it was old African, but there are other words from what could be Elizabethan English and also what I think were Spanish terms. All of this is delivered in the accent and cadence of the fields making it very difficult to understand.

But people were talkative. Wherever I went in Port Royal or St. Helena's Island, the former slaves would talk to me assuming we spoke the same language. Then they would discover I was as strange to them as they were to me.

On landing in Port Royal I had no real direction. I went to the encampment where the First South Carolina Volunteers was being formed. Drawing myself up into what I thought would be a dignified military posture; I addressed the sergeant on duty at the front of the camp.

"Good afternoon sir, I would like to enlist."

"You would?" he responded in a drawn New England accent and inspected me from top to bottom. "And who might you be? You're not one of these local niggers… Don't talk like one anyway. You a house nigger?"

"No sir. I am from British Canada. I have…" before I could say anything more, he cut me off.

"British Canada?" His hand rested on his pistol holster.

"Yes sir. North of Michigan and Ohio."

"We don't like England. They side with the Secesh. They trade with them and their ships run our blockade. They buy Secesh cotton and pay for it with English guns. Being English doesn't do much to recommend you."

"As that may be, I have come to enlist and to join the fight."

"Didn't know they had niggers up there. You wait right here boy. I need to talk to my lieutenant about you." With that he indicated to an armed black private to guard me. Once the sergeant had disappeared into the maze of tents and buildings, the guard lowered his rifle.

"You be from up nort'. You run 'way?"

"No I was born in Canada. I was always free."

"Lord almighty. You de fuss freeborn man I meet. Why you come here?"

"For the same reason you picked up that gun. I want to fight. My father was a slave."

"Kin you read an write?"

I was not disturbed by his question. It was not the first time I was asked. Fugitives arriving in Buxton all wished to know if we were literate and if they could be taught the basics of reading and writing. Try though he might, Absolom never mastered these skills. I think there may be a certain age after which the brain will not accommodate the alphabet. No matter where I eventually went, whether it was with Colonel Higginson or General Sherman, the question was always the same. Both the Colonel and the General were of the opinion that if we were to make good citizens out of the Contrabands, education was the one sure way to do this.

As we talked, the private set the butt of his rifle on the ground and cradled the barrel with its bayonet in the crook of his arm. He asked question after question treating me like an exotic animal until the sergeant came back and shouted at him. He almost dropped his rifle from the fright, as he did not see the sergeant coming up behind him.

"Goddamn it William. This man could be a spy and you're treating the son-of-a-bitch like some long lost brother. Are you as dumb as you look or dumber? You put that rifle square on his belt and if he moves you blow him a new belly button. Do you hear me?"

"Yes sir."

"Not sir. I ain't no goddamned officer."

"Yes sergeant. I'se sorry sergeant."

"You come with me," he said motioning me to follow and explaining nothing more. William looked confused that I would be ordered to move after he had just been told to shoot. He did not shoot and eventually the sergeant and I arrived at the duty officer's tent. I was left to stand in the sun while the sergeant went inside.

I could not hear what was being said within the tent, but in a moment the sergeant appeared, held back the flap and told me to go in.

After the strong sunlight, I had trouble seeing. The tent had a portable writing desk and four chairs. It also had a small table and a camp bed with neatly made linen along one wall. Sitting in two of the chairs were another sergeant and a corporal. They were listening intently to a man seated behind the desk who was giving them instructions concerning the next day's training drills. Dismissing them, the man behind the desk turned to me and addressed me in a thick backwoods language.

"Y'all want to be a so'd'er? Sergeant Royce says you're an Englishman?"

"I was born in British Canada and lived there until I decided to come here to sign up."

"What'd you do there?"

"I worked for a newspaper."

"One of them nigger rags?"

"No sir. I was with our town's leading newspaper."

"Floor sweeper?"

"No sir. I was a reporter."

"A nigger reporter?" Here he used a term I was not pleased to hear and will not write. "Don't lie to me, boy."

"Sir, I have no thought of lying to you."

He handed me an old newspaper and told me to read the first story I saw, which I did. After a minute of reading, he grabbed the newspaper out of my hand and told me to wait outside. Once again I found myself standing in the strong Carolina sun as he hied off to speak to someone.

After twenty minutes Sergeant Royce came for me and bade me follow him once more. This time I was seen by a captain who asked me the same questions and gave me a book of poetry to read from. I was tempted to embellish with my acting skills, but from the severity of the look on the captain's face I decided against such foolishness. But again the officer appeared dumbfounded and I could see I was about to be handed on.

Finally, I was brought before a colonel.

Making my presence known to the regiment's senior recruiting officer, Colonel Fessenden, I presented my letter from Rufus to Colonel Higginson and a hastily scribbled note from Frederick Douglass. He read them over then beckoned me to come closer.

"I am heartened that you have come to join the Cause." The way he intoned the word "Cause" made it seem holy. "Colonel Higginson is away for several days, but as I recognize the name of Frederick Douglass, and assume the other is of equal importance, I am sure he will want to speak with you before we enroll you in the regiment.

"In the meantime, I will send you off to help teach school. There is nothing like a little teaching to focus what you know." I was then referred to a young white woman named Laura Towne and her companion, Ellen Murray, who had opened a school for Contrabands.

Ellen Murray was a quiet woman, who shared roots with me in Canada, and was much under the influence of Miss Towne. It was obvious from the brusqueness of Miss Towne's demeanor and manly gate that Miss Towne was in charge of the household. Miss Towne took the lead in all things and oversaw the operation of the school directing Miss Murray in her daily teaching activities.

There was another teacher at the school as well. She was Miss Charlotte Forten. Miss Forten was a Negress and I believe may have been one of the first, if not the first, teacher from our race to instruct the Contrabands.

I thought I was lucky to be tossed in with an educated female member of my race. Although many of the Geechee women were very pretty and exotic by any standard, I felt uncomfortable around them. Our differences were vast and their language nearly incomprehensible. Often, I found them too childlike in their dreams. Rumours would fly one day granting every freed slave forty acres; next it would be treasure of Confederate gold; and the next Father Abraham himself was coming to bless each and every one of them and to welcome them personally to freedom. The local women subscribed to these stories as though they were confirmed fact. But not Miss Forten. She was severe with them and tried to instill a sense of equilibrium. It was her mission and it left no time to dally with me. In our short acquaintance, she made it known that I was an interloper and hindrance who was waiting on orders to go off and play the men's game of war.

Miss Towne was much more entertaining. She laughed easily and smiled almost constantly. If she was not the picture of a female teacher I had painted for myself, Miss Forten certainly was. But Miss Towne cared deeply for her charges and recognized the need to teach reading and writing above all else. But, she also laughed and shared fun with the women without caring whether it diminished her importance.

Despite my academic abilities, I was put to work doing manual labour around the school. When it was too much for me to do by myself, I was allowed to ask one or two of the Geechee men to help. In this way I came to know several of them and discovered, that like me, they too were waiting to be called up into the regiment.

My summons came sooner than theirs. Colonel Higginson sent for me ten days after I arrived.

"Rufus Stephenson's letter arrived several days ago, but it took me until yesterday before I reached it in the pile that was awaiting me. He speaks very highly of you. So, you would like to join us in our crusade? Splendid Frederick. We can use you. Do you have any training in arms?"

I told him I had not except for shooting rabbits with an old fowling gun.

"That should not be a concern. But I believe you may be too valuable to waste in adventure. First I want you to undergo infantry training then I have something in mind." With that he addressed Colonel Fessenden. "See he is enlisted immediately and starts drilling tomorrow."

My interview over, I was led away and placed under the care of Sergeant Royce who had been impressed with the reception I received from Colonel Higginson. "Maybe we can be friends with the English after all. You went to school?"

"Yes. I attended Sectional School 13 in Raleigh Township in Upper Canada."

"I would like to hear more about that," he said as we almost strolled to the private soldiers' bivouac in the encampment. "How many kids went to school there?"

"Somewhere around seventy or eighty depending on the year."

"Whew!" He blew out his cheeks in surprise. "That's a lot. How many grades?"

"Right through to the finish of high school. If you wanted to, you could go on to university. A friend of mine who was ahead of me in school just graduated from King's College in Toronto as a doctor."

"He was black?"

"Yes." I could tell Royce did not believe me so I tried to soften the impact of this knowledge. "I think he's the first Negro medical doctor to graduate in Upper Canada."

"And nobody said anything?"

"No. I know there was a man named Largill who tried to stop the settlement where I grew up and tried to force Negroes out of Chatham by attempting to bring laws against us, but he failed. He published the newspaper that competed with the Planet where I worked."

"I see now. The man who owned your newspaper thought if he hired a nigger to write for him it would drive the other fellow crazy…"

"You never met Rufus Stephenson if you think that. He hired me because I could listen and write. Nothing more."

"Was there a white school near you?"

"It was closed because we had better teachers."

"Well where'd the white kids go to school?"

"Most of them moved over to our school. Some went in to Chatham if they had…"

"You mean to tell me white kids and nigger kids went to school together? I don't believe that."

"Well, you can believe what you want, but I am telling you the truth."

"And nobody said anything?"

I explained that the parents were glad just to have their children educated. Those people coming from England and Scotland were of a class that did not receive much schooling themselves and it was just as important to them as it was to the fugitives.

For the next month I marched, did close order drill, learned the commands, a bit about tactics and marched some more. We did not see any action at that time although one contingent went off to attack the Florida coast.

In the spring of 1863 my turn finally came to go to Florida and the Indian River country. It was not a big campaign and we did not fight anything that could be called a major battle. But we were constantly sniped when we were on picket duty.

The Geechee men were fearless in the face of the enemy. They delighted in their retribution and it was not unusual for one to stand his ground, reloading his musket and firing when the odds were strongly against him. I do not recall any retreating in the face the enemy and some carried their bravery to absurd proportions.

One time, we happened upon a farm that had gone unmolested until our arrival. Livestock was running loose, there were preserves in the pantry and smoked meats hanging in the smokehouse. One of the Geechee men cornered a young hog and placed a rope halter around its neck planning on taking it back to our camp to butcher it. He held the other end of the pig's rope with one hand and carried his musket in the other. Other Geechee men took the hams and were employed in eating slices of that meat as we marched on toward the next plantation.

Midway through a cane field rebels hidden in the woodlot bordering the field opened on us with musketry. And I watched in amazement as Edwin, the Geechee pig man, carefully set his musket down, tied the rope to his trouser belt, straddled his hog, picked up the musket, sat on the stoat and commenced to fire in a steady rhythm from his sitting position.

Later, Edwin, told me, "I ain't losing that pig. I love pork too much." And the pig marched home with us.

A month later, as spring turned into summer and the heat descended on us, I received an order to attend Colonel Higginson.

"Frederick, I have been thinking about how you could be of greater service than merely as a rifleman. I want you to come with me tonight while I go forward to scout the lines."

As evening commenced its descent upon us, I reported to Colonel Higginson's tent. He was now wearing a private's clothing and carried a musket instead of an officer's pistol. He also had a big Bowie knife, of the kind favoured by the enemy. For all I could tell, he was an ageing private. I was dressed in the same manner, but he ordered me into a filthy suit of clothes that had been abandoned by one of the Geechee in favour of a soldier's uniform.

"If we come across a rebel picket and are captured, then you do your best to sound like a Contraband or they will kill you. Davis has ordered that all Negroes be killed out of hand if they are found in uniform." After a thoughtful pause, he continued. "It would probably be best if you learn how to speak and walk like a slave. You are too erect and proud. Best if you could learn to be a little more servile, then you might be able to move freely inside the Secesh lines."

This last notion bothered me. I did not know what the colonel had planned for me, but it sounded more dangerous than facing the enemy in battle and the thought of it made my palms sweat.

We set off from the edge of our camp on horses and moved quietly until we arrived at our pickets' outpost. The outpost itself was little more than a crude abatis of felled trees with the branches sharpened and facing outward. It would not stop the enemy if he made a determined charge, but if he had no support it would deter him by making him think about what he was attempting to do.

Our adventure was completed without incident. We learned the enemy's cavalry and batteries were gone from the vicinity inviting us to march on poorly defended Rebel positions with impunity. With the first pink light in the east we were crossing back into our lines. At the time I did not know it, but these intelligence-gathering excursions were a regular feature of Colonel Higginson's life.

CHAPTER SEVEN

September 25, 1878
After thinking about the war, I sat down on Sunday night and wrote the following letter to Mrs. Lincoln. Writing it reminded me of writing editorials for Rufus. I do miss that task. It made me think in ways we do not often force ourselves to.

> Mr. Frederick D. Macdonald,
> C/O General Delivery
> Buxton, Ontario
> Canada

Mrs. Abraham Lincoln
Pau, France

September 25, 1878

Dear Mrs. Lincoln,

In your initial letter to me you indicated you wished to know how coloured soldiers felt about serving the Union cause. My answer is complex, but not hard to understand. It combines bitterness, revenge, the wish to become full American citizens, the desire to assure a future for their children, and the wish to be declared men once and for all.

From what my reading tells me, the Rebellion was predicted by the Constitution.

I grew up with the simple belief that slavery was of the utmost evil, which is the only possible philosophy for the son of a fugitive to hold. What I did not know, until I joined the army, was how the vox populi and politics complicated what should have been a very simple issue.

Complications by no means condone the institution. Still, one of the biggest surprises I encountered in my quest to understand slavery's longevity has been Chief Justice Taney.

Taney was the man who gave credence to and enforced the slaveholders' contention that certain types of men were not fully human and could therefore be deemed chattel.

Long before the situation eroded into warfare, Taney made public his personal view of slavery by freeing his own slaves. This occurred in 1818 leaving thirty-nine years until his infamous Dred Scott Decision.

I must tell you the Scott Decision terrified both freed men of colour and fugitives. It even frightened those of us who lived beyond the borders of the United States because it declared your nation's law above the rights of foreign subjects and the laws they were governed by. The very idea that Negroes, no matter their citizenship, could be declared possessions to be held universally without rights was odious.

As a British subject, born free and expecting to live my life without trouble, the knowledge that the moment I crossed your borders all of my liberties were negated and I was subject to being gaoled and sold, frightened me.

Please understand I am no lawyer. Your husband would have had a far better understanding of these matters than I.

Chief Justice Taney appeared to be an abolitionist, or at least a friend of the coloured man when he freed his slaves, but something changed in him.

It is apparent that if he had one great fault, it was that he loved the law to the expense of his humanity. The Constitution, for him, was something celestial. I believe he saw men as transitory upon this earth, but the law as immutable and enduring. This unflagging faith forced him to read areas of the Constitution concerning slavery as being beyond any possibility of flaw and therefore beyond amendment.

These legal factors affected the coloured soldier who desired to serve in many ways.

Although we wanted to fight, we were cautious of promises coming out of Washington. It was widely accepted amongst the coloured population that we were still not viewed as full men when we were finally allowed to spill our blood on your battlefields. This was borne out when our rate of pay was three dollars a month less than that of a white soldier.

Like many other coloured troops, I chose to refuse this payment rather than accept my status as something less than an equal of those for whom I might die. General Sherman offered to make up the difference for me out of his own pocket and I cannot tell you how much I appreciated his generosity as he was not being paid regularly at the time, but it was not only for me that the three dollars was important. It was for all of us and it had to be paid by our government.

The legal structure for the continuance of slavery remained in place until 1864. After the repeal, I was under the misapprehension that with the death of the Fugitive Slave Act, the Dred Scott Decision died with it. I assumed that in appointing Mr. Chase to succeed Chief Justice Taney, part of Mr. Chase's instructions would have been to overturn the decision in question. It surprised me to discover recently, that the Supreme Court only reversed itself a few years ago in 1873.

I have listed the major complaints that would have sapped the morale from any soldier. Because of these, I was astounded at how many men, myself included, faced the enemy's fiercest fire with joy in our hearts. Perhaps this proves the response to the Civil War was a moral crusade against such an evil that the cause outweighed any complaint.

We lived in bad conditions throughout the war. I often risked many forms of death, as did my fellow soldiers: disease consumed us; we were exposed to the weather; we were massacred at Fort Pillow; fed to the enemy in the torpedo's bowl at Elliot's Salient; and there were a thousand other demonstrations. Yet, as I have already said we went willingly to the fight.

For me to speculate as to your husband's motives for withholding us from the fight until the middle of 1863 would be incorrect. I can only add this: your husband must have lacked confidence in his nation.

Serving under General Sherman, I was present for a number of privileged conversations and made privy to several notes of personal correspondence. Although I cannot divulge what was said or the contents of letters from various correspondents, I will tell you that I was more aware than probably any other private soldier of the ongoing machinations of various members of the Cabinet and your husband's efforts to deal with them.

General Sherman, it is safe to say, suffered from the same pressures from Cabinet as did your husband, and beyond that from family. He was true to your husband and the nation in all things and I believe his loyalty stood him in good stead with your husband and encouraged the bond between those two great men.

It is as hard to explain a man's willingness to endure shot and shell, as it is a president's decisions to someone who has no experience of either. The noise, confusion and terror do not transcribe onto the page. Without offering offence Mrs. Lincoln, I will endeavour in future letters to describe my personal experiences in terms you will hopefully comprehend, but I fear they will not carry the true realities of war.

I hope this note finds you well and enjoying your time in France.

Your faithful servant
Frederick Douglass Macdonald

CHAPTER EIGHT

September 29, 1878

Eden must have been a vast plain. Why else would God give men eyes that look forward into the distance rather than on all sides as if we came from a forest? If I accept this proposition, it belies the bible. I have often thought upon the English naturalist, Mr. Darwin, because of this. I have read his works and tried to resolve my own conflict between the beliefs taught to us in church and his understanding and promulgation of evolutionary theory. My only solution has been to establish a meeting point midway between the two views.

This is what I was thinking about as our train passed through the friendly portions of Western Virginia into the mountains of eastern Ohio. With the looming hills I quickly formed the opinion that I do not like mountainous country.

This new train of thought was caused by the close darkness of the mountains even though it was a spring afternoon and the sky was clear. My home country is one of golden fields and changing shades of green not the muted hues of the piney woods. At home, the horizon is at the far limit of my sight and when the sun shines, it shines from true sunrise to true sunset. This was my first real experience with mountains. On my way to Baltimore, I slept as we passed through northern New York and its Catskill range. While other people speak lovingly of mountains and their beauty, I do not like having to strain my neck at an uncomfortable angle just to see the sky; I do not like living in shadow for a good part of the day; and, I do not like having places where my enemies can hide within arm's reach.

At the end of April 1864, Colonel Higginson sent for me as he now often did. I donned my slave's costume and armed myself with nothing more than my wits. As I passed Sergeant Royce on my way through the camp he took in my dress asking, "Going out again tonight? Well, you are more than earning your stripes. You should be promoted, and I will ask the captain to promote you as soon as he can."

We tried to keep my activities as a spy secret, but once I crossed a picket line in these rags and was recognized as the "British Nigger", I was exposed to the whole camp. I fretted that word of a Negro operative in the vicinity would somehow leak out to the Rebels, but nearly four centuries of keeping secrets from slaveholders was enough to ensure no hint ever made it to their ears.

"You did not need to dress for a mission tonight. That is not why I called you in," he said after he returned my salute. "I have something I want you to consider carefully before giving me an answer. I have received a request from a General Dodge. He is a corps commander with General Sherman out west.

"It seems they are freeing large numbers of slaves as they work their way through Tennessee. General Dodge feels these people could be mined for information about the activities of their former masters. However, he believes they would be more forthcoming with a member of their own race. I have listened to you speak both as the educated man you are, and in your disguise. You can pass for a field hand or house servant anytime you want. This could be of benefit to our western army. Would you consider volunteering for the job?"

It was true, I could now pass for a Geechee as long as I kept my head about me and remembered the character I was playing. The men of my company had helped me considerably in learning to speak Geechee. They were generous with their time, but their instruction was not without humour. Nothing hindered them in feeling free to laugh at my mistakes and to tease me until I perfected a strange word or complicated phrase. They were also smart enough to trade their own tutelage for lessons in reading and writing.

I took a week to come to a decision. What spurred me to accept was the fear that my trip down from Canada was being wasted. From all appearances, coloured regiments were being withheld from the real fighting to the north and I wanted to contribute my blood or, better yet, some Rebel's blood. Despite the brilliance of the Negro troops at Battery Wagner, many generals were still reluctant to admit that coloured soldiers could best the enemy. Among those of whom I have had heard this said was General Sherman. In fact, it was common knowledge among the coloured army, that the General hated the former slaves and would have nothing to do with them.

Because of this, I was surprised to learn one of his corps commanders was seeking the help of a Negro.

When I made my decision, I went to my friend Sergeant Royce and asked him to pass the word up to Colonel Higginson that I wanted to see him.

"So you are heading west Frederick?"

This took me by surprise. I had not said anything about the enquiry and was sure Colonel Higginson had not. Somebody, an orderly or perhaps a non-commissioned officer, overheard our discussion and bandied it about.

"How did you hear about it?"

"Edwin told me." The hog soldier must have gained this knowledge from someone working in the officers' quarters, but it was no use chasing the source. It would have been easier to jump up and catch a skein of high-flying geese out of mid-air. When I didn't reply he tried again. "You going to go?"

"Yes. I want to fight and there is more promise of battle in Tennessee than there is here."

"I would have liked to spend more time with you. You taught me a lot. Maybe when the war is over we can visit. I'd even like to go up to British Canada to see your country." He meant it too. Royce did not like the demands made by bigoted whites on others of their race to hate Negroes. He made his own decisions. But his journey north would never be made. He was transferred to the 45th United States Colored Troops, promoted to lieutenant and died in the fighting at Chaffin's Farm later in the year.

I would have liked to get to know Sergeant Royce better myself.

When I was granted an interview with Colonel Higginson, he already knew what I was about to say and hushed me. "Since you have been with me, your behaviour and efforts have been exemplary. I wish I could grant you a commission, as God knows, you deserve it. But, I can't. I can, however promote you to the rank of sergeant and am doing so immediately."

Such a response from the colonel was flattering and unexpected. I had only recently been appointed corporal.

Before winter closed the fighting for the year, the fight for Chattanooga had taken place. Our troops successfully stormed Lookout Mountain and Missionary Ridge. As I passed through in May, signs of the fight were not yet hidden by the blossoming of spring. Wherever I turned there were burnt buildings and shell holes. The buildings that suffered the most seemed to be the fine homes of prominent Rebels and the military provisioning factories that supplied the Secessionist army.

Blue uniforms were everywhere. They were on the streets and standing guard whenever you came to a crossroad. Our soldiers were the only white men of fighting age that I saw. There were plenty of local women, but they had little to do with us and would not look directly at me. There were also the children of Rebels who did not share the hesitation of their mothers and older sisters in expressing their hatred.

Even though I wore the blue coat with my new sergeant's chevrons on my sleeves, I was treated with disrespect. For many of our troops I was like the proverbial monkey in the zoo and they stared at me when I walked the streets. Some even went so far as to turn around to watch me after I had already gone by. I considered this a product of a coloured soldier being so unusual in the western armies. Within the Army of the Potomac, coloured troops were being seen more regularly. In the west I was still a rarity.

The orders I carried assigning me to General Dodge bore enough stamps and seals that even the most illiterate private could not fail to be impressed. I also found that by speaking with my natural accent and vocabulary, I could force my way past all but the most obstinate sentry and he only held me up long enough to call an officer. Once a man with bars on his shoulders appeared, I knew I would be on my way sooner than later.

This was helped by the fact that I did not hesitate to put on an air of importance and mention the names and ranks of men I had never met.

After more than a fortnight of wearing travel, I arrived at one of the rear encampments of Sherman's army during the assault on Resaca.

All eyes were turned toward the fighting and men were holding their muskets a little tighter. This is where I saw my first Henry rifle. I would quickly become acquainted with these fast-firing weapons, but did not come into possession of one until just before Bentonville.

I presented myself to the duty officer of the first encampment I stumbled upon. He was an Iowa man who looked upon me with disdain, but I was becoming used to this and wasted no time reflecting on it while presenting my orders to him.

Within moments a captain with a more generous spirit was directing me to General Dodge's headquarters. As a final gesture, he offered to send a private with me as a guide.

General Dodge was in the throes of fighting his portion of the battle and I could not disturb him. He was one of those men whose task of the moment consumed him to the exclusion of all else. It took another three days before I was able to present myself. In the meantime, I was issued a rifle and enrolled temporarily in Company H of the 7th Iowa Infantry.

When General Dodge finally had time to see me, a corporal took me to him. A captain was also present, but during our interview he did not speak.

At first all General Dodge did was return my salute and look me over. I waited in silence. His eyes were of the kind that searches a man for his intent. Finally he spoke.

"Sergeant, you come highly recommended from Colonel Higginson. I am not familiar with your former colonel. He says here you can read and write and that your appreciation of intelligence matters is keen, but he does not give me much of your history. How well do you write?"

I gave him a brief résumé of my schooling and career as a reporter.

"It would be best if you did not tell General Sherman you have been a reporter if you ever meet him. Has Colonel Higginson told you what I require?"

When I answered that he had, General Dodge continued. "Right now we have lost count of the number of former slaves who are fleeing the plantations and private homes to follow our army. General Sherman is in the habit of speaking with some of them occasionally to obtain whatever insight they have into the movements of the Rebels. Many of their masters have taken up the gun against the Union. What the slaveholders don't countenance is that their former property is more aware of the actions around them than the slaveholders give them credit for. General Sherman feels a white man will lie to him as quickly as look at him. Nigras, on the other hand, share an interest in defeating the South and will tell all that they know and more.

"Aside from collecting information, we need you to talk to these people to convince them to return to their former homes so they can be fed and cared for. The plantations need to get up and running again or no one in the South will eat next winter. You have to tell them, if they go back we'll make sure they are paid for their labour.

"Make it clear, if they follow us, we cannot feed them and we can't hire all of them. Also tell them they are slowing us down."

He went on to outline the objectives of the coming summer's campaign, which was already underway. General Sherman wanted Atlanta and we could not take it if we were burdened with half the countryside's population. He was about to dismiss me then, almost as an afterthought, he added, "If any of the young men see your uniform and want to enlist to fight, tell them they can, just not in the Army of the Tennessee. We don't have time to train them if we are going to gut the South before the Rebels can prepare defenses. There are lots of Nigra recruiters around signing men up for the eastern regiments where there are proper training camps and supply depots."

With that, he bade me good afternoon and dismissed me into the care of the silent captain. General Dodge's manner had been brisk and professional, but not contemptuous. I felt this was a man of business who was bound to accomplish what he set out to do.

Saluting I turned and followed the captain from the General's tent. Once we were in the open air, he introduced himself.

"I'm Captain Mortenson. General Dodge has delegated the responsibility of dealing with the freed slaves to me. There are thousands of them and we have to get the situation under control quickly or it will develop beyond our means to deal with it. I will depend on you a great deal sergeant. No one has ever done this before so we do not have history to guide us. Each step we take will be a test."

I understood fully, yet the mission disappointed me because of the obligation to engage in bloody combat I felt I owed John Brown.

We went to Captain Mortenson's tent and spent the afternoon discussing our first steps. He outlined what was already being done and it seemed to me his efforts were perfectly satisfactory. Still, the engagement of a coloured man might pry more secrets loose. After we had been alone for a time, I was calling him by his first name, Hakun, and I became Fred. Outside of his tent, he was still captain and I sergeant.

We decided to set up a mobile office at the rear of each advance column. It would be staffed by: one junior officer, a sergeant, corporal and two clerks who could serve as writers. All that would be required was a tent and transportation. The personnel could be drawn from the casualty lists of men who were not too severely wounded. Captain Mortenson would conduct the interviews to see that the men were of the right temperament and attitude to deal with the freed men.

Our process was simple. Runaways would be invited to come to our tents. It would all have to be by word-of-mouth because so few could read. I would be in charge of that. Wherever we could settle for a few days, I would don a dress uniform and parade myself through the town or village encouraging the people who were following our army to talk to me and ask questions. I would then point them to the closest interview tent. In the tent, the officer in charge would make sure the freed men were offered coffee and maybe a plug of tobacco if we had any, but the army was moving so fast that supplies were often slow to catch up and we had nothing to give. If the subject had something interesting to offer or appeared reluctant to talk to a white man, I was asked to speak with him.

These efforts began producing information immediately. We were able to identify farmers who provided hay for Wheeler's cavalry and one man, a former house slave, overheard his master telling the mistress that he was going to join General Johnston at Altoona. With the advance information that the Rebel army would be waiting at Altoona, General Sherman was able to turn Johnston's left flank and force him out of his position.

While we were enjoying these successes, we were not aware they were unappreciated by those personal enemies jealous of our Generals Sherman and Grant. After barely a month of operations we were disbanded. No reason was ever given.

It was the view of troops on the line that General Halleck had tried to steal credit for Grant's victories at Fort Donelson and Shiloh, and that he tried to impede General Sherman at Chattanooga, but was unsuccessful in all. The public in the North knew the names of both Grant and Sherman and would admire them even more in the coming months. For the moment, Halleck satisfied himself with sneak attacks like a sniper firing from a thicket, and one of the targets he hit was our modest enterprise.

In the end, I returned to the 7th Iowa in the 1st Division and was with them under Brigadier Sweeney.

After months of manoeuvres we were finally stopped at Kennesaw Mountain. We could not flank the mountain, which was General Sherman's favourite tactic. By this one simple means, he avoided much bloodshed. But we were still moving toward Atlanta.

On the morning of June 27th we could no longer adopt this strategy. Geography dictated that we must now fight and General Johnston held the heights.

Kennesaw Mountain ran from the southwest to the northeast across our line of march. I remember looking up at it and thinking it was the tallest mountain I had ever seen, although I know we had crossed larger mountains to get to the foot of Kennesaw.

Our battle ended with one big attack. We had been fighting for days with the Secesh and it seemed like whenever we drove the Rebels from one position, they would reveal another by unloading canister in our faces. This was to be one determined push to unseat Johnston from his perch.

We had just passed the solstice and the long roll woke us from wherever we had fallen asleep. No one bothered with tents. We lay, uncovered, on the ground with our blankets close by to be pulled over us when the chill of the early hours made us shiver. The weather was hot, but with the cooling of the night, it felt as cold as on a winter's eve.

After passing Hood's right side near Big Shanty and forcing his retreat, we found ourselves at the north end of Kennesaw. The mountain seemed to have two summits, which would have to be taken. I learned later that arrayed around the northern side of this mountain, General Thomas of Chickamauga fame had our right flank and General Schofield had his.

Despite being a sergeant, I had no standing within my company. Our sergeant was Albie Chatterton. Albie befriended me when I returned to the regiment and we shared cook fires and bivouacs. Lining up in preparation for the fight, he saw that I was nervous. Although I had been in small skirmishes in Florida, Tennessee and now Georgia, this was to be my first major fight and I did not know what to expect. Even though this is what I thought would pay my debt to Brown, the prospect of a big fight frightened me badly.

"You'll be fine Fred," Albie whispered to me so the other soldiers wouldn't hear. "No one who is sane is anything but afraid. Just try not to think too hard on things and do what you were trained to do."

More than his words, I appreciated his calm voice. This must be how a horse feels when it is coaxed out of a burning barn with soothing words. It does not know the meaning of the words, but their tone conveys the message.

All along the Secessionist line a few muskets cracked, taunting us. Still we held our ground. Officers looked at their watches, then up the mountain to where we had to go. No one was happy about this, but no one would refuse to go. We had faith in Uncle Billy. Some men had more faith in him than in God. We believed he would not spend our lives foolishly and without gain even though we might never see it.

Where we could see the muzzles of guns pointing out from their emplacements, we could also see the severe downward angle they were depressed to. There was the stink of urine in the air as some of the men wet themselves in fear. When I looked up I could see one battery aimed directly at me and I knew that as soon as we commenced our charge, I would be no more. Because of this, I had a terrible time controlling my own bladder.

Then it was eight o'clock, the appointed hour and the drums and bugles sounded the charge. I pointed my musket toward the summit, its bayonet shining in the beautiful morning light, and roared like a lion. With that one yell all fear left me and my only desire was to be at the Rebels. I do not know if I wet myself then or later.

Along with my fellow soldiers I climbed hard. Our battle cry, the beat of our feet and the occasional curse of a man who stumbled was the only noise. Then the rebels opened on us. Holes, where clusters of men once were, appeared in our lines, but we could not stop. Our company reached a line of rifle pits and the Secesh inhabiting them cut us down with a number of volleys. I do not know how many. My own Enfield was empty, but my bayonet was ready. Somehow I made it to the line of pits along with the other survivors of Company H. Once we were on them, the Rebels leapt up, fired in our faces, then turned their muskets around and swung them like clubs. I closed on my first man and waited until the butt of his gun flashed by my face, then I skewered him under the breastbone. He slid onto the ground and I had to put my foot on his chest to pull the knife out of him.

Another Secesh killed a young private to my left with the discharge of his gun and was in the process of turning it around when I lunged for him. Because he was to my left and I am right handed, it was an awkward attack that missed its mark. Just as I pulled back, a shell burst over our heads and I felt the hot slice as something tore my face asunder. It stunned me momentarily, and in that instant, the Secesh brought his rifle down onto the crown of my head and I collapsed to the earth with all things fading from my sight.

CHAPTER NINE

September 29, 1878

Entering my experience at Kennesaw into this diary caused me to re-member certain details of the battle for the first time since we fought it. The terror and bloodlust I experienced has always been with me, but if I find myself starting to think about them, I force those thoughts aside and continue with my day. It is other, smaller details that now come to mind.

One of those remembrances is waking up in the field surgery and the de-light in finding myself alive. There was also the accompanying memory of the dizziness, sick stomach and headaches that beset me for several weeks afterward and which I had forgotten until I set pen to paper.

However, I do not remember being rescued by Albie. One of the privates in our company told me that after the Rebel clubbed me he was in the act of reversing his bayonet to finish me when Albie shot him. I was left to lie until the battle was finished. This was the safest thing for me, because no one would be bothered to assault a man who was already down when there were plenty of soldiers standing.

Writing about my role in the war has made me curious and I began to wonder how General Sherman felt about that battle. His detractors called Kennesaw a failure, but I do not see it as such. As one of the wounded whom nearly did not survive, I still believe he did the right thing. He con-ducted so many battles and they proved successful for the most part. Not only that, many were accomplished with as few soldiers killed as he could manage.

I have not asked the general about his role in the war. He did write a bi-ography three years ago which answers many questions about dates and movements. Still, like me, he must have deeper views he can only share with someone who trod the same campaign trails.

In light of this, I dashed off a short note to him at the start of the month asking whether he would care to give me his views on that fight.

Life here on the farm goes on, but I get so wrapped up in these journal entries that I forget I have done other things in my life and will do more. At the moment I do not know whom I will give this biography to when it is completed. I would not wish to bore the General or Mrs. Lincoln with my impoverished recollections. They were privy to much more important events, so I guess I will give it over to Eunice to read then pass on to one of Harriet's boys.

We continued harvesting this week. Benjamin had his own crops to bring in and could not help with my harvest. But because my turnip planting was so small this year, I hired young Lincoln. At ten-years old, he is old enough to start working in the fields and his dad appreciated the gesture. With both of us digging, we were able to load six, bushel baskets from the one-acre patch this morning. After lunch, we washed and stored the turnips in the cold cellar. I gave Lincoln two dimes and one half-dime for his efforts and he was completely happy with that. I still have some onions to bring in and if the weather holds that should be done next week and I will hire him again. That will leave me with little more to do before the snow flies.

Earlier this week it rained, so I spent several days in the workshop planing and squaring the planks for Reverend King's bookcases. I had some nicely seasoned white oak, which I took out of my back woodlot several years ago. By all rights, it should be expensive because I had to haul the raw log into town to have it sawn. The sawyer at the local mill gave me a fair price, but still he has to make a profit. Now, with the steam mill Benjamin and I bought, we can do our own sawing next winter and either add that profit to our own purse, or in cases like Reverend King, produce the finished furniture for considerably less. I may just give the bookcases for both the school and the reverend's home to him as a gift. Right now I don't need extra cash and the school could use the donation. I will talk to Eunice to see if she is in accord.

Eunice has been in a good mood lately. I think she may be brightening up. I hope this time it will be for good because I worry a great deal about her.

Morgan is coming for dinner tonight and that always cheers her. After Albert died, Eunice came home from wherever she had been to live with Morgan in their father's old house. I think it was a great comfort to her to spend her mourning in familiar surroundings. It would have been too hard to live alone in the home she and Albert shared. With all of the families going back to the United States after the war, I was surprised she was able to sell the farm. Fortunately, there were a small number of people who felt like me – we did not trust the American people to treat Negroes any better as freedmen than they did as slaves. Since the insurrection, this is being borne out.

Recently a story appeared in the Toronto Globe that caught my eye. In Ohio a crowd broke into the Erie County gaol on September fourth and pulled William Taylor out of his cell then hanged him. The story did not list the cause for this mob retribution, or whether Taylor was a coloured man, but I am sure he was. This is not the first time Ohioans have meted out punishment without a trial and I am sure it will not be the last.

Even though bigotry is alive and well here in Ontario, particularly with those new immigrants who feel the need to be superior after generations of living in the British lower classes, I have never felt my life was in danger. When all the farm work is done for the winter, I am considering the possibility of taking Eunice to Toronto to visit the shops and friends. There are many performances by some very fine actors and singers that take place around the Christmas season and it would entertain her immensely if we were to attend a few of these. I will write to see if I can obtain tickets for these performances.

Over the years, my marriage to Eunice has been one that would try many men.

When I arrived home from the war in the summer of 1865 my first ambition was to put the farm back into production. Say what you will about the Americans, they know how to get things done and their energy infected me. I had many plans to expand the buildings, the numbers of our livestock and our land holdings. While I was fighting, I saved my money avoiding the perils of alcohol and women. By war's end I had a tidy sum, which I converted to a draught and mailed home to my mother being fearful of robbery on my return journey.

After getting what little crop was left off the fields I settled in to turning our farm back into a working establishment. Mother and Harriet tried their best while I was away, but it was sufficient only to feed them and produce small amounts of produce for sale. After mustering out, I was delayed in returning home until mid-July and did not get a full crop planted so the winter of early 1866 was a bitter one.

Despite the privations, I found myself swept up in the news that Canada was about to become a country of its own.

No one made any pretense that the joining of Upper and Lower Canada with the Maritime Provinces was anything other than a reaction to the large numbers of trained troops on our southern border. My fondest wishes were for the General and decent men like Albie Chatterton, but I was willing to defend this country against them if I had to. When the first Fenian threats arose, I presented myself with my honorable discharge papers to the 24th Kent Volunteers and was accepted into the regiment. But I was never called up even though members of the regiment were sent to Windsor to guard the border on several occasions.

With the spring of 1866, I was able to plant nearly thirty acres of barley and oats along with fifteen of root vegetables. I also put in two apple trees, two pear trees, and two sour cherry trees, but did not expect them to bear fruit for at least three years.

As time permitted, I began to visit Morgan more frequently than was called for. My real reason was to see Eunice. I never forgot that morning when my heart stood still and despite marrying Helen, and Eunice preferring Albert to me, I still loved her as feverishly as I did when we were children.

First, she was reluctant to speak directly to me. She stared off into space saying only that she was very tired. I thought it was a physical ailment. Buxton had just had an outbreak of smallpox and I wondered if that in some way she was affected. Still there were enough bright days in which she smiled and addressed some comment to me.

Morgan could see what was going on and became my voice in his sister's ear. He crooned my name and spoke sincerely of my merits. Gradually she would address me directly and we even came to holding conversations. The only subjects that could not be discussed were the war and what she had done during those years. But I did not care. My joy lay in the fact that she was speaking solely with me.

Martha was not pleased with the attentions I paid Eunice. She thought her too dark with too many unanswered secrets. It would be best, my mother said, if I did not pursue Eunice. But I felt an uncontrollable love for Morgan's sister that would only be extinguished once she took me into her heart and loved me as ferociously as I loved her.

We often attended church together. Martha and Harriet would accompany us, but Martha would be grim-lipped and withhold all but the briefest of greetings. When we were at home, I would implore my mother to be more Christian toward Eunice, but all she would say was "That girl is going to hurt you and hurt you badly. I've heard things about her and what she was up to in the States and you don't want that troubling your life. Just let her go."

But I could not. I thought about her while awake and working, and dreamt about her whilst I slept. I did not want to let her go and the thought of us having a happy life together warmed me when it was cold.

Over the fall of 1866 we grew closer. I spent most of my free time at Eunice's home. A distance had grown between Martha and I and a schism was opening with Harriet as well. I grieved more over Harriet than my mother because I truly loved my sister and did not want to lose her. It was my opinion there was a meanness to Martha and that she had closed her mind to Eunice, but I felt Harriet would come to see the flame burning in my heart as something true and good.

By the middle of the 1867 winter, I had my own chair in front of Eunice's fire. It was not long after that we began talking about the possibility of getting married. Looking back now, I realize that it was I who spoke mostly about marriage. Eunice never introduced the subject and did not do much to encourage me. Her outlook was simply that if I wished to marry and look after her, that was acceptable, but she neither sought nor desired it.

This was something I refused to see at the time. I moved about in an unreal world blind to the reality of Eunice. Despite the fact that we talked, she evinced no real care for me. Often I would talk for an hour or more and she would simply stare into the fire while Morgan answered for her when an answer was needed. I suppose I should hold him responsible. He did nothing to dissuade me and, looking back now, my marriage to Eunice would relieve him of responsibility for her. I do not think this factored into his thinking. As I have previously written, Morgan was and is a decent man. I believe he simply wanted his sister to have someone who would care for her after the devastation of losing Albert.

Our farm was becoming more organized and by the fall of 1867 it was going to show a profit as long as the markets held their prices. Starting in mid-August, I was making weekly trips into Chatham with wagonloads of produce that I sold on Saturday mornings. I was always careful to pack the wagon so the vegetables would not be bruised during the shipment. It was no use trying to sell my vegetables in Buxton because almost everyone who remained after the war was also a farmer.

It was on one of these trips that I first discussed buying our boarding-house with my banker.

People around Chatham knew me from my reports in the Planet during the war. This caused a lot of Chatham's citizens to seek me out on Saturday mornings. The extra purchases helped to impress Mr. Raymore, whom I already knew and was friendly with. When it came time to close the deal on the Grand Avenue property, he did everything he could in his power to help me.

Now, with the future looking so promising I began thinking seriously about asking Eunice to marry me. I waited for the annual winter lull in our work then went to her home on a Sunday afternoon after church.

I drove mother and Harriet home from the service and only stopped at the door.

"You're going to see her again I suppose?"

I bleated out a "Yes" and tapped the mule lightly on its buttocks. This was before we owned Sam and Billy.

"My son, you are a fool." I now know I could not argue with this assessment. But, I did not wish to advance this conversation further by telling her my plans, so all I said was "I know Mother, I know."

Eunice accepted with neither joy nor sadness. It was almost as if she was repeating some earlier assent that only needed repeating. I, on the other hand, was so filled with joy that I did not perceive her consent as acquiescence and for the rest of that day I planned our nuptials only vaguely aware, that once again, I was the one doing all of the talking.

March twenty-first, the spring equinox, was a day I felt would be lucky for us. So I set the date and felt content that life would now be as I dreamt it should be.

Martha refused to attend the wedding, which caused a lot of talk in the community. She was too strong-willed and sometimes I despise her for it. Harriet did attend. Not because she liked Eunice, but she felt the same way about me as I did about her and she did not want me to go to the altar alone. Morgan gave Eunice away and Benjamin was my groomsman, although he too was not happy about my marriage.

Reverend King performed the ceremony at Morgan's home and he earnestly tried to convince my mother she should attend. Martha was steadfast, accepting no argument. Instead, she spent the morning packing her belongings to move to a cottage in Buxton. She refused to sleep under the same roof with Eunice.

Morgan hosted our wedding supper. People from the village came to wish us well and give small gifts. Afterward, Eunice and I went back to our farm alone. Harriet joined Martha in her new cottage. After my husband's privileges, we settled down to sleep.

Some time later, soft weeping awakened me. When I reached out to touch Eunice and comfort her, she violently jerked away toward the wall and curled herself into a ball.

CHAPTER TEN

A response from General Sherman to my query about his views on Kennesaw arrived this morning. John Edwards brought it out to the house. It is a long and friendly letter, which I scanned through to give John the gist of the correspondence. Later, in the barn, I read it again more thoroughly and enjoyed reading it.

W. T. Sherman,
817-15th St.
Washington, D.C.

Mr. Frederick Douglass Macdonald,
C/O General Delivery,
Buxton, Ontario
Canada

September 17, 1878

Dear Frederick,
I am in receipt of your letter dated September 1 instant. It is curious to say that both you and Kennesaw Mountain have been on my mind. Then, I find you and I are thinking of exactly the same things. I thought this only happened to people who have been married a long time.

Disregard my impoverished humor. There is little enough jocularity at my headquarters here in Washington. Most of the soldiers I deal with are careerists who plot every sneeze for its benefit.

Because of the stifled atmosphere, I seek other fronts to challenge and enjoy myself with. Now I attend more theatrical performances and musical demonstrations. I have seen some exceptional singers of late and have attended the salons afterwards, which allow me to meet them and they are glad to meet me because of my continuing fame. In November I will travel to Boston for the new Gilbert and Sullivan operetta, "HMS Pinafore". Many fanciers of musical theatre have been awaiting this since it was premiered in London and reviewed in that city's Times newspaper last spring. Lately, I find myself drawn more and more to New York for the city's business and cultural life. I often make the journey alone as Mrs. Sherman feels it a bit frivolous and is busy with priests and monsignors preparing our son, Thomas, to become a Jesuit.

Thomas graduated earlier this year with a good career in law ahead of him and I fully supported this. Then his mother held sway and, true to her Irish roots, sacrificed her oldest son to the priesthood. I am not in favor of him joining the clergy. I believe the church has too much influence. Mrs. Sherman knew I was not happy with this, yet she went ahead and committed our son before he had a chance to experience much of the world. In my view, the Church is an institution where a man with no family name or wealth can seek to attain some prominence. Since the war our wealth and family connections have become the envy of America and Thomas has the personal advantage of this. He has explained his reasons to me, but I feel they are not his own opinions. They sound like those of the clergy. What is a father to do when his son is grown to manhood?

Recently, I was a guest of Mr. Samuel Clements who lives in Hartford, Connecticut and is more popularly known by the nom de plume, Mark Twain. He is indeed as witty as his writings indicate, but more than that, I found his social observations to be accurate and telling. I recommend you read his work, but you need not indulge in his children's adventure story, Tom Sawyer, to get the full flavor of his writing. I believe he is a more successful essayist than novelist. Over cigars, he told me that he once served in a Missouri Confederate militia at the start of the war, but did not fully comprehend that battle was more than a fine uniform and polished sword until they killed a man by accident. After that he went west and it was a good thing. He is the kind of cynic we need to force the healing of this country and to prevent the Secessionists from gaining renewed momentum in our society.

It surprised me to learn that one of Clements' close friends is a Negro farmer, John Lewis, who tills the farm next to Clements' country home. Because Clements is a Southerner hailing from Missouri by birth, I naturally expected that he would choose not to associate with Negroes. I told him about the friendship between you and me, and he seemed pleased. We talked about the problems now facing our country and both of us agreed that the Negro question forced upon us by slavery is probably the most urgent to resolve. Clements said he is considering a new novel that will contain a slave as a major character. This is a very radical idea and I worry for his safety.

In regard to your question about the Kennesaw Mountain fight, a lot of people decry it, from the comfort of their hearths as a complete failure on my part. I have never looked on it in that light. It was simply a different kind of battle than what we had been doing up until that point in the Atlanta campaign.

The greatest problem with war in mountain country is the disparity of vertical interval at which you must fight. Someone is always on the low ground. If that army is to be successful, then it cannot be by flanking the enemy. With time you can surround and starve your opponent out of his positions, but for us time was an unaffordable luxury.

It galls me that so many good men were lost at Kennesaw in the same way they were killed at Shiloh and Vicksburg. But that is something I have to accept responsibility for and I would not be a commander if I could not do that. What we obscure with the hindsight of historical sunshine is the fact that this was war, a brutal war and one in which we were in danger of losing not only a battle, but our country. In many instances, I could attain my objective, whether it was to make a junction between two wings of our army or overwhelm an enemy-held position, with a small number of casualties. Still, there were times when only an out-and-out, frontal charge could do the job. I am sure those who criticize me now for the losses at Kennesaw would be even more vicious in their attacks had I left Kennesaw alone and let General Johnston use it as a base from which to block our entrance into Atlanta.

As it is, I consider him to have taken the day because he escaped to fight on. Perhaps the only happy event for me was that President Davis lost all confidence in Johnston, whom I considered to be a very good general, and removed him in favor of the incendiary Hood. Once Hood was in command of Atlanta, I knew he could not hold it the way Johnston would have and it was a pleasure to push him out of the city. I have met Hood since the war and in our interview he admitted that this was so.

Your part in all this has gone unsung. This letter will confirm to your grandchildren and their grandchildren that you were an important factor in the downfall of Atlanta and subsequent campaigns although at the time I assigned you the task of being an agent within the city, I was sure you would not live to see me enter it or meet me again.

The night we first met, my generals urged me to go to bed and see you the next day. McPherson's death earlier in the day was still tearing my heart out, but I was restless and wanted to explore the things that were on my mind. These generals were the same who told me the idea that you acting as a spy within Atlanta was not a good one and viewed the contribution you might make as limited and with long odds against achieving any handsome advantage. Because they had been correct in their advice about most things, I gave them some credence, but I also had an instinct that told me the intelligence you might provide could prove to be of some considerable tactical importance if you survived to give it.

The conversation about having a Negro spy developed while we were still attempting to unseat General Bragg from Chattanooga. At the time, our fight was against regular army units and I could not see any advantage to it because we had no such person with military training. But, the thought stuck in my mind. I was also faced with the thousands of Contrabands fleeing their plantations and clogging my supply lines. We had no orders regarding their legal status to allow us to deal with them and had to consider them as property under the law until a different legal character could be pronounced. That is when I asked General Dodge to look into someone who could help with the Contrabands and who might be of useful service in collecting intelligence from them as we advanced through the South.

The Meridian campaign that we fought between our advances at Chattanooga and Atlanta was a diversion for us. I saw the need to keep navigation open on the Mississippi, which I used to convince Grant to allow me the expedition, but I also needed to eliminate the Rebel forces at my rear if I were going to carry out the ambitious plan of cleaving the South in two. I sought to ensure that there was not enough strength remaining to the south and west to cause the Georgia incursion to fail.

Aside from the strong recommendations of our generals, I had got in the habit of talking to Contrabands who had recently escaped their plantations. I found them to be willing accomplices to my desires. Much of the news they provided was of a better quality than that of my own officers who could do naught but look across the lines through glasses and try to guess what the enemy was up to.

In speaking with them, I found they were quick-witted and appreciative of the time accorded them. In this they behaved with dignity and aplomb. My experience of a Negro's wit was infrequent as I came from a free state, but whilst manager of the Lucas, Turner and Company bank in San Francisco, I was acquainted with the story of Henry Sampson.

Sampson was a slave of unusual intelligence belonging to a Colonel Chambers. We made use of him at the bank where he was taught to read and write by one of our tellers, Mr. Reilly, and eventually elevated himself to the point where I felt it worth my while to pay him two hundred and fifty dollars a month. His work was dependable and before long, he was able to purchase his own freedom, then that of his family and brother.

Slaves on the plantations I visited while a schoolmaster in Louisiana, were no less intelligent, but they did have to be much more devious to make any headway in the world. In the main, they had to be Janus-like, presenting only one of their two faces to those who owned them.

During all of our actions in the South I took every opportunity to speak with Contrabands. They perceived me as some kind of messiah: wanting to help me and our movements as much as possible. They would come to our pickets and tell them where the enemy was hiding and who was helping the enemy. This was not done with impunity. If a man or woman were suspected of passing intelligence along they would be beaten or hanged. This still did not deter the slaves and they continued to seek us out right until the cessation of hostilities.

Even before our meeting I had used agents to collect information. But you were the first Negro that I worked with, who was trained as a soldier and could tell the difference between a Napoleon and a Parrott gun.

I half expected you to shuffle into my camp on that first night. Long experience suggested that those of the sable race all behaved in a like manner putting the more subservient of their Janus faces forward when dealing with a white man. Watching from beyond the influence of the lanterns, I let you wait. I wanted to measure you.

Rumors had been circulating from the time you arrived from the East. You were portrayed by various of my general staff as a man who could not know the true situation because you were British in origin. There were others who insisted you could not be trusted because of the same, then there were those who would not believe a Negro had the intelligence to accomplish anything other than the menial.

In those first moments, before coming out of the shadows, I studied you in much the same way I would a horse. Although still grieving I could not let sorrow cloud the day and I wanted to know whether you could only run a furlong or the full mile. You stood at parade ground readiness and there was intelligence in your eyes that took in everything you saw and which I believed evaluated facts quickly. It did not take me long to rate you as a steed capable of running the mile, and more, with ease.

We all fall into the trap of comfort. I don't like to be trapped, but even I am occasionally cornered. Before you spoke I was expecting, and therein lies the trap of expectations, to hear the voice of a field Negro or at best a house servant. Instead, I was introduced to eloquent speech with distinguished elocution. My first reaction was that I should employ you to instruct several of my generals in erudition and rhetoric. God knows they could have used it. Dodge had provided me with a docket on you and as I told you, I was aware you had been a reporter in your home country. He did not send me any examples of your writings and so, I supposed you to be one of those who managed to scrawl a few incorrect facts onto a page then hand it over to your editors to correct the spelling and insert the commas.

This all gave me a start and I almost ruled you out as a spy, wondering if you could even personate a nigger. You seemed assured that you could and if you remember, the first mission I gave you was to dress in the cast offs of a field hand to go among them and bring me back news of what they knew. That you had already succeeded in your earlier work with Captain Mortenson was assurance that you would accomplish this too.

Recently, I met your Colonel Higginson at a function in New York. I remembered his name, but for a few moments it eluded me as to where that particular acquaintance developed. When I did recall, we had a satisfying conversation about you. One of the anecdotes he recalled for me was your attempts at learning how not to be British. Stories of you circulated, and apparently do to this day, of the strange Negro who spoke like a white schoolteacher, but could not wrap his tongue around the simplest working phrases from the field.

My expectations were more than met when you reported back to me that a runaway felt safe enough to tell you where a hundred barrels of gunpowder were buried in the woods to the East of Atlanta and that he knew right where it was because he helped bury it.

That confirmed you could accomplish the mission successfully. But we both knew, as the siege of Atlanta progressed, the Rebels would be looking for anyone passing intelligence to Union troops. Already there had been incidents in which innocent people were lynched after being accused of spying. All it took was someone to point a finger. J'accuse if you will.

I did not feel our second meeting got off to a good start. Why General Davis believed Captain Berton is beyond me. Normally, Davis was more perceptive than that, but when Berton called you my barber and offered your services to Davis, the captain went beyond the accepted bounds of good humor. That incident and the verbal drubbing I mistakenly gave General Davis caused him to hate you beyond his normal hysteria over Negroes.

Several times, and especially after Ebenezer Creek, I was tempted to censure him for his racial antagonism. But, other than that, he was a competent commander and I did not like to remove commanders mid-campaign and still do not see the efficiency in disrupting the progress of a campaign. Your support for his decision at Ebenezer Creek convinced me that his was strategically determined and only partly driven by racial hatred. If anything, he was callous.

Captain Berton paid the price, however, and was sent to a frontline unit. He did not fare well there either. Before we could occupy Atlanta, a Confederate sharpshooter took him when the captain failed to keep his head lower than the parapet.

I wrote to Mrs. Sherman after Kennesaw that 'I begin to regard the death and mangling of a couple of thousand men as a small affair, a kind of morning dash.' The press got hold of that and made it sound like I cared not for those men. In truth, I was becoming mightily sick of war and facing Atlanta, I would have given the most generous terms for surrender so as not to face losing even more fine men. The idea of sending you into the city did not please me, but I knew then it was what I must do in order to have the best information possible. I steeled my heart for the task, but almost became crazy when I was told Berton had ordered you to cut General Davis' hair, because the general requested a barbering.

When I came upon you, interrupting this bad farce, I was highly angered that you were treated in such a bewildering manner. The look of incomprehension on your face and General Davis' rude manner told the tale of Berton's poor joke.

I do not know where Berton concocted that story from, but I believe it was to make me look foolish for having placed my trust in a Negro. Whatever the reason, he perpetrated it on you and General Davis, and I have had enough trouble from men named Jeff Davis.

Seeing you look around helplessly for some relief from the situation infuriated me. Berton knew you were not a servant and the unhealed gash across your face was testament of you being a fighting soldier.

While this was going on, my brother John was pressuring me to join the ranks of those Republicans who believed President Lincoln was soft on the rebel politicians and their officer corps. He wanted, they wanted, Mr. Lincoln to punish the Secessionists by forcing them back into the Union then to withdraw the common rights of a citizen from them until they earned the trust of the government. I received a number of letters from John during the Atlanta campaign assuring me Mr. Lincoln was about to lose the fall election and that the Republicans were looking for a new man. He also pointed out his party's willingness to forge an alliance with select members of the Democratic Party who supported the war.

I received one newspaper clipping from him, which I still have, sent by a supporter in Wisconsin that states openly 'We hope that a bold hand will be found to plunge the dagger into the Tyrant's heart...' The editor who wrote that needed a rope placed about his neck.

But I could not give much time to these considerations. You and I had a siege to break or we would only be serving our president the cold gravy of defeat.

A siege is harder on men than the out-and-out charge of direct battle. Atlanta was wearing us down and the fact that the siege looked to be endless until we cut the rail lines at Macon was doing more damage than good. Even Mr. Lincoln was suffering from it. Our poor president was a good man and deserved better than he was getting from that pack in Washington. At least General McClellan was for finishing the war and reuniting the country. It was suggested by the Copperheads in the House that we make peace at any cost. I believe they were supported by many Democrats in this notion of capitulation. It was then, and is now, paramount to treason. So, it was a good thing that General McClellan was awarded his party's nomination with such a resounding confirmation.

Copperheads dared not show their faces in the theatres of action. I think you would agree we would not have tolerated them. But, they held some sway in the North and in Washington and, of course, the government of Mr. Davis encouraged them.

Vallandigham was a traitor and Mrs. Lincoln was right in that. It is not well known among the citizenry of our country, but in mid-1864 there was a near revolt in Chicago and the Northwest due to the efforts of this low cur and his associates. They were trying to organize the secession of the Northwestern states to take them out of the war. It only failed because a plot was discovered to free the Confederate prisoners at Camp Douglas in Chicago and the camp was reinforced.

General Grant learned about the plot from General Rosecrans. It was developed by these Sons of Liberty who held a meeting in the Canadian city of Windsor in April. That in itself should have been enough to justify the invasion of Canada West. But, I respect Mr. Lincoln's judgment in that. We did not need to fight Britain and already we were close to war with France over their invasion of Mexico. The Union had neither the resources, nor the will, to carry on conflicts with these two great powers. It was only a matter of time until we beat the Rebels, but we could not defeat both the Rebels and the British or the British and the French. The president simply set the watchdogs out and we knew every move that was made.

I don't believe spies were ever more important than in this war and will not hold them in the same contempt other military men do. If not for courageous men like you, the war would have dragged on and cost untold thousands more lives.

Crossing the lines must have been difficult and you undoubtedly have many tales to tell that weren't included in your reports. I would like to know how you actually managed to worm your way through the pickets guarding Hood's advance works. Would you honor an aging general with the specifics of your adventures in Atlanta?

As it is growing late and I must meet with President Hayes tomorrow morning I will end this communication for the moment. Mrs. Sherman sends her regards and I look forward to reading your next letter.

Your friend,
W.T. Sherman'
(also signed Cump by his hand)

Rain today. I spent the morning carving an attractive headpiece for Reverend King's bookcase. The pattern I have chosen is grape vines and leaves with flourishes. I have to sharpen my gouges and chisels every half hour or so because the wood is so well seasoned, but the work progresses nicely. I don't know why I should be able to carve as well as I do. When I begin to work, I am nervous that it will look childishly ridiculous. Then when I am finished, I am amazed it turned out so well. But it is not always what I planned when I started out.

CHAPTER ELEVEN

October 6, 1878

Sneaking through the lines into Atlanta had a certain amount of danger to it, but once in the city, people were so concerned with the ongoing bombardment from our guns that a lone Negro hurrying as if on some business for his master attracted no attention.

After the ridiculous joke perpetrated by Captain Berton on General Davis and I, General Sherman took me aside and we spoke for nearly an hour. I could not see the importance of much of the conversation. He asked about my background and family. When I told him about the loss of Helen and our baby, he fixed me with his eyes and did not speak for a moment. Then he said, "I lost my son Willie last fall in Memphis to the typhoid. Even now, I cannot think of him without tears forming in my eyes."

We spoke for a while about our respective families. I told him Absolom died just before the start of the war and he confessed not truly knowing his own father who died when the General was nine years of age.

"Thomas Ewing admirably stepped up to undertake my education and be as much of a father to me as he could, but the death of one's own parent when one is so young has lasting effects I feel until this day, no matter the kindness extended by others. I was fortunate to have Mr. Ewing as I have seen how people generally shun children who have lost their father to protect them. It is as though the offspring are diseased and unwelcome in society."

Rumors about General Sherman having become crazy at the commencement of the Civil War made me wonder how stable he was now. I could see the looks some of his staff officers threw in our direction and they concealed little. I am sure the General had his purpose in allowing me to become so close, so quickly, but I did not see it at the time. Now I know those few hours bound me to him for the rest of our lives. Yet, at the time I thought the death of a child so recently surely must have served to unhinge him once again.

"It seems," he said to me, "that men like you and me, and Mr. Lincoln, are destined to do the things needed to assure our country, but that we must pay a price. I wonder at times, if it is not some kind of divine levy that our children, like the first born of Israel, must be sacrificed.

"Mr. Lincoln lost his son William as well, which you must have read about in the papers." I noted that the General did not use the same familiar nickname, Willie for the president's son that he applied to his own lost child. "I did not know the president very well at the time, but I do know he was as badly hurt by the death of his son as I was of mine. And, as I am sure, were you."

We talked quietly and it was only after I left his presence that I realized we had ceased to behave with military deportment during our meeting.

The General's orders were simple. I was to enter the city to estimate the number of troops defending Atlanta and inventory the number and types of batteries available to the Rebels. I was to keep my eyes open in particular for any signs of movement, be they from re-enforcements or troops making ready to withdraw to a more defensible position.

I was also given the name of a Mr. Peter Lawson who was a friend of the General's from before the war and who in the past, had indicated that because of his Union sympathies he would help the General. My first action once I entered Atlanta would be to find Mr. Lawson and seek refuge among his slaves. The General believed Mr. Lawson would give me the passes I needed to move freely about the town.

The General then provided me with details of a joke they played on a fellow student at the West Point Academy years before and which no one else knew that he and Lawson were its authors. I was to use this as a bona fide proving to Lawson that what I said was true.

Once I received my orders from the General, I circled Atlanta to the east giving the front a wide clearance, then I traveled southwest at an angle to intersect the railway line which ran north from Macon and provided the city's defenders with provender and ammunition. By following this line, I was able to walk right into the heart of Atlanta without hindrance. The going was so easy I even considered jumping aboard one of the slow-moving cars, but decided not to tempt fate.

Travelling by night I covered a distance of nearly one-hundred-and-twenty miles in five days. My biggest concerns were the militiamen and paddy rollers who patrolled the roads and nearby woods looking for fugitives trying to escape to the Union lines. Only once did I come upon any of these cowards.

On my third night I began to angle my way toward the southern edge of the city. I was perhaps forty miles to the southeast and had been sleeping rough as I went. Thorn thickets were the best cover to lie up in during the day. Stories from the fugitives in Buxton educated me in what to do to avoid capture and I regularly rubbed onion and wild garlic onto my feet and wore it in my clothing. As it was August there was an abundance of these plants all around me.

In the distance I could hear the ongoing cannonades from both our batteries and Hood's. Above the artillery din, as dusk was settling on this night, I could also hear the baying of hounds. They were closing in and growing louder as each moment passed. I made myself ready to leave my daytime roost and was working my way toward the road when their howling first reached me.

Their pursuit did not frighten me as I was in good cover and the worst I might expect was a beating for running away, then my return to Mr. Lawson, but they passed me by in pursuit of another poor soul, and in half an hour I was on the march again.

Just before dawn on my fifth day, I arrived in the southern part of Atlanta where the rail lines enter the city. I was hungry and tired, but I had reached my objective and now had to set to work.

The south side of Atlanta had suffered only slight damage so far; it was the north side that was virtually in ruins. Not one building that I saw as I moved north through the city had escaped our barrage. The guns must have been permanently sighted to cover different parts of the city, because as I approached a Union shell would explode here and there in the dark. At daylight the bombardment picked up. Many buildings were now burning, but civilians and soldiers both worked hard to keep them contained. Occasional rain showers had dampened the ashes but did not extinguish the fires. Because of this, there was the overall smell of wet ash added to by the smell of decaying flesh. There were dead horses and mules lying in the streets. Negroes with dray wagons tried mightily to remove them all, but the efficiency of our Northern war machine was such that they could not keep up. Rescue crews attempted to plumb the ruined houses to remove the corpses of the human victims, but they could not search every ruin. Only those homes and commercial buildings where someone remained alive to call for help and report others trapped within were searched. The rest were left until they could be dealt with. In many places there was only the slightest evidence that a street had traversed the ground. Building rubble lay atop torn earth and identification of a laneway came from something as simple as a foot of undemolished brickwork running in a broken line with another section of foundation or wall a little further on.

Destruction of this immensity was beyond my ken. Although I had seen the harvest of battle, I was not prepared for such ongoing horror wrought upon civilians. I could shut my eyes and stop my ears to it, but I could not quit breathing and with every breath, my stomach heaved.

After a morning of this, I could take no more and sought the shelter of a standing wall where I put my head down and divested myself of the contents of my nearly empty stomach. I had a small bottle of water in the blanket I was carrying and as I pulled it out to wet a piece of flannel to wipe my face, a man's voice called out.

"Goddamnit. Get away from that wall. Can't you see it's about to fall over."

I had never even considered the possibility. My stomach had taken over my ability to think. The man was correct. I realized now that the wall had wavered to my touch and if I had leaned hard upon it, it would have come down atop of me.

"Come out from there you dumb nigger. We need some help here." The speaker was in his late twenties and wearing the uniform of a Rebel officer.

My first inclination was to grab him by the throat so I could choke the life out of him. Then, I remembered my role.

"Yassuh. I jus' bin sick, but I be fine now. I be right there." Since joining the Army of the Tennessee and working with the Contrabands of Tennessee and Georgia, I had come to understand they spoke a different dialect from the Geechee of the coast. Unlike Geechee, every word was English, but shortened for field use. Because of the training given to me by the coastal Contrabands, I was able to pick up this western manner of speaking much more quickly than I had the coastal. Not knowing whether this young officer was very bright, or how much he paid attention to the speech of slaves, I was careful to make sure my diction would resonate properly.

"Come with me. There's people trapped in the machine shop near the roundhouse." I followed him past two broken locomotives. One was lying on its side ten feet from the track and the other had its cab completely blown apart. There was steam leaking from the boiler of the engine with its cab gone. Where the cab had been, the control-levers and valves were missing disabling the tank engine completely.

He set me to work removing bricks and timbers from the rubble that had once been the machine shop. It looked as though a hurricane had pushed the building over as all the bricks were lying in a fan-shaped pattern. Here and there a driving wheel for some tool protruded above the rubble. Seeping upward through the bricks was the strong odor of turps. Also arising was the weak voice of a man calling for help.

I noticed the officer had backed away to a safe distance from the wreckage, but was watching me intently.

"Can you still hear him?" he shouted referring to the buried man.

"Yes suh…"

"Well hurry up then. Those fumes could take fire any minute." I was not happy about my situation. Even though the man, or men, below me were my enemy I was not about to let them roast alive. These were working men with families not soldiers who accepted death as possible result of their employ.

"Sir. I'm working as fast as I can." I responded throwing the bricks off to the side, but being careful not to hit anything that might spark. My hands were not those of a preacher or rich man, but a farmer turned soldier and I thought they were tough enough until I set about digging with them.

The fingernails tore away into the quick and the bomb-sharpened edges of bricks cut deeply into the pads.

It was no lie that I was working as fast as I could. I wanted to free these men and get away from the liquid that was causing the smell before it exploded in my face. There was no way of knowing how much of it was interred within the building, but I assumed there was at least a barrel hidden somewhere in the rubble.

Ten minutes of hard work took me to where I found a shirted elbow. It moved, and so I dug furiously until I had uncovered the upper part of the man. In another few minutes I had him free and was carefully picking him up and carrying him clear.

He was coughing and choking from the dust. In between fits, he thanked the officer for getting him out. I was beginning to regret my efforts. Then, as I set him down, the brick mound erupted into flames. Hideous screams poured out tearing through the air above the noise of cannon shells for two or three minutes before the rubble bier fell silent.

"Pick him up," commanded the officer. "Take him to the hospital." He could walk, but needed help so I slung his arm about my shoulder and supported him that way. In truth, I did not know where a hospital was located and I did not have to feign ignorance in seeking directions.

"Sir, I don't know where's there a hospital. I come from the south side of town an could find him one there easy."

"Oh for…" here he took the Lord's name, "sake. Go up this road here and turn right at the church. It's about a quarter mile along. Ya'll know which way is right don't you?" I admitted I did and was off more carrying than helping the wounded man's walking.

By the time we arrived at the hospital, my patient had not said ten words to me, and those were only terse directions. He did not thank me for digging him out. Those words were reserved for the officer whom I decided I would shoot if given the opportunity. I was glad to be rid of the machine shop victim, but as I turned to leave a young woman in a nurse' costume told me to help carrying a dead man on a stretcher out to a wagon. The wagon was going to take him to the cemetery in the northeast section of the city and was being driven by an older Negro.

A young coloured helped carry the body to the wagon. He did not want to talk as he was in a hurry to get back behind the shelter of the hospital walls. I could not blame him. When a projectile whistled overhead to explode nearby we dropped the body and dashed to hide under the thick plank bed of the wagon, along with the elderly driver, before the shrapnel descended back to earth. Shell fragments fell all around after the initial explosion so we remained hidden until we were sure the hissing thumps had stopped on the deck of the wagon indicating it was safe to come out.

"Can I ride along with you?" I asked the older man once we had finished loading the corpse.

"Climb on up… Where you going?"

"Marse Lawson's."

"Don't know him. He live near here?"

Arriving at the cemetery gates, I climbed down off the wagon and judging by the sun made further north into the city. Forty-five minutes of walking and carefully stepping my way around razed buildings brought me to a common well where three slave women were loitering and gossiping while drawing their water.

"Hello ladies," I began addressing the prettiest of the three. "Where would Marse Lawson be living?"

"What you want him for? I'm much more fun." This caused the other two to break out in a cackle of laughter.

"Ah, I'd like to be staying, but I've got to deliver a letter to him or my own Marse William'll whip me dead."

"You no fun boy," then, "he live up that street there. Big yellow house. About half a mile."

Winking at the pretty one, I set off in the direction indicated and after ten minutes came upon a two-story, yellow frame home with large windows on both the main and upper floors. Knowing the trouble I could find myself in by arriving at the front door, I went around back to seek the slave's entrance to the main house.

Set back at the rear of the property and hidden by the main house were two slave cabins. In former times, they had been neatly kept, bespeaking the habitation of house slaves. Now they were all but destroyed by artillery fire. There was shell damage to the roof of the main house, and I discovered the back wall was almost completely shot away. Cannon balls had destroyed the summer kitchen and exposed the winter kitchen. All around the buildings, the ground was furrowed and pocked by shells. Underfoot, shards of metal made walking dangerous if the walker had no shoes. The bomb fragments were in various states, from rusty and mostly buried to shiny and lying on the grass like some discarded children's toy. An old woman, as round as she was tall, was chopping kindling on a block at the rear of the house. She was rending parts of a broken wall into useful faggots for her stove. Looking up at me, her face registered impatience and anger at my audacity in disturbing her work.

"What you want boy?"

"Marse Lawson at home?"

"Who be asking?"

"I've got a message for him from an old friend. Now be he home?"

"You bess tells me and I give it to him."

"Sorry mammy. I've been told to tell no one but Marse Lawson himself." With this she stood up and stared at me. No one was going to get by her.

"I can wait all day mammy. But this be important and Marse Lawson'll be mad enough to whip you, if you hold me up." From her "Humph" in response, I could tell Marse Lawson had never whipped her because she was an important part of the family.

"Ya'll wait here," she said driving her hatchet into the chopping block. Waddling up a set of temporary steps, she disappeared into the house. Returning a few minutes later she was preceded by a tall, balding man whose posture told of military training.

"You have some sort of message for me?"

"Yes sir. An old friend asks you to remember the time you and he stuffed Bill Rosecrans' shoes full of old papers…"

October 7, 1878

The story told to me by the General was that he and Lawson decided to have a lark at Rosecrans' expense. On learning from a senior cadet that there would be an unannounced inspection in the middle of the night, Sherman and Lawson proceeded to stuff the toes of Rosecrans' boots with old papers and rags so his feet would not fit into them. For good measure they added a dollop of glue to the wadding. By doing this, they rendered the boots useless for immediate wear, and indeed only after much effort with sticks and hooks was Rosecrans able to clear the blockage. The prank proved popular among the cadets and for a long while afterward cadets locked their shoes up at night in fear the mysterious perpetrators would strike at them. Sherman and Lawson also hid their footwear and never admitted culpability.

"Come with me." I followed the man into the house, and so did the mammy. Lawson led me into his study on the ground floor telling the woman politely he would ring if he needed her. As she turned away, I saw a hard look in her eye that gave me pause.

Taking a set of spectacles out of his pocket he turned to me and held out his hand. "Please give me the message."

"I am sorry sir, but it is not a written communication. I memorized the message." As I slipped from field hand English into my normal speech, Lawson who was the same height as me took a step back as though I made to strike him.

"My God, you truly do come from Cump." At that time the name was foreign to me. We called the General Uncle Billy and assorted other names, but enlisted men never used the shortened version of his middle name. "Please sit down."

Lawson drew the blinds on the windows of the study and locked the door.

Settling into a chair beside his desk, I explained what I needed from him without revealing my mission. I believe he understood my reticence to tell him what I had to do. Knowledge of that nature was lethal. He consented to let me live with his slaves and to give me a pass that would allow me to travel about Atlanta on my own without hindrance. Then, thinking ahead, he surprised me by asking if I had any skills we could use to explain my presence.

The carpentry that Absolom taught me was put to good use. Lawson told the other slaves and white neighbors that I belonged to his sister in Macon and was on loan to try to keep the house in repair until the siege was lifted and then complete any construction occasioned by the ongoing bombardment. It was a viable excuse for my presence and I set to work immediately upon the conclusion of our interview.

As a carpenter, I was able to wander the city seeking building materials and hardware. There was not much of either available. Everything was dedicated to the defensive works surrounding the city. The scarcity of lumber and nails sent me further afield and I made note of regiments and divisions, cannons and mortars.

At the same time, I worked on rebuilding the summer kitchen and closing up the holes in the roof. For this the ancient mammy, whose name was Nora, was happy and began treating me in a friendlier manner.

I had a few bad times when soldiers wanted to know what I was doing near the batteries, but I explained my presence with my fascination for seeing the big guns fire. Whenever they were fired and I was nearby I buffooned a jig-like dance to show my glee. It never occurred to the artillerymen that I would know anything about their equipment and function. I was, after all, a "dumb nigger."

As August entered its final days, I came upon definite signs that a movement was underway. Whether it was to move to new fortifications or to abandon the city, I did not know. Three quarters of a mile from the Lawson home, there was a battery of twelve-pound guns and I had taken to hanging around them when I was out and about. It was here I overhead a conversation between two gunners.

"Cap's got orders to clear out tonight. He wants us to put up a couple of pilgrim guns then bring these here south through the city." A pilgrim gun was nothing more than a log painted black and mounted on the remains of a wrecked gun carriage. From a distance observers could not tell the difference between a log and a cannon barrel, so they would refrain from assaulting a position thought to be heavily defended with artillery.

"Where to from there?"

"On to Alabama."

Looking up, one of the gunners spotted me and cursing pulled out his pistol. "What're ya'll doin' here?"

"Sir, I'm just waiting to see you fire the big gun."

"Goddamn ya," and he aimed his pistol at my head. I raised my hands up to cover my face. Then, laughing, he discharged his gun, but not at me. The ball passed near enough for me to feel the wind, but I was too close to the shooter and the thunder of the shot blocked out any other noise.

As he cocked the Navy Colt again, the other gunner interfered. "Let him alone. He's been coming to watch the guns fire for weeks and dances every time they go off."

"You like the guns, nigger?"

"Yes sir. I like them fine and hope you give them Yankees hellfire with them."

"Damn right we'll give 'em hellfire. Now you get 'way from here before I shoot ya'll for real."

I took his advice, but as I walked away another pistol shot rang out. This time the ball sang by my head missing me by inches. Not wanting to give him a second chance, I ran weaving snake-like among the rubble. Two more shots followed, but the range was too extreme for a pistol. I remember hoping he could not reach a carbine or rifle.

That night throughout Atlanta there was a constant rumbling of wheels and shuffle of infantry boots.

As the night grew long I inched back toward the forward positions and discovered they were abandoned. The shortest way to reach General Sherman with the news that Atlanta was his for the taking was directly across the space between the former Confederate positions and our lines. I did not wait to say goodbye to Lawson, but immediately slid down through the dirt on the forward edge of the parapet. Trying not to make any sound in the dark to attract musket fire, I crawled on my belly across the five hundred yards dividing the lines.

Crawling that far quietly took nearly three hours. I would crawl a yard and pause to listen for any indication that I had disturbed the pickets. Finally I was within hailing distance of our lines. I knew it would be deadly to call out without cover, so I searched around in the ruined earth for a shelter of any kind and finally felt a tree stump that had been up-ended. Hiding behind this I shouted to the soldiers manning that section of the front.

'Hey... Hey. I am Sergeant Macdonald. I need to cross back through the lines.'

The sentries responded as I expected they would. They fired into the dark in the direction of my voice and I was gratified to hear their balls thunk into the dirt several yards away.

"Stop firing and get your sergeant. I need to report to General Dodge."

"Can't be one of ours." I didn't know at the time, but General Dodge was wounded in the forehead after I began my mission and had been placed on leave.

"Get your sergeant or your lieutenant. They can ask Dodge about me. I am not armed and will stay here until you get an answer."

Shuffling ensued and a voice called back. "Don't move or I'll shoot. Ya'll jess keep talking to me so I know you're out there."

I did while making reference to everyone I knew in the lower ranks of our army. Shortly a new voice joined our conversation. "You say you're Sergeant Macdonald. What do you look like?"

It was a strange question but I answered. "I'm five foot ten inches tall and I have black hair. I was wounded at Kennesaw and have a big scar down the right side of my face and a badly broken nose. And I'm black."

The new voice took the Lord's name in vain then said "Get him in here quick before the Reb's get him."

"Do not worry about the Reb's. They have left the city and are heading to Alabama."

Now it was important above all else that I get this news to headquarters and General Sherman, however, no one knew where Uncle Billy was encamped and it took me the rest of the night to find him.

CHAPTER TWELVE

November 19, 1878

Rain, rain and more rain, then two nights ago the weather cleared and the moon came out. The fields are sodden and the stubble inundated in places. Yesterday, throughout the day, I saw mallards paddling and feeding in the deeper puddles. Hopefully the ditching Benjamin and I completed earlier this spring will let the fields drain quickly. In the meantime, I have been working on the bookcases. They are almost ready for assembly. Reverend King's are more elaborate than those for the school, but I would be proud to have either set in my home. Yesterday I spent the day planing the backing boards to finished size then rabbeting them so they would lock together nicely and give the entire structure the strength to bear the weight of the books that would call them home.

During the night, I heard a large flock of birds pass overhead. At first I thought they were geese, but their talk wasn't as harsh and demanding as the honking of a goose. They were loud enough to awaken me from my sleep and I went to the window, which was opened a crack, and watched as they continued to pass low over the house. Their chatter was insistent. At times almost melodic. Then they began settling into our field on Thompson Street: huge, bluish white snowflakes in the moonlight cupping their wings to drop onto the earth.

Swans come into our region twice a year, once in the spring and once in the fall. They stay for a day or two; in the spring eating bugs and new shoots; and in the fall the grain and kernels of corn remaining from the harvest. Then, when the wind is right or they are rested enough, they fly away as one. In the fall they turn south toward the lake and follow the shoreline. I suppose they use it as a guide to take them to Point Pelee where the distance over open water to Ohio is shorter for their journey to the winter nesting ground in the United States. Every spring, they land here once again before heading off in a northwest direction. I don't know where they go from here or what their final northern destination is, but they fly with all determination and from the thousands of birds we see landing every autumn, I believe that ambition is rewarded.

It took ten minutes or more for the entire flock to pass overhead. I am not sure of the time because I was reluctant to light my bedside lamp to check. Sitting in the rocking chair in the corner of the room, I listened for nearly an hour until all of the chortling from the field had died away. Only then did I return to my bed.

In the morning I was up before Eunice and instead of making coffee and breakfast, I pulled on my clothes and gumboots then set off along Wellington Street. The fields were too wet for me to go across country and the tree line along the road's edges afforded me some cover as I tried to sneak up on the birds.

Normally the swans came in dozens and hundreds, but this was the largest flock I have ever seen. There were thousands upon thousands of them, maybe as many as ten thousand, and the field was a moving blanket of white. I have not seen this many living things gathered in one place since the war.

Had these been geese, I would have brought out my gun and tried to bag one or two before they flew out of range, but I have always liked swans and wished them no harm. Benjamin or Morgan would not hesitate to shoot as many as they could. It wasn't that I did not like their flesh; it's just that they seemed to be the most pronounced minute hand of the year and I had no desire to interfere with that timepiece. In another way too, swans are more dignified than geese or ducks. It is never a choice for me and I take great, if fleetingly rare, pleasure in their company.

Settling behind a big maple overhanging the edge of the road I watched with interest as, like any army, the swans posted sentries while the others fed. When I arrived, hundreds of birds waddled away from me looking exactly like a wave receding over the sand. Now that they could not see me, they flooded back to peck at choice seeds floating in the water or lying in the mud.

After an hour I was surprised by Eunice flapping her way along the opposite side of the ditch separating me from the flock. She was clothed in her grey Mother Hubbard and gumboots. Her hair was wild and uncombed. She had taken to plaiting handfuls together then tying each into a four-inch long shock so that her scalp showed through between them. The wooly braids danced crazily with every step she took as she ran toward the main flock. She had something collected in her apron and I soon realized they were rocks because when she came within range she started hurling the stones trying to hit the birds.

"Get away. Get away you sons-of-bitches. That's my corn you're eating…" two more stones. "No one said you could have that food. No get away from it." Her eyes rolled in her head and did not alight on any target for more than a second or two. It was then I realized she was weeping as she attacked.

I stood up and stepped out from behind the tree, which hid me not only from the birds, but also from her. Calling her name, I clambered down the embankment of the ditch and waded across the deepening waters to the other side.

Whilst I was doing this, I kept calling her name and telling her the birds meant no harm. She ignored me at first and continued to pursue the swans, which now had taken to the air. When I emerged onto the field, she was fifty yards ahead and running away from me as fast as the muck would allow her. Her apron still contained stones and she threw them whenever she got close enough to hit a clutch of birds. Doggedly I followed gaining as we went.

Several minutes passed before I finally caught up with her. She still had not paid me any attention. Reaching out, I placed my hand gently on the shoulder of her throwing arm to encourage her to desist. Before I could stop her, she spun around and hit me on my jaw. The hand she hit me with held a rounded stone that had the same effect as a club.

Eunice's hand drew back and she stared into my face not with recognition, but with wild hate and bloodlust. My head was spinning from the first blow and I knew if she hit me again, she could possibly kill me. I brought my right arm up to block the blow. After it landed without doing any more damage, I reached out to grab her wrist. Her strength could only be described as maniacal. It took me all of my might to restrain her until she calmed down. Then the glint of recognition flowed slowly into her eyes and I relaxed the lock of my arm although I did not dare let her go yet.

After a bit, I placed my arm around her shoulder and guided her back toward the house. She still had not said a word to me, but cried softly and I could not tell if it was for me, or out of self-pity, or for something unseen and unknown to me.

At home, I wrapped her in a blanket and brought her rocking chair to the stove so she could warm herself. Both of us were chilled and shivering. After adding a few pieces of hot-burning apple wood to the firebox, I placed the kettle on to make tea, then went to change out of my wet trousers.

From the kitchen I could hear her. Up until this point she had not said a word directly to me, nor had she uttered anything intelligible. Now she called Albert's name loudly and cursed the Confederates who killed him.

News of Albert's death did not reach me for more than a year. I was encamped outside of Atlanta at East Point, just before we set off for Savannah, when the letter arrived. It was one of eight letters that made it to me all in one mail call. Martha wrote to say that he was among the dead of the 54th Massachusetts men, but she had no details as to how he died. That letter carried the names of two others of my friends who were killed in the war. After that, no letter that could reach me would arrive without an inventory of the dead from our village. Sometimes it would be just one while after a big battle, the names would roll on endlessly. Occasionally, there would be a correction and a man would be moved from the killed list to simply wounded, but that was rare.

Even though years have passed, I still have no knowledge of how my childhood friend met his fate and don't suppose I ever will. I do know that I miss him immensely and wish his happy face could appear once more at my back door.

Once again in the kitchen, I set up a small folding table beside Eunice's chair, added tea to the pot and brought cups and cream and sugar to set upon the table. Eunice was rocking slowly as I did this but stopped when she saw a cup of tea had been prepared for her.

"Thank you," she said, as she seemed to come back into the moment.

"What happened? What did you think you were doing?" I asked. Not to be a scold but to see if she could explain what happened so we could treat her.

"I don't know," she responded in a weak voice before taking a sip of her tea. I added extra sugar knowing that the sweetness would aid in her recovery. "All I know was I was in the field and you were with me bringing me back to the house."

"But, I heard you call Albert's name a few minutes ago while I was in my bedroom getting dry clothes."

"Did I? I must have been thinking of him."

"Do you think of him often?" I wanted to pry. It is cruel, but I wanted to know that I was lost to her. Of late I have spent time remembering and daydreaming about another woman who treated me kindly and whom I should have pursued.

"I try not to. It does me no good to dwell on him, but I cannot help myself. When I least expect it, when I am sewing or cleaning the house," it had been months since she actively cleaned our home, I have added those chores onto the ones I already perform. "His face appears before me. I can feel and smell him. His voice comes ringing to my ears. And I remember other things and those are the only times I feel pleasure."

We talked about Albert for a while longer. Strangely, I grew happier as we spoke and before long I forgave Eunice for trying to kill me with the rock. It was almost nine o'clock and still we sat side by side remembering our lives and talking about how different they might have been if there hadn't been slavery and there hadn't been a war and if hundred of thousands of men hadn't died.

Billy and Sam still needed feeding, and Buttercup had to be milked before I could settle down to working on the bookcases. I wanted to finish them this week and they would take three days to apply the finishing coats of paint and varnish after I assembled them. Reverend King had stopped by to ask that I paint the bookcases for the school a cream color. I was disappointed because I believe a beautifully grained wood like oak should be finished with a simple varnish that lets the nature of the wood show through. But then, I could see his point. Paint would add durability although our students do not destroy things, there would be wear from even gentle usage.

It was in my mind to bright finish, as the sailors say, the bookcases for Reverend King. He had asked for a simple design. I have not told him of the carving work I was doing nor have I told him that the bookcases destined for his house were to be a gift from me.

Eunice had calmed herself and was now quite happy, but to be on the safe side, I added several drops of laudanum tincture to her last cup of tea then walked her to the bedroom and tucked her in before going to the barn.

Billy and Sam were glad to see me and I quickly got them oats, adding an extra measure of feed as a reward for their patience. Buttercup was in a state and only tolerated me because I washed her udders and relieved her of her milk. The extra hours I made them wait meant that the stable was filthy and it took me an hour to muck it out. With that done, I spread new straw to give the floor some warmth because the weather was growing colder.

The headpiece of Reverend King's bookcase was sitting on my bench waiting for me. I had about three hours worth of work to do before it was ready for finishing. It was the last bit of work and once it was attached to the top, I could begin applying the varnish. The air was ripe with moisture that would cloud the varnish so I would let the weather dry out before completing the finish on both the school's and Reverend King's work.

About two o'clock, I heard John Edward's voice in the yard. He was calling to the house, so I left my work in the barn and indicated that he should join me in the workshop.

"I've got some tea boiling."

"Can't say I wouldn't welcome a cup. It is raw out here." He had Lincoln with him. And Lincoln gave me a big grin. "I appreciate you hiring Lincoln to help you. It's about time he started earning his keep. If his appetite gets any bigger, we're going to have to buy a farm to feed him."

"And you," I thought without charity.

"You got a letter from Mrs. Lincoln." He handed me a packet that was much thicker than the usual communication, and then waited for me to open it.

Using one fat ham in an unsuccessful attempt to nudge the headpiece aside, he loosened the vice and pushed it clear so he could plant himself upon my workbench with his mug of tea in hand. He gave no thought to the work or his son or me other than to settle in to listen.

Mrs. Abraham Lincoln,
Pau, France

Mr. Frederick Douglass Macdonald,
C/O General Delivery,
Buxton, Ontario
Canada

November 2, 1878

Dear Mr. Macdonald,
I thank you for the alacrity with which you replied to my initial letters. Surely with operating a farm, furniture factory and real estate holdings, your time is highly valuable and I will try not to ask too much of it. Still, I struggle to understand all that went on and where my place in the history of those years shall be. It would comfort me a great deal to know that it is alongside Mr. Lincoln's in the question of the war and the emancipation of America's slaves. After all, I was his major influence during the war years and he took my guidance to heart in all but a few matters. It was me who made it plain that McClellan was of no military use and had to go. And, I all but authored the Emancipation Proclamation by dictating idea after idea to my husband. One of the few things I failed in was getting him to rid the government of that horrible Stanton. To this day his ghost plagues me.

It is common knowledge that I came to France in order to take my person out of the influence of my son Robert. He is the one who accused me of being insane and who locked me in an asylum. Even though Stanton died some time ago, I believe it was his continuing control from the other side that turned my son against me. Thank God I had the help of my friends and lawyers the Bradwells or I would still be incarcerated at that awful Bellevue Place.

My departure from my fair country's shores should not be construed as cowardice. I have faced a great many dangers in my time. I have lost my beloved husband and all but one child. Even that remaining son is now lost to me although he still lives.

You may not know it, but I have also faced the enemy's guns just as you have. In the summer of 1864 when Jubal Early snuck north from Virginia through the Shenandoah to attack us in Washington, I was one of the staunch matrons of that city who did not panic or flee. More than that, I accompanied Mr. Lincoln out to Fort Stevens where together we faced the bullets of Confederate sharpshooters.

It is strange, but it is the heat of those days that remains uppermost with me. Washington was a bestial place at best in the summer months and ridden with fevers. Many people perished from the Yellow Fever and malaria. Mr. Lincoln and I were lucky in that we seemed immune to the improvident night air that causes these agues. During the height of the summer we never stayed overnight in the presidential mansion if we could help it, although during Early's threat we lived in The White House for protection. The air was more beneficial to one's health in the country at the Soldier's Home, but even there, throughout that July, the climate was unbearable and I fear the heat ruined a number of my dresses and gowns.

How soldiers could bring themselves to run to the attack in that heat, I do not know, but they did. It must have been one hundred degrees during the day. I saw many of the rebels in light shirts without collars and their sleeves rolled up instead of proper uniforms.

At first General Early moved against Baltimore and we believed the rebels would be defeated there. But General Wallace did not have sufficient troops yet under his command to turn the rebels at the Monocacy River. The troops General Wallace did have were Hundred Day recruits and very few had any experience of battle.

It was at this time that Early revealed himself to be nothing more than a common brigand when he ransomed the city of Frederick for an outrageous sum threatening to raze it if the money was not paid.

After beating General Wallace back into Baltimore from the Monocacy, General Early turned toward Washington. Mr. Lincoln and I had always expected any attack to come from the south or west, but someone had the foresight to construct a ring of fortifications completely encircling the capital. Among these was Fort Stevens that lay directly in the path of the enemy's advance from the north and it was here that I became a true battle veteran.

Mr. Lincoln would not take me out to see the battle at Fort Stevens until he considered the situation stable. Capture did not frighten me as I was sure that no matter how treasonous the rebels were, they would still behave as gentlemen if they somehow managed to seize me. Mr. Lincoln commanded that I stay in Washington and not roam. Rebels were already being reported within the city's precincts on the Saturday. Instead, he placed me under what amounted to house arrest with Lizzie Keckley as my warder. He also left instructions with the White House guard that no one was to provide me with a carriage or any other means of transport. He did not trust me, and looking back on those exciting days, he was correct in this. I would have made my own way to see the fighting.

We were still waiting for reinforcements from General Grant. I did not know that Grant considered the troops manning the forts around the city sufficient to deter Early. He was also counting on General Hunter to arrive from the west to add to our existing army, but Hunter was lost or waylaid.

When the battle at Fort Stevens started, I believe we had somewhere around two hundred men manning the guns. Of these, a number were convalescent and should not have been depended upon. But when their test came, they shone like stars in the heavens.

In the evening, after Mr. Lincoln returned from Fort Stevens and accomplished his business in the War Office behind our mansion, he rested long enough to tell Lizzie and I about the horrible lines of civilians fleeing with all that they owned down the Seventh Street Road in advance of the rebels. There were hundreds of these poor souls hoping to find succor and respite in the capital. As he described scene after scene, Mr. Lincoln's eyes would grow moist with grief. It was hard for our eyes not to mist up as well and more than once Lizzie uttered a cry of compassion.

On the Monday before the battle got underway, the reinforcements Grant at last sent from Petersburg began arriving at the Sixth Street wharf. Taking our son Tad, who loved soldiers and anything martial, Mr. Lincoln went down to meet the men who had so recently been on the front lines. According to Mr. Lincoln, Tad loudly 'huzzahed' them as they came ashore with the Greek cross of the Sixth Corps emblazoned on their caps as a symbol of their fidelity.

My husband sent our son home under escort and joined the march from the city to the fort in his carriage. Soon, Mr. Lincoln and our Black Horse Guard were at the head of the column leading our troops right up to the fort's gates. It seemed as though the entire city followed these brave men as an ocean of civilians swirled behind the tramping infantry.

Confining me did have an unintentional benefit. I was able to see how wonderful American manhood truly is. After Mr. Lincoln passed, thousands of wounded men left their hospital beds to man the ring forts. As if that were not enough, I espied Quartermaster General Meigs leading more than a thousand armed civilians to aid in the defense. Later I learned that these were employees of the War Office.

Behind them came the sailors of our navy and their civilian dockyard workers. No Secessionist was going to set foot in the capital without paying in vast amounts of blood.

On the Monday of the battle, Mr. Lincoln felt the situation was still too unsure to allow me to attend Fort Stevens, but the next day, he personally escorted me out in our carriage. Along the way, we stopped at a field hospital to visit some of the wounded men. It seems to me that they appreciated this small effort and those who could, greeted the president and I with warmth and deference.

We were separated from our mounted guard on the journey, but they caught up with us at the hospital and after more than an hour, we continued on to the front lines.

This was one of the few times I was glad Stanton was with us. To control the crowds who desired to wish our soldiers well, he had issued strict orders that no one was to enter the fort without a written pass from him. Neither Mr. Lincoln nor I had such a document, but we did not expect this lack to cause any problem as Mr. Lincoln trumped Stanton in every manner. However, the sergeant of the guard had his orders and demanded our passes.

He was polite and firm, but very frightened for he did indeed recognize his president. Still, his orders were 'With no pass, you cannot pass.' Mr. Lincoln was doing all he could to restrain his laughter at the situation, but he did not wish to insult the young man who was doing such an efficient job.

Finally, giving Secretary Stanton a knowing look, the president suggested that Mr. Stanton could solve the dilemma quickly. Stanton took his meaning and hastily scribbled a pass on the back of a carte de visite then presented it to the sergeant who looked relieved and let us go forward.

I did not know battle could be so exciting. The noise and smells were overwhelming, but the crackle of musketry and flash of the cannon set my heart to racing. I could feel myself getting caught up in the rhythm of the fight and studied every procedure, movement and action.

It amazed me that although we had more artillery pieces, the rebels, used theirs to better effect. A young cannoneer explained that our guns were in fixed positions set to sweep designated areas of the field while the rebels could move their batteries at will to where ever they were needed. I was concerned that this gave our enemy an unfair advantage until the young artilleryman pointed out the lack of protection for the rebel gunners as compared to the security afforded by our earth and stonework.

Attaching myself to this new professor, I watched with fascination as our gunners aimed and fired their weapons at several houses about a mile away. Once a gun had relieved itself, the attendants rolled it down an inclined ramp and washed out its barrel, dried it, then reloaded it before pushing the huge machine back up the ramp and into firing position. All of this was accomplished under the shelter of the thick parapet walls.

In the meantime, Mr. Stanton cowered in the fort out of the way of the fighting, but Mr. Lincoln placed himself up on the parapet with the riflemen and artillery gunners. His large frame clothed in his yellow linen coat must have made a tempting target for the Secessionist sharpshooters.

My artillery instructor, who by this time had been detached from his unit when his officer saw whose questions he was answering, told me that the Confederates were very good marksmen and that they were armed with English Whitworth rifles. These had large telescopes attached to them and were deadly accurate at nearly a mile.

The president was escorting Zachary Chandler around the upper works and pointing out different aspects of the battle to him. My husband was not unfamiliar with strategy and tactics having served in the Blackhawk Wars when he was younger.

Suddenly, Father's sleeve puffed out as though catching an errant breeze. I could see, from where I stood, that a bullet had passed so close as to make a hole in the President's jacket. Then I heard someone yelling 'you old fool get down' Mr. Lincoln grinned, knowing it was shouted in the heat of the moment.

My husband needed to appear fearless in front of these young men. He could not ask them to forfeit their lives were he not willing to risk his own. However, at that moment, I wished he would not be so brazen about it as he dodged another bullet.

After making some remark about a lucky shot, I learnt that the bullet, which missed him, caromed off a canon barrel and wounded a soldier in the leg. Mr. Lincoln made a jest of the Rebel's poor marksmanship. Men who overheard my husband judged the remark cavalier, but knowing Mr. Lincoln, I knew cruelty was the farthest thing from his mind and any such pronouncement was a mockery of the Rebel's skill rather than disregard for the wounded man.

Though the battle periled us all, I was soon caught up in it again and eventually made my way onto the ramparts to watch the final act as we drove Early from the field. As our manly battle cry leapt from a thousand charging throats I could not keep myself from joining in and was exposed for the longest time to the muskets of the Rebels hiding in the nearby houses. When I heard the artillery commander order a change in the aiming point of his cannons to destroy those houses, I begged to be allowed to fire one of them at least once. But this was serious business and I recovered quickly enough to know it was not my place despite my importance.

As darkness fell, Mr. Lincoln and I repaired to our carriage and made to return home to the mansion. Before the driver urged our team on, a captain of the horse guard approached without dismounting and addressed both the driver and president.

'Please be careful not to lose the escort. Even though we have driven them back the way they came, there may still be rebels on the loose in the city. We do not wish ill to befall our president,' and with that he doffed his hat and gave the command for our column to start moving.

We were no strangers to the idea of a possible assassination. Just a few nights before a stranger in an odd uniform followed the president home to the Soldiers' Home at the end of the day. In another attempt, someone loosed the bolts in our buckboard's seats. I was thrown out of the carriage and required several weeks of treatment and rest to regain my good health.

It was easy to believe the incident was merely an accident or negligence by a sloppy mechanic. But when someone fired a shot, clearly in an attempt to kill Mr. Lincoln, it was not so easy to dismiss.

At first my husband considered it an unreported accidental discharge by a soldier who did not wish his incompetence to come to the fore, but the next day Mr. Lincoln's hat was recovered and in the crown there was a through-and-through bullet hole.

When it became apparent the war was ours, we began to relax and after Lee surrendered at Appomattox, all thoughts of this manner of conspiracy left us.

We considered assassination a political tool that might possibly be used by the South in its desperation, but in no wise did we think one person might go to the effort to organize the attacks on Misters Lincoln, Seward and his son Frederick, without the sanction of a surviving government. The way in which it was carried out was cowardly and unfeeling.

I was in the box with Mr. Lincoln that night, as you are undoubtedly aware. But let me step back to paint you a better picture.

The day had been fair and warm with the lilacs in bloom throughout the city. Mr. Whitman, the poet wrote that he could now not smell a lilac without thinking of that day. It is a shame this beauty should be tainted with the memory of such horror, but I feel exactly the same way.

After his weekly cabinet meeting, Father took me for a drive in our carriage in the afternoon. The city seemed to lift on the wings of joy now that our triumph was nearly complete. We just awaited the news that General Sherman had completed vanquishing the Rebels and expected that momentarily.

Young soldiers flirted with the better classes of young women and older officers bore out their standing as gentlemen in their treatment of the city's matrons. I felt that the dresses worn by the women of our city were newer and happier in character. Those worn at the same time in Richmond must have been frayed and tattered. Still, here in our happy capital city there was a smile on every face and the Rebels earned everything they received. I often fancied in the following years that, had I observed the visage of that murderous Booth, I would have known in an instant his intentions. But that was not true. All I saw about me was gaiety and delight and my heart swelled with the same.

Each moment of the day is with me even now. We were late in arriving at the theatre and the performance was already underway. As we entered our box above the stage, the artists correctly halted their work to acknowledge Mr. Lincoln and the orchestra played 'Hail To The Chief. '

Mr. Lincoln graciously bowed to this and the actors and actresses began again where they had stopped.

We did not hear Booth enter our box. Like a viper, he slithered up behind the president and placed his pistol against my husband's head. I can only imagine how badly he must have been trembling knowing that his name would take its place alongside that of Judas Iscariot. How could he not be aware of the infamy he was about to commit?

Now, with retrospect, I was glad General and Mrs. Grant were not with us. Major Rathbone and Miss Harris were not as desirable targets and so, once the murder was complete, Booth had no reason to do more damage.

When Booth entered our box, Mr. Lincoln was enjoying a great laugh at the performance. It had been many years since my loving husband was able to enjoy himself fully and as I stole the occasional glance at his face I could see the enjoyment and happiness transforming him once again into a man so easy to love.

He held my hand throughout most of the performance and I was delighted to have him do so. He was holding it when the shot went off and in that instant, I felt a small tremor go through him and I knew, without looking over toward him, that my husband had taken his leave of this earth.

Pushing past me, Booth made his leap onto the stage. Would that he had broken his neck instead of merely a leg. Then he was gone.

I do not remember screaming anything, but I have been told by several people present that I did. After that, all was pandemonium as a doctor attending the performance was rushed to our box and arrangements made to take Mr. Lincoln to a more comfortable place where the physicians and men of state could gather to wring their hands helplessly. If the murder illuminates only one thing it is that a president shall never die alone or in peace.

My husband was taken to the house across the road from the theatre. It belonged to a Mr. Peterson and I am grieved to have left him such a legacy.

News of the cowardly act traveled quickly and all elements of Washington society, from the poorest to richest, were dismayed and saddened by it. Dr. Abbott and Lizzie Keckley told me later that the Negroes of the city wept openly in the streets and crowded around the house where the president lay. Dr. Abbott went on to say that it was like the end of the world without the world actually ending.

I do not know where Major Rathbone got to at that moment, but I was led by Miss Harris and several others whom I do not remember to the house and room where my husband lay. I could endure only a few minutes with him before my emotions overcame me and I would have to leave the room. At some point Secretary Stanton entered the chamber.

Secretary of the Navy, Gideon Welles, told me later that Secretary Stanton had made himself inconvenient at the home of Secretary Seward who was also attacked. Welles indicated that Stanton charged into Seward's home after the attempt on his life and began shouting contradictory orders until one of the physicians attending Seward and his son told him to calm down and be quiet.

Stanton traveled from the Seward home to the Peterson house and assumed his bullying posture again with me. At one point as I wept for my dear husband he yelled at me and told anyone who would listen to 'get that damned woman out of here and don't let her in again.'

Without shame my son Robert, who should have protected his mother, let Mr. Stanton punish me in front of the entire world. I now think he later came to understand how his father would never have approved of his behavior. But Robert was always one who sought the protection of the strongest and with his father dying, he instinctively went to Stanton's side despite the fact it was evident Mr. Stanton was insane with rage.

He kept me from my husband in his final moments, as if in doing so, he was punishing not only me but Mr. Lincoln as well. I believe Mr. Stanton bore such hatred toward the president that he had to extract his vengeance even at the moment of our good man's death. Mr. Stanton was a weak man who, in life, could not overcome the president's willingness to forgive the Southerners. Stanton and his ilk wanted their revenge tenfold and fie on anyone who would deny them that even if they were dying. I sometimes wonder if the hand of Stanton did not share the trigger with Booth.

So you see Mr. Macdonald, I too have faced the fire. More than that, I have faced the grief of widowhood brought about by a murderous ball and the wrath of political enemies too weak to strike at the president himself, but not his wife. To protect my country and my husband's name I would do it again. I do not seek to usurp Mr. Lincoln's place in the history books, I simply feel it right that I share it for all that I did and was to him.

Yours sincerely,
Mrs. A. Lincoln

CHAPTER THIRTEEN

November 24, 1878
When I was young we did not have a saddle horse at home. The earliest work animals I remember were two bullocks that pulled our plough and wagons. Then, as our farm developed and Absolom built his various businesses, he purchased a team of mixed-breed work horses to replace the oxen, but I rarely rode these animals and only then without the benefit of a saddle or bridle. Because of this, I was a poor horseman. But in Atlanta, the General would become my teacher and I progressed under his tutelage until I was acceptable.

The night I made my way back through the lines it was dawn before I found the General's headquarters. He moved them almost every night and did not always advise his troops on his movements. One private, upon suddenly seeing him emerge out of the dark, did not believe he was who he said he was. The General was dressed in an old, grey flannel shirt and his jacket and pants were covered in mud. He looked as little like a commanding general as possible. The young picket actually pointed his rifle at him and was discombobulated when the General started to laugh as though this were the finest of jokes.

He was asleep when I reached the house in which he had set up his headquarters. As was his usual practice, he had spent almost the entire night before pacing, talking and dictating orders: wearing out two writers in the process. Sleeping and eating were not important to him and he did both only when he could not avoid them.

Captain Nichols recognized me immediately and shook my hand in welcome, which pleased me. When I told him that the city was now abandoned by Hood's troops, he immediately went to wake the General.

"Well, my prodigal has returned," he chuckled as he rubbed the lack of rest from his eyes and indicated to an orderly that coffee was needed. It was somewhere near seven-thirty in the morning when I was admitted to the house and I was surprised when the General suggested that the addition of whiskey to his coffee would be welcomed. I did not turn him down when he offered me similar hospitality, even though I did not normally take liquor. I would soon learn.

"There is news? What's Hood up to?"

"General, Atlanta is yours for the taking. Hood's men abandoned their positions last night and were marching south when I last saw them. As best I could tell, they were blowing up what was left of the city as they went. I crossed through the open stretch between Atlanta and the First Illinois'

Battery M and met no challenges from the rebels. Only our men opened on me, but I was sheltered and safe until they found an officer who could identify me."

"Well that is certainly news worth waking up for." He then ordered breakfast for both of us and we sat eating as I told him everything I had learned from troop strengths to my opinion of the Southerners' morale. He interrupted occasionally to ask a question, issue an order or summon a courier to take intelligence to one of his subordinate generals on a distant flank. When I was finished he thanked me warmly and asked me to stay close to headquarters. I joked about smelling like an old goat and he gave me permission to bathe, but almost as soon as the words had left his mouth he was ordering his wing and divisional commanders to attend him as soon as possible. I took this as a sign I could go to wash and maybe sleep a little.

Sleep did not last long. Within two hours drumming began and there was a mad scurrying of officers and enlisted men. An hour later the advance columns of our entire army were moving forward across the barren ground that separated us from the rebels only yesterday. By the end of the day, we occupied all of Atlanta and the railway line as far south of the city as Macon.

There was no sign of Hood or his minions anywhere in the city. A delegation of citizens with Union sympathies rode out to surrender officially. It was more a courtesy than a necessity.

Hood's men had been thorough in their departing destruction. In the northern districts of the city, our cannonades had accomplished near total destruction. Toward the centre of town, the damage was considerably lighter, but some sections were in much worse condition than when I first passed through in early August. Toward the southern edge of the city there were still a number of unmolested buildings. Many were private residences, but some were factories and depots with warehouses loaded with cotton awaiting shipment.

I marched with Albie Chatterton. Whilst spying in Atlanta, Albie looked after my equipment and clothing for me. We tried to stay near the General, but Albie's divisional position prevented this, so I detached myself and caught up with the headquarters staff staying close without being in the way.

We were in Atlanta four days before the General sent for me. When I reported, he took my salute then smiled and offered more coffee, this time without whiskey. We discussed the changes I could discern in the city. Then he asked if I had a mount available to me. When I replied that I did not, he told me to have Captain Nichols provide me with a suitable horse. I did not tell him that a suitable horse would be docile, blind and lame in at least four legs.

The captain was ahead of the request and as I emerged from the meeting with the General, he produced a lively, sorrel gelding. I did not know enough to tell which breed this horse was, but I did know it was full of nervousness and required a more proficient horseman than me.

An ostler held his bridle expecting me to mount the horse. "Captain Nichols, I'm not a horseman, what do I do?"

Nichols laughed and showed me how to mount the animal, which he said was named Gaylord, "... but you can name it anything you want once you get to know it."

We spent an hour with me on the horse, the ostler leading us in circles while Captain Nichols, along with four or five others giving good-natured advice on how to steer the beast. Occasionally, Gaylord would start and I would lie across his neck grabbing his substantial mane which felt like thin telegraph wires. Gaylord sensed that I was not the commander and took it upon himself to go where he would when the reins were handed to me. Although he had been castrated and was therefore without sex, I had come to think of Gaylord as male. I also rechristened him with the unkindly epithet Blackheart, but later changed that to the more favorable Pal.

"Press your knees into his flanks on both sides and draw back on the reins. He'll stop." It was the General on his own horse: Lexington.

"Hell. Phil Sheridan was worried that once you were mounted you'd take his command. But, I can see there is no need for fear there. I'll telegraph him to stand down right away. He can take the day off and get drunk. We are going into the city this morning and I want you to ride with me. Do you think you can do it?"

I assured him that I would try to follow in his wake, but that he should check often to make sure we were both still there and that I was not left riding shank's mare.

Lexington was a beautiful horse appearing to be as strong and handsome as his reputation made him out to be. Mounted upon his back, the General's appearance changed. Despite the campaign clothes that sometimes confused sentries, he was as handsome and distinguished as any hero by Sir Walter Scott. As we rode through the ruins of the city I was able to keep up with the General and he proved himself to be an apt instructor. Had not secession and the war intervened, the students at the Louisiana Military Academy where he had been headmaster would have been lucky indeed. The General's abilities as a teacher rivaled those of my own Reverend King and Mr. Rennie. The General was able to see the humour in any situation, but was sensible enough to know when to make a jest and I was the butt of many of his jests that morning. I did not take offence, however, because each small joke was accompanied by precise and friendly instructions on how to accomplish the manoeuvre I had just failed at. In all, it was more like a Sunday morning pleasure ride, than a survey of destruction.

"You know sergeant," he and I were riding together ahead of the other officers and escorts in our party, "I am not happy to be here in Atlanta for the reasons we have come. Atlanta was once a beautiful city, but has since become a larder for the rebels and because of that, I have to destroy it. They must learn there is no romance in war and that rebellion is the greatest sin against our democracy. We are going to show them what war means. I think I have the confidence of the president and General Grant to pursue my next campaign, but first I'd like to know what you think. How should we conduct this war?"

Generals should not ask the advice of sergeants. That he would do so embarrassed me and made me stop Gaylord. Lexington took a few more strides until the General brought him up as well.

"General, I am not sure what to say. I have opinions, yes, but they are not educated. They simply come from my heart."

"I'd like to hear them regardless."

"General sir, I believe that now we have General Hood on the run, we should follow him and destroy as much of his army as we can. I do not believe we will profit from waiting."

"I agree with you sergeant. Much has been lost in this war because generals did not follow their enemies to destroy them when they had a chance. That has been a Godsend to Lee from men like Hooker and Burnside and even Meade. But I believe we are in a unique position having taken Atlanta. I am thinking of leaving Hood to Thomas. If we do that, then we can gut the Confederacy."

"The only way I see of doing that sir is to drive a wedge down to Mobile Bay. We already have the territory east of the Mississippi and the Meridian campaign made our backs safe. If we can fight our way to Mobile, then we will have sliced off another important piece of the rebel territory and denied them a deep water port."

"That's true sergeant, but I am thinking of bigger stakes. What's your opinion of the morale in the ranks?"

Morale was not a problem, I told him. If anything the troops took great heart from the fall of Atlanta and were ready to follow their general anywhere. Not to sound too sycophantic, I told him that before we went anywhere, the men would like new uniforms and boots along with other provender, but generally, we had the forward motion of an important victory and the men recognized that.

He did not tell me any more about his plans. We returned to our survey of the city. I could tell he was taking in every detail so he could decide on how to best carry out his plans. Then as we were riding back to our headquarters, he asked me about my childhood.

I told him about our war games and the other amusements we undertook in our free time. For some reason, I also told him how Absolom's surviving son from his first family, Rueben, died of meningitis shortly after arriving in Canada West and that the young nurse who was sent to help him with his dying son was to become his new wife and my mother. He commented that all that loss would have destroyed a lesser man, and that praise gave me enormous pride in Absolom. When I came to telling him about Albert, the General asked if I thought Albert would be suitable to help in the work I was doing. In truth, I had not even thought about the possibility. I allowed that he might be very good. People liked him, he was strong and intelligent and he had once been a slave, which was more than I could lay claim to, so he would have the sensibilities to deal with and read the different situations he would encounter. On the other side of the slate, I knew that he would require training of the kind Colonel Higginson had given to me.

When this conversation occurred, I did not know that Albert had been dead and buried more than a year.

"If you would like, and you think it would be of use, I can request his transfer to our command. I am sure with our capture of Atlanta, even Secretary Stanton would not refuse such a simple request. Please provide Captain Nichols with all your friend's details when we get back." My heart sang. To have Albert by my side would make life, and death if necessary, easier.

"Are you ready and willing to undertake more special assignments for me in the coming months? These may be more dangerous than anything we have attempted."

"General, I think we over-estimate the cunning of the Rebels. Because they can see me only as a slave they don't ascribe any intelligence to me as a coloured man. This is my great shield."

"When this war is over Sergeant, you should consider a career as an actor playing the great roles. I would imagine you could make a highly believable Othello."

"I believe this is enough acting. I would like to get back to being a farmer and cabinetmaker. How could the false drama of the stage ever compare to what we are doing now?"

The General laughed and said I hit the mark with that statement. We spent the rest of the tour through the city talking about his childhood and his family. By the end of the day, I felt the Sherman's of Lancaster were neighbours I had known all my life.

Two weeks later I reported to the General that Albert was killed on the

Carolina coast in an action there. Our conversations about Albert had built him into the hero he was to me and the General appreciated and admired our friendship. Knowing it was Captain Nichols' duty to send all such requests to Washington, I addressed him directly by telling him there was no need to pursue the matter further. It was the captain who broke the news to the General.

General Sherman did not interrupt his meeting with Generals Slocum and Howard. Instead he told Captain Nichols to have me wait saying that he wanted to see me when his conference was over. After an hour and above the noise of the headquarters, I heard the General tell an orderly that he would see me.

"Captain Nichols told me your news. I cannot tell you how saddened I am by the loss of your childhood friend. It is the curse of what we do Frederick. Those fellows in Washington and Richmond think this is nothing but glory and that death comes to us like some scene from a heroic painting. Women swoon at our uniforms and toss roses at our feet and kisses to our cheeks. But none of them, not the women and not the politicians, see this as the worst job on earth. We are not the dogs of war we only die like them. No one sees us cut down by canister in a blink to lie screaming in our own offal. I can only hope your friend did not suffer. I will tell you that those responsible will not escape unpunished. The South started this but you and I will end it for all of us."

I did not see the General for two weeks after that. Then, he asked me to leave Atlanta and head east to determine whether there were any rebel forces in the vicinity. I was now convinced we were going to strike for Mobile and needed to determine any opposition we might encounter.

Hood and Forrest went north and General Johnston was out of favour. General Wheeler's cavalry had become more a roving band than an effective army. Still, they were a threat if used properly. I reported all of this to the General when I returned to Atlanta in the first week of October.

Walking through the city on my way to the General's headquarters I passed the well where I first encountered three slave women in August. Gaylord had been left in the care of Captain Nichols who seemed to have a greater affinity for the horse than I. It would not be credible to have me riding in my role as a slave. Since the fall of the city, I saw the women on occasion and had taken to nodding to the pretty one. She was beautiful by any man's standard.

It was readily apparent she was of pure African descent. Her skin was carbon black and I had been in the South long enough to know that light skin among the members of my race was highly prized even though many hated the skin of the Whites. Her face was pear-like in shape, except with the pear being turned upside down, and it was topped with short wiry hair held in place by a piece of red, yellow and brown patterned rag. Unlike her two companions, she stood six feet in height and was pleasantly built, but most unique about her were her eyes. They were similar in shape to a Chinaman's, wide at first then narrowing to a point and ending, like a happy splash of paint, on an upward stroke.

Since losing Helen, I had not thought much about women. The war and soldiering consumed me. That I was an attractive man did not elude me. A number of women had fluttered their eyes and made it known my attentions would be welcomed. Believing these attentions had a way of interfering with a man's plans, I chose to avoid entanglements. In Atlanta this changed. I was now sure of myself, and where I stood in the Army of the Tennessee. We were, for the moment without a fight to fight and it had been a long time since I had the pleasure of a woman's private company.

Her back was turned to me as I approached, but I could see from the elevation at which her waist bent, that she was not either of the shorter ladies.

"Sister could you bring up some water for a thirsty man?" She turned and when she recognized me she smiled brilliantly and offered me what she had already drawn. There was a tin cup tied to the well by a piece of twine and she dipped the cup into her bucket and handed it to me.

"I remember you. You was the nigger looking for Marse Lawson's house."

"Yes. Yes I was. You have a good memory."

"I should. I marked you weren't no everyday nigger and now you don't sound like one."

"Well, this is how I normally speak."

"Where you from? Up north someplace? Ain't no ones talk like that 'round here."

"You're right" Revered King would punish me with lines for using contractions in my speech, but here I found myself falling into the habit more and more even when I wasn't personating a field hand, so I corrected myself. "I am from up north. So far up north you have only heard rumours about it. I am from Canada West."

"What state's that in?"

"It is not in any state, it is a different country…"

"Like the South trying to be? When they break off?"

"No. We were never part of the United States. We are a different country altogether."

"Well, you shore sound different. You a slave there?"

"No. My dad was a slave here in the South, but he escaped."

"For sure? I heard about folks getting away, but I thought that was all rubbish made up by some nigger want to sound important."

"No. It was true."

"I'll be…"

She told me her name was Song and she belonged to Marse Milford Henderson. She still lived in his home looking after Henderson, his wife and two daughters. There was no place else to go unless she took up the sporting life as she called it. We talked for another few minutes, but I had to report to the General. I asked her if she came to the well every day and she allowed that she did. When I heard this I promised that on the first day I could I would ride by and visit.

"You got a mule?"

"No. I have a beautiful brown horse named Gaylord." She was impressed and for the first time since I acquired the animal I took some pride in him.

"Go on. You ain't got no horse."

CHAPTER FOURTEEN

November 30, 1878
Today I finished the bookcases and tomorrow Benjamin is going to help me deliver them. Often I find myself wishing I could live in a larger city where this type of work would be in demand. As much as I like farming, it does not hold the same appeal furniture manufacturing does. Absolom would be aghast if I had ever made these thoughts known while he was alive. He held that owning land was the best investment we could make in our new country and all else should be secondary to it. Because it served him so well, I have tried to follow his example and it has done me well.

With the bookcases completed, I am faced with the happy task of making Christmas presents for Eunice, Martha, Harriet and her two children Rebecca and David. Rebecca turned eleven years old a few months ago and David is nine years old. Both are charming children and as I have none of my own, I feel like they are my own son and daughter.

Rebecca is a serious child. I think she will become a schoolteacher eventually. Harriet's letters show my niece to be inclined toward history and literature. But for all that, she is a little girl and Harriet has told me she still loves to play with dolls so I will make her a perambulator shaped like a sleigh. I can paint its body and wooden wheels with gay designs, and Harriet can stitch up a mattress out of quilted material.

My nephew David is an easy child to make toys for. He has taken up cricket and baseball. I have a good supply of ash and will make him both a cricket and baseball bat.

Baseball will soon overtake cricket in popularity here. I enjoy the sport myself. Like me, Benjamin and a few other veterans learned baseball in the army. When the weather is fine, we sometimes gather at a vacant field near town to play a game. Often there are not enough old soldiers to make up two teams and so we've begun teaching some of the younger men and older teenagers. We are now finished playing for the year. If we get cold weather soon, we will play shinny on the pond behind Benjamin's house.

We played baseball frequently in the army whilst encamped. I proved to be reasonably good and could hit the ball most of the time when it was pitched to me. Because I could also throw accurately, I played second base. That way, if the opposing team made a hit up the middle of the field, I was often able to catch the ball and hurl it to first base or home plate in time to count the runners out. This made me a popular choice when picking players. While in Atlanta there was an ongoing game. When any player had to leave to stand guard or perform some other duty there was always a group of players ready to take part. So the teams who started playing the game in the morning were not necessarily the teams who finished them in the evening.

It was a good sport to while away the time and it gave me the opportunity to meet and befriend soldiers from a number of different companies in our regiment. As it turns out, I had already developed a modicum of local fame. Men knew who I was, but had only a slight inkling about what I was doing for the General. Comments referring to me as the General's 'pet Nigger' were now rare. While many still treated the Contrabands with disdain, I was becoming accepted as one of the men. Our officers treated me with courtesy, if not respect. Most of the private soldiers who came from towns and cities were also kindly toward me. If the harsh comments came from any one corner, it was from the farm boys who had never come into contact with a Negro before. They could be vicious in their language and a few times I had to show I was ready to defend myself.

From time-to-time, I would disappear from the game for several days. My comrades knew enough not to ask me where I had been or what I was doing. Eventually, I would make my way back to take up my position at second base.

South and east of Atlanta, the land starts to flatten out. The mountains were left behind in northern Georgia and the rolling red hills begin. I was expecting to see groves of palm trees by this point, but was disappointed in that. My expectations were built on my experience of the coast. Nonetheless, I was just as intrigued with the long-needled pines that prevailed throughout the area. The land looked to be good for crops and many of the plantations I passed were neatly kept. Grain, corn and cotton were growing well. Along with my study of any troops and defensive positions that I encountered, the General had required me to assess the progress of the harvest and quantities of livestock. I explored this region two more times for the General as he could not believe the rebels would open their doors so completely.

Between journeys and baseball, I spent my time interviewing local slaves seeking any information that would serve us. I was also assessing the men for inclusion in a new group the General wished to form. When I spotted a likely looking man among the slaves, one who was fit and big, I enlisted him in our Pioneers.

The General asked for enough men to make two separate battalions. It was obvious these would be going with us wherever we were bound, but the General had not let slip his plans or our destination.

Pioneers dug, chopped and lifted for us so our troops could be free to fight. They were glad to do so. They received pay, food and clothing in return. They also received the unannounced benefit of personal pride. When you encountered a Pioneer or group of them in camp, they walked with straight backs. No longer were they slaves or subservient. These men had purpose and if anyone was ambitious to begin the next phase of our adventure, it was the Pioneers.

Song helped in this, as she knew many local men who fit the bill. As word spread that there was a coloured soldier recruiting, the front of my tent was mobbed and I had to post several privates to keep order.

Throughout the month of October there was an over all sense that something of large import was about to happen. Reports of Hood's army arrived almost daily and they indicated he was moving to the north and west. Mostly these consisted of the intelligence that his cavalry, under General Forrest, was harassing our supply lines. They weren't doing much damage, but still our forces could not bring them to battle. Hood seemed intent on moving toward either Memphis or Nashville. A few camp rumour merchants had it that he was attempting to seize Vicksburg so the Confederacy could once again control the Mississippi, but this was quickly discounted. Veterans of that fight knew how difficult it was to capture that city with a well-provisioned and rested army and looked upon Hood's rag-tag band as not being up to the task.

Finally, early one afternoon while the heat of the day was still on us, I received an order from Captain Nichols to attend the General. Leaving the camp and our game, I located the General's headquarters in the large Neal House on Mitchell Street. It was an impressive brick edifice with six columns supporting the front portico, a cupola and two wings for additional rooms giving enough room for himself and his staff. It was evident, even from a cursory glance, that this was why the General chose it.

The sentries let me pass up onto the columned gallery where I waited for admission. Captain Nichols came out to greet me and asked me to wait while the General finished an interview with one of the local doyens. We could hear her through the opened front windows as her voice rose and fell.

"General, they tell me you are going to burn my house and that I must leave."

"Madam, I am afraid that is so."

"But my husband was your friend many years ago at West Point. Surely that must count for something?"

"Is your husband dead?"

"No sir."

"Then why does he not come to see me himself?" From the tone of his voice we could tell that the General already knew the answer to this question.

"He cannot."

"Why ever not?"

"Because he is away from home."

"Ah. He is away tending to business?"

"Yes."

"And what business would that be? The last I spoke with him, he was trained as an artillery officer. Has he perchance changed employ?" This flummoxed her momentarily.

"You know damned well where he is."

"Then madam, he is my enemy and I will treat him as such."

"But my children and I have done nothing to deserve this."

"That is not true. Have you not knitted socks for the Confederate army? Haven't you and the other women of this city rolled bandages for use in Rebel hospitals? Don't your children call my men names and curse them in the streets. Madam, as much as General Hood, you are the enemy and it was you who started this damnable war. You must now be prepared to pay the price."

"But this is cruel and terrible." She then caught sight of me, and the look on her face changed from one of desperation to raw hatred. "I should have known not to expect any grace or mercy from a Yankee. You have come to destroy us and set the niggers over top of us.

"I see your boy out there. He is costumed to masquerade as a soldier. None of those goddamned niggers can be soldiers. They aren't smart enough. God, they can't even speak English. Yet you use them to fight against good Christian men. General Hood was correct when he said you could not defeat us except by turning our own property against us."

We did not need to see the General's face when she said this. It was the one accusation his normally good nature would not tolerate. He did not accept it from General Hood and he would not accept it from this city wife with pretentions of grace and good manners.

"Had my wife said those things to me, I would have dealt with her severely. But you are not my wife and it is not my place to treat you in any other way but as an enemy citizen. You have three days to take what you can carry and leave your home. If you need food, we will provide it, but on the fourth day you must be gone because your home will be burned whether you are in it or not. Now good day to you madam, I have other business."

She screamed at the General, but stopped almost as soon as commencing as he must have turned and walked away from her. After several minutes she exited the house by the front door and in passing me spat in my face. Captain Nichols arrested her on the spot and the guard took her away.

"What will my children do?" was the last I heard from her and I was gratified to hear Captain Nichols hiss at her "You should have thought about them before you attacked a Union soldier."

The General then made me wait and I suspected it was because his mood had been soured by the incident, but when I was admitted to his office within the house, Generals Slocum and Howard were in attendance. I was not expecting them and their presence conveyed the importance of what we were about to discuss.

Slocum was my new corps commander. As a testament to General McPherson, General Sherman chose two good leaders to replace him. Slocum was one and General Howard the other. Both had experience in big battles. Both fought at Gettysburg and Howard lost his right arm at Fair Oaks. This wound endeared him to us and offset the fact that he was a deeply devout Christian who brought evangelism to his command and expected much the same from his officers and soldiers.

Upon my entrance into the office the three men turned to look at me, but only the General smiled. I could not determine from the others faces what they were thinking or thought of me. All three looked weary, but only Sherman's face displayed a tinge of humor along with his exhaustion. It was as if he had worked hard and could see success in those efforts.

I saluted the three and they returned my salutation with nods.

"Gentleman, this is the man I have been telling you about. Master sergeant Macdonald has been a boon to this army since he joined us after Chattanooga. Sergeant, I assume you already know who these officers are, but I will introduce you nonetheless. This is General Howard and this is General Slocum."

Neither offered to shake my hand and I had no expectations of them doing so.

"Macdonald was the man who brought me the news Atlanta was abandoned and has been important in enlisting and developing the Pioneer battalions you are about to use. He is a trained observer and a very good one at that. I would suggest that anything he tells you, you can believe. When he is not sure or does not know the answer to a question, he will tell you outright. We've all been punished by people who need to show they have the answer all the time."

This quip brought the slightest trace of a grin to General Slocum's face. He served under General Hooker on several occasions. Camp rumor had it, that General Slocum tried to resign; not once, but twice; upon learning of his being posted to Hooker's command once again. It was bandied about that only President Lincoln's refusal to accept his letters of resignation kept Slocum in the army.

General Howard's face was immobile.

"Sergeant Macdonald was trained in intelligence matters by Colonel Thomas Higginson."

This surprised Howard who looked up registering the first emotion to cross his face. "Higginson. The one who financed Brown and led a Negro regiment over on the coast of the Carolinas?"

"The same. Colonel Higginson and the Abolitionists were quicker to see what should have been apparent to us all. And that is the Negro was and still is perfectly placed to develop intelligence the enemy does not even realize the coloureds understand. I have worked with Sergeant Macdonald for more than two months now and can attest to his effectiveness. And, in case you have any concerns regarding his capabilities, I ask him now to give you a resume of his schooling and the training he has received since enlisting in our army."

I proceeded to explain my history as the son of a fugitive and the formal education I received at the hands of Reverend King. I was careful to omit my career as a journalist. Then General Slocum interrupted me, addressing me in Latin.

"*Nos mos increbresco huic bellum inter frater vel nostrum Res publica mos intereo.*" (We will to grow strong in this war among brothers or our Republic will perish.)

To which I replied "*Ego operor non vereor nex of Res publica pro nos es validus per vox in nostrum pars.*" (I do not fear the death of the Republic for we are strong with right on our side.)

Slocum laughed loudly and applauded my quick response. I could tell Howard was favourably impressed as he watched me from behind his beard and Sherman beamed as though it was his own son who had just amazed his teachers.

"Carry on sergeant," Slocum commanded. "Sorry for the interruption."

I explained how Colonel Higginson singled me out when he recruited me and began my education in intelligence the moment I finished infantry training. I described how the colonel personally escorted me through an artillery battery explaining the different types of guns we saw, their munitions and what they did. His thoroughness included a familiarization with the different Confederate uniforms we were likely to encounter in our region and how to determine numbers at a glance. Most of all, he trained me to take in every detail in a scene and to recount as much as I could hours later. I eventually came to the point where I only needed to walk through a room to be able to write down its content and the location of every item in it a day later. We employed mnemonics to enhance my memory. I also told the generals how I became highly skilled with a knife, as that was the only weapon a slave might be likely to carry.

Both men were impressed and congratulated me on my abilities.

"Generals, I want you to use Sergeant Macdonald freely in our next campaign. He will provide you with the best intelligence available. Make sure he has couriers whenever he needs them. His needs will be a priority. You will also keep me informed of his location at all times.' Then Sherman laughed, 'I do not want you to get him killed and that is an order."

Howard and Slocum questioned me for another half hour before I was dismissed to return to the ball game. As I left I realized I still did not know where we were going, but if we were burning the Confederate woman's home in four days, that was when we were leaving.

CHAPTER FIFTEEN

December 4, 1878
Few people ever see a great army on the move unless they are part of it,
opposing it, or victims of it. I feel sympathy and remorse for the victims of it, but it is often the case that those opposing it cast themselves
as victims for the benefit of easing their loss. So it was when we cut the
telegraph wires binding us to the safety of the north and marched east from
Atlanta.

For two days before we marched away from the city, the buildings making
up the heart of Atlanta burned. Periodic fires had broken out all through
the week before and little was done to extinguish them. One facet of any
city not often accounted for until too late is the availability of liquor. Men
drank on duty and off, carousing through the streets setting fires to private and public buildings alike. The General issued orders indicating most
private homes were to be spared along with churches, but any building
used to produce or store materials that could aid the rebels was to be put
to the torch or knocked down with powder. Our soldiers only grudgingly
acknowledged his restrictions and continued to set alight private homes
at the slightest provocation. Throughout the nights leading up to our exit
from the city, flames burned successively higher and higher. During the
day you could not see the sun for the smoke. But at night the illumination
was such that you would have had to be blind to lose your way. At all times,
your throat was raw and dry, your voice hoarse. Each breath choked you as
if some man had wrapped his hands about your neck and was strangling
you. The noise was beyond deafening as the shouts and cheers of our men
mixed with the fire's unrelenting roar and the crash of magazines and factories as they blew up.

From the vantage point of a hill near Decatur, I glimpsed only a small portion of the vast array of our army and even that looked like a river of blue
flooding over the countryside, driving a world of dust before it.

Gaylord and I marched east with General Slocum's Left Wing. I had been
taken from the 7th Iowa and attached directly to General Sherman's headquarters with Captain Nichols as my commander and his first orders to me
were to accompany and serve Generals Slocum and Davis.

The weather was cold with a slatternly rain that cut across your face like
a slap that is more insult than hurt. The bad weather settled in after our
fourth day en route to Milledgeville. I was now comfortable riding my
horse although he still had a mind of his own and would sometimes stop
for no apparent reason. Then I had to use my spurs to goad him onward.

When it started raining I wished I were marching instead, because riding generated only a fraction of the warmth our walking muscles created. Someplace along the line, my waterproof had been lifted from my equipment and I hadn't missed it until the weather turned. At least the heat of a good march trapped in a wet, woolen uniform was some comfort. Several times during our first days in column we dismounted and walked our horses because of the mud in the roads and I was thankful for the opportunity. My limbs were stiff from the damp and cold and it took several minutes of exercise to get the blood flowing enough to loosen them. Our wagon trains carrying supplies were expressed into the middle of our column whenever they fell behind. Although more convenient for the artillery and foot soldiers to walk on ground not yet churned into mud, the supply wagons were better placed in the center of the column where they could more easily be protected. We still feared attack from guerilla bands operating in the area and with no support apparent from our rear we were vulnerable. Also, there were rebel forces situated in both Milledgeville and Macon and they could do great damage if they got loose. To our benefit these circumstances spurred our foragers, whom we referred to as "Bummers", to work early and hard. They did this much to the chagrin of the Secessionist citizenry.

It had been the General's idea that this war should always cost the enemy something. If they would not pay with the lives of their soldiers or the surrender of their politicians, then the bill due would be redeemed in personal property and provender. Many of our men collected the most unimaginable items. It was not unusual to see a man who had lost his hat wearing a woman's bonnet to ward off the rain and cold. I am sure there was also much personal treasure dug out of the dooryards on some of these plantations. For many of our enemy we came almost as a surprise. They were expecting us, but not as quickly as our movements allowed for and so did not bury their jewelry and gold efficiently. A bit of freshly turned earth was enough to commence an excavation to rival any performed along the banks of the Nile. We had, in our companies, men who could virtually smell loot and the deceptions forged to protect it.

Many Southerners lived in an unreal world in which they believed regal manners and haughtiness formed a shield. At one point, nearing Shady Dale a Southern woman, the dame of her plantation, blocked our Bummers entrance onto her property. When the sergeant in charge of the detail demanded to know what she was hiding, the woman replied, "Sir, I hide nothing from you."

"Are you sure you have no Confederate generals seeking refuge under that great petticoat of yours?"

But she did not see the humor in this. "Sir, you may not talk to me that way. I am a Southern lady and will not stand accused of lying."

"It is precisely because you are a Southern lady that I do not believe you. Now please stand aside."

When our men searched her house and barns, they captured two wounded Rebel soldiers. The sergeant's good nature having been abused, he ordered the smokehouse emptied, the hen house destroyed with all the chickens given to the slaves and that the slaves be set free. Then, he burned her house and drove off her cattle. The woman, in tears, accosted the sergeant as he made to ride off. Turning to her he simply said, "You do not speak well for the South's gentility."

Almost two weeks into our campaign, we captured a bundle of newspapers from Milledgeville. From it we learned that General Beauregard, who was presumed lost in the wilds of Mississippi or Alabama with little hope of joining our columns in battle, was urging the citizens to rise up in defense of their state. Little did he know that the people were not so inclined. We talked of this around the campfires at night and came to the resolution that revolution was easy as long as someone else footed the bill. Once it came time for the average Southerner to dig deep into his pocket, he wanted to renegotiate the fare. We could kill his sons, but we could not steal his niggers for the niggers had cost him cold hard cash.

The other information imparted by the newspapers was the fact that Macon suffered from a snowstorm. These were not the deep snows we received in Canada West, nor were the temperatures as cold, but because of the rarity of the event, havoc seems to have ensued and I believe to this day that the dusting, as we would call it here at home, kept the Rebels from actively pursuing us.

My days were spent riding among the freed slaves trying to determine where the enemy was. There was a lot of speculation, but no hard fact.

One report I heard time and again was that the Negroes had been abused by their masters and their hounds and were deathly afraid of those dogs. Bloodhounds were used to track runaway slaves and escaping Union prisoners of war. Often, at the end of a chase they were loosed upon their quarry to do whatever terrible damage they wished. General Howard must have read the same reports because we received copies of his orders through General Sherman's headquarters that "...all bloodhounds and valuable dogs be killed".

We did not know of a certainty, but suspected from the lack of action on this march, that the enemy was disorganized. From one captured rebel we learned that "... there are so damned many generals in our command, you couldn't throw a stone without hitting one and having it skip off him to wound three others."

This was good news. Too many people giving orders only creates confusion in any situation and in a military instance, it is disastrous. We hoped that many more Southern gentlemen insisted on their right to be generals.

Our columns were an amazement. Everything we needed, or could conceivably need, we carried. We had wagons specifically dedicated to map makers and photographic services; there were hundreds of cooks and armourers: so if a man was lost, he could find his way; if hungry he could be fed; or if his rifle broke it could be repaired. The planning for our endeavor showed us to be the most modern army in the world.

Among the amazing feats performed were the actions of the Pontoniers of the 58th Indiana regiment of engineers. The night before we crossed the Yellow River, men of that regiment struggled all night by the light of bonfires, to put not one, but two bridges across the stream, which measured about one hundred and fifty feet in width. The bridges were placed upon canvas-sided pontoon boats straddled by heavy timbers, then decked with chess and safety rails.

I was personally gratified to learn that working along with them in that night, many of the men I recruited into the Pioneers had cut their way down through the steep slope of the riverbank to give our troops and supply wagons a beneficial grade in their approach to the bridges.

One of the repercussions of our passage, as in our earlier campaigns, were the numbers of slaves being swept up in our wake. General Sherman did not deny them and even treated them with a degree of courtesy some soldiers found embarrassing. Hundreds joined our march and soon we had a major city of homeless Negroes following behind us and getting in our way. This caused the occasional outburst on the part of officers and soldiers. Many of the former slaves were simply trying to help, but their good intentions were more a detriment.

When General Slocum asked me for my views on the situation I could only comment that "...we are stuck with them until we reached our destination. They are too frightened to return to the plantations they left and see us as their single guaranty of freedom."

General Davis, who was now commanding the Fourteenth Army Corps, did not see it this way and urged General Slocum to purge our columns of the "black swarms". It was no secret that General Davis disdained coloured people. He made his views known on a number of occasions and came within moments of striking me when Captain Berton played his childish prank. Glaring at me, he told General Slocum, "... this situation will only get worse the deeper we go into Georgia. How do you expect to feed and cloth them? We are scavenging clothing for our own troops out of the cupboards of the homes we overrun."

But General Slocum chose to abide the stream of Negroes travelling with us. General Davis issued an order when we reached Eatonton, just before Milledgeville, that our wagons would no longer be permitted to carry "useless Negroes."

General Sherman had another view. He frequently asked Captain Nichols to have me find a local Negro elder. Once again, he did not trust the whites of the neighborhood we were now travelling through to be truthful. I witnessed several of his meetings with these venerable men and can report that no one was ever more courteous to them than the General. But, the flood of slaves running away from their plantations had grown to untenable proportions and threatened to drag our army down. With each meeting, the General asked the elders to spread the word that the slaves should stay put and freedom would follow "... as surely as night follows day, when we bring these Rebels to their knees."

I believe the General was naïve in his appreciation of how widely the slaves were able to speak with each other and how desperately they wanted to be free. After interviewing hundreds of them it became clear their intelligence was limited to their own plantation and maybe those immediately neighboring. Because of this, I undertook to tell as many of the slaves as I encountered that they would be better to stay on their plantations. In the hopes that we could convince the slaves they were free and that they should trust us in our efforts to keep them from clogging the roadways, we worked out a schedule of payment that plantation owners had to pay if they wanted work done by their former property, but could not put it into effect right away. This provided no relief to our situation, as the general feeling among the slaves was that freedom was defined by geography and distance from their masters.

Of more help was the rumor spread by the plantation owners themselves. They told their Negroes that the Union soldiers stabbed, shot and drowned the slaves of Tennessee and did the same thing in northwestern Georgia. This frightened the slaves and their fright was not helped by the fact that when our men took it upon themselves to loot a farm, they sometimes included the few paltry possessions of the slaves in their depredations.

It was around this time Song found me. We had become separated in the final days before leaving Atlanta. She told me she was going to come with the army. It was the only way she would ever escape to the north, so I knew she was probably among the camp followers, but did not know whether she was with our wing or Howard's. My duties prevented me from visiting her in the last days of our residency. Whilst riding by an encampment of women who were of some questionable reputation, I heard my name called.

The last time I heard that voice was in conversation with her when she sent a message to our headquarters via an old house servant whose command of English was probably better than his master's.

Upon arriving at the gates of her home, she rushed out and informed me that a strange young woman had accosted her only the day before. From a distance, she looked like any other Negress, but when you got close to her, it did not take a sharp eye to discern that she was white with her skin stained dark with oils; and the hair was dyed and damaged to mimic the kink of our race.

I reported this to headquarters, but the young woman eluded capture. I bore her no animosity and wished her well, knowing the possible fate that could await her. I also understood that she braved not only the Union's wrath, but the censure of her Southern white friends and intimates if her adventures ever became widely known. For such was the contempt of the Southerners for their slaves that even personating one for the benefit of the Southern cause was not considered an acceptable ruse.

"So that's the fine horse you bragging on. Where you been? I be looking on ya since we left home." I apologized for not finding her sooner and told her I had been busy with our campaign. This did not impress her and she bade me dismount, which I did.

"You got to get me away from here?"

She was carrying a slop bucket and it was obvious that she was now acting as a servant to the sporting women who had their own wagon.

"You've got to help me or I'm going to die." Desperation rang in her voice. I could see her working out something in her head. It was clearly an untenable situation for her to be stuck in.

"Have you got someone to go with right now? Someone who can help you until I can get back here and get things arranged so you can travel safely?"

"No. Just them girls and they treat me worse than Marse ever did."

"I'll be back in a day or two. I have to get back to headquarters now." I had six dollars in my pockets. That was half a month's wages of a private soldier. I reasoned it should see her through until I could get back and I didn't need it. With it, she could buy food and find accommodation. I also wrote a pass for her to allow her to travel freely with our columns.

She thanked me for the money and pass and urged me to return swiftly. Then I rode off.

Meeting her disturbed me. It had only been a few days since we left Atlanta and already her situation had deteriorated to the point she was in jeopardy. I decided I would try to find her a position as a laundress with headquarters so I could look after her until we reached safety. It would be at least another month before we arrived at our destination, which we now knew to be Savannah on the Atlantic coast.

Truthfully, I had started to miss her company. She was very handsome and practical. Our conversations, for that is all they ever were, showed her to be eager to learn. I vaguely promised to teach her the alphabet and to read and write. Now I know this promise to have been wrong and made more out of self-interest than in any larger spirit. I hoped to keep her close to me until I could come to some decision about us. She was physically attractive to me, but what held me back was the recently acquired knowledge that Albert was dead and Eunice was free to choose another husband. With dead certainty in my heart, I knew that man had to be me.

December 7, 1878

As we continued on our path toward Milledgeville, the state government was preparing to flee. This was the information I was carrying back to headquarters when I encountered Song. A day before I slid through the lines into the city dodging the few cavalry troopers in the area. It proved a simple thing to do because I was on foot and dressed in my usual slave garments. Talk was all about bemoaning the fact that the brave leaders who promoted the Confederate rebellion had fled into the night. Rumors abounded and stories repeated to me at various times on this incursion pointed to, among other incidents, two senators who spent five hundred dollars each to board a private carriage so they could skedaddle in comfort.

In learning of their actions, I came to share General Sherman's view of politicians as a lower class of people I would not wish to associate with, except out of dire necessity.

Milledgeville was the capital of Georgia at the time, but the capital has since moved to Atlanta. I feel that the move of 1868 was a slight directed toward General Sherman and the people of Georgia seem defiant in rebuilding that seat of rebellion.

When our men marched into Milledgeville there was little to mark it as a capital except for the State buildings. A few paltry shots were fired in its defense, but Wheeler's cavalry had departed and the streets were open to us. In short order they were crowded with blue uniforms and what passed for blue uniforms. Soldiers invaded the citadel of government and staged theatrical sessions of the legislature and even went so far as to personate a trial of Georgian senators.

Wherever we marched in the South, we always found our way to the warehouse containing each town's stock of liquor. Because of this, Milledgeville paid a heavy price, but the saddest aspect was the destruction of the State's fine library. Men who could barely read stole books and burned them. Others used them for sanitary purposes. I was saddened because each volume so destroyed meant people who cared would not have access to some of the greatest words ever set down. Among the volumes I saw trampled beneath our soldier's feet were those of Shakespeare and Donne who had nothing to do with the current rebellion.

I turned my back on the destruction and rode out to our camp on the Beulah Plantation between the Oconee River and town. All along the way, there was hard smoke in the air from the destruction of cotton fields and burning barns. The worst smoke came from the oil-soaked ties of railroads. A track-tying party was underway with as many as three thousand men lifting the railroad tracks and ties off their bed then burning the ties to heat the rails until they glowed as red as Lucifer's eyes. Once the rails were hot enough the infantrymen, who seemed to make a specialty of this, twisted the rails beyond use. They called the results 'Uncle Billy's Neckties.' I believe the General took an impish delight in the name.

During our stay in Milledgeville, I encountered the General only once. He was in high humour and was even accompanied by Stephen Burns, the reporter from the New York Observer.

"Sergeant. Come over here please." The General had a broad smile on his face. He was pleased with the progress of our march and with his troops having taken the Georgia capital at very little expense. "Sergeant, this is Mr. Burns. Mr. Burns, Sergeant Macdonald. You share Scottish names, but I fear not quite the same grandparents. Mr. Burns, Sergeant Macdonald is attached to my staff in special capacities. He is not a cook or valet. If you mention him in your reports before this war is ended, I will have you shot, but for now, I think you should get to know him as he is as valuable as many of my generals and has a remarkable story to tell."

The General's introduction frightened me, for my anonymity was my strongest defense and I did not trust any reporter.

From the subsequent look he gave me, I could tell Burns did not appreciate either me, or the General's sense of humour. It was also evident he did not wish to get to know me. His hand was never extended, nor did he ever address me by my rank. When he finally sought me out in Savannah he spoke my name simply as Macdonald and did not ask me questions so much as demand I provide him with information. When I answered those demands truthfully, he acted as though he did not believe me.

I parted company from the General and his reporter shortly thereafter.

Whilst in Milledgeville we received two disturbing reports. The first was that several of General Kilpatrick's men who had been captured by Wheeler's cavalry had been murdered after they surrendered. Their throats had been cut, some almost to the point of decapitation. The other, and this became known only as we were departing the capital, was the news that torpedoes were being planted in our path.

These infernal devices were long copper tubes packed with powder and ball shot, then set to explode out of the ground where they were hidden. The slightest touch set them off and the result was the loss of a foot, leg or worse. We had never seen these before and they put fear into all our hearts. It was one thing to be honourably shot or cut down by cannon fire, but to be assassinated days and weeks after the murderer fled the scene was unthinkable.

General Sherman ordered that Confederate prisoners clear the ground ahead of our march. They wasted no time in protesting the inhumanity of it. General Sherman responded with the point that it was no more inhumane than using the torpedoes in the first place. General Slocum told us at a meeting that Sherman had been so appalled by these devices he tried to contact high-ranking Confederates to negotiate a cessation in their use, but there appeared to be no one in command.

We left Milledgeville on November 24 having been there less than a full day. I was not sorry to see it go, nor did I mark it as anything other than another town that needed to be brought to heel. The politicians were all gone and there were few admitted Rebels left to confront.

The weather was cool, somewhere around freezing, and dry for our leave-taking. A good thing about the low temperatures is that the ground froze and supported the boots of our infantrymen for a short while until their constant tread kneaded the Georgia clay into a muddy bog. Then, they moved into the fields alongside the road kicking down any fences or walls in their way. Our orders were to destroy everything in our path and if we had stuck to the roads, much of the farm works would have remained standing.

This countryside was laced with creeks and small rivers requiring us to re-build bridges or establish pontoon bridges. In places even the rough corduroy of logs had been taken up and burnt by Wheeler's retreating men. Captain Poe and his engineers commanded the situation and the waterways barely slowed us down.

General Kilpatrick's horsemen formed a flying wing that operated beyond our lines chasing Wheeler off. One of their missions was to free prisoners held by the Rebels in their beastly prison camps. If we were all of one accord, it was that these camps should be liberated as quickly as possible and the prisoners brought back to health. There was not a man among the fourteen thousand in our wing or in Howard's legions who had not heard the story of Camp Sumter near Andersonville and would kill any Rebel guard or officer found to be keeping our comrades in those horrible conditions.

Reports of another stockade called Camp Lawton came from various sources and the cavalry was dispatched to free those men. By the time

General Kilpatrick's troops arrived at the camp, they found it emptied and abandoned. We did not know where the Rebels had taken those men, but if we could free them we were bound to regardless of the cost.

Freeing the captives was one thing we were not successful in. The health of several escapees who entered our camps bespoke of them not as men, but as the dead who had not taken notice of their condition.

A few days short of three weeks into our campaign we were drawing close to Savannah. Travel had slowed due to the marshy quality of the ground and the increasing number of rivers and creeks that traverse the region. Wheeler's cavalry had also slipped behind us and were raiding our rear daily. As we approached the bridge over Ebenezer Creek, General Davis required my presence post haste.

"Macdonald, you may finally have the chance to prove you are good for something to this army. Those goddamned niggers are piling up in our wagons and on our rear again. If we don't get shut of them, Wheeler will have a devil of a good day with us. I want you to proceed back along the column and warn them that they must separate themselves from us. Tell them they are doing more damned harm than good."

"General sir, I will try, but we have already tried to talk them into breaking off with us and it has been no good. Even General Sherman has not been able to do this."

"Sergeant, I do not care what you do, but they will not cross that bridge tomorrow even if I have to set the torch to it myself."

"Yes sir, General." I left his camp feeling that I had been given a task doomed to failure before I even attempted it.

In the morning our column approached Ebenezer Creek over a long causeway roofed by the branches of large tupelo and cypress trees and bordered on either side by fields flooded from the rains. The cypress branches were strung with the Spanish moss that grows everywhere here and in the gloom of a cloudy, late-autumn day the scene of maybe a thousand sad Negroes trudging along took on a foreboding, ghostly quality that still makes me look over my shoulder in empty rooms. There were six or seven hundred Negro women and children as well as their men threaded throughout the line of march when we came to a halt.

I turned Gaylord and spurred back to the head of the column to determine what was the matter and discovered that the Rebels had torn the planks off the deck of the bridge and burned them. It would take several hours for the engineers to make the bridge fit for travel once again. This was the opportunity for me to press our need for independence from the runaways.

Riding quickly along the lines of infantrymen and teamsters, at times I came near to being knocked into the waters. The weather had warmed to well above freezing, but the rain continued to fall. In Milledgeville I had foraged a new waterproof coat and so was now comfortable. As I approached each group of Negroes, I could see the terror written on their faces and felt as though I was lying to them when I begged them to return to their farms with the promise freedom was close to hand. One man with a wife and three children clinging to him was obstinate in his determination that they go forward with the army.

"We're going to cross over that river there and are going to be free and there's nothing you can do to stob us." He and his family moved forward toward the bridge leaving me to wonder how I could ever fulfill my orders. Short of shooting him there was nothing I could do.

After an hour of imprecation I gave up my attempts to turn back the flood. Instead, I quietly rode Gaylord down their lines observing them and the determination on their faces to leave their homes for a promised land they knew nothing about. I would have felt sorry for them, but my own father had fled to that promised land knowing naught about it either.

Toward the end of the line I met Song. She was looking healthier and more able than when I had seen her nearing Milledgeville. I presumed she must have found food and accommodation away from the women she was serving. When she recognized me she leapt forward to wrap her arms around my left leg nearly pulling me out of my saddle. Her actions startled Gaylord and he backed away from her as if I had reined him back.

When he recovered I told her not to make any more sudden moves as this horse was nervous and I could not always control him.

"I'm sorry. I'm just so happy to see you. Been waiting on ye to come back for me."

"You can go up to headquarters tomorrow and not worry about having to ride back here in the column." I had made arrangements for her to become a laundress for the headquarters staff. Many of the officers were happy to help me in this request.

"Oh blessed be the Lord. When should I come?"

"In the morning," I told her. "But now I have to go along. There's so much to do." I told her how to find me in the headquarters camp the next day and patted her hand to give her comfort then Gaylord and I cantered off back toward the bridge.

Provost troops were stationed at the entrance to the bridge and were turning back the crowds. They were from New York and were not men I had served with. Stopping me at gunpoint they demanded to know who I was and where I stole the uniform and horse. It was a corporal who held me in place.

"Corporal," I growled in my best parade-ground voice and unmistakable

English. "If you hold me up one second longer you will be taking night guard for the rest of your life on some God forsaken picket line in the Dry Tortugas. You'd best look at these stripes and listen carefully…" But he did not. He reversed his musket so the butt end was pointing toward me and raised it to strike me off of my horse.

Gaylord became my staunchest friend in that moment by canting us sideways of his own accord and taking us just out of striking distance. I pulled the Navy Colt out of my sash and all in one motion, cocked it and aimed it at the corporal's head. "Corporal I cannot miss from here and you are seconds away from becoming just another dead man. Put your rifle down and do not make any more trouble."

I was gratified to see a flash of doubt pass over his eyes. Then he slowly lowered his rifle and I lowered the hammer of my pistol, but did not lower the gun itself.

"Yes I admit it is a bit strange to see a Negro in uniform. Especially the uniform of a sergeant, but I guarantee you, I am what I say."

One of his privates came forward to calm him, as he was still halfway between accepting my word and fighting with me. "He sounds like the genuine article. You never heard no nigger talk like that before have you?"

The corporal grumbled his agreement and came close to me. I still held my pistol so it could be brought into play at an instant's notice. "We got orders not to let niggers pass here. Have to turn 'em all back."

"Follow your orders then. Mine are to talk them out of following us."

"Not doing much good."

"No."

"You can go on across."

"There's a woman I gave a pass to. She's going to come across tomorrow morning to work at headquarters. My name is Macdonald and the pass will have it written on it." I took out a scrap of paper and a pencil and wrote my name and Song's then gave the note to the corporal. "Let her through. She is expected in General Davis' camp, but don't let any more through."

He tucked the note into the breast pocket of his blouse and indicated that I could pass. The rebuilding of the bridge was finished and companies were quickly crossing it in columns four abreast. I tucked in behind one company and crossed the bridge onto what I take may have been a small island.

Stopping on the east bank below a low embankment, I dismounted and talked to some engineers who were working on hauling pontoon boats to the next crossing. An hour later I was riding toward that crossing.

Less than a mile from where I landed on the east side of Ebenezer Creek, the Pontoniers had bridged Lockner Creek. The two waterways formed a natural barrier to anyone striking eastward. I was well across the pontoon bridge on Lockner Creek when I overheard soldiers in the column exclaiming that the first bridge was gone. Wheeling Gaylord around, I could see roils of smoke rising into the air above the trees and from the rear the huzzah of men who had succeeded in accomplishing something.

I charged back to the first bridge over Ebenezer Creek and pulled back on the reins at the remains of the bridge I had crossed an hour before. The decking was gone and the trestlework that had supported it was in flames. Soldiers were standing around on the eastern end of what had been the bridge. Some were cheering the destruction, but others were pointing and calling to the western bank of the stream.

Trapped on the far side were hundreds of runaway slaves. Most of them were women and children with no way to cross. All was madness as men splashed into the river and tried to swim, some of them sinking from sight before making twenty yards. Others were clutching logs and branches thrown to them by soldiers on the east bank and many men were succeeding in their efforts. The women and children were not so strong and would not attempt to swim the distance. A few men built small rafts for their families out of flotsam and were able to transport their wives and children, with difficulty, to safety. I watched as one woman, holding an infant fell into the water to be slowly separated from her husband. She remained above the top of the water for a few minutes then her struggles weakened. First, she let go of her child in the slow moving current and then she herself slid below the surface. A compassionate soldier swam to the child and carried it back to the shore, but there was no hope for the mother.

All of this was accompanied by a terrible wail from those on the far bank. They were crying "Don't leave us. The rebs coming. The rebs be coming," and such things. There was nothing they could do to save themselves except to flee back along the causeway on which they had come. I called to them to do this, but most stood there like wild animals frightened into immobility. A few tried to enter the creek and were drowned of an instant.

Many, helped by the kinder soldiers who would not be part of abandoning these unfortunates, made it across the river and onto the dry land. They were exhausted but felt they were safe. I looked among those resting on the banks of the creek and up the incline where the land firmed up, to see if Song had somehow made it across, but I did not find her.

From behind the runaways on the opposite bank, the popping of carbines could be heard. This was cause for a general hysteria, and exhausted or not, the Negroes on our side of Ebenezer Creek were up on their feet and heading for the Lockner Creek pontoon bridge.

Gaylord carried me swiftly to the pontoon bridge where I encountered once again the New York provosts.

"Get across. We have orders to cut this bridge loose as soon as the last company makes it to the other side and niggers be damned." It was the corporal who was speaking. He and his men were holding those who had crossed the first bridge back. Every wagon was searched above and below before it was allowed onto the span.

"You can't leave them like this," I yelled at him.

"I can't do anything about it. General Davis sent word saying he would have me and my men shot if we allowed one nigger to cross the river."

Behind us the screaming threaded its way through the trees then along the road like the swamp's malicious spirit.

A sudden outbreak of carbine fire caused a rush on the bridge as the last wagons and company began to cross. The provosts used their rifles at port arms to hold and push the crowd of surviving Negroes back onto the road. Two men stood ready with axes and at a command from the corporal, the provost troops fell back onto the bridge and fired a volley above the heads of the crowd while the axe-men swung their blades and the bridge began to drift free leaving me and the runaway slaves trapped on the edge of the broad creek.

CHAPTER SIXTEEN

December 8, 1878
From across the creek I heard my name being called. Albie Chatterton
was standing on the opposite bank waving his hat and beckoning me to
cross over while I still could. Behind me the sound of shots from Wheeler's troopers was growing louder and I had no doubt they had forded Ebenezer Creek and were now on my side of the water.

Death was certain if the Secesh caught me. Their government had condemned any Negro caught in uniform to summary execution. Stories of
how the rebels had murdered the surrendering troops at Fort Pillow the
previous April were well known.

Turning in my saddle, I was just in time to see the first mounted troopers
gallop around the bend in the road several hundred yards away. Spinning
Gaylord to face them, I unslung the Sharps carbine I carried with me and
fired at them. This was as much to give them pause as to clear the action
because I knew that in a minute I would be neck-deep in the water of Lockner Creek and any charge left in the breech would swell making the rifle
unusable.

All around me hands were taking hold of my saddle and bridle. Women
held their infants up begging that I take their children across to safety.
Grown men with tears in their eyes pleaded for the chance to cross. Groups
of two and three individuals were on their knees praying together. I pointed to the opposite shore where dozens of soldiers were throwing anything
that would float into the water for the fugitives to hang onto.

A few took advantage of the flotsam and ran into the water until they were
up to their necks, then clasped whatever they could and awkwardly kicked
toward the safer shore. Others held onto me as if I were some lone, magical
talisman that would prevent Wheeler's men from capturing them. Their
desperation was retarding my escape. I pulled my pistol out from my sash
and threatened those holding me back.

"Let go. I will not be able to help you if they kill me, which they surely will
if they catch me on this side of the creek. You will have to let them capture
you. There is nothing I can do for you now, but we will come back and kill
them all."

Most eased their grip on my horse and tack, but a few still held fast. These,
I am ashamed to say; I kicked away. Once clear, I urged Gaylord into the
stream. He must have sensed the urgency because without hesitation he
plunged in and swam lustily toward the place where Albie stood cover for
me with his rifle aimed over my head at the oncoming rebel cavalry. As the

creek deepened, I held the pommel of my saddle with one hand and my pistol above my head so the charges in the cylinder would not get wet, with the other. Then we were climbing into the shallows and I slid back onto the saddle as we emerged from the water.

Wheeler's men were now shooting through the crowd toward us. It was hard to tell whom they were targeting, but we could see bodies falling and hear their cursing between shots. Albie was loading and firing at the horsemen and managed to knock one out of his saddle. This brought them up short and they raised their aim to begin firing across the creek. There was only limited cover on our side and we were outnumbered. I swung Albie up onto Gaylord's rump behind me and we dashed toward a line of hastily constructed abatis where our rear guard had formed a skirmish line.

Only a handful of runaways were able to cross the second creek. Before night fell, we watched as the rebels herded their slaves back in the direction they had come. That morning we had started out with more than a thousand trusting Negroes and now there were fewer than a hundred. Most of these were men.

"Thought you were a dead man," Albie jibed in his nasal, mid-western accent. "Ya'll keep doing that to me and I keep showin' up an' bailin' ya'll out."

"And I cannot thank you enough for that either. But where did you come from? How did you get here? You were with General Howard when we left Atlanta."

"Oh. I came with a detachment guarding a bunch of wagons sent over by Colonel Parrott. Figured while I was here, I'd look up our favourite colored sergeant. Some of the boys on provost duty said they seen you by the bridges earlier, so I come back for a look-see. Good damned thing I did too."

"Well I am more than glad you did. We are going to have to get out of here."

"They ain't comin' over now. They'll take them runaways back to where they can pen them up."

"We had better get moving anyway. Captain Nichols and General Slocum are going to want to hear about this."

Albie and I walked along the road together beneath the cypress for a mile with me leading Gaylord. I now had two friends in the ranks whom I could depend upon: Albie and Gaylord.

Gaylord was turning into a better friend than I ever thought he could be when we first met in Atlanta.

By this time the early December dusk began settling upon us. I begged my leave of Albie urging him to catch up with me at headquarters where we could share a bivouac for the night. After cleaning beneath Gaylord's saddle blanket to remove any twigs or pebbles that may have lodged there during our swim, I mounted my horse and set out to find our divisional headquarters in the growing dark.

It took three hours to catch up to General Slocum's wagons. General Sherman was not with them, nor was Captain Nichols. They had gone on ahead earlier that morning with the advance companies of our wing. We were nearing Savannah and General Sherman was a man who liked to see the lay of the land himself. For all I knew, he could be demanding the surrender of the city that very day, but that would not occur for two more weeks.

General Slocum's tent was always easy to find. It glowed continuously from several oil lamps burning inside and had two guards posted out front. What made it even easier that night was the shouting coming from inside its canvas walls. I heard it even before I entered the clearing where headquarters had been set up.

"Goddamnit. He is not going to get away with this. I expect you do to something about this general. To abandon that many runaways like that is a premeditated cruelty. It's murder! General Davis had no right to do that. It is criminal and I will not let it go. If you don't do something about that infernal old Copperhead, the press will…" I was just in time to see Major Connolly, the aide to the Third Division commander General Baird, storm out of General Slocum's tent and into the night.

That General Slocum accepted such abuse from a subordinate without disciplining him gave me cause to think that the general was considering action against General Davis. It was very clear, however, that General Slocum had been informed of the day's events and it was in his hands now.

I decided to hold back from speaking to General Slocum that night and to keep myself available as an eyewitness. But, no one from command ever sought me out. Even General Sherman asked me, only in passing, if I thought Davis was correct in removing the bridges. The only one who spoke to me in any detail about Ebenezer Creek was the reporter Stephen Burns.

At a distance of some miles to the east of our bivouac cannon fire was underway. We took this to be the line defending Savannah and that the rebel artillerists were dueling with ours. To the southeast General Howard's wing had made a lodgment across the Savannah-Ogeechee Canal. Our goal was in sight and for all concerned, we had arrived at our campaign's destination. No one said anything, but many of the men were thinking that because we were so close, we could have brought the runaway slaves left behind at Ebenezer Creek to safety.

We did not enter Savannah directly so much as we seeped into town. When we arrived on the outskirts, it was evident that General Hardee had decided to put up a strong defense. We did not know how many men he had, but we were sure they were far fewer in number than our two combined wings. Still, they held us at bay.

There were a number of small victories in the siege of Savannah. Men of the Fifteenth Corps' Second Division under General Hazen assaulted Fort McAllister and completed its capture in less than a quarter of an hour on December 13th.

Hardee was an excellent general. Probably one of the best the South had. He had written several books on warfare and was respected by both sides. I think this may have unnerved General Sherman a bit, because he decided to summon the division that General Foster had just landed on Hilton Head Island.

It was about this time we also learned that General Thomas had all but destroyed General Hood's army at Nashville in Tennessee. This was cause for celebration amongst our men and some of the more verbose predicted the end of the war in a few days.

We were not aware of it, but General Beauregard had made a junction with General Hardee and those two brilliant soldiers hatched a daring plan to sacrifice Savannah, in order to save Hardee's army.

For a week before their escape occurred, we learned later, rebel engineers strung old rice boats together across the Savannah River to make their own pontoon bridge connecting the south shore, via two islands, with the north shore. This would provide them with a safe exit from the city we were not aware of.

The rice boats were anchored in the current using the iron wheels of railroad wagons as anchors. The discovery of this provided the answer to a mystery that had daunted us since our arrival on the edge of the city. Dozens of wheel-less rail wagons were found suspended in the air supported by balks of timber. We could not comprehend the use that such massive amounts of iron would be put to. Prognosticators assured us the wheels were being smelted down into cannon balls, but someone pointed out that if this were the case the skies above Savannah would be glowing red at night from the furnaces. We were sure some evil use was being made of the wheels, but no one of my acquaintance made even a close guess as to the real purpose.

Mail arrived in our camps for the first time since leaving Atlanta. I received three letters from Martha informing me on the condition of the farm, the village and our neighbours. Only one line gave me any news of Eunice and that was simply the fact she was living at Morgan's home. Despite the paucity of information about Eunice, I was glad to receive the letters as I had been away from home for a longer period than ever before and was beginning to find myself growing homesick.

General Hardee had an assured escape route if he could cross the river. For some reason General Foster was almost reluctant to deploy his division to block the roads leading north into South Carolina. They remained unobstructed by General Foster's Hilton Head Division when they should have been sealed off. General Sherman recognized this and in an effort to provide Foster with the time necessary to move into place, the General sent a stern and threatening surrender demand to Hardee. But, Hardee did not accumulate his reputation by being timorous. Instead, he coolly replied that they would fight it out if necessary and that he, Hardee, had conducted his campaigns by the rules of civilized warfare and he expected nothing less of General Sherman.

I was not within earshot of the General when that reply was received, but I would have liked to be. The General's temper was legendary and could be educational if you were not the object of it.

Shortly after lunch that day, General Sherman sent for me. He was already aboard a small steamer called *Harvest Moon* in the roads and they were holding its departure on my arrival. The General had decided to go to Hilton Head to personally inspire General Foster to move.

"Sergeant, glad you could join me. Do you still remember how to speak to the Negroes along this coast in their own language?"

Before I could even answer, we were under way. The General inquired about my well-being and asked how I was getting along as a horseman. Then he excused himself and disappeared into the ship's cabin. Captain Nichols, who continued the conversation, explained that the General wanted me handy in case he got the opportunity to talk with any local Negroes. Then the captain urged me to take advantage of the seamen's mess.

When I entered the room where five sailors were eating at one long bench, it fell silent. Before it did, I heard the men talking about having General Sherman on board and how much they admired him. Once I crossed the threshold into the cabin, all eyes turned to me and the Negro cook who was serving food shook his head as I walked up to the serving window.

"Goddamnit boy. You knows better to come in here expecting to eat with the white men."

The thought never occurred to me I would have to eat elsewhere. "Where do I eat?"

"You come around to the cookhouse door and I'll fix you up, but you can't eat here."

Not wanting to cause trouble for the General, I left to do as instructed. On my way back through the ship's interior passage toward the deck, I bumped into Captain Nichols. He asked me what I was doing. He thought, he said, I was having my meal in the mess. When I explained to him that

I had been told to leave, Captain Nichols excused himself and went to the officers' wardroom.

A second later I heard General Sherman explode and he came storming out into the passage with his napkin still tucked into his belt.

"Come with me." And he drafted me in tow as he swept along the corridor and into the seamen's mess. The five men and the cook nearly dissolved into fits of hysteria as the red-haired Vandal of the South exploded on them.

"Who in the name of…" here he blasphemed, "told this man he could not eat in this mess?" No one owned up to it so the General marched up to one young sailor and pushed his face to with an inch of the sailor's nose. "Was it you?" The sailor bleated his innocence. The General turned to an old salt. "Was it you?" The old salt was even more discombobulated because he knew how much the General could do to make his life a misery.

Finally, the cook admitted his guilt through the serving window.

"When a soldier in my command says he is hungry you feed him. I don't care if he's black, white or purple. You feed him. This man has done things for his country that would make your mother turn white, and he will not be taking any b******t from you or any other goddamned cook. Now get on with your business." Then the General turned so only I could see him and winked at me. I almost missed his smirk as he brushed by.

The journey took the *Harvest Moon* down the Savannah River into Ossabaw Sound. It was slow going at first because the rebels had taken up the cobbles from Savannah's streets and dumped them in the river to create obstacles to impede any attack from the sea. They had also converted a number of their torpedoes for use in the water where they floated just below the surface. Coming into contact with one could produce a hole in the bottom of the *Harvest Moon* big enough to sink her in a few moments.

We reached Hilton Head late in the afternoon, but in time for General Sherman to light a fire under General Foster to get him to block the Carolina roads, but it would take a day to move his troops fully into position. We were turned around and returning to Savannah before the sun had fully set.

An hour out of Hilton Head the *Harvest Moon* eased onto a mud bank on the falling tide. The ship's captain advised the General that we would be here for at least seven hours until we passed slack tide and the flood carried us off the bottom. We were in no danger and had not Savannah been tottering, we would have had an enjoyable, if enforced, evening of leisure.

This was not to be. General Sherman requested the use of the ship's boat, which in this case was Admiral Dahlgren's barge. He also commandeered enough sailors to row it to our destination, then accompanied by Captain Nichols and I, stepped down into the boat.

With one of the sailors, a local man, acting as pilot, we set off through some salt marsh. The pilot said this would take us into Savannah without having to risk the open waters of the sound. The wind was building and with it the waves, so this seemed a prudent tactic.

The General was in surprisingly good humor despite the setback of the grounding. Shortly after leaving the ship he turned to me and asked if I were nervous.

"No General." Before I could get any more out, Captain Nichols joined in.

"Oh no. He's not nervous. Why should he be? He's just experienced his first shipwreck with our fearless sea-going, pirate leader; we're lost in a marsh someplace on the east coast of somewhere between South America and the frozen polar wastes; and he can't see where he is going because it is pitch dark. General, we've been in worse positions before so why should he be nervous?"

The General laughed then pulled a bottle from his satchel and broke its seal. He took a long drink, hand it to Nichols, then me and finally to the boat's crew.

"Not a waterman huh sergeant?"

"Not really General. The closest I get to this much water back home is when the low fields flood." This wasn't strictly true. I have sailed on the Great Lakes and we keep a rowboat in a small marsh near Buxton for water fowling, but the good-natured atmosphere of our plight inspired me to join in the fun.

Traversing the salt marsh was easier said than done. We were still at it when the sun broke the horizon. Head winds and reversing currents made it difficult to make any headway. During that night, Hardee managed to escape with his entire army across his floating causeway and Mayor Arnold along with several members of Savannah's government tried to surrender to General Sherman, but they could not find him.

That was how Savannah fell into our General's hands.

CHAPTER SEVENTEEN

December 13, 1878

> "Savannah, Georgia,
> December 22, 1864
>
> To His Excellency President Lincoln,
> Washington, D.C.
>
> I beg to present to you as a Christmas-gift the city of Savannah, with one hundred and fifty heavy guns and plenty of ammunition, also about twenty-five thousand bales of cotton. – W.T. Sherman, Major-General."

If I were to receive a city as a Christmas gift, I can think of none better than Savannah. As much as I despised the aspirations of the Confederacy, I could not help but love and admire the elegance and beauty of this city.

Savannah almost seems to exist as an act of providence. When we arrived at its gates the city was already one hundred and thirty-one years old. It survived the revolution and because of its location away from the coast, being seven miles up the Savannah River, hurricanes do not seem to affect it. Fire has not plagued the town the way conflagrations seem to frequently raze other cities. I was gladdened the citizens of Savannah did not heed General Beauregard's call to resist our armies. That meant we could leave the city and its twenty-two lovely squares unmolested.

Not having been to New Orleans, I cannot speak to that city, but many of my comrades who have visited both New Orleans and Savannah assured me Savannah is the more gracious of the two, with New Orleans having the faint air of disrepute.

It also seemed a city of tolerance. During our travels from Atlanta, we observed that most houses of worship were Baptist, Methodist or Pentecostal. Savannah had its share of these denominations, but also made room for Catholics and even Israelites. A local man told me the Jewish temple was among the oldest in all the Americas. This gave me some hope that after the war Negroes would find a welcome here, but that does not now seem to be.

The houses of Savannah reflect the wealth of this city. These were the homes of cotton and silk merchants and shipping owners. Many were stone and brick and appointed with complicated ironwork. Often delicate in its execution, the ironwork has a number of purposes. It serves as a screen to preserve the privacy of the families within, and as trellising for what must be magnificent gardens. As we were only in Savannah at the start of the winter months, the gardens were dormant, but I could tell from the nature of the beds and the care of their design that, when in bloom, the gardens must be a source of joy to whoever beholds them.

General Sherman had taken one of the best homes as his headquarters. It belonged to the cotton broker Charles Green and was completed the year the Rebellion commenced. In an effort to preserve it from pillage, Mr. Green rode out to greet General Sherman and offered the General his house as a headquarters. The ground floor of the two-storey home is entirely covered along its front with elaborate wrought iron. An Italian friend fighting with the New Yorkers told me the entranceway, which covers the full two stories, resembles the entrances to the great castles in his homeland.

It was in the halls of this house the General was further disturbed by the newspapers from New York on several accounts. The first incident occurred shortly after Christmas.

Every morning I rode from where I camped outside a nearby cemetery to our Madison Square headquarters to be of service to the General. Upon arriving at the house, I met a private who was carrying a bundle of newspapers up from the river wharf where a steamer had just arrived. Included in the dispatch were the New York Times, the New York Observer and the New York Post. All were dated December twenty-second. Newspapers from Washington, Baltimore and Philadelphia would arrive later.

Thanking the soldier, I collected the bundled newspapers from him and proceeded onto the porch to let Captain Nichols know I was there and to lay the papers out on the hall table. As I was unfolding them the General came to the door of the study without seeing me and asked if the papers were there yet. When he did notice me he stopped for a moment and we chatted, then he asked me if I had a chance to scan the columns. When I replied that I hadn't, he took the three newspapers and started to look them over.

As was to be expected, the papers were full of General Sherman and his nearly bloodless victory over Savannah even though by press time on December twenty-second it was not an accomplished fact. Still, I think he enjoyed the notoriety. As it was New Year's Eve, his fame would give him something to celebrate.

Suddenly, the General's lilting face turned somber and his eyes began to moisten. Telling me to wait in the hall, he returned momentarily to the ground floor study. I could hear a soft sob from within, but dared not enter without an invitation.

"Sergeant. Come in and close the door after you."

When I entered the room I was struck by the fact that he had taken the time to pull the draperies closed.

"I have just learned that my newborn son Charles died on December fourth. I haven't even held him. It was on the second page of the Times. Just a few paragraphs saying that he died just short of twelve months of age and then some about the loss of Willie." Here he took the Lord's name in vain, but I could not charge that against him. The depth of his distress was obvious.

"Forgive me Frederick, but I sometimes think there is a malicious God who has set out to test me. It is the cruelest jest that I receive this news from the papers before I hear it from Mrs. Sherman."

"I felt that God had tried me too when I lost Absolom then Helen and our baby one after the other. Even today, I cannot understand His reasoning in taking a newborn or why He layers one sorrow on top of another."

"Maybe it is to plumb our depths to see if we measure up to some yardstick. Surely Mrs. Sherman has suffered enough. I know I have. Everyday I miss my Willie and wish it were I who had succumbed to the disease instead of him. Even now, were I to be killed on the battlefield, it would be somewhat easier for her because it is an expectation of a soldier. But to lose a child? You know yourself. When you lose a child you lose your future and isn't that future what we truly value above all else."

This was a conversation I had had with Absolom. He and the General were very much alike in their understanding of our place in the family line.

"Sit with me awhile Frederick. I don't feel like settling in to work just yet." We sat, undisturbed for an hour, in the study's two big armchairs. Very little was said. The General offered me a drink, but when I declined he refrained from having a glass on his own. I did not know what to say to him. When I lost my kin, I was empty and could not think of one thing to say about them. It was as though a blow had stunned my emotions and by not speaking about them I could avoid their loss. Because I felt this way, I could not offer the General any condolences that would mean anything. I kept my counsel and did not intrude upon his thoughts, but sat looking out the window, as did he.

"I should write to Mrs. Sherman," he said startling me. In the quiet of the study, I had waited for any indication that I could do something for him, but he simply sat slouched in his chair with his head supported by his right hand. Occasionally, a tear would streak his cheek. Until this announcement that he needed to write his wife, he uttered few words.

"Wait for a moment Frederick." I was not going to leave my friend in despair until I knew he was starting to surface from the deepest point of his mourning. "I would like you to take this down to the outbound steamer for me and make sure it goes off today."

He wrote quickly, dipping his pen nib, with smooth motions, in the inkwell on his desk. At the end of each line, he blotted the ink dry before starting on the next. As he wrote, his demeanour changed for the better. When he had written all he was going too, he folded and sealed the letter.

"See if you can catch the steamer before it leaves. I will try to wire Mrs. Sherman as well, but am not sure where she is at this time." Promising to catch the boat before it departed I began to turn and as I did, he clapped my on me shoulder and thanked me. Then he called out to Major Ewing, his aide and brother-in-law.

Our northern newspapers delivered another blow to the General shortly after New Year's.

General Sherman was not used to being taken by surprise, but on this day he was completely unprepared when Secretary of War Stanton was disgorged from a packet onto the dock. Secretary Stanton claimed he was there to "...take the air," but no one accepted his story, least of all the General.

For all his fierce, war rhetoric, Secretary Stanton was a myopic, lumbering dumpling. It was when he commenced speaking that he became commanding. Soldiers guarding the steamer landing were quick to come to attention when they recognized him. Having only seen engravings in the newspapers, I did not quite believe I was encountering the real Secretary until an officer addressed him and guided his party along the dock.

A carriage took him to the General's headquarters where he insinuated himself. Runners preceded him by a few minutes so the General at least had that little grace. As desperately as I wanted to know what precipitated this visit, I was not within earshot of any conversation, having been asked to vacate the main house. However, I had a good idea as to what was behind the visit.

A day after we returned from Hilton Head Stephen Burns, the New York Observer reporter, sent me a message asking me to meet him in Washington Square. As our headquarters were located on the west side of Madison Square, Washington Square was the farthest away from the Green home of any of the town's squares.

"What happened at Ebenezer Creek? You were there weren't you?"

I admitted I was, but his abruptness put me on my guard.

"Well, what happened?"

I told him that a number of people were trapped between the creek and the charging cavalry when the first bridge was taken up and the trestles burnt and that the same thing happened at the pontoon bridge.

"Whose fault was it?"

"I don't know for sure if there is any fault to be apportioned."

"It must be somebody's fault. Was it General Davis?"

"I don't know. I didn't see the general anywhere nearby."

"You must have received orders from someone."

"I was not involved in the dismantling of the bridges. My orders come directly from Captain Nichols who received them from General Slocum."

"But you work for General Davis too don't you?"

"Only occasionally am I loaned to him. If I take orders from anyone other than General Slocum, they come from General Sherman."

"But you were working for General Davis that day?" He kept coming back to General Davis over-and-over again during the next half hour. I believed, and still believe, General Davis was entirely responsible for the calamity, but I did not hear him give the order and only had the word of the Provost detail that any order was given. Because of this, I would not say a word against him.

"You know Davis hates niggers, don't you?" he continued to push.

At this point I decided there was no profit in continuing our conversation and so I rose from the bench and excused myself.

"Listen you black-assed son-of-a-bitch. You don't walk away from me until I have finished, do you understand?"

I didn't respond immediately. Instead, I surveyed him to adjudge my next move. He was young enough and looked like he could be strong, but I doubted he would do anything physical, but if he carried a weapon he could be dangerous.

"If you are armed Mr. Burns, I would advise you to defend yourself. I have a pistol with me and will not hesitate to shoot you down if you utter one more insult. Now if you wish to defend your honour, I would suggest you challenge me and we settle your insults right now. If you do not, I would advise you never to speak with me again and to refrain from any attempt to impugn my name. Should you do so you had best go armed from that moment on."

The colour drained from his face and he couldn't speak. He was a man who was used to abusing others. He was also used to having them, out of manners or fear, quail in the face of his bullying. Like all men of such a nature, he was not accustomed to his victims holding their ground and returning his invective threat for threat.

It was plain he was looking for someone to attack General Davis so he could file a report on what was said. My early training as a reporter made me wary of his motives. Even today, I am sure Major Connolly informed him of the situation. The Major had plainly threatened to report the incident to the newspapers. That the Major did not claim credit for the information was no surprise. It would cost him his career and possibly his commission as well if it became known he was the author of any incriminating story. However, I was equally sure Mr. Burns viewed me as just another dispensable darkie.

When Mr. Burns did not respond, as I expected he would not, I turned and walked to where I had tethered Gaylord, mounted my horse and rode off.

Mr. Stanton was occupying General Sherman's time fully so that I rarely saw the General over the next two days. When Secretary Stanton finally recognized that the General kept a Negro soldier nearby he became intrigued and asked the General for permission to interview me.

"General Sherman tells me you are very bright for a member of your race."

That was not the way I would have phrased it, but then I did not wish to contradict this powerful man. I have always felt that I was no more than average for any race, but I did have the advantage of a good education. So I thanked him for the compliment.

"I am not used to speaking with such an erudite colored man. So I will not hold back on my questions..."

"I will try my best to answer them as fully as possible, sir."

"Thank you... Sergeant I was given to understand General Sherman did not have any colored troops in his army."

"Sir, he doesn't have any colored units. But I was seconded from the First South Carolina Volunteers to help deal with the flood of runaway slaves."

"... And I understand that you have been performing a second task, collecting intelligence?"

When I admitted to being a sometime spy the Secretary's face lit up. "Could General Sherman not use more men like you?"

"Sir, I believe my ability to glean information comes from the fact that it has been abroad among the enemy that our army has no Negroes in its ranks so our enemies do not expect me."

"... But surely your security is not the only reason General Sherman refuses to have Negro soldiers?"

"Mr. Secretary, we moved like lightning through the heart of the Confederacy and succeeded in dealing a substantial blow to the Rebellion. The speed with which we travelled prevented us from taking the time necessary to form and train colored units. We did make use of able colored men as Pioneers who already knew how to handle a shovel and build roadway. I also know that General Sherman is correct in his assumption that the runaway slaves we encounter are not ready to become full citizens, which they would demand if allowed to serve. More than once he has said within my hearing that..."

"Yes. Yes. I have heard him say what you are about to. Yet I fail to understand how you, a member of the colored race, can accept anything less than full manumission?"

"You would not let your children run the republic, and the enslaved Negroes are like those children. First they need education and property to be responsible for. I have seen that the great crime of the Rebels is to keep their slaves in a child-like state while propagating the myth that colored people were not capable of learning or managing knowledge…"

"But that will come with freedom and responsibility."

"I am afraid I disagree sir. Education…"

"Well, I guess I have been told," and he chuckled at his own humour, but his eyes were hard. "General Sherman tells me you are an educated man and I am beginning to believe that. Let us agree to disagree on these points. Believe me when I say that wiser heads than yours have considered these matters and are sure this is the correct course." He paused for a moment and gave me another smile that indicated he no longer wished to debate this topic with me. "I am sure it will all work out in the end. What also continues to concern me is that General Sherman has refused to declare himself for the Republican Party. I cannot fathom how he can declare himself to the cause of freedom without espousing the principles of our party and abolitionism…"

"Sir, I think you misread our General. If anything, he is an abolitionist of the first-rank who probably does not speak the language, but his actions tell the tale…"

"Don't contradict me Sergeant. I know what I have seen and heard." I expressed an apology and he continued. "It is believed in Washington and Richmond that General Sherman dislikes Negroes. Had not his war record been so good, we might have suspected him of more insidious emotions."

We were moving into dangerous territory. I would have liked to end our conversation as abruptly as the ending of the one with Mr. Burns, but this was a man whom I was bound by law and military use to respect and treat with dignity. He was second in the land only to President Lincoln and as such I recognized his right to dictate to me in any way he pleased.

"General Sherman is the most patriotic man I know, but he does not espouse the political aspirations of your party because he views politics as a morass of contradictory efforts that get in the way of achieving our final victory over the Rebels. In regard to his treatment of Negroes, I can assure you Mr. Secretary, never has a man been more courteous or friendly to my race and for that we would follow him anywhere."

Now, I realize that my frankness was not in the General's best interests. I could see Secretary Stanton took note of my comments but did not address my view of the General's political understanding.

"Do other Negroes feel the same way as you?"

"I believe they do."

"If we brought together the leaders, the ministers and spokesmen of the coloured people of Savannah, what do you think they would tell me?"

This was a challenge I could not answer with certainty. I had it expressed to me that General Sherman was a great man who treated the former slaves with courtesy whenever he had occasion to meet with them, but there a number who wished to follow their freedom with a strict segregation from the white population. They wanted nothing to do with a race of people who had caused them so much pain and anguish and I feared they would tell him this.

"Mr. Secretary, sir, I have seen General Sherman treat with coloured men and women almost since the first day I knew him. He has never evinced anything but graciousness toward them and, for that matter, toward me. If there is a Brutus in our midst who believes in the holiness of his blows, let him come out of the shadows and accuse General Sherman and I shall stand for the General…"

"My God! All this intelligence and Shakespeare too."

Ignoring his comments, I continued. "I believe you have been misled in your understanding of the situation by the newspapers you quote. If you were to query any leaders of the Negro community or churches, you would find a unanimity of approbation for General Sherman."

Secretary Stanton turned his face from mine and paused to reflect on this. Then said, "that is a capital idea. I will have General Sherman instruct you to assemble the local coloured leaders and we will answer this question."

A slight smile spread across his face and he changed the course of the interview. "What about his supposed murderous outrage a few weeks ago when General Davis sacrificed thousands of Negroes to enemy troops?"

"Mr. Secretary, I was present and there were not thousands of coloured people involved. There was less than a thousand and many of those made it across both Ebenezer and Lockner Creeks. I was charged with discouraging runaways from following us and, as a soldier and Negro, I understand the military necessity of not burdening our columns. Wheeler's cavalry troops were immediately behind us and had been harassing the tail end of our column since we left Milledgeville. The waterways at Ebenezer and Lockner Creeks offered a natural barrier to major troop movements on Wheeler's part.

"I, and many others who were present, believe we could have delayed removing the bridges until the runaways got across. But sir, you have to remember General Davis had gone on ahead and was not present to see what his orders fomented or how much time was available before the arrival of the main body of Wheeler's men."

"You believe that this was a tactical necessity and not a malicious act?"

"Sir, I do not know what was in General Davis' mind. So you know where I stand, I will tell you that he is known as harboring hatred toward my race. Also, I personally have born the brunt of his invective, but whether his racial feelings were his motivations I cannot truly say because those creeks were a definite tactical impediment to our enemies."

"You seem to be truthful Sergeant and I appreciate your candor, but the newspapers do not back your version of the events nor do they conform to your view of General Sherman and his relations with our newly freed colored citizens."

Secretary Stanton ended our conversation here and excused me. Our interview had taken place in a smaller side room at headquarters so it was up to me to leave the room. As I stood the Secretary asked me to stay close by. General Sherman, he assured me, would be sending me to invite the leaders of the Negro community to a meeting.

The meeting with Secretary Stanton did not go well. I failed to convince him of my General's good intentions and I failed to explain that the incident at Ebenezer Creek was more complex than the newspapers made it out to be. I felt badly because I saw the tragedy that unfolded and there was nothing I could do about it. Those people whom I threatened with my pistol and kicked away from my horse still haunt me. When I have an awful day with Eunice, they visit me at night and I continue to feel impotent to help their ghosts.

An hour-and-a-half after being dismissed, Captain Nichols entered the stable office with a list of men to invite to a meeting at our headquarters the following evening.

There were twenty names to be contacted. I spent the rest of the day and part of that evening riding the streets of Savannah extending invitations. Everyone accepted.

On the appointed night our guests all arrived within fifteen minutes of each other. They were dressed in their best suits as befitted their own positions and that of their hosts. A larger room than the ground floor study was needed so the meeting was moved to the second floor where the ballroom was set up with tables and chairs along with water, tea and coffee. As each man entered the room he was greeted by one of two officers delegated to that duty. Adjutant-General Townsend was present and took notes. Mr. Stanton made his own record of the meeting and I was positioned at a small writing desk to make a record of the meeting for the General. It made me think back to John Brown and another gathering a scant six years before.

Before we commenced, General Sherman asked me to simply observe and record, but not to interject.

The meeting of January twelfth began with introductions. First General Sherman introduced Secretary Stanton then each of the guests rose, introduced himself and contributed his story. This took slightly more than an hour. Many of the stories were so similar the same hand could have written them. Secretary Stanton appeared to be growing impatient, but good manners prevented him from urging the speakers along.

Finally all the speakers had been heard from and one, a dignified man of about seventy years of age, rose and addressed their hosts.

"As I told you a few minutes ago, my name is Garrison Frazier and my friends here have asked me to act as their spokesmen."

"Thank you for your time, Reverend Frazier." Stanton began addressing the gathering as much as speaking directly to the standing orator. "I appreciate your coming to meet with me like this. I would like to clarify the situation of your people as they see their future in the United States once this Rebellion has ended. But before I do I would like to be certain that you understand what has happened with the Emancipation proclamation."

In the most condescending of tones, Stanton proceeded to ask Reverend Frazier what he understood of the congressional acts and presidential proclamation freeing the slaves in the Rebel states. Reverend Frazier's response was considered, balanced and one that would have been the envy of most lawyers.

Stanton continued to ask similar questions with the evident hope that Reverend Frazier would stumble in his discourse, but the old man confounded the Secretary and answered in clear, unequivocal statements. Unable to trick him up, the Secretary then asked whether the freed coloured would prefer to live among the whites or in communities by themselves.

"We would prefer to live by ourselves, for there is a prejudice in the South that will take years to get over..." Later we learned that every one of the guests except one missionary from the North agreed with Reverend Frazier.

This was not the expected answer and the mood of the room cooled. Mr. Stanton changed tacks and began asking about Rebel threats to arm their slaves, but Reverend Frazier quickly discounted this.

None of the notions the Secretary arrived with bore any fruit and it became evident that Mr. Stanton was desperate to buttress his views by finding some fault. Turning to General Sherman, he asked politely that the General vacate the room. The implication was clear. Mr. Stanton believed that the General's presence curtailed open speech.

"Now. State what is the feeling of the colored people toward General Sherman, and how far do they regard his sentiments and actions as friendly to their rights and interests or otherwise?"

Reverend Frazier brought himself to his full height and looking Secretary Stanton directly in the eye with defiance, because he grasped very early on what the Secretary was attempting, began to speak.

"We looked upon General Sherman, prior to his arrival, as a man, in the providence of God, specially set apart to accomplish this work, and we unanimously felt inexpressible gratitude to him, looking upon him as a man who should be honored for the faithful performance of his duty. Some of us called upon him immediately upon his arrival and it is probable he did not meet the Secretary with more courtesy than he did us. His conduct and deportment toward us characterized him as a friend and gentleman. We have confidence in General Sherman and think what concerns us could not be in better hands."

When he finished this broadside, Reverend Frazier remained standing. His eye did not waver from the Secretary's, and it was the Secretary who looked away.

CHAPTER EIGHTEEN

December 14, 1878
The children's toys are finished. The perambulator is too large to be wrapped so it will have to be hidden from sight until Christmas morning. Eunice covered the bats in brightly coloured paper with ribbons and bows and Mother will take all of the gifts with her when she goes to visit Harriet on the twentieth.

I copied the letter that arrived from Mrs. Lincoln on November 19 and forwarded it along with a short greeting to the General. In my note, I mentioned I was setting down my reminiscences of the war and our actions. Today I received the following response to that letter when I picked up the mail.

W. T. Sherman
817-15th St.
Washington, D. C.

Mr. Frederick Douglass Macdonald,
C/O General Delivery,
Buxton, Ontario
Canada

November 29, 1878

Dear Frederick,
I bid you a happy Thanksgiving and hope this letter finds you well. It is quiet at home today, as Mrs. Sherman has gone to St. Louis to be with our daughter Minnie. I could not afford the time for such an extensive trip and so have stayed behind for this holiday. I celebrated it with my brother John, whose duties kept him here in Washington as well. The enforced leave gives me time to catch up on my personal correspondence.

Thank you for the copy of Mrs. Lincoln's letter. It shows her to be a feisty woman who knows her own mind. I was interested in her views on Secretary Stanton although I am certain he had nothing to do with the assassination.

You report that you are striving to set down your memories of the war and our campaigns. When you are finished I would be happy to receive a copy of your recollections.

If there is one thing I have learned, it is that eyewitnesses to the same event often deliver compellingly different versions of the same story. When I wrote my memoirs a few years ago I was thankful not to have to depend solely on my own memory. Much of what I wrote came from my daily diaries and the copies I had made of my orders, telegrams and letters with various people.

These did aid me in refreshing my memory and once I had a piece of paper dealing with a certain subject in my hand, that day or event came flooding back to me as though it had just happened. Be that as it may, I still received letters from our associates in the war who attempted to correct my versions of events.

A lot of men who served on both sides of the Rebellion wrote their memoirs and I will suggest to President Hayes that we should establish a national library where these diaries could be lodged for the use and edification of future generations. I have no doubt that yours would make extremely interesting reading and provide insights that will not be found elsewhere.

If we could develop a library for just such a purpose, would you consider contributing a copy of your memoirs to it?

Since my last letter, I have not only been busy with my office, but also with helping to organize several veterans' events. Your name came up in conjunction with a reunion we will be holding in Chicago next November and it was wondered whether you would make the trip down to that city. Please accept my personal invitation to attend the affair. However, if your wife's health prohibits you traveling to join us, I understand and once again, please keep me informed of your activities and plans.

Sincerely,
W.T. Sherman
Signed by hand, 'Cump'

It was a kindly note and when I picked it up at John Edwards' General Store, I had no compunction about reading it aloud to him. The reference to Secretary Stanton eluded John until I explained that Mrs. Lincoln had mentioned the former Secretary in her letter. Our Postmaster was intrigued by the idea that I was writing my memoirs and asked if he could read them. I told him when they were finished I would show him parts of it and this satisfied his curiosity for the moment.

When I set out to write these recollections, it was to set the facts straight in my head so I could report to Mrs. Lincoln in a sensible manner. I also thought my niece and nephew would be interested in learning about my part in ending slavery by putting down the Rebellion. Like the General, I find myself to be a little vain about it. Now, I begin to see this as an opportunity to present my memories of our efforts with General Sherman's army to the world at large. In light of this I will continue with my narrative…

The rest of our stay in Savannah was more salubrious. The General spent his time remaking old acquaintances and I settled into a routine that was almost office-like in its hours and duties.

Savannah was both welcoming and antagonistic toward us. In general, the people liked our soldiers and the soldiers behaved themselves because of this. There were many harmless entertainments. Distressingly, there were also a number of sporting houses of bad reputation throughout the town where men, who were so inclined, could take their ease.

I could have visited several of these because they contained coloured women, but I knew what the treatment was for the pox and did not wish to undergo such painful humiliation. As we could see the end of the war was within sight, I decided to continue saving my pay to improve the farm or to invest somewhere. Another incentive was that, like everything else in Savannah, the price of sin was climbing exorbitantly almost every day.

Rebel men who fled the city to fight with Hardee were acknowledged to be our enemies, but the women left behind were more often than not, treated as though they were our own daughters. Three general officers from Hardee's corps even asked General Sherman to assure the safety and well being of their families, to which the General graciously consented.

Because of this, it infuriates me that those Southerners who threw themselves on his good offices should now disparage and tarnish General Sherman's name. To this day the adults roundly curse him and the children are taught to fear him. According to many parents all that is missing are horns, a tail and a pitchfork. He has replaced the bogeyman under the bed. The General was and is still billed as the great vandal and yet there is no real call for such slander. I have marked this down to the Southerner's frustration over the erosion and defeat of their Rebellion.

All through the holiday season and into January we awaited instructions from General Grant. At first, he ordered us to move by sea to Virginia to open another front on Richmond. General Sherman appealed this and it took some time to hear back, but when we did Grant rescinded his original command and allowed us to take our armies up through the Carolinas.

I believe part of the impetus for this decision came from General Halleck, who although not a friend of Sherman's was a pragmatist. He understood that a great deal of time would be lost in assembling the number of vessels necessary to complete this manoeuvre and more could be gained from another bold move rather than sending men to further entrench around the Rebel capital. When General Grant acquiesced to Sherman's original plan he urged us to move with all speed.

While General Halleck was supportive of our moving north through the Carolinas, he was also motivated to write to General Sherman over the situation with the Negroes. Burns' pen had injected its poison into the pages of his newspaper and his stories were widely believed.

Washington's opinion of General Sherman was that he was a Negro-hater.

Apparently Secretary Stanton did nothing to dispel this idea and Mr. Lincoln was concerned with our reported treatment of runaway slaves. In all, we must have freed somewhere between twenty and thirty thousand of the wretches, but the reports indicate we accomplished far less and abandoned four times that number to their fates.

From Savannah there was little we could do about the damage to Sherman's reputation. The northern newspapers went uncontrolled and were fed untruths by vanquished Southerners. Not one editor took the time to consider the sources of the rumors they chose to print. The only publications that came close to the truth were those of the enemy from Richmond and Charleston as they reported our progress across Georgia and our activities in Savannah.

Throughout early January General Howard's wing had transported by sea from Savannah to Beaufort on the South Carolina coast. General Slocum's wing moved overland along the Savannah River toward Pocotaligo where the two wings would make a junction then drive north toward Columbia. General Sherman left Savannah by sea on January twenty-first to join Howard and I went with him.

Beaufort was another city of great charm. As it had remained loyal to the Union throughout the war, it had not been subjected to any damage. The splendid homes remained intact, but we did not have sufficient time to inspect these, only seeing them from the water as we disembarked to move inland immediate upon our arrival.

Many people in the North were grateful for our march through Georgia believing we were divinely inspired to punish the Rebels. We did not punish them unduly, but destroyed their ability to make war on the Union. South Carolina was a different story. The widely held belief among our soldiers was that South Carolina was the seat of secession and its citizens should be the ones whom we punished.

On the first part of our incursion, we passed from Beaufort through the low country behind the coast. This could have been extremely dangerous as Wheeler's troopers were somewhere up ahead of us and we believed they had joined with Hardee's army. The land all around was flooded from the winter rains and we travelled over raised roads that concentrated our companies making them targets for artillerists. What we did not know, and fortunately for our advance, was the Rebels were falling back away from us toward Charleston and Augusta to protect those cities whilst our real goal was the city of Columbia.

We were rapidly moving away from the coast and our Pioneer Battalions were doing a magnificent job of laying corduroy road through the swamps and muddy bottoms along our track. They were carrying us forward at a rate of ten miles a day, and this frightened our enemies.

Finally, at the Salkehatchie River General Hardee decided to make a stand and ten thousand of his men dug in along the riverbank. The thing we feared most happened, the enemy's artillery caught us on the raised roads. To dislodge the Confederates, we could not complete a frontal assault along the roadways, so our infantry waded into the cold waters of a flooded swamp and, holding their muskets above their heads, chased the entrenched rebels out of their positions. This was accomplished with the loss of only a few of our soldiers.

We built bridges and more corduroy roads right through the heart of that swamp. When General Johnston heard about our feat he was moved to exclaim "…there had been no such army since the days of Julius Caesar." We felt pretty good about our progress and believed the war was nearing its end. Many of the men hoped that in a short time, after gutting South and North Carolina, we would link up with General Grant and be in the final fight to kill the infamous Robert E. Lee.

I did not have much to do. As the General did not view me as a servant, but a member of his headquarters, I was not attached to any regiment or company. I was at loose ends trying to be as helpful as possible. Because of the nature of the countryside, there were not many plantations about and consequently, not many runaway slaves. We would occasionally encounter a single man or a small family of fugitives and I would question them, but the information we gleaned was simply that Hardee's men and Wheeler's cavalry had passed by and bragged on how they were going to murder us in the next fight.

General Sherman was living out of his headquarters' wagon as there were not many suitable buildings in the vicinity. Those we came across, we burned. Every afternoon, the General's wagon would come to a halt on some partly dry, heap of earth. There the teamsters and attending company of infantrymen would unload the tents, tables, chairs and other bric-a-brac that made the set-up useful, then proceed to establish the General's roost for the night.

The rest of us were left to shift as best we could. I became proficient in buttoning two dog tents together to form one shelter large enough for Gaylord's tack and me. The ends of this were open to the weather and so the only way to get a night's sleep was to curl up like a newborn in the center of the tent with drainage trenching encircling me.

A courier arrived at our headquarters late in the afternoon of the sixth day of our march. He demanded to see General Sherman without delay and was shown into the General's tent. A little while later, he emerged and returned along the road to Savannah. General Sherman came out shortly after his departure. The General appeared shaken and, although not distraught, seemed dazed.

He sat by the fire talking with Major Ewing and several other aides. There was no mention of the dispatch, but it had to have been very important to shake him like that.

The next day Captain Nichols and I travelled side-by-side. Over the preceding months we had become good friends and often rode together during campaign movements. He eased his mount to his right until his knee was almost touching Gaylord's left flank.

"I saw what was in the communication that arrived last night and don't know what to make of it."

Because of the severity of the General's reaction to the intelligence, I thought that Grant was taking General Sherman away from us, or ordering us to turn toward Richmond as he had tried to do once before.

"It was a letter from his brother John, the senator. He has asked the General to become the next president of the country when Mr. Lincoln finally steps down."

"How can he do that? He needs to be nominated, then elected?"

"The General could easily dominate any party convention as he has all but put down the Rebellion single-handedly. Look at how much support Little Mac got last summer and he was not a very good general."

"I know, but do you not think people might be tired of wars and generals? This Civil War was supposed to be over very quickly, in a matter of months. And it was going to be fought without many casualties on our side. It didn't turn out that way. Most people in the North do not even want to fight."

One of the tasks we had while in Savannah was chasing off recruiters. They flooded the city almost before we entered its precincts and began rounding up Negro men. Recruiters were paid agents who provided substitutes to wealthy Northerners so they could avoid the draft. If a man could find a substitute to take his place in the ranks, then he would not have to fight. The Recruiters told the liberated slaves that they had to fight in the Union army and began caging them for shipment north to Boston, New York, Washington and Baltimore. It was nothing more than slavery under a different guise. If the prisoners had reached those cities, they would have been 'sold' to the highest bidder. Recruiters had no right to do this and freed slaves had no obligation to enlist. I took part in several expeditions to break open these new slave pens. It was felt my presence would restore some confidence among the Negroes and lend some veracity to our troops' explanations that the enlistment of the former slaves would be purely voluntary and no one could force them to fight. I took pleasure in holding several of these Recruiters at gunpoint and threatening them with all manner of consequences. When we herded them back aboard a northbound paddle wheeler many were still complaining and asking who would be making up for the financial losses they incurred when we interrupted their trip to Savannah.

The draft was not a new issue. Just before I joined the Army of the Tennessee our navy had to shell New York City to quell a riot by the Irish who did not wish to fight or be part of the national draft. So to say that the people of the North were happy with the war and content with its conduct was not accurate.

"Not only are the people growing tired of the war and those of us who are fighting it, think about the General and what he thinks about politicians," I said in further rebuttal.

"Well you are right on that. How could I have forgotten?" and we both laughed at the very idea of Nichols forgetting and General Sherman accepting any position that brought him closer to the political class than he already was.

South Carolina's citizens were not aware of the special animosity we held for them. One of the first town's we encountered after leaving the coast and driving away Hardee's men was Barnwell. It was put to the torch by General Kilpatrick's cavalry and he quipped that they had changed its name to 'Burnwell'. While the town succumbed to the flames, Kilpatrick held a farce in the local hotel under the deception of a ball. Instead of inviting the townsfolk, he hosted a number of Negress' and danced with them throughout the night. It was said that General Kilpatrick was partial to coloured women and dallied with them often.

The General did not try to stop the abasement of Barnwell. He had the measure of his army and knew any attempt to stop our soldiers from seeking revenge on the home of secession was futile. Instead, he made sure the women and children were safe then let the town burn. This was a change from the man who tried to protect Georgia's private property from total depredation.

On the evening of February fifteenth we were poised before Columbia. In the previous days we had captured many small hamlets and destroyed the South Carolina Railroad. These demonstrations severed the communications between Richmond and Columbia, South Carolina's capital. During the last few days before entering Columbia our biggest worry was not Hardee and Wheeler, but the remnants of Hood's Army of Tennessee. Although they had been soundly defeated at Nashville before Christmas, there were still enough men and equipage to cause problems if they could link up with a sound commander.

It is rumored that General Hood was in disfavour having been driven from the countryside surrounding Atlanta and being badly beaten at Nashville. Some of our men were willing to bet that General Bragg or General Beauregard would be given the overall command. A number of our officers felt there was a chance General Johnson would be called back into action in an attempt to delay us.

As we entered Columbia, no intelligence was forthcoming as to who would lead the remaining Rebel army. What we did not know was that as we entered the city from the south side, General Beauregard was departing from the north. We were also not yet aware that the Southern commander had replaced General Wheeler with a new cavalry commander, General Hampton, who also departed with Beauregard, deserting his first defensive position.

It was cold and the north wind was up as Captain Nichols and I followed Generals Sherman, Howard, Blair and Logan across a pontoon bridge into the town. Rebels had burned the bridge across the Congaree so our engineers and Pioneer Battalion were forced to float a new crossing into place. The town had already surrendered, but we could see that South Carolina's capital city was already alight and had been burning for period of time before our troops entered the city.

A long row of cotton bales was blazing furiously. Several people, among those who welcomed us, were quick to say that retreating Secessionist troops set the fires in the cotton and the armory. Also, they weren't sure, but they thought the Niter Works were either on fire or damaged beyond repair. It turned out that they had been moved out by rail before the line was completely closed.

Our entry into Columbia was like a scene from the bible in which the Messiah is surrounded by the halt and the lame. Only in this instance it was the newly emancipated. When they were able to get close to Lexington, they reached out and touched his flanks while those near to the General stroked his legs and feet with veneration. Some of the crowd even went so far as to leap up to pat the General's hands as he held his horse's reins.

Our arrival took on the overall atmosphere of a fete. Only a few white Union sympathizers, or sycophants trying to curry favour, were to be seen. Most of the crowds were Negroes, and those who weren't praising the Lord or testifying were busy passing out gallons of spirits to our men. The blue-clad soldiers wasted no time in consuming the offerings and before we crossed into the city a goodly number of them were drunk and capering about.

Our baggage wagons were rumbling into Columbia when a raggedy man and his companion stepped out of the crowd and presented themselves to the General. The men were escaped prisoners of war who made off from the holding pens at Columbia's insane asylum and thereby avoided being shipped by train to other prison camps. One of the men, Major Sam Byers had written a lyric poem called "Sherman's March To The Sea". It was immediately popular with soldiers and civilians across the country and, as far as I know, the only song about our march that the General approved of and enjoyed. I think he was very pleased to be referred to by the ancient accolade of "Chieftain".

From the moment we entered the city we were plagued by enemies who either slipped into town unseen or remained hidden until they came out to do their damage. They were reported to be setting fires all around the town. General Sherman had required that our army not engage in the destruction of private property. We were to destroy targets of military importance only. The General gave his word on this to the mayor of Columbia and to any resident seeking his protection.

Certainly, many of our men were involved in what eventually became an uncontrolled riot. There was too much liquor flowing, but we watched as agents of the South also helped to put their city to the torch.

In the evening of February seventeenth the town began to burn in earnest. Our troops operated the city's fire wagons and pumps. Most were involved in trying to quell the fires and, along with the civilian townsfolk, passed buckets of water up from the river. The General himself came out of his headquarters and directed the efforts of our men to fight the blazes, but the wind took the embers and spread them from house to church to store to office block unleashing a flood of new fires.

It was during this time that I killed one of our own soldiers as he and his comrade tried to molest a young woman. However, my power was limited in saving the many coloured women who were subjected to the same treatment and worse.

The burning of Columbia took place over General Sherman's objections and to his chagrin.

By morning, little remained of Columbia that was usable as a town. My heart was saddened at the destruction, as was that of any man of good conscience. We were soldiers not barbarians and did not desire to be stained as such. We simply wanted to move on to fight our last battles and to destroy the consumption that threatened the very health of the Republic.

CHAPTER NINETEEN

December 17, 1878

Before we had a chance to carry our campaign much beyond Columbia, Burns' pen was again spreading its vitriol. This time, I believe someone must have contained his slanders somewhat by threat because he wrote of our leaders that "… true Generals Sherman, Howard and others were out giving instruction for putting out a fire in one place, while a hundred fires were lighting all around them. How much better it would have been had they brought in a division or a brigade of sober troops and cleared out the town…"

Mr. Burns failed to mention what we all saw, which was the action of Rebel agents who set about destroying the city whilst allaying their own guilt through the complicity of the Northern reporters.

When we left the ruins of Columbia, we were unhappily forced to carry Mr. Burns with us.

There was a great collection of unfortunates who chose to abandon Columbia with our columns. Along with our constant irritant, Mr. Burns, Miss Marie Boozer accompanied us. She was reputed to be the most beautiful woman in the South, but I never did have the opportunity to see her, so I will withhold my opinion.

My position with the General's headquarters served to cosset me. Although aware of many incidents of cruelty toward the citizens of South Carolina, I did not see or participate in any outrages. I was, however, given the charge of an execution we performed near the village of Camden on the North Carolina border.

The condemned man, Thomas Corcoran, smuggled a pistol into a meeting with General Howard. Mr. Corcoran requested the appointment to ask for the protection of his property. During the engagement, Corcoran removed his pistol from its hiding place, pointed it at the general's face and pulled the trigger. The pistol misfired and guards seized the assassin. It was a single-shot, dueling pistol not fit for the task, but I suppose he felt it was a weapon of honour suited to his purpose. It has crossed my mind that the weapon's own sense of honour prevented it from firing and thereby taking part in a cowardly murder.

Major Ewing placed me in charge of the detail responsible for killing this man. At first I thought we would shoot him, but Major Ewing indicated to me this was an act of treachery by a civilian and did not merit a firing squad. We would hang him.

Canvassing the men who would help perform the task, I discovered that they were all like me: no strangers to death, but only familiar with death through sickness or on the battlefield. We did not know how to successfully hang a man making it quick and as painless as possible. Because we were on the march, we did not have the time to build a proper gallows, so it was decided to hang him from a tree limb.

I knew that he needed to be dropped a distance to ensure his neck broke cleanly, but I did not know how far that might be. As the sentence was to be carried out expeditiously, I decided to make the man stand on the bed of a wagon and then have the horses pull the wagon out from under him. I reasoned a drop of at least three feet would be sufficient to snap his neck.

We set up the execution site the night before, moving the wagon into position beneath the tree limb by hand. A carpenter built a set of removable steps up to its bed as well as an additional platform two feet in height and placed in the wagon for him to stand on. I thought this would give a sufficient drop. In the morning a team of horses would be limbered to the dray and one of the privates would drive them away. Before finishing for the night, we draped the rope from the limb. One of our men, who had been a sailor on the Great Lakes measured and tied the slipknot into the hemp then suspended it allowing three feet for the drop.

On the morning of the execution the picket aroused me earlier than the rest of the camp and I sent him to get our party up and dressed. I let Corcoran sleep as long as possible. He did not know this was his last morning, although he knew he was bound to die. I considered this a final kindness.

With my detail assembled, I caused reveille to be blown by the bugler and the assembly sounded by our drummers. We formed part of General Hazen's Second Brigade into a three-sided square around the tree. The senior officers from headquarters were the last to gather. They took their leisure smoking their first morning cigars in order to steel themselves.

Corcoran was awake when we went for him. He had been under guard in a special tent set up away from the regular encampment. The guard called him out of the tent, but he would not come. The guard called again and still there was no sign of movement. I told three of our detail to remove the tent. Corcoran was revealed, curled on the ground and moaning softly whilst rocking back and forth.

A surgeon had accompanied us and was quick to check the man over. When he pronounced him fit and uninjured, the surgeon pulled a flask from his pocket and urged Corcoran to drink. After a minute, our prisoner composed himself, but still had to be helped to stand. Once upright a corporal pinioned Corcoran's arms behind his back with a length of rope.

We marched slowly toward the tree and the wagon. The regimental band played the Death March. Confined in a square of four guards, Corcoran stumbled and then made water in his pants. Although the distance from the guard tent to the wagon was less than one hundred yards, it took five minutes to cover. For the final twenty yards, Corcoran could do nothing but stare at the dangling rope. His progress in this last walk was halting and he tried to pull away from the inevitable climb up onto the wagon's bed.

Two guards all but carried him up the steps and placed him squarely on the platform. Corcoran collapsed twice before we sought a plank to tie him to so he would remain standing in an upright position.

I asked him for any last words, but he could not speak. He had not said a word during the entire procedure from our arrival at his tent until he was hanged. His face lost all colour and his breath came in a staccato of sobbing. Waiting for him to compose himself was fruitless. After a few moments I placed a burlap sack over his head and the corporal who was aiding me noosed him. A padre was praying feverishly from the ground beside the wagon. Then, more for the assembled troops than for Corcoran, I read the execution order aloud. When I finished the brief, the corporal and I clambered down the steps. Two privates pulled them off to the side so the man would not strike them in his fall.

Shooting a man with a gun is one thing. It is over in an instant and in battle is easy enough. But hanging a man requires that you look into his eyes and his terror infects your soul. My heart raced so hard as we stepped down from the wagon I thought it would burst. But this was my duty and others had performed similar acts before me so I knew I would survive. As I pulled the burlap down over his face the look in his eyes and my own knowledge that I was the last thing he would see made me wince.

A slight wave of my hand to the private driving the wagon was the order for it to be driven forward. Only then did we realize that we should have tied his legs together. Corcoran tried stepping backward to stay on the wagon, but the noose tightened and dragged him into mid air. Instead of falling and snapping his spine as I intended, he swung out and was left to dangle, legs kicking and choking noisily through the burlap cloth.

Several soldiers in the hollow square, men who had seen horrors beyond compare, commenced retching. Corcoran was in horrible pain and needed to be dispatched quickly. I whispered to the corporal that he should grab the man by the legs and pull down hard. When the corporal tried this he only succeeded in pulling against the spring of the limb so there was no firm resistance to break Corcoran's neck.

Finally, I took my pistol from its holster and moving to where I could make a clean shot, prepared to shoot him. As I began to raise my arm, a hand stopped me. General Hazen's adjutant, Colonel Martin, shook his head indicating that nothing more was to be done to correct the situation.

It took Corcoran ten minutes to stop kicking and shuddering. By this time, the burlap cloth below the noose and the collar and shoulders of his shirt were soaked in blood from the chafing of the rope. After half an hour the surgeon pronounced him dead and the troops were marched past the hanging corpse as a reminder that discipline, for anyone who transgressed grievously, would be terrible. We then placed him in his coffin and buried him in the grave we prepared the night before. A wooden marker was placed on the mounded earth so his family could find him and rebury his body where they chose.

Our plan for North Carolina was to fight the different Confederate forces singly before they could join together to make a large enough army to seriously threaten us.

Hampton's cavalry constantly harassed the rear of our columns and the weather did not let up to allow us maneuvering room across the land. It took General Kilpatrick several days to get his division across the Peedee River. But the weather, from my understanding wasn't the only impediment to our progress.

As a well-known womanizer General Kilpatrick had few peers. Even on campaign he was making continual assignments with numerous ladies. This time, however, this peccadillo nearly cost him his freedom.

Although I never saw the legendary Marie Boozer, she caught the General's eye and fancy. I am sure her motives were not altogether romantic. Her carriage carried not only her, but a mountain of luggage, some of which we were sure contained the valuables she wished to keep safe from our foragers. There was no better protection than that of a Union general. The men of our wing felt that the inattention brought about by Miss Boozer's attentions caused General Kilpatrick to be careless in his duties.

Shortly after crossing the Peedee, which was the border of North Carolina, General Kilpatrick and his cavalry encamped. The General divided his division into three columns in order to block Hampton's men from reaching Fayetteville where they might make junction with Hardee's Army and possibly Hood's.

Sloppiness and eagerness on the part of General Kilpatrick resulted in his headquarters being left open to attack. General Kilpatrick did not spend as much time solidifying his encampment and guard details as he should have. That, and his desire to race back into the arms of the voluptuary, left him particularly exposed. Shortly after dawn on March ninth, the rebel General Butler attacked Kilpatrick's encampment from the west and General Wheeler stormed it from the rear across a range of swampland.

General Kilpatrick was caught short in his drawers. Apparently Miss Boozer was also clothed in her flimsiest attire giving the men who took the time to look a very good understanding of her attractions. General Kilpatrick took to his heels and disappeared before the rebel horsemen could capture him.

One of the wings dispatched to block Wade Hampton's escape was forced to come to the rescue of General Kilpatrick's camp leaving the road open to Fayetteville for our enemy. Many of the men in General Howard's camp took delight in the thrashing our pompous little cavalry general took that morning.

While this comedy was playing out on the road to Fayetteville, more momentous events were afoot. The rebel government finally settled on a leader for their men. They reinstated General Johnston. Had they left him in place at Atlanta, all of the destruction and easy conquest on our part might never have occurred. But we were not to learn of his appointment for several more days.

At Fayetteville we divested ourselves of more camp followers sending them by steamer down the Cape Fear River to Wilmington. These included Negroes, and whites who felt it unsafe to remain behind in their homes after befriending us.

I cannot get over the fact even the best historians declare the surrender by General Lee at Appomattox the end of the conflict. Men were still dying after Lee's surrender and would for several months to come.

In the Army of the Tennessee we knew the end was close, but the thing was not finished yet. Our prayers asked that General Johnston would not force one last great scene of destruction. So far, both Generals Johnston and Sherman had avoided the murderous continual fighting that cost so many lives in the Eastern Campaign. We were proud and thankful this campaign gave us no Cold Harbor or Antietam to stitch onto our battle flags.

Still, the General was determined to see it through. Every day we awoke with the knowledge that he would fight if necessary. By the second week of March, except for daily skirmishes, we had not yet had to wage a major battle in the Carolinas, but we knew one was coming. From here on out, regardless of the weather, we proceeded stripped of all unnecessary gear.

At Averysboro everything changed. Quick to recover from his drubbing, General Kilpatrick encountered a line of skirmishers along the Raleigh Road on the ides of March. These forced his troops to dismount and build breastworks in the swamps bordering the road on the north side of the Cape Fear River. As our cavalrymen confronted the Rebels, they came to face a new group of infantry who turned out to be General Taliaferro's division. These troops had been driven off the coast and marched inland to become part of Johnston's army.

The fighting went on all night with General Kilpatrick requiring reinforcements from General Slocum before the battle could be turned. The Confederate line wasn't broken until the next day. Instead of a minor engagement, as we had been experiencing since leaving Atlanta, Averysboro turned into one of the biggest battles of the campaign.

Averysboro showed there was still a great deal of fight left in the rebel army and that vexed us. We had become too confident in our strength and this was shaken when we were finally tested.

During this part of the Carolina campaign, I was used only occasionally to collect intelligence. Stories about me had spread and Hampton's troopers knew to be on watch for "Sherman's nigger spy." Every Negro in the vicinity was forced to stay home where their masters could identify them. One or two slaves suspected of being me were lynched on the spot. I was told, by one house servant, the feeling among the rebel soldiers was they would sooner hang ten innocents than miss out on destroying one dangerous agent.

We were of the opinion it was us who would end the war and the sooner we ended it the better. Because of this, I was ready to fight and the chance came five days after leaving Fayetteville.

As General Slocum's wing advanced along a road that ran from Fayetteville to Goldsboro, we began encountering more and more rebel cavalry who attempted to delay us. Our numbers were too vast to be deterred and we poured along until we were brought up abruptly just south of a small town named Bentonville.

Ranged before us was all of General Johnston's army.

Stretching across the Goldsboro Road and blocking our way were what appeared to be ten brigades of infantry supported by artillery. South of the road, the enemy's left flank was protected by dense swampland that they judged to be impassable. North of the road at least a dozen brigades were hooked around to confront and contain our left flank. I have never seen such a vast sea of men.

In light of this we began fighting with our shovels building breastworks as quickly as we could fling the earth up and out of the ground. The rebels would not wait forever. At 2:30 in the afternoon the world fell apart when infantry began pouring over the tops of the rebel fortifications.

I was with the 61st Ohio having just delivered a communication to their commander, Captain Garrett, when the attack commenced. Even by this late point in the war I had never been on the defensive against such a force. Fear chilled my heart as thousands of men, all intent on killing me, came screaming toward my position screeching their horrid yell.

By this time in the campaign I had acquired a Henry repeating rifle and was firing as quickly as I could. It was plain that the only recourse I had to save myself was to create an impenetrable wall of lead and the hope that my comrades were doing the same thing. We loaded and fired continuously until the order to fall back was passed along the line. So many cartridges had been fired through it, that the barrel of my rifle burnt my hands when I touched it.

As embarrassing as it is to tell, I took to my heels and ran at an oblique angle aiming for a wood where I could see numbers of our men turning to face the oncoming enemy. I thought my legs were full of shell fragments they pained me so badly, and I was convinced my lungs were shot through, but I reached the wood uninjured.

From the safety of the woods it was like watching a flood as the Secesh infantry insinuated itself between, then engulfed companies and regiments who were still trying to hold the line. At times only a flag or burgee held aloft told us where a unit was still fighting.

The Fourteenth Corps Hospital, which had been erected earlier beside the creek to the north of the Goldsboro Road, was almost overrun before the wounded men could be evacuated. I heard stories later of how ambulance drivers cut the traces of their wagons and fled on their horses leaving their human cargo to be captured or killed.

If anyone ever tells me again that all is well in a battle and things proceed in an orderly fashion, I will be tempted to shoot that person. There is no order and, in a big battle like this, no order giver who truly knows the situation. It is all smoke and noise and one man killing another.

After the war, I would meet men who fought for General Grant starting with the Wilderness and surviving right through to Cold Harbor. How they survived these maelstroms I do not know. How they kept their sanity after the insanity of a big fight was beyond my comprehension. Still they appear now to be sane and sober men.

As an observation, it may be that your gravest moments come when you are paralyzed with fear and your salvation comes when you hand yourself over to death. Then you can move and think without fear because you have accepted that in a moment you will be one of those bodies being trampled beneath men's feet. It is this that saves you if you are to be saved at all.

Once I turned in the woods along with hundreds of other blue-coated men and started to fire back, I felt a sudden calm within me. I knew we could not stop the onslaught and so accepted my death as inevitable. But, I knew that before I died I would make a good account of myself.

At this point I was not sure what company or regiment I was part of. There were men from every unit crowded into the woods. Later I learned that Albie Chatterton was fighting in these woods as well, but he was badly wounded and I never saw him again. The rebels kept up the pressure on us until we were dislodged, but our retreat was less skitterish than earlier and we fell back with some order. The right wing of our army was driven more than half a mile to the west from its original position, but they still had the swamp to their backs. Our left wing had been turned and they were now well south of the Goldsboro Road.

They would maintain this position as the night fell. We were all exhausted and expected the fighting to decline and cease with the coming of dark. The rebels had different ideas, however, and we heard demonstrations by them continuing below the road until very late. Even though we were not under direct attack, none of the men around me slept.

We fought for the next two days and by morning of March 22nd; General Johnston's army had all but left the field.

It was not clear at first whether we defeated the rebels or merely chased them off. The fields and woods were covered with bodies and there were a goodly number of wounded enemies strewn about. We recovered as many of these as we could and our surgeons treated them with kindness.

There is a great amount of cleaning to be done after a battle. Men are to be buried; wounded tended; abandoned or captured weapons to be collected and stored; enemy stores to be sorted through and either re-assigned to our men or destroyed. As part of our army did this, many more men set off in pursuit of General Johnston and the survivors of his army.

On the third day of the battle, I reported to General Slocum's headquarters. "We thought you were among the dead sergeant. We've been looking for you."

"I was fighting with a number of different units. It seemed like every time I prepared to set off to find headquarters, the Johnnies took it upon themselves to attack my position and I found myself fighting in positions from which I could not easily extricate myself."

"Be that as it may sergeant, General Howard has need of you." And so, I returned to his staff headquarters leaving the final fights and skirmishes to others. I did not mind this as I had seen enough and was bitterly tired of war.

After the end of the fighting it was time to rest. Food, clothing, mail and money caught up with us. Following a bath in the cold water of the creek on the northern edge of the battlefield, I donned a clean uniform and felt myself a new man.

Before we confronted the rebel army we hoped it was possible to bring the campaign to an end with negotiation. Intelligence received on our march north from Fayetteville told us General Johnston was back in command and, even if his masters in Richmond did not know it, he understood the futility of continuing the fight. Still he chose to do so. The result of his tenacity was the last major battle of the Civil War.

Since the receipt of his brother's letter, the General was quieter although he would, for no apparent reason, curse all politicians. Those who did not know what had been communicated remarked on his weariness. Some of our men had taken to calling him "Crazy Billy". The more charitable majority blamed his condition on the loss of his infant son. We who knew, and that was a very small number, could see that he viewed the invitation to become the Republican candidate as an insult. I don't believe for a moment he regretted rejecting his brother's offer. He once said that "Goddamned politicians started this war, they left it to us to fight and now they want me to join them to help bathe them in the sad glory of the men who died. Do they think I am such an opportunist?"

Near the end of March, General Sherman quietly boarded a train and disappeared for five days. No one knew where he had gone except Generals Slocum and Howard and Sherman's own aides. When he returned his spirits had lifted and he seemed in better humour than we had seen him since leaving Savannah. Even the politicians faired better when he deigned to speak of them.

Returning to General Howard's wing, General Sherman collected his headquarters staff together to reveal that his recent trip away from the army was to meet with General Grant and President Lincoln at City Point. I was on the fringes of this gathering, unsure as to whether I should be there or not. No one shooed me away so I stayed to listen to what the General had to say.

"We should be grateful to have a man like Lincoln leading us. He has a clear vision of what the future holds and if you are as tired of this war and the rights of states as he is, then you will be glad to know it is just about shut.

"The one thing President Lincoln was firm on was that we finish this with as little bloodshed as possible. The time of killing is drawing to a close and we are to welcome our Southern brothers back into the fold."

Looking toward where I stood on the perimeter of the circle, he continued, "We are all tired of the question of cotton and niggers. Without the latter the former cannot exist. We have done our utmost to destroy the first and to help the second. Now it will be up to other men to ensure that what we have accomplished will remain in place."

Sherman had not been told that his proposed plan to give every freed Negro forty acres of land and a mule to work it was already being abandoned by Secretary Stanton.

"General Johnston is somewhere up ahead and I hope he understands the hopelessness of his position and will treat with us to settle on the generous terms our president would have us offer. If they were offered to me, I would be on my way home tomorrow morning." This statement developed a happy chuckling among the collected officers.

"I believe General Johnston has as many as thirty thousand men gathered near Raleigh. Let us pray he chooses not to use them, but if he does we must do again what we have striven so hard to avoid. We must shed a great deal more blood, so let it be theirs and not ours. Regardless, pray for a peaceful ending to this war."

The end of the war was closer than we thought. Whilst the General was at City Point, we were resting and preparing to follow General Johnston to Raleigh to prevent him from joining with General Lee's army. But three days after our general returned to us, Richmond fell and with it all hope of a Confederate nation.

On April ninth a rider tore through our encampments screaming the news that General Lee had surrendered to General Grant. It was cause for celebration and mysterious supplies of liquor were suddenly in evidence while fiddlers sawed at their instruments and soldiers danced with each other.

We were not finished yet. General Johnston was still out there with a considerable force. Even though all odds were against him, he was not a man who would lay down arms easily as we had just seen. The day after General Lee's surrender we were marching again in pursuit of the foe.

Mild skirmishes and attacks by Confederate sharpshooters marred our advance on Raleigh. With our imperturbable chase, General Johnston fell back abandoning the state capital. Raleigh fell to us on April thirteenth without much of a fight and the next morning the war ended for us.

Rebel delegates approached General Sherman and asked to negotiate their surrender. At the time, they suggested a ceasefire to forestall any further bloodshed. This was quickly assented to and General Sherman offered to meet with General Johnston to arrange the terms ending our hostilities.

Turning to General Howard, General Sherman asked if he might borrow me to act as a bodyguard during the negotiations. I was flattered and happy to know that I would be back in his company.

CHAPTER TWENTY

December 22, 1878,

Just as we were boarding the train to leave for Durham where the surrender talks were to take place, General Sherman was requested to enter the telegraph operator's office. He spent nearly thirty minutes speaking with the operator. When he emerged his face was ashen and his manner so brusque you would swear that the man who emerged was different from the fellow who entered.

The distance from Raleigh to the station at Durham is twenty-five miles, making it too far to ride over and return the same day so we took a train. General Sherman sat alone for the entire trip staring out the window and only speaking when he needed to give an order. I sat at the back of the car for entire the journey, pleased to be included in this momentous occasion.

Something of terrible importance must have occurred to affect the General this way. We had seen him toss off dark moods moments after bad news had been delivered. Within minutes of learning that a flank had been turned or a cavalry charge rebuffed he would return, if not to his normal jesting self, at least to a better-natured version of his person. Whatever this was mired him for the duration of our trip.

General Johnston's headquarters, as far as we knew, were in Greensboro so Durham was roughly halfway between the two encampments. I am not sure what I was expecting upon our arrival. General Sherman had been so quiet, I assumed that there was a death in his family that he had just learned about, but then he did not appear to be in a confidential mood as he was in Savannah when he descried the loss of his son from the newspapers. In consequence, he told us nothing of what he expected from the rebels.

Kilpatrick met us at the station with horses for the final leg of our journey. I was given a saddled mule and rode well behind the main group of officers until the General signaled that I should come forward and accompany him and his advisors.

The cavalrymen who met us were in great spirits as we all should have been. They joked and laughed with much exertion. When they spotted a poorly horsed group of Confederate troopers, they taunted them until the General ordered them to stop.

Forty-five minutes after leaving the station at Durham we were met by a delegation of rebel officers. Central among them were Generals Johnston and Hampton. Where I understood Lee to be a strongly handsome and large man from the etchings in the newspapers, Johnston was small, but well turned in his grey uniform. Above all he had the look of being ever ready for battle. Each strand in his beard was in place. The skin of his cheeks and brow freshly scrubbed and his beard carefully trimmed and shaved. His face was set in grim countenance, but not a visage that was unhandsome or imbued with hatred. Most of all, his eyes captured everything that went on around him while dedicating their main focus to General Sherman. Here was another great chieftain, of that I was certain.

The greetings between the two were cordial enough. I was surprised to hear that General Johnston's voice was deeper than his size prescribed and it was melodic as many Southern voices were. General Sherman still spoke with his high-pitched, Ohio-bred accent, which although softened by years away from his home state, proclaimed his birthright. General Johnston suggested they repair to a homestead nearby where they could commence their discussion.

Mr. and Mrs. Daniel Bennett met the two generals at the door of their home. Surrounding them were their four children. I hoped, as I am sure their parents did, that the children would carry the memory of the men they saw this day for the rest of their lives. Before retiring to another building on the property, Mrs. Bennett very quietly told the children that when these men were finished, the fathers of their friends who were away fighting the war would be coming home.

The house was decent enough although of unpainted frame construction and only three rooms. It was a credit to Mrs. Bennett that the family's home was immaculately kept. The two generals settled into the large front room and General Sherman asked that all except General Johnston leave.

We presumed this was so the two men, who had never met, could take the measure of each other and speak candidly.

As I later understood the discussion that took place inside, General Johnston asked for the same and better terms that Grant gave Lee. Johnston felt he was not backed into a corner tactically and had some limited leeway to make requests and demands. General Sherman, who had been fighting solidly for six months was overjoyed to have an end in sight and was willing to make concessions, but discussion ground to a halt when General Johnston suggested they bring in a representative of the rebel government.

"My government does not recognize the legitimacy of the rebel government and so will not negotiate with them," was Sherman's reply.

When the two officers exited the house, General Johnston had the same look of consternation about him that General Sherman had earlier that day. Sherman had not fully recovered his composure although the meeting and negotiations seemed to have gone well and lasted several hours.

With a few words of appreciation and the confirmation that they would meet again on the morrow, we mounted and rode back toward the station.

At the station General Sherman caused our train to remain stationary so

254

he could address our full attention. We were all in a giddy mood and full of congratulations to ourselves for this meant we were now sure we had survived the war.

"Gentlemen, gentlemen," he began. "This morning I received news that will make this both the happiest and saddest day of this war. First, I wish to tell you that General Johnston and I have agreed to cease all fighting until surrender negotiations are complete. He will be telegraphing his government..."

At which point one wag, who will not here be named, spoke up to general laughter. "That's if he can find them."

"Yes, Major ********, if he can find them he will ask for the authority to act on behalf of not only himself and his present army in North Carolina, but for General Taylor in Texas and Louisiana, and the armies of General Forrest and Maury in Alabama and other places.'

With this announcement there was a rousing round of applause with some of the officers leaping to their feet and cheering.

"Now it grieves me to advise you that last night President Lincoln was murdered in Washington."

Pandemonium broke out in the car. Several of the same men who had only a moment before cheered the end of the war had their revolvers out and were shouting for death to the cowardly rebels.

"Please settle down. Put your weapons away." It took a full three minutes before order settled back onto the car again. Only then did I become aware I was weeping with my own pistol in my hand and death in my heart for any rebel who dared cross my vision.

"All the details are not yet known. What I have been informed of is that an assassin crept up behind him while he and Mrs. Lincoln were attending the theatre. The assassin shot him once in the brain and got away. At the same time another member of this murder conspiracy stabbed Secretary Seward and his son, but both survived. And we have been advised that there may be an additional murderer on our trail. Because of the loss of Mr. Lincoln, Vice President Johnson is now the president.

"General Johnston has assured me this was not the doing of any man in the rebel military and we know enough of his sense of honour to believe him. When I showed him the telegram he was visibly hurt and as shaken as though it was his own president this had happened to.

"When we arrive in Raleigh, I want the Provost Guard increased and all liquor that can be found confiscated. If our men decide to take it upon themselves to strike out I want it made utterly clear that no act of revenge will be tolerated.

"I expect to learn more when we arrive in Raleigh and will keep you informed of any new facts as I receive them. For now I would suggest you offer a prayer for Mr. Lincoln."

There was not the flash of violence we expected. A few men called for revenge, but the tears we saw were tears of sorrow not of anger.

On the following day we returned to Durham and the General once again met with General Johnston, but this time Johnston had John Breckinridge from the defunct Confederate government with him to oversee his end of the negotiations. Both were fixed on the political rights of the returning rebels. General Sherman agreed to broach the subject with our government in Washington and included the rebel suggestions in the draft memorandum he telegraphed to our capital.

I was not close enough to Breckenridge to hear the entirety of his statement as he rode away from that meeting, but I did hear him say something about General Sherman being "…a hog sir. Yes sir, a hog. Did you see him take that drink." This I thought most ungracious for a man who should have dangled at the end of a Union rope.

"President Lincoln made it clear at City Point that the rebels were to be welcomed back," our General began when filling us in on the day's events. A number of his staff were not happy that the rebels would suffer no consequences, other than what had already passed, for the four years of bloodshed and heartache they caused. "This has been a war in which the president painted the broad over-strokes and dictated the outcome. Even though he is no longer with us, I feel obliged to honor his wishes."

Many felt the final draft of the agreement was not what the country wanted. What the General saw as generosity and compassion on the part of the Union was interpreted as a confirmation of the rights of slaveholders to hold onto their human property. It also seemed to acquiesce to the rights of individual states to make their own decisions and go their own ways. This is certainly not what we had fought for and I do not think the General meant his agreement to be understood thusly. But in Washington it was.

This was also not what Secretary Stanton wanted, and it enflamed his already smouldering feelings toward the General. The secretary soon set his emissaries, chief among them General Halleck, to work undermining and defaming General Sherman in the New York papers.

What Secretary Stanton did not intimate to the scribblers who were furiously wreaking their revenge on General Sherman, was that the General had not signed a binding treaty, but was only making recommendations and leaving it up to the political lords of Washington to amend and finalize it.

The situation was not helped in any way when Secretary Stanton all but took over the government ignoring the other members of the cabinet and essentially rendering President Johnson impotent in the matter of the final surrender. Stanton ordered General Meade and the Army of the Potomac to close on General Johnston's rear from the north and to block his escape as though there had been no ceasefire.

I was the recipient of this information several weeks after it occurred. My friend and former school chum, Dr. Anderson Abbott apprised me of all the goings on as he was stationed in Washington at the time and heard of them through various offices and his own contacts within the newspapers.

At the same time Secretary Stanton was howling with madness at Sherman, Halleck sent a telegram containing the falsehood that Jefferson Davis and the Confederate cabinet were making good their escape with millions of dollars in gold and were quite prepared to bribe an amicable Sherman to allow them to pass. Upon receipt of this ridiculous story, Secretary Stanton gave it credibility and went with it and other suspicions to the press to denounce General Sherman for his unpatriotic behavior. The secretary stopped just short of calling the General a traitor. Newspapers like the Chicago Tribune did not.

For weeks, as our campaign drew to a close, there was talk that the Democrats would court the General for the presidency. It was widely believed the executive position was open for the taking and many thought Secretary Stanton saw himself on the throne as the succeeding Republican. I know General Sherman was a man of peace and mightily tired of the war, but I could not see him as a Democrat supported by not only the general party, but also by the much despised Copperheads. He did not espouse their values and even today I feel that he acknowledged a debt to Mr. Lincoln that demanded personal loyalty and loyalty to the less radical arm of the Republicans. If his reaction to his brother John's letter suggesting that he run for the presidency in the next election was any indication of how ambivalent he was toward the idea of political office, the notion that he would accept a Democratic nomination was ludicrous beyond words. Still Secretary Stanton chose to attack and demean him, hopefully cutting off any aspiration to office.

He had come and gone almost before any of us knew he was there. General Grant arrived by train in our camp to sort out the mess. Grant did the best he could by Sherman, but he could not milk the venom from Stanton's rhetoric. The one great kindness he did for our general was to allow him to resume the negotiations.

On April 26, General Sherman returned to the Bennett home to treat with General Johnston once again. It was a difficult meeting. Johnson still wanted more than Sherman could offer. He was as tenacious a negotiator as he was a fighter. Sherman could offer nothing more than the terms Grant had given Lee. They continued to spar for an hour until an impasse was declared and, at General Johnston's suggestion, our General Schofield was brought in to "...fix the question".

Before Grant left Raleigh, he approved the new terms for the Confederate surrender. It had been a near thing as Grant only allowed a further forty-eight hours in the ceasefire after which hostilities would recommence.

With the new agreement in place and awaiting ratification, we could begin to feed our former enemies welcoming them back as ones who had simply gone astray and who now saw the light. More than that was to be left to the government.

The morning Grant departed, the railroad brought the first of the newspapers bearing the condemnations of our general. Among them was a vilification by Mr. Burns who would later go on to line his own pockets by publishing a history of the march. I was among the soldiers lined up for the privilege of buying a fresh piece of news when the two men in front of me began cursing the vendor and passing the papers back to the crowd without paying for them.

Printed on the front page of every publication were Secretary Stanton's lies. We would not pay to read these and we would not allow them to be sold to unsuspecting buyers. In a moment a lantern appeared in the hands of a private and despite the protests of the vendor, he splashed the coal oil from the lamp's reservoir over the newspapers on the vendor's cart then set them alight with the wick.

"If you don't want to go up with this trash, I wouldn't say anything," threatened the private. The vendor retreated a safe distance to watch his stock burn. This is the only time I willingly took part in setting a fire.

It was not until much later that we learned Stanton had ordered General Sherman's removal, but that Grant had refused to do this and indeed did not even mention it to Uncle Billy.

In the end, General Schofield was left to oversee the return to peace in Raleigh and we were ordered north to Richmond. General Howard had already been appointed to oversee the newly formed Freedmen's Bureau. All agreed that he was the ideal for this position, but many held doubts the government would aid him in his task. General Sherman also took leave of the army, albeit only temporarily, going south to Savannah and making sure its citizens were still being fed.

We left Raleigh on the morning of April 30 beginning our long march toward the rebel capital, which now rested in the hands of General Halleck. We would have liked to get our hands on his neck. Instead, we were meeting more and more of our former enemies.

How quickly a heart turns when that heart is left to answer its own voice.

Our men greeted the rebels with sympathy and compassion. We fed them and spoke softly to them in admiring voices.

"Never talked man-to-man with no nigger before." One of the scrawny Johnnies told me when I offered him coffee. After a few minutes of discovering which battles we had been in and where we might have shot at each other, he looked up saying "Maybe we was wrong. You have a good heart and sharp mind. I wasn't expecting such gracious treatment from anyone let alone a colored fella."

I encountered this sentiment time and again, but never from a Confederate officer. Officers were aloof and felt they had the right to treat me with disdain, to which I advised them to "...go to Hell," and denied them any victuals. It was the men who never owned slaves and worked like slaves on their own land before the war who treated me with more manners than their superiors. In a short time, I came to understand they were not fighting for the regal life of the few Southern gentlemen, but because they felt we had no right to invade their homeland.

The march on Richmond was more brutal than any we had performed in Georgia or the Carolinas. When the rain wasn't driving hard, the sun was baking us. As we were approaching Petersburg on the south side of Richmond, the heat and strain of the march began to overcome our men and they fell in great numbers along the sides of the road. Some died in this manner and others had to be transported to our night's bivouac in ambulances.

Sherman's Army was not allowed into Richmond by order of General Halleck. He sent troops to stop us from crossing into the city. At one point, a group of our men were faced down by a Union battery charged and ready to fire. We could do naught but await the arrival of our own chieftain.

When Sherman returned, he was quick to deal with General Halleck. Halleck wished us to pass in review in front of him. Stung by this insult, General Sherman replied that the only way we would enter Richmond would be under General Grant's orders and when we did, General Halleck had better look out.

On May 11 we marched through Richmond and passed General Halleck's headquarters. He was not there to receive a salute if any had been given which it was not. The soldiers of the Army of the Potomac cursed and berated us. Fistfights broke out along our route. Our officers refused to quell them and ignored the imprecations of those officers stationed in the town under Halleck. The rebels treated us with more dignity than our comrades in arms. We were ready to fight as an army and if that had happened there would have been horrible results rivaling the great battles.

We paused long enough to inspect the rebel capital, camping north of the city. The acrimony felt by the Potomac soldiers declined and we were allowed to tour the city to see the different sights.

For the next week we marched as though we were on a holiday tour rather than a military manoeuvre. We paused at Fredericksburg and Chancellorsville to walk over those battlegrounds. Our eyes followed the terrain with experience and some of our regiments who had actually fought on it before being sent west described the events to our anxious ears.

Before encamping at Alexandria, we paraded around Washington's tomb at Mt. Vernon and saluted the famous old man. Men were telling each other how proud he would have been with our efforts to hold the Union together.

General Grant overlooked the insult to General Halleck. I believe he may even have enjoyed it and thought it warranted. He sent word to our troops that we were to prepare for a final Grand Review to honour all those we lost and all that we accomplished. We were excited by this prospect, but we were chagrined at the state of our uniforms and footgear. Some of the men were barefoot and others had only a blue blouse or jacket to prove we were soldiers of the Republic.

Before the parade, some uniforms arrived at our camp, but not enough to go round. Officers who had personal money went to tailors, but the rest of us became the poor cousins of the Army of the Potomac who were immaculately dressed. The men laid it down to Stanton's hatred of Uncle Billy and most, including me, believed this was more than likely true but impossible to prove. Without sanction our soldiers agreed that the clothing we campaigned in, would be the rags the public would see us in. If they did not want to honor us for our sacrifices, that would be their business.

Once we set up camp across the river from the capitol, a shift began to take place. The newspapers that had called for General Sherman's head to be mounted on a pike at the gates of the city were now softening their language. Some, like the wily Horace Greeley, even admitted that maybe Secretary Stanton was overstating the General's generosity in the surrender negotiations and that the stories of Sherman being bribed in the escape of Jefferson Davis and his government was 'flapdaddle.'

But Secretary Stanton was not yet finished with our General. He arranged to have General Sherman called before the Senate Committee on the Conduct of the War. This committee would have done the witch hunters of previous years credit. Headed by Secretary Stanton's crony from Ohio and leading Radical Republican, Benjamin Wade, they attacked our General from all quarters but could not breach his resolve. The General made us very proud by not cringing under this blistering fire and then regrouping and letting go with devastating broadsides of his own.

I only spoke with the General twice once we made camp in Alexandria.

The first time he called me to his headquarters.

"We'll be on the march again two days from now. This time it will be our last opportunity to swagger and sway as we have a right to. I want to make sure you are there and I have a favour to ask of you. I would like you to ride escort with Mother Bickerdyke in the parade."

The venerable woman had been responsible for saving many men through her practice as our head nurse. She had been stern when she needed to be, bullying everyone from recalcitrant physicians to General Sherman himself; and compassionate with her charges. Many young men slipped away in her care whilst she held their hands with such tenderness that they believed she was their own mother. To be allowed to ride beside Mary Anne Bickerdyke was no imposition it was a compliment.

When I accepted the task, the General thanked me for my agreement then laughing, invited Captain Nichols in. Nichols was no longer a captain, but had been promoted to major as was befitting his service. The General motioned him to close the door as he entered and poured three glasses of whisky. Then raising his glass to the pair of us said "To you and all the men who made General Sherman." Tossing his drink off in one long swallow, he smiled commented on the quality of drink available now in Washington and said he would see me after the review.

The first day of the Review was splendid. General Meade's Army of the Potomac positively glistened in the spring sunshine as the bands struck up happy marching tunes. Crowds lined Pennsylvania Avenue as the flag bearers of the first units stepped out.

I could not get close to the reviewing stand, but knew that General Sherman was up there with Generals Grant and Meade as well as President Johnson and the entire cabinet. Oh to have been able to watch Secretary Stanton squirm, now that the press was seeing his true value and from his proximity to such a fine and honourable man as Uncle Billy.

Soldiers marched past the dignitaries all day. Cavalry and artillery batteries rumbled to the cheers of tens of thousands of citizens. But there was one group who did not display with the others.

The coloured troops who fought many battles and shed so much blood were nowhere in sight. I expected to see them take their place in the heart of the country by marching with their comrades, but they were not permitted. If the General had not placed so much trust in me and befriended me, I would have boarded a train back to Canada that day.

For the last time, we heard the long roll calling us out at five a.m. on May 24. For the last time, I fed, curried and tackled Gaylord. Suddenly I was overcome, because until now I had not realized that at the end of the march today, I would turn him back to the army and he would be sent on to new duties. The other men around me gave me room when they saw my tears and heard me talking to my friend of a thousand miles. Many others were bidding their farewells too. Then I mounted him and we pranced to the yard where the parade marshals directed me to my position.

Mother Bickerdyke was not there yet, but in a few minutes an ostler led her up to me and Major Nichols introduced us. It was difficult for her to reach across to take my hand because she was mounted sidesaddle facing left and I was on her right. But she managed it nonetheless and gave me a warm handshake then thanked me for, "… being so generous in agreeing to escort me." How do you tell someone like her that the privilege is all yours?

We shuffled around in our positions waiting for our own band to signal the start. I was nervous. Already people were rushing up to place flower wreaths on the pommels of our saddles. Gaylord seemed to be enjoying himself and proved to be a gentleman by waiting when a young woman asked me if she could feed him an apple. Only after I assented did he delicately bite the fruit in two and lick both pieces into his mouth without once touching her hand. We were waiting on General Sherman who would lead us past the reviewing stand and give the order to salute the dignitaries.

It was already warming up when we moved off. The sky was a brilliant blue. I had not taken note of the colour of the sky in a very long time, but today its richness flooded me with happiness and pride. It was as though the very gods were saluting us.

Our men marched for a full day past that one point. Our salutes were perfect in their execution and the lack of uniforms did not detract from us. We were indeed the warriors who trampled out the grapes.

When I entered the room in the War Office he was using as his headquarters I saluted. He smiled, and quickly returned my salute. Taking up a thick file from the General's desk, Major Nichols nodded to me then left our company. With the Major gone, the room was silent. For days entire continents of sound had overwhelmed our lives. The satisfied clatter of victory in the streets, the happy shouts of soldiers and the tramping of two hundred and fifty thousand, boot-shod feet that went on for three days were all part of the landscape our ears perceived. But now, in this room with only the two of us present the loudest sounds were made by the dust.

Before I arrived the General had been working behind his desk. Now he flanked the big oak table in a manoeuvre that carried him around its right end to the two visitors' chairs that were placed in front of it.

I was disconcerted and did not know how to behave: nor how I should feel. We were no longer on campaign working out the problems of the daily fight, now we were at peace with nothing left to do but say farewell. It was hard imagining a continuing friendship since we no longer shared a common purpose even though I loved him as a father and felt sure he considered me in a more favourable light than simply that of a subordinate. The General would go on serving his country and I would return to mine. Tickets for the train home were in my haversack – Absolom's carpetbag having long since been lost.

"Sit down Frederick." He pushed one of the chairs back for me and settled into the other. The weariness of the past four years had already started to leave his face. And although his fine red hair was a little thinner than when I met him nine months before, he had a small smile of welcome upon his lips. He could now go on in his occupation without the presence of death hovering over his every decision.

Looking directly into my face he said, "I wanted to see you one last time to say thank you. Without the information you brought back from beyond our front lines I would have been blind many times on our march."

"That was my duty, sir…"

"And I understood it to be nothing less. But, you went far beyond your duty. You could have contented yourself with a life in camp or simply followed on the march. After Goldsboro, I wrote Secretary Stanton for permission to grant you at least a field commission. I can't think of another man who deserves it more, but for some reason Mr. Stanton declined my suggestion.

"I fear I know why too. At first I thought it was his personal hatred of me. Although the Secretary pushed me hard to incorporate colored units into The Army of the Tennessee and to give full political rights to every liberated slave we came across, he is frightened of you and your people.

"It wasn't until he arrived in Savannah that I fully understood this. Up until that point I was naïve in my expectations and did not see the hands of Stanton and Halleck working against the simplest things we were trying to achieve. That's because we were isolated, off in the southwest corner of the Republic and well out of the view of the public for the moment. But as we gained momentum moving through Georgia, the press took notice of us and no politician likes it when a soldier gets more ink than he does.

"Reverend Frazier's support of me during the meeting at the Green House in Savannah was the final turning point. Mr. Stanton held a great contempt for colored people even though he espoused the cause of emancipation. Suddenly, with such a well-spoken man telling him to his face that many Negroes did not want to associate with their former white masters, Secretary Stanton was confronted with the truth. And that is your people are not the ignorant and less intelligent of our species. Certainly, given the opportunities of education and the chance to own their own land, the colored population will prosper.

"This was an idea Secretary Stanton and the rest of the Republicans who pushed so hard for emancipation and the punishment of the South, never considered in their calculations.

"Later, it occurred to me that this frightened Mr. Stanton. He saw that his expectation of a docile people, grateful for a few political bones tossed to them was entirely wrong and because of this he had to take control before the situation got out of hand. He had to kill the child in the womb.

"With more than one hundred and fifty thousand colored troops under arms and experienced in combat, Negroes now had a potent force with which to make demands. What that force lacked was an officer corps of men like yourself who could step up to take command and direct armies to whatever purpose. Mr. Stanton could not let that corps develop. He and Halleck did not trust you, so they cooked up a plan whereby leadership would be denied to the Negro troops. No man would ever be allowed to rise above the rank of sergeant.

"A few commissions were granted recently, but they are inconsequential and to people who have no battle experience." I knew this well because when I stopped to see Dr. Abbott at the Iowa Circle Contraband Camp, Martin Delany was there strutting in his new major's uniform and bragging loudly for all the world to hear how he was the first Negro commissioned at that rank in the army. I had refused to salute him.

Now the General inspected the toe of his shoe avoiding me like a child does when it is held responsible for what is about to be said. "Grant had a man in his command, Christian Fleetwood, who was a sergeant major under General Terry at New Market Heights. Fleetwood stood his ground better than any other soldier that day and led his comrades to success.

"I know both Grant and Terry recommended him for a commission and I also know that Secretary Stanton has turned both requests down.

"Mr. Stanton's original plan failed him. All he saw were the vast number of votes he could bring to his party, working on the idea that the Negro population would be so grateful for emancipation, they would automatically vote Republican in any and every election.

"I sincerely hope he is in error on that account.

"Now the war is over, we will start disbanding the coloured regiments without even so much as a thank you.

"I was chagrined when the Grand Army of the Potomac marched in the review without one of its Negro regiments being represented. It is something I will take up with Grant. It was probably not his decision. But, it is also something that we should apologize to those men for." Here the General paused for a breath then changed the tack of the conversation. His eyes had become wet as if a great sorrow was trying to escape through them.

"What are your plans? I assume you will head home to Canada?"

"Yes sir. No one is there to work my land and I need to get a crop in or it will be too late this year to take off any kind of harvest."

"I deeply wish you could stay. If we are to have a chance at making emancipation work, we need men like you." Here he paused again to let his gaze wander out the window.

"It would be asking a lot. For black men in this country, things will appear as if they are getting better and that a future will be given to them, but that will not be the case. To have a future Negroes will have to fight like hell against the bitterness of the South and the prejudice of the North.

"Truth is, Frederick, I think we won this war only on the battlefield. We beat Bobby Lee and Joe Johnston and Sidney Johnston and all their armies, but we did not conquer the South. We just took their guns away for a while. Their animosity towards us is going to fester until they feel it's possible to make another attempt. For that we are going to pay a heavy price in the coming years and it is the colored people who will bear the heaviest of that burden.

"It was my hope that if we treated the Southerners well, they would feel welcomed back into the Union. But Stanton and all the rest who never fired a shot, nor had one fired at them are bully for punishing the South. Personally, I believe we have done enough punishing to last a century.

"The South still wants its independence and will win it one way or another. In the coming years those Secessionists who have some political capital left with their people will try to dominate the House and Senate and I fear they will succeed.

"If they succeed they will make all of the rules and punish Northerners and Negroes alike. Anyone who is not of the South had better watch out.

"Here in Washington, there is a madness to move colored people into positions of responsibility that they don't have the education or the experience to succeed in, and in some cases positions they do not want. It is difficult to understand this, but I see the hand of Stanton behind it. I am sure he feels that by undertaking a campaign like this, he will guarantee the rights and security of Negroes in our country.

"I am frightened he is wrong in this. I believe the Southerners will seek the revenge on the Negro that they cannot have on the North. Men like Forrest will never see your people as equal and will never treat his former stock as fully human. How could he? He made his fortune selling slaves."

Now a trickle of tears worked its way down the General's wrinkled left cheek. "Frederick, I think it is a good thing you are going home even if I will sorely miss you. I know if I ever need you I can call on you and we will strap on our battle harness and set right whatever needs it. But for the moment, I cannot declare war and take up arms against those who were so recently our enemies. I have forgiven them and now I have to make good on my promise to accept them back into the Union and my heart.

"When we set out in 1861 to end the rebellion, I foretold a long and bloody war. Many people thought I was crazy and some even called me that to my face. Now I know they were wrong and I was right. Maybe, I have that other sight that lets me look into the future and the future I see for Negroes in my country is not a good one. The South has already come to hate me, but they will hate your people more. My advice to you, dear friend, is to get out now while we are celebrating, because after this is all over, a curtain will fall quickly.

"Since we took Atlanta I have come to consider you my friend. Right from the first, I've always known that anything I said to you in private would never be repeated. When you are famous, it becomes rare to have someone like that. Although he is more like my older brother, Grant and I have the same kind of friendship. But I was always nervous about the things I said to him because he had a duty to run the army and crush the rebels. If he thought that my craziness was returning, then he would have no other choice but to treat me like a subordinate rather than a friend.

"I will fondly remember the nights that my heart was happy to hear you had successfully made it back through our lines and were coming to my headquarters to report what you discovered.

"You know me. I am not a religious man, but I sometimes think it was a divine coincidence that you arrived at my camp on the day my dearest friend McPherson was killed. The day I received that news, my heart was torn apart and I wondered how much more I could take. It was only ten months since we buried Willie and suddenly McPherson was gone. Perhaps I have always known deep down that I need strong friends.

"During my life there have been times when I could feel myself weaken. When failure pursued me." He was now addressing the silent motes of dust rather than me. His eyes locked onto an unremarkable spot on the floor as he spoke and he worked at his left thumb, fiercely rubbing its nail with his right thumb.

"It happened in California and again and again in Saint Louis and Louisiana. Often, this took me dangerously close to becoming totally crazy. When no one would listen to what I had to say and even my brother mocked me, I slipped over the edge at the start of the war. Especially after Bull Run when the goddamned rebels whipped us. Mr. Lincoln felt I had done a credible job, but I did not and had no confidence in Cump Sherman. At least I did not dive into the bottle like that son of a bitch Hooker.

"Mr. Lincoln was not a general, but a politician. He was unique in that he could measure the real worth of a soldier beyond the accomplishment of political goals. With no support from Halleck or any of the other general staff over me, I felt I had no future, but I did in Mr. Lincoln.

"When we began to win under Grant, I grew healthier. I could feel myself healing. By the time we finished in Vicksburg I knew that I could trust my instincts and that carried me through the Atlanta campaign despite losing Willie.

"Now it's all over and I will never be crazy again, but only thanks to Grant, McPherson, Lincoln and you."

Tears were now flowing freely from his eyes, but he was not weeping and I felt as though he was mourning the unseen future.

The General continued on for several minutes. In a corner of my heart I knew this was the last time I would hear his voice and see his animated face as it told stories of its own. Like the hollowness that followed the deaths of Brown and Absolom, my soul emptied until it rang like a long-abandoned seashell upon some beach. Then, he begged my forgiveness for such a short leave-taking and stood up extending his right hand. I brought mine up to clasp his, but instead of pumping it in farewell, he drew me close and took me in his arms, holding me for the moment. His hand gently patted my back and I responded in kind. I believed I could smell thousands of miles of dusty track and rivers of blood and yet I felt a curious warmth, a pleasant contentment wash over me. Tears rolled down our cheeks to mix as they dropped onto our jackets. In that single instant, all we had done became history.

EVERETT JORDAN'S STORY
STORY
BOOK THREE

CHAPTER ONE

28 December, 1878
According to Lincoln Edwards, his father had committed no act to cause Eunice to lash out the way she did. According to John Edwards, he was simply delivering a letter from the General. Eunice obviously descried him coming down the road from the kitchen window. She was dressed in her winter coat when he arrived and started to scream at him as soon as he pulled into the lane. He must have wanted his fee for delivering my letter very badly because he should have turned his wagon around without getting out.

It happened while Benjamin and I were down on the lakeshore.

We were water fowling. The lake and mouths of several small creeks are still ice-free and a number of local ducks remain to feed. With our crops sent to market and the fields prepared for winter we have little to do and spend our time hunting and visiting with nearby friends. The roads are still a bog, but soon they will be frozen and covered with enough snow that we can travel as far as Chatham and Dresden in my cutter.

Our plan was to visit each creek and if we weren't lucky enough to shoot any ducks, we would come back by way of the south field to see if we might chance upon any of the rabbits that live in the stubble.

At the end of the summer, I treated myself to a new double-barreled gun. It was ordered from the T. Eaton Company of Toronto. I wrote to the store after having it recommended by Rufus. They were prompt in their delivery and I am quite pleased to shop this way. I have written Mr. Eaton with a list of other requests to see if he might supply them and what his prices are.

The gun is superbly balanced and a much more delicate and elegant firearm than any of the military muskets and rifles I had grown used to during my service.

When I left the army, I felt uneasy about owning another gun, but that feeling eventually passed as I realized a gun has no brain. Any evil done with a gun is always accomplished by a man. So, I acquired a heavy, old, single-barreled piece. When I decided to purchase the new double-barrel, I gave the old one to Benjamin as a way of saying thank you for being my friend through the years. He was delighted with it and we now hunt together as often as we can.

After I ordered it from Toronto, I was not sure I had done the right thing until the baggage master at the station sent a note announcing a parcel had arrived and he was holding it for me. It was delivered to the Buxton Station a mere three weeks after I posted my request and draught.

By lantern-light this morning, we tackled Billy to the smaller of our two field wagons and set off in the dark toward the lake. We had our lunches with us as we intended to stay out all day, and I had filled a flannel-wrapped bottle with coffee that we drank with some bread and pork as Billy towed us along in the dark. His eyes must be better than either Benjamin's or mine because his hooves find the road on every step. In truth, I trust Billy so much that on early mornings I have sometimes continued to sleep letting the jack take me into the village.

At the corner of Central Road and Wellington we started to veer right, but I called out 'haw' to Billy and without pause, he turned to the left, away from the village and south toward the lake.

Lake Erie has a fearsome reputation at this time of the year. Many sailormen, including an entire crew of Macdonald clansmen, have died in the monstrous fall storms that plague these waters. Still, every year, ships fail to arrive in port, especially in the fall. I will not travel after the end of September by steamer, deeming it much safer by train.

It was still dark when we arrived at the culvert across the first creek. Benjamin and I shared the remains of the coffee and waited on the light. Billy occasionally shook his harness producing a soft jingle we hoped would not warn off whatever game was about. Finally the first graying began and we slid from the box to the ground and tied Billy's reins to a low tree branch. There was soft grass all around the base of the tree for him to eat and he was content to wait there as we went about charging the guns in preparation for our sport.

Our boots made crackling sounds even though we trod as gently as possible. The mud was crystalline with ice from the overnight cold. With the sunrise, it would melt and become slick again. Leaves covered the paths, but they were only partly frozen. We could walk across this carpet noiselessly because the leaves were sodden.

At this time of year there is no smell to the woods. Earlier in the fall, the oaks give off a peppery odour that I begin looking forward to in the final warm days of summer. Now, there is no smell and few sounds we do not make ourselves. Before breaking through the thicket of scrub bushes rimming the shore, there was only the wind and cawing of crows.

We stopped and listened. Benjamin preceded me so he could get the first shot off. If the birds were frightened to flight before he was ready, the chances of him missing were far greater because of the weight of the gun. There was soft clucking as two pairs of small black and white ducks took turns up-ending to catch minnows or pick up snails off the bottom. They did not see us as we edged out into the open where we could both shoot. The ducks were about thirty yards from where our path opened up through a grove of sumacs. Winds had knocked all of the red leaves off the bushes so our arrival was quiet as we came upon the mouth of the creek from the east. The north wind meant that once the birds took wing they would fly directly in front of us, passing from left to right.

It only took a second for the ducks to see us, but that second's grace meant Benjamin and I could get into position. Benjamin was able to take aim and shoot the lead male bird. It's wings stopped folded up as he fell unmoving into the long grasses beside the creek. I shot the female of that pair and male of the second. All landed on dry ground while the fourth duck, the lone remaining female, cleared the trees then circled far out over the lake before disappearing into the grey black morning.

Half a mile away is the mouth of another creek. These are not vast flowing rivers, but small watercourses, which are mainly dry except during spring run-off and fall rains. Still, there is enough current at these times that over the years the waters have worn through the soft clay of the bluffs bordering the lake creating ravines that drop a hundred feet over a distance of a mile.

Billy had not finished grazing the grass around his tree, but resigned himself to moving when he saw us breaking through the thicket. We spent the rest of the morning visiting our different hunting areas. By eleven o'clock, we knew that there would be no more ducks until evening and so we stopped by the side of the road and built a small fire to boil more coffee and cook bacon.

During lunch, we decided to see if there were any geese still dropping into the corn stubble. "I saw some last week up the Central Road so they are still around and I wouldn't mind one for Christmas. Would really like a swan, but I'm sure they all gone south."

"Too bad for them," I said, thinking I said it under my breath, but I evidently had not. Benjamin looked at me wryly then laughed. I had not told him about the huge flock of swans that visited only a few days before.

Geese would not be landing in any of the nearby fields. We needed dirty weather to bring them down. The sun was strong and the sky unlimited blue. Surely they were flying, but so high only the archangel Gabriel could bring them down. Still, we did not want to go home to the chores that were always waiting.

We decided to stop in Buxton at Morgan's smithy. Several weeks ago, Benjamin asked Morgan to make a new set of becketted blocks for his barn loft and he thought they should be ready by now.

The ride into the village was slow and enjoyable. Billy's pace was unperturbed. We told the same stories we have been telling for the past dozen years. Even though they never change there is comfort in hearing them over and over again. It is like they confirm our place under heaven. Neither Eunice nor Benjamin's wife Mary joins in. They roll their eyes and cluck their tongues when we start telling them. Eunice complains they waste my time and leaves the room if possible. But, Mary finds humour in our repetition and allows us to carry on.

Before we arrived at Morgan's forge, we made sure our guns were unloaded, covered in burlap and hidden in the wagon bed. Although I doubt they would, we didn't want any of the village children finding and playing with them. Although they are only hunting guns, they can still do much damage to a person if they are discharged at a close range.

"You boys get any birds?" was Morgan's hello to us.

"Nine. Four black and whites, five canvass backs."

"Want to trade for some nails? I just got a keg of rose heads in."

When we agreed, Morgan filled a small bag with a pound of the square nails. We passed the time gossiping about friends and former neighbours who returned to the United States after the war. We rarely heard from them, but Morgan just received a letter from a girl he liked when we were young. She had gone back with her parents in 1866 to find relatives. They lost touch, but her letter informed him she had married and been widowed. She wanted to know if Morgan, who has never married, was still in Buxton and whether he was married.

I barely remembered her. Her sudden appearance from our past made Morgan uncomfortable so we teased him about ordering a wife by mail. Morgan, who is a shy man, was suddenly very embarrassed, but we would not let him go. He is my brother-in-law but he is also a close friend. He is happy to tend his forge and stay out of his sister's path. I knew he would forgive me for the teasing as he could tell it was only meant in fun and not maliciously.

There is always a pot of coffee resting near the coals on the forge. It never runs dry nor is it allowed to get in the way of the work, but it is also never moved far enough away from the fire to cool. Morgan is in the habit of sipping coffee all day, though I cannot understand how he can drink that much or tolerate its tar-like consistency. I like coffee, but Morgan's coffee is only consumable in the first hours of the day. After that it burns my stomach and makes me uncomfortable. Despite this, we accepted cups from him and stood around holding them while we talked. I did note Benjamin also avoided drinking the liquid.

Morgan's smithy is warm with a pleasant, smoky smell. I rarely visit in the summer because of the heat that builds up from the forge, but it is a welcome sojourn in the fall and winter.

Morgan was glad of our company because he set down his tools and filled his own cup. Business has been slow but it does not seem to bother him. I believe he is a great man for saving all the pennies that come his way.

When we arrived he was busy making a variety of ironware to sell later. It keeps him busy and having common stock enables him to fill orders quickly. He is very perceptive in his business thinking. The work he does keeps the forge employed every day creating hinges and shackles. These he makes to standard sizes, which saves time. He also creates wares that work together. If you purchase a shackle, he will also sell you the chain that fits with the shackle and the blocks and hooks and bolts to form a complete set of tackle. I admire his thinking in this and have asked to invest money in his company more than once, but he rebuffs me every time saying it is not advisable to take money from a relative, even one as removed as an in-law.

As we laughed at the jokes and taunts, the door of the smithy flew open to admit Paul Crispin, one of the village boys.

"Mr. Macdonald, you have to come quick. There's something wrong with Mrs. Macdonald. She's hurt Mr. Edwards."

I flew out the door without thinking to ask young Paul where Eunice was. Benjamin and Morgan were right behind me. Benjamin shouted at Paul asking the location and the response was that bad things had happened at my home.

Urging Billy to a steady trot, the three of us rode off with Morgan shouting instructions to his apprentice and Benjamin asking for more information that Paul did not have.

CHAPTER TWO

28 December, 1878

Under normal circumstances, I would never whip Billy, but my chest tightened the way it did when the first rattling sounds of musketry announced the enemy was afield and battle was imminent. All I could think of was protecting Eunice. As we raced down Central Road, forcing Billy to go as fast as he could, I did not care anything about John Edwards, although in my heart I knew it was wrong to feel this way.

My fears for Eunice have been growing all fall. At times I would come into the house to find her sitting, sometimes standing, and staring at nothing with her eyes unfocused and thin lines of spittle dripping from the corners of her lips. In the middle of the night I could often hear her crying and talking to herself. Most of what I heard was without sense. There were times, however, when I understood the words. Much of it had to do with the war and Albert. A lot of her conversation I took to be raw imaginings. One of the recurring discussions was the shooting of a Negro soldier somewhere. I don't know if or where this occurred or how she had knowledge of the incident, but it bothered her sleep regularly.

Tragedies should never happen on beautiful days. They should be reserved for those when the weather is in sympathy with the event. As we covered the distance from town to the farm, the sparkling air caused tears to seep from the corners of my eyes. Benjamin was beside me on the seat and Morgan was behind us doing his best to hold on in the wagon bed.

Other than Edwards' wagon and untethered pony in the yard nothing appeared out of the normal. The pony, still harnessed to the rig, was slowly grazing, working its way around the corner of the barn. Bits of green grass are still growing in the protected areas where the wind is blocked and the sun can warm the earth.

From the time we left Morgan's forge to arriving at our house, no one said a word. Benjamin watched me without turning in my direction, his face rimmed with worry. Once I looked over my shoulder to make sure Morgan was still in the wagon and he was staring straight ahead so rigidly it was difficult to tell whether he was furious or upset, then he wiped his eyes giving away his true feelings.

Upon entering the yard, I could see the house was closed up. There were people moving about inside, but I could not tell who they were. Our wheels ground the dust into powder as we halted dramatically. Billy, awash in a sweat-infused lather, turned to look at me through the steam rising from his back. It was a though he understood there was a crisis and would be looked after in time when the full depth of events were comprehended.

God bless Benjamin. He led Billy into the barn unlimbered and dried him. He caught the postmaster's horse and disconnected it from the wagon then stabled it as well. Benjamin also took the time to fill two nosebags with oats.

Inside, Mary Munro was fussing in the kitchen and Peter Allan, a large white constable was guarding Eunice's door, beyond which there was an unsettling quiet.

"Mr. Macdonald," Allan said rising to meet me. "We need to speak about your wife. She attacked John Edwards earlier today with a set of shears and threatened to cut Edwards' son's head off." Allan's voice was gentle carrying no malice toward me or finding fault with Eunice.

"Is John hurt badly?" I asked, sense and gravity starting to return.

"He's cut quite badly on his arm, but the injury is not lethal. The boy, Lincoln, who was riding along with his father, wasn't hurt."

I liked Peter Allan. His broad English accent and the decent way he treated people made him a favourite of more than myself. There had been incidents in which constables persecuted and injured local Negroes, but Allan was never one to indulge in such. He treated our women with respect and befriended more than one resident of Buxton.

"Your wife is ill though. I don't know what is wrong with her, but there is definitely a medical problem and I think she may not be right in the head. Mrs. Munro has given her a large dose of paregoric elixir to calm her, but I am afraid she is going to need more than that. Mrs. Munro says that Dr. Abbott looks after your family, so I have sent a wire to him in Chatham asking him to come. I hope that was all right."

"Does John need a doctor?"

"I don't think so. Mrs. Munro sewed him up and gave him a dose of the elixir as well. We put him in your bedroom. Lincoln is with him and I think both of them are asleep."

"Good. I will take him home as soon as he is able. But, I do not expect Dr. Abbott before tomorrow." Then, "Will there be charges?"

"I do not know. It depends on Mr. Edwards. If he wants me to write a charge sheet, I will have no choice but to charge her. However, I will talk to him. It is obvious to me that she is not in control of her wits. Perhaps you can talk to him as well. If it is a matter of treatment then I can see no reason to pursue this further and will not."

"Thank you. I will speak with John. Is Eunice awake?"

Allan's hand gently cupped my elbow and led me to Eunice's door before turning me loose. Beyond the wooden panel I could hear soft whimpering. Because the door was built from thick slabs of poplar, it was impossible to tell whether it was an animal or human making the sounds.

Slowly I edged the door open. The memory of Josiah Smith is still strong within me, the incident having happened only three months before. And, I wished never to see another human suffer so.

Eunice was lying on the bed with her heavy quilt gathered closely about her. She was moaning softly and did not recognize my presence. I had not been in the room for weeks. The experience with Smith prepared me for the worst, but all was fine. Eunice's bedroom was clean and very neat. Beside her bed, on a round maple table that I built for her was a kerosene lamp and her father's bible.

I was surprised she had taken the bible out. She told me several years ago that God abandoned her when he killed Albert and she did not want anything to do with the Divinity. "If I go to Hell, then I go to Hell. All I want is to burn in that Hell with Albert."

This statement sent me reeling to the barn. Even in death Albert was still the man she slept with every night and the man she made breakfast for in the mornings. Eunice did not treat me badly in any other way, but she made me understand I was only a source of bread and water for her. Now I understood that I had wasted my life for a love that would never grow. That in fact, it was a dead seed sewn onto salted earth.

For no reason that I can explain, I still love her and take bitter pride in maintaining our marriage. I wish it were not so. Over the years we've been together I have often tried to convince myself to find another woman, but I made vows to cherish and honour Eunice. These were made even before we married. My memory is clouded by so many other events; but these vows were clearly, and without doubt, committed in my heart that morning on the ramparts of our imaginary Chapultepec.

Coming to the edge of the bed, I sat softly so as not to startle or frighten her, but she did not move. Reaching out, I stroked her hair the way you would gentle a much-loved horse. Still she did not move. We sat that way until the light faded from the day with darkness sifting softly through the room and the blue night growing without fanfare outside the window.

I was reluctant to shake her, fearing that if I did she would wake with a start and do herself some unintentional harm. I concluded it was not sleep she was enchanted by, but a deeper unconsciousness. My heart tried to reach her without words, but it was no use. In the end, I gave up and quietly left the room to her mewling.

Mary and Benjamin were sitting at Absolom's table with Allan and Morgan. Teacups were spread before them and Mary was in the midst of pouring more tea into Allan's cup when I closed the door to Eunice's room. She looked up, they all looked up, expecting me to say something. There was nothing for me to say, so I told them she was still sleeping although I did not believe this myself.

Sitting down to join them, Mary rose and took another cup down from the cupboard setting it in front of me. Morgan spoke first. There was fear in his normally placid voice.

"How is she?"

"Asleep. She didn't wake up and I thought it would be best to let her lie until whatever is affecting her passes."

"She didn't say anything?"

"No."

"She has not spoken since we put her to bed," Mary said, "but then she has had several large spoons of paregoric. She will probably sleep until morning."

"Maybe we had better speak to Edwards," Allan offered when Mary finished. "He made some sounds a short time ago. I do have to determine his intentions. But finish your tea first. This has been hard on you. It is unfair that God has burdened you with this."

Tapping on the door of my bedroom, we were surprised to hear Edwards answer by telling us to come in. He was lying on my bed and Lincoln was curled up next to him. I was expecting an explosion from him but he surprised me.

"How's Eunice? Is she okay?"

"Fine John. How are you?"

"I'm good, but Lincoln was shaken up. He doesn't understand what's happened."

"I do not think any of us do."

"Well it's plain she is very sick. Is Dr. Abbott going to come to see her?"

"I hope tomorrow. Do you need a doctor? I can arrange for Dr. Abbott to see you when he arrives, but that won't be before tomorrow.\"

"No. Benjamin's wife is a good seamstress. She's sewn me up nicely. There's a little tingling in my hand but nothing more."

We continued on like this for a few minutes. All the while it was becoming more and more apparent that John had no interest in signing charge sheets against my wife.

"Do you have any idea what cause Eunice to attack you? Did she say anything?"

"She didn't say a thing at first. I had the letter from the General in my hand and was reaching out to give it to her. I think I said I would see you later about the fee you pay me for bringing the mail out, but I don't remember if I did or not. She just grabbed me by the wrist and pulled me half way out of the cart and began stabbing me with her scissors."

"As she was stabbing me, she started yelling that she had already killed me so why was I following her. Do you know what she was talking about?"

I confessed ignorance to the question and suggested that we would have to await her awakening. Then we sat silently for a few minutes until Allan came to the door of my room to say Mary had more tea ready and we should go into the kitchen to have some. We covered Lincoln with a quilt then silently trooped out of the bedroom.

CHAPTER THREE

Dec. 28, 1878
Late this evening Mother arrived. She took over from Mary and began shooing people off to their homes. After making sure John's arm was treated with a poultice to draw any poisons out, she wrapped Lincoln in the quilt from my bed and sent father and son home with Peter Allan in Allan's trap. I would deliver John's cart to him in the morning. Mary and Benjamin stayed for a late supper then went home as well.

It is a rare occasion for Mother to enter our house. Her absence has been of her own choice. There is no affection in her heart for Eunice and has never been since we were children. When I needed to, or simply felt like visiting with my mother I would go to her house in the village where she would put on the tea and bring out her baking so we could chat, but out of politeness our conversations only touched on Eunice or what she was doing.

Outside the house it is all silence and the moon casts a shimmering light over the fields. Up in the village only three lamps break the dark. It is easier to stare out the window and contemplate the perfection of God's gentle night than think about my wife lying ten feet away and it is God's own truth that I do not know what I shall do.

"You cannot live like this…"

"I know, but I also do not know if there is an alternative. She is not an old horse I can take out to the pasture to shoot."

"Son. Nobody is asking or suggesting you do that. There must be other ways. I know it is unsavoury, but I do ask that you consider a mental asylum."

"I cannot do that mother. If needs be, I will look after her here. We have enough money and I can sell the house in Chatham to pay the costs of bringing a woman in to help with her. Maybe Mrs. Bell would come."

The thought of an insane asylum causes my stomach to heave. It has been suggested to me that these are dark and inhumane places; and the men and women who inhabit them less than animals. A mule or cow or pig would be looked after better. Stories abound from the days when Fort Malden was the asylum for people of the region. I have seen the men toiling in the fields with my own eyes and am aware they do so for no pay, just room and board. Mr. Dickens paints a very grim picture of charity hospitals, asylums and poorhouses in England and I can only think this new Canada is the same if not worse. I can well imagine barracks with naught but straw on the floor and no place for private functions or bathing. Mr. William Hubbard, my friend in Toronto, has written to me of how the inmates of the Toronto Lunatic Asylum were forced to open a cesspool under the direction of the asylum staff, who would not aid them, and had them remove thousands of barrow loads of their own filth. I do not know if women were so employed, but I would give Eunice the gift any soldier is willing to administer to a badly wounded comrade before I let her suffer that. Eunice is a proud woman and could not tolerate that life. It would mean her death in a very short while.

"She would help for a short time," Mother said speaking of Mrs. Bell and rescuing me from these dark thoughts. "But, that will not last long and there is no woman in the village who has the time to look after her as well as her own family." She did not add that most women would not feel very charitable toward Eunice, but I understood the implication.

Mother looked at me hard, challenging me to make the decision she desired. As much as I loved her, I could not. Not until I knew everything. That was something the General taught me. Do not move your troops until you know where the enemy is, what he is doing and what you will do.

"Perhaps there is some medicament that will relieve her symptoms. I am expecting Dr. Abbott by the morning train…"

"Don't forget there will also be Edwards to deal with. He is friendly now, but I fear that will not last long if Eunice is not locked away in hospital."

As I let this sink in, the only sound in the room was the ticking of the big clock on the wall above the table. Its slow, unimpeded tick-tock foretold the eventuality of some future, but not what that future would be. Mother was correct. Our postmaster was another story and I am afraid he will demand what he thinks to be justice as the shock wears off. There is little I can do about him until he makes his intentions known. Edwards' reaction to the attack was something I considered done, but now I must also worry about that.

"Well there is nothing to be done tonight, so it is probably best to go to bed and wait until Dr. Abbott gets here."

Mother went to the spare room I built after taking over the farm at the end of the war. At the time she did not think it was a good idea to invest money in something so frivolous, but now she makes no comment.

Even after the worst of battles I was never so glad to see a day end.

December 29, 1878

With less than three days before the New Year, the end of the year is now more than a threat. This past year has become one that I will be glad to see the back end of. It snowed overnight and the fields are filled and white. Small drifts have developed along the fence lines, but many open areas are swept clear of the dry snow by a slight northerly wind. The yard between the house and barn has very little covering and I was able to feed the animals and milk our cow without hindrance.

Eunice awoke during the night. She was confused, barely making any sense. I gave her more elixir to ease her back into sleep and sat watching over her until it was time to do my chores.

When I returned to the house Mother was making breakfast. Of late Eunice has avoided cooking as much as possible. Most of what we ate was produced by my paltry skills with the frying pan. Food prepared by another has always smelled good to me, but now its aroma is almost divine.

I tackled Sam and Billy. They seemed in a good mood and glad to be getting off the farm. As we passed through the village, I supposed that their step brightened as if to show off to the other animals tethered along the street. It seemed they were announcing their importance and the importance of their mission. Sam's ears perked up and stayed that way all through the village. Both mules lifted their tails slightly and I let them break into the slow trot they were so desirous to step into. Once clear of Buxton they slowed a little on their own and we settled into an even, match-step pace that carried us along nicely.

When we stopped in front of the single-story building that serves as our station, both jacks shook their harnesses. Their jingling carried in the morning air. I placed blankets over them and fed them, then wrapped my heavy fur coat tighter around me and settled in to wait.

A little while later, the train eased into the station from the east and I could see Dr. Abbott's slight figure through the carriage windows as he moved down the aisle and onto the platform alighting into the chill air. He was carrying a rich-looking black Gladstone and was dressed in a fine wool coat with a shearling collar and a hat that matched his collar.

Mrs. Lincoln had presented Dr. Abbott with the president's shawl as a thank you gift for helping the president's family after the assassination. It was something Dr. Abbott never spoke of and which I never felt comfortable asking him about although I had known the story for a while and we considered each other friends.

"Frederick, how are you? Your telegram was a shock." Then as he swung up into my wagon he commanded me to "… tell me everything that has transpired. I need as much information as possible." So as we began the homeward journey, I unraveled the story of the past few months.

When we reached the farm, he was frozen. I ushered him into the kitchen to let Mother take care of him until I had looked after the mules. Returning to the house, I found him plying his skills with Eunice.

She was pale and lying upon her bed. The effects of the elixir left her almost lifeless as Dr. Abbott checked her pulse and prized her eyelids open far enough to look underneath them. While he was doing this, he was asking her questions. 'Did she know her name? Did she know his name? What day was it? What was the next holiday we would celebrate?' Her answers were incoherent and often just one word.

Picking up her hand, he flexed each finger so it bent at the knuckle. I could not tell whether he was satisfied with the results, but he looked up and indicated that I should leave the room as he began to unfasten the bodice of her nightclothes.

I waited in the kitchen for him to complete his assessment, feeling as impotent as I did on the morning Helen died. When he closed the bedroom door gently behind him, he had a perplexed look on his face.

"I am not sure how much is insanity and how much is the paregoric. How much elixir has she been given?"

Pushing the bottle forward on the kitchen table I said, "a spoonful every four or five hours."

"No more?"

Mother looked down at the oilcloth on the table then unrepentantly at Dr. Abbott. "I've been giving her a spoonful almost every hour to keep her calm."

"Mrs. Macdonald, a spoonful every hour will do more than keep her calm, it will incapacitate and endanger her. For the moment, I think it is best that we do not give her any more."

That she had so willfully administered this drug was almost beyond my comprehension and the look on her face told me she would continue to do so if Eunice showed any signs of giving her trouble.

"I need her head clear enough to talk to her, but that will take some time."

Nothing needed further saying. As I did not feel like fighting with Mother, I offered to make breakfast for the doctor and he smiled his assent. While I busied myself with the cooking duties he asked Mother about her general health and then talked about social activities in Chatham. Christmas was less than a week past and the congregation at the First Baptist Church was in its annual tizzy of singing hymns and cooking vast meals.

Disappointed in Mother's behavior, I offered to take her home while Dr. Abbott stood watch over Eunice.

The trip was not a pleasant one. Mother digs in her heels and sulks when she does not get her own way. Nothing was said all the way into the village and she climbed down from the wagon and headed into the front yard of her house before I could fully come around to help her down. She entered her front door without a word and closed it behind her indicating that I was not currently welcome.

At least the silence of the ride home was welcome and even pleasant as the sun broke through the clouds to dance in dazzling diamond sparkles across the fields. I forced myself to think about other things as we covered the short distance home. It was getting close to the time when I would have to make decisions about new crops to be planted in the spring and which of our fields to let go fallow this coming season. Just as we were turning into our lane, I also realized that there was a letter waiting for me from the General or at least Edwards had one. Once we knew what we would be doing with Eunice, I would stop to see if I could do anything for John and to collect my letter.

In the hour it took me to deliver Mother to her home, the temperatures dropped appreciably. Because of this and the increasing amounts of sun, I was sure the barometer was climbing and there would be no more snow for a while. The air was too dry and the cold temperatures would not allow snow to form on the lakes. To get a major snowfall the wind needs to be out of the southern quarter. But the morning was still.

Dr. Abbott was sitting at the kitchen table reading one of my books. For some reason, maybe it is due to the process of getting older, I have started to collect more and more books on every subject I can imagine. Sitting on my shelves is Mr. Darwin's "Origins Of The Species", and a condensed version of Baron von Humboldt's five volume"Kosmos", the completed works of Mr. Dickens and the poetry of Milton, Pope, Blake and Whitman. William Shakespeare's plays and sonnets occupy an entire shelf of their own. My library has grown in such volume as I will shortly need to build another set of shelves and will use the set I built for Reverend King as their model. In the few fantasy moments I allow myself, I dream of adding an entire room to the house to act as a library and refuge for contemplation.

Since I began writing this diary I have come to realize I enjoy the act of writing more than I ever did as a newspaperman. The freedom I find in thinking about the things I wish to consider; the puzzles set before me by the likes of Mr. Darwin, and responding to them is something I did not encounter in the day-to-day drudgery of reporting. Now it serves to bring me unqualified joy.

I finished my recollections of the war earlier in the month and will now finish a copy for Mrs. Lincoln. This memoir should serve to inform the president's widow about my time in the army.

Dr. Abbott made a pot of tea and was sipping it while he read. The teapot was enclosed in one of Eunice's knitted tea cozies. After doffing my boots and coat, I joined him at the table.

"She's still asleep. That was a heavy dose your mother administered, so I suppose she will be asleep for hours and we can use the time to talk about what needs to be done."

"I don't want her in the asylum," I began. "Slaves were kept in better conditions. In the lunatic asylum no one cares whether they live, die or simply rot. When I was in Amherstburg I saw how they kept the inmates at the Fort Malden Lunatic Asylum. Eunice would never..."

"... Times are changing Frederick. These places are far better than anything you've seen and there is a new provincial asylum in London, which is run by a very good man. Dr. Richard Bucke."

"Are the inmates still forced to work?"

"They work, but they are not forced to. It is part of the treatment. Dr. Bucke believes that work is an essential to healing and recovery, but if a patient does not wish to work or is incapable of it, then they are left to other treatments."

"Do you know this Dr. Bucke personally?"

"We've been colleagues for several years now and have a number of mutual friends. He is even writing a biography of my friend Walt Whitman. I admire his efforts and his integrity. Eunice could not be in better hands than his. Dr. Bucke is a humane physician but conservative in that he doesn't ascribe to every new theory brought forward by the more dubious members of our profession. Still, he is very progressive with treatments that work. But it hasn't come to the point we should consider committing her yet."

"When will we know? I can't watch her twenty-four hours a day. I have a farm to run. If I can keep her here with me while she recovers then I can make arrangements to have a woman come in to help."

He warned me of the possibility that Eunice may never recover. Something, beside the paregoric was seriously wrong with her. Looking directly into my eyes he asked if I knew anything that might account for her illness. I do not know, but suspect something happened during the war years, when she traveled in the Union Sates looking for Albert, to cause her such anguish now. She would never talk to me about the time from when she sold out and left Buxton until she returned. Whenever I asked her, her eyes would grow teary and she would turn away. For days afterward she would not speak and would sit at the table staring out the window while twisting a forelock of hair.

"You know the war damaged people beyond the wounds we could treat. In the Contraband Hospital in Washington I saw all sorts of dementia brought on by battle or privation. More than one of our patients ended their own lives. We were lucky enough to stop some before they could succeed, but often they would try again once we ceased watching. The next attempts were usually successful.

"Look at your friend Josiah Smith." At the very moment he said this, I had been thinking about Joe and wondering if Eunice was not suffering from something similar. "I am positive that something he saw or did in the war prompted such a violent reaction. We saw that in soldiers and civilians as well. Now we are seeing some kind of delayed reaction in people who endured more than God intended them to. But what has Eunice seen or done that would provoke a similar fit?"

"Maybe she will tell you. We do not speak much these days and never about the war. I gave up asking her. Do you think this Dr. Bucke could get her to talk about her past experiences?"

"Maybe. It would be worth a try. If you wish, I will write him a letter after I talk to Eunice to see what course of action he would suggest."

I agreed to this plan and we settled down to wait for Eunice to awaken. He with his book and me with my nightmare.

December 30, 1878

Eunice was groggy most of the day yesterday, but she began to arouse herself late in the afternoon. I was surprised it took so long. The amount of the elixir must have been enormous: Enough to threaten her life. Still, she came around slowly asking for water first, then begging for a pot of coffee. Her eyes were still shiny with the paregoric, but her manner lacked the concentration of a fully conscious person. I looked in on her periodically as did Dr. Abbott. Me more to service her physical needs, he because of his concern for her safety. I would have emptied her chamber pot except that it had not been used.

Even though the light had gone completely from the sky, I did not consider it evening. Supper was not yet on the table. Around five o'clock I apologized to Dr. Abbott excusing myself to feed the animals and muck out the barn.

Many people do not like to shovel manure and soiled hay. I have heard them complain about its stink and the backbreaking effort it takes to lift fork-full after fork-full into a barrow then wheel it out the doors and onto the manure pile. Some have even gone so far as to call it 'nigger work'. But, I do not see it that way. I enjoy the effort and feel proud when I can look from front to back in our barn and see a clean, orderly home for the mules and the cow. The repeated work of shoveling without having to think takes me away, if only momentarily, from this nightmare. And I like the smell. It is the healthy smell of well cared for beasts and more honest than the sour perspiration of many men who sweat from mendacity.

I worked by lantern light for an hour. After washing her teats, I sat down to milk our Jersey cow, Buttercup, who produced a bucket-and-a-half of rich milk, which I poured into my new DeLaval separator. This machine has saved me hours of waiting for the cream to rise and reduced the potential for spoilage to almost nothing. After a few minutes of turning the weighted wheel, I had a pint of perfect cream and several quarts of milk. Because of it, I am considering adding more cows and developing a small dairy business along with our cash crops. It would provide additional year-round income. Dr. Abbott will also be pleased to have the cream with our porridge in the morning.

With my work in the barn finished I bade the animals good night and returned to the house.

There was a light coming from Eunice's bedroom window and by it I could see the distinguished physique of Dr. Abbott sitting on a chair near her bed. Although it appeared he was speaking with her, I could not see Eunice nor could I hear Dr. Abbott's words. When I came into the house I made sure to stamp my feet a little louder than usual so they would be aware of my return. I did not want to hear anything of the discourse between them. Eunice had caused me enough pain with her behavior and I did not need to increase that by delving into her secrets.

I began supper and did a little housework. There have been so many people through the house in the last twenty-four hours that they could not help leaving a minor mess. It was nearly seven-thirty when Dr. Abbott came out of Eunice's room.

"She's in a very bad condition. If you can't get her to eat, she will need to be treated in hospital before we can take her up to London." I knew that she had not been eating properly lately, but thought that was just her habit now. "I think she is trying to starve herself to death. She claims she doesn't need any food, but that she's getting enough liquids. However, that pot of coffee you made her earlier is sitting on her bedside table untouched and the glass of water has only been half drunk. I checked her chamber pot once when she dozed off. She has not produced anything since she took to her bed."

"Could somebody have emptied it?"

"I don't think so. Certainly your mother didn't. No. I believe that when she drank what she did, it was absorbed into her body completely. If she has a favourite meal, you might try making that for her, but it is important you get her to eat before she cannot."

At the best of times Eunice could do the work of a man but not require the same amount of food that Benjamin or I would eat, even after an easy day. Her clothes hung on her frame waiting for new flesh that would never develop. Occasionally I would arrive in the kitchen to find her sipping a cup of tea and pecking at half a biscuit, which she would eventually abandon. I did not know if she favoured her morning meal. She never evinced any desire for a later repast of meat or fowl. She would cook a chicken or roast of pork for me then if she were feeling polite, would sit with me while

I ate it. I suppose if she likes anything it is a light salad of cucumbers and vinegar and that is what I wished I could make her, but it is the wrong season. We do keep a keg of pickled cabbage so I spooned some onto a plate and sprinkled it lightly with sugar. I also poured her a glass of cold tea and added a small drop of bottled lemon extract to it, then took both the plate and the glass in to her.

She was lying on her side under the covers in her bed and I could see her knees were pulled up to her chin. Sitting on the edge of the bed I stroked her hair until she opened her eyes.

"Eunice, the doctor says you have to have something to eat. You are getting dangerously weak."

"Not hungry."

"Please Eunice. You need to try to eat something."

"Leave me alone." This came out as a low, hissing growl imbued with hatred. After years of this melancholia I was growing tired of her surliness, but resisted the desire to slap her.

Using the spoon I pushed the shredded cabbage onto the tines of the fork I brought with the tiny meal then brought the food to her mouth the same way you would try to feed a reluctant three year-old. She hesitated a moment then opened her lips and teeth to accept a bite. Her jaws did not move. She held the vegetable in her mouth without chewing or swallowing, then she slowly pushed it out with her tongue and I only managed to catch it with the fork before it spilled onto the coverlet.

"Try a little tea. That might help your appetite..."

"Don't want it..."

"You've got to eat something."

"Let me die."

"No!" I threatened lowly. "I cannot stand you anymore with your self-pity and self-hate. You ruined your life because you would not accept the fact that Albert is dead... That he was killed in the war. And now you're ruining mine. What do I need to do? Dig up his body to prove he is gone?"

"I know he is gone. There was enough proof." With that she pushed my hand holding the plate aside knocking its contents onto the floor.

Without looking at me further, Eunice turned her face into her pillow so she could not see me. There was no reasoning with her, so I left the room to fetch a broom and dustpan. It is unchristian of me, but I was thinking her death would not be unwelcome. In that most uncharitable moment I prayed to God he would take her right then.

After cleaning up, I sat with Dr. Abbott talking about old friends and our experiences during the war. It was too late to catch the eastbound train back to Chatham so he is staying overnight and I will deliver him to the station in the morning. I showed him to the guest bedroom and we put out the lamps in the kitchen. He has been very good to Eunice and I do not know how to thank him for all his kindness.

Sometime afterward, I got up and saw that the light was still on in his room. He had taken the book he was reading to bed with him.

December 31, 1878

Our situation is one that did not do much honour to the birth of our Lord. It is sad that such days should occur. Although she was never one for socializing, which she knew I enjoyed, she would accompany me to the homes of our friends in the village. This year is one celebration in which we have seen few people.

Eunice remains in her bed, only coming out for her physical necessities and to wander throughout the house at night. By morning she is back under the covers. Several times I have awakened to find light seeping from beneath her door. I believe she may be reading. If she were simply staring at the ceiling, then she would not need the light. At least it shows me that her mind is actively working. Occasionally, I also hear dishes rattling in the kitchen, which means she is eating something, but I never rise to join her.

This morning I picked up Mary Munro to look after Eunice then drove Dr. Abbott to the station so he could at least spend New Year's Day with his family. He sent a wire to Dr. Bucke at the Lunatic Asylum before he boarded the train and then was off. "We should," he told me, "hear from Dr. Bucke in a day or two. I am sure he will accept Eunice, but you had best prepare yourself for a lengthy time of hospitalization. These things are not cured overnight, if at all."

January 15, 1879

What I was not prepared for was the amount of time it would take for a positive answer to come back. I knew the Christmas holidays would slow things down, but I did not expect the answer we received from Bucke two weeks later.

Dr. Abbott sent the letter by regular post saying he has received word from Dr. Bucke that there was no room at the institution for any more patients. This caused me great concern and I immediately began making plans to go to see Mrs. Bell so I could ask her to come, at least for the short term, to help look after Eunice.

My heart was, however, gladdened when Rufus Stephenson made the pilgrimage to Buxton to visit without any invitation. He had heard from Dr. Abbott, after encountering him outside his offices on William Street, that I was confined to my home by Eunice's condition. Rufus loaded his cutter with a few small gifts and some food and arrived at my door unannounced.

We had not seen each other since the Christmas before. He was busy in Toronto most of the time representing our riding in the provincial parliament. So there was a great deal of catching up to do.

I was a little afraid Eunice would try to disrupt Rufus' visit, but she remained deathly quiet in the confines of her bedroom.

Rufus was in a grand mood. He enjoyed the twelve-mile journey from town and made it plain that he planned to spend the night. We talked about politics, books and business. The Fenian threat from south of the border was once again raising a scaly head. This time in the far off newly created province of British Columbia as well.

Information indicates that western members of this unwholesome organization were forming attack commands in Montana and Washington states. Rufus says there is some concern that they will join up with the Métis rebel Louis Riel who is now living in Montana. Rufus fears that Riel has not finished doing his damage.

Although I have not indulged in spirits since my days with the General, I felt so good I allowed Rufus to pour me a small glass of whisky from the flask he brought with him. He also brought me a collection of books and an interesting pamphlet from a group of men in England who are attempting to create a complete dictionary of the English language. They are looking for interested amateurs who would like to read the great works of literature to help reference the definitions of words. It might be something I could entertain once we know what course the future will take with Eunice.

Rufus' stay buoyed my spirits in a way nothing else has in a long time. I was sad to help him load his cutter for the return journey. He looked quite happy in his big lap robe and furs. The sun was shining and he was off on an adventure. I wished I were going with him.

Just before he called to his horse to begin the journey he turned to me and asked if I were interested in coming back to the newspaper. It would give me something beneficial to do with myself if I found the loneliness to be stretching out and sawing at my soul.

I said I would think about it, and indeed the thought of once again producing something that people think is important appeals to me. However, I don't want to give up this house and my fields. Mostly, the treatment we received at the hands of scribblers like Burns turns me away from ever undertaking the profession again.

CHAPTER FOUR

January 26, 1879

I had completely forgotten about the letter John was trying to deliver when Eunice attacked him. It was waiting in the same parcel of mail that contained Dr. Abbott's note about Dr. Bucke's reply. The note from the General contained Christmas wishes. The wait also had the added benefit of a Christmas letter from Mrs. Lincoln in the form of a fancy card and second letters from both she and the General that just arrived.

The day was cold so I did not linger to read the letters beyond opening them in front of Edwards and reporting briefly on their content. I felt I owed him that. Sam drew me home and after stabling him I made a pot of tea to warm me up then settled in the kitchen to read the latest news. Eunice was asleep in her room. And I began to read again the letter that just arrived from the General.

> W. T. Sherman,
> 817-15th St.
> Washington, D.C.

Mr. Frederick Douglass Macdonald,
C/O General Delivery,
Buxton, Ontario
Canada

> January 10, 1879

Dear Frederick,

I am in possession of your manuscript sent in early December. It is a remarkable piece of work and it gives me a window into my behavior during the Georgia and Carolina campaigns. It also sheds light on the actions of several people like the Secretary of War and the correspondent Burns.

You have created an important document with this. I believe it is one of the most balanced pieces of reporting to come out of the war. In particular, I admire the effort you made to treat General Davis fairly. Another might have taken the opportunity to assuage a personal hatred and take revenge for the slights I know he committed.

I also enjoyed your account of learning to ride properly. In the nature of things we all just assume that everyone can do the same things we can. It never occurred to me until Captain Nichols had to give you riding lessons that you were not comfortable on horseback. Still, I laughed heartily at your rendition of the story.

You made no mention, or I do not remember, of the woman named Song.

I suppose you did not wish to discuss her, as she was part of your personal life. However, I wish you had. If I had known there was someone of importance to you, I would have brought her into my headquarters where she would have been looked after. If you would like, I could have our troops in the area make enquiries to see if she survived the war. That at least would ease your mind somewhat.

Burns was a constant problem for me. He was mendacious as hell, but I dared not turn him loose into the wider world with what he knew. It did not surprise me to read that he cornered you and tried to force your hand. I wish I had been there to witness your final treatment of him. I believed the man a coward and you proved it. What you may also have suspected and what I can confirm now, is that he despised coloured people. His alligator tears over Ebenezer Creek hid his hatred toward the Negro and the only reason he pursued it was for the sake of a story that would make our army look bad. I believe he may have been firmly lodged in the Copperhead camp. Burns was also one of those men who viewed himself as all-powerful and the way he chose to prove it was by attempting to destroy those in higher positions than he. You and I never talked about the end of the war, but I know that at the time he wrote a number of stories critical of Lincoln, Grant and me. Whether you read them or not, you did not say. Burning the New York papers in Raleigh was a good indication you could not be fooled. Still, I could picture Burns in his office gleefully planning to knock us off our chairs with his articles. Fortunately, the people of the country are smarter than that.

The account of your conversation with Secretary Stanton was illuminating. Bracing you like that was callous. I am sure he expected you to vent against my hatred of the Negro and was disappointed when you did not. You made yourself quite an enemy there. Your telling of the meeting with the Savannah elders gave me pleasure. I saw the official record of that meeting, but don't recall whether you gave me a copy of your notes. If you did, forgive me for not remembering, but I certainly enjoyed reading Reverend Fraser's comments and closing remarks once again. It sounds like Mr. Stanton found his trip wasted on all counts.

With your permission, I would like to have these memoirs copied by typists and distributed to a number of the officers you served with. Many grew to like and respect you, and they often ask me about you. In particular, Major Nichols sends his best wishes and asks that you write him directly when you have the opportunity.

The news of your wife's health is distressing. Have the doctors been able to diagnose her condition? We have some very good physicians here in Washington and if you wish, I can make arrangements for her treatment at our army hospital. Please let me know what aid I can offer.

Finally, I have received two communications from Mrs. Lincoln. The first was a very nice illustrated Christmas card. These are very charming and welcome at holiday time.

The second was a letter that is causing me some worry. It is disconnected and rambling and at times incoherent. In it she talks about being advised by spirits. She believes she is in contact with her dead husband and sons and they visit daily to warn her that malevolent spirits are destroying her remaining happiness. She goes on to say that she has sought the help of Europe's leading spiritualists, but they are ineffectual. Because of this, she is considering a return to the United States. A number of years ago, I heard rumours she was involved in séances and necromancy, but I was not interested in gossip. I am not sure what to make of this, nor am I sure of what we can do to help her.

Have you received any letters from her since the one dated November second?

There is little more to write at the moment. Now that the holidays are over, we will be getting back to business here in the shop. I am still faced with the Indian situation in the west and am not sure yet how best to resolve it. I wish it would resolve itself on its own, but I know that will never happen, so I must try to develop a solution. The government has brought everything between the Atlantic and Pacific under its control. And as in the old days, they still will not negotiate in good faith with the different tribes. Because of this they expect my army to accomplish their promises to the white settlers.

So you see, nothing much changes.

Mrs. Sherman sends her regards and wishes you and your family well. I have not told her your wife is ill and will wait to hear more on her condition before I do.

Sincerely
W.T. Sherman
Signed by hand: Cump

The fancy card from Mrs. Lincoln was colourful and a delight. It was folded in half so it would stand upright on the table. I left it there for Eunice to see when she awoke. It might make her happy for a moment.

Mrs. Lincoln's next letter was more distressing. The handwriting appeared as though the writer was palsied. There was not one smooth line or loop in the entirety of the short note. It took several minutes to read it and make sure I understood it completely.

Mrs. Abraham Lincoln,
Pau, France

Mr. Frederick Macdonald
C/O General Delivery,
Buxton, Ontario
Canada

December 17, 1878

Dear Mr. Macdonald,

This note is to let you know my enemies have found me here and I will be returning to the United States as soon as possible after Christmas. It is only from there that I shall be able to mount some defense.

I would like to thank you for your correspondence and will write to you with my address when I know my situation better.

Sincerely,
Mrs. Abraham Lincoln

CHAPTER FIVE

June 1, 1879

A place has been found in the London Lunatic Asylum for Eunice. We are to deliver her on the fifteenth of this month. I am so relieved this will now come to an end. She has become a danger, not only to herself, but to me as well. I have hidden all the scissors and knives out of fear she will creep into my room while I sleep and slay me. For my own protection I have taken to barring the door with a chair wedged under the doorknob.

I was sinking into my own hell of despair before the letter from Dr. Abbott arrived. Spring has come and almost gone. What should normally have been a happy season has had a filter placed over it. The sun does not seem to shine as brightly and the winds maintain an arctic element. From the end of January onward our home has been its own battleground and the only time peace reigns is when Eunice has a demand to make of me that she hopes I will accede to.

At the beginning of March she requested paper, pen and ink. I asked her what it was she intended to write. "The truth," was her only reply. So I provided her with a ream of writing paper. Since then I have heard nothing more of whatever it was she was meaning to set down. I would be surprised if she actually wrote anything. Her mind flits like one of the little hummingbirds at our honeysuckles.

Mrs. Bell has been a godsend. She has spent more than ten of the past sixteen weeks with me. Her husband asked that she return to Chatham twice to help him with chores around the boarding house. He does not begrudge me her assistance as some husbands would. It seems he is able to place himself in my situation and does nothing but wish me well.

Surprisingly, my mother has offered her help once again. I thought she would refuse when I cautioned her not to adjust Eunice's dose of paregoric for her own convenience.

"I heard the doctor," was Mother's terse reply. "If I wanted to kill her she would have been dead a long time ago and you would have been saved all of these sorrows. But that is not what you want. So I will help you look after her to give you some little comfort, my son."

She was good to her word. When Mrs. Bell went home at the end of April, Mother came and looked after my wife as if she were Eunice's servant. On Dr. Abbott's bi-weekly visits, she listens attentively to him and carries out his instructions to the letter. Still, no warmth passes between Mother and her daughter-in-law. I wonder if Mother actually ever considered Eunice to be part of our family. I doubt it.

The aid of these two ladies allowed me to accomplish some work. A

Chatham woman, Mrs. Babcock, for whom I built a mahogany table, approached me with another commission. This time she wanted an armoire in the French style. She asked that it have space for a number of her husband's suits with the trousers hanging straight down and not folded double on the hangers. It also had to have six drawers for socks, handkerchiefs, under things, shirts, collars, cravats, and a small chest for his jewelry.

Designing this cabinet took nearly three days. Part of the slowness came from the fact it was one of the few things I did this spring I truly enjoyed and did not want the process to end. I was extraordinarily pleased when she approved the plans. We agreed that the exterior and drawer fronts should be made from black walnut while the drawers themselves be fabricated from poplar. I had quantities of both woods seasoning in the barn and was glad to be able to sell some of it.

Poplar is an easy wood to work. It cuts and sands cleanly. Once it is properly seasoned, it does not shrink or expand much with changes in the weather, nor is it inclined to warp. Walnut is the same, but very much harder and time must be taken when carving it. I worked slowly on the decorative headpiece carefully sculpting a shell motif into the apex of its triangle, beading it and affixing molding along its upper edges.

In all it took me three weeks from start to finish and it was an exceptionally beautiful piece. The last step in the process was several layers of two-pound cut, white shellac applied with clean muslin pads. In between each coating I sanded before applying the next layer. It took several days, but I built up ten coats giving the armoire a deep shine that will endure for generations.

Mrs. Babcock was delighted with the piece when Benjamin and I delivered it to her. She immediately began planning more furniture. Her family has money from a property they hold near the village of Oil Springs where oil was discovered just before the war. Apparently the property has eighteen wells on it pumping the smelly, black tar day and night.

I would be happy to have more commissions from her. She pays well, never asking for credit and the work provides me needed relief from Eunice.

I also bought four more milch cows in partnership with Benjamin. We now produce between twenty-five and thirty gallons of milk every day. Some of our milk is bought in the village, but most of it is sent into Chatham on the morning train. Benjamin wants me to commence the study of cheese making. As he still cannot read I must do the learning from books and journals then teach him how to perform the necessary tasks. Except for reading and writing, he is a smart man and learns very quickly. Taking the ability to read and write away from him was a crime.

June 7, 1879

Today I purchased the tickets for next Monday's train. Eunice must present herself for admission on Tuesday morning, so we will take the late train up to London and stay overnight in a boardinghouse belonging to a friend of mine. Very few hotels there will accept Negroes as guests. Clerks in obviously empty hotels have told me there was no room or I was not welcome because I would upset their other guests.

Dr. Abbott will join us at Chatham. Dr. Bucke has invited him to have dinner and stay on the grounds of the asylum. It was decided not to upset Eunice, but to try to keep everything as normal for her as possible.

June 16, 1879

I have just returned from delivering Eunice to the London Lunatic Asylum. My strength is completely depleted. Never have I felt like such a traitor as that moment when she realized she would not be coming home with me. Doctors Abbott and Bucke forewarned me she would likely become outraged and violent as that had been her history. Instead, she just stared at me with tears in her eyes.

"I want to go home."

"Mrs. Macdonald, it would be best if you stayed here for now. We can help you here," Dr. Bucke intervened. He placed himself between Eunice and me, and I understood that he was positioning himself to be ready to defend me. A large man dressed in a white attendant's uniform stood by, as well, in the event she had to be restrained.

We began our journey with a lie. I explained to her Dr. Abbott was able to make an appointment with a physician who was famous for treating cases like hers. I elaborated on the treatments he was likely to perform in order to return her to normal. With the small talk distracting her, she did not take note of the amount of clothing and number of possessions I was packing into a small trunk I had purchased for her. It was far more than would be needed for an overnight journey.

Although she normally liked to travel, Eunice did not want to go. "I am fine. I don't need to go anywhere and I am tired of Dr. Abbott. Another doctor is not going to do anything for me. Please just give me time to think."

"Eunice, you hurt John Edwards badly and threatened his son. That is not normal behaviour."

"I thought he was a man I once saw who meant to harm me."

"Who was this man?"

"It was a long time ago. During the war. He was a Secesh soldier and he should not have been."

"What do you mean he should not have been a Secesh soldier? What did he try to do?"

"Kill me."

"They were all trying to kill us. The life of a nigger was not worth anything to them. We were just property and if by killing us they could deny the Union war material, they would do it without a second thought. I saw that time and again in Georgia and the Carolinas."

"But he should not have hated me..." With that she rolled over in her bed facing the wall where she had remained while I prepared her luggage. It was the first time she had ever spoken of doing anything during the insurrection and I was curious to learn more, but she would not speak of it further.

On the train we sat at the back of the car. Most people ignored us, but a few glared openly in our direction. During the war I had experienced the same thing. My fellow soldiers often could not see me as a man. Rumours had flown about the encampments in the coloured regiments that during the fight to take Battery Wagner white federals fired on the returning survivors of the Massachusetts 54th for no other reason than that they were Negroes. I have no reason to believe this except that I read it in reports by a man named George Stephens in the Anglo-African journal. He claims to have been there and there was confusion all about. Then when the 3rd New Hampshire came up to reinforce the 54th in the dark and smoke, they emptied their muskets into the Massachusetts men by mistake. There were other instances in which Negro troopers were disdained and openly hated by our fellow Union men. I myself experienced it on more than one occasion.

Still, open hostility has been on the increase. I have heard more than once that in a town on the other side of Chatham, local ruffians brag 'the sun will never set on a living nigger in our town.' Nothing, the likes of the murders that are occurring in the American South, has happened yet. So for the moment I will not countenance the rumours, but am disturbed at this new and unfavourably changing landscape.

I could see Eunice was becoming agitated. She looked around the coach with wild eyes, not comprehending where she was. She began to rise and I gently forced her back down into her seat. She brought her face up to look directly into mine and I could see she did not recognize me. Some private world beckoned her and she had entered it. Fearing the worst, I took the bottle of elixir from the carpetbag I carried and poured a tablespoon full, which she drank without complaint.

At Chatham, Dr. Abbott boarded the train and sought us out. By this time Eunice was dozing with her head pressed against the pane of the window. For the next few hours we steamed along in pleasant conversation with the newly greened countryside resplendent as we passed hardwood forests and beautifully ploughed fields showing the new growth of this season's crop.

Dr. Abbott was excited. He had received word from Dr. Bucke that an old friend was awaiting him at the asylum, but Dr. Bucke refused to identify the friend. It was to be a surprise.

When we arrived at the station in London, my friend Alexander Hamilton was there to pick Eunice and I up with his wagon. Dr. Abbott was met by a buggy from the asylum. I remember thinking as he departed that he looked particularly joyous with the prospect of his surprise friend.

During supper, Eunice brightened up and spoke pleasantly with Alex and Mrs. Hamilton. Afterward the Hamilton children came in and entertained us with what they were learning in school. There were two girls about eight and eleven years of age and one boy who looked to be twelve or thirteen from his size, but amazed us by accounting ten as his true age. The girls recited poetry. One piece was a pleasant rhyme about angels and the spirits of children who pass in infancy. The other was Lord Tennyson's "Charge of the Light Brigade" with all the dramatic gestures and histrionics the child could muster. The young lad recited the spellings of dozens of difficult words.

Alex gave us a bedroom with a single double bed in it. I put Eunice to bed and took off my waistcoat, shirt and trousers, then taking a spare blanket stretched out on the floor. My bivouac was not the most comfortable, but I was able to sleep. The day's trip must have exhausted her because she did not stir during the entire night.

In the morning, we arose to see the Hamilton children off to school then Alex, with a conspiratorial glance, helped me load Eunice into the wagon and drove us to the Asylum on Highbury Avenue. London had grown considerably from the last time I was there. Where the river was once the heart of the town, the commercial centre and new residencies were all moving away from the public wharves to the areas around the train station; and there were now many fine, brick buildings.

We arrived mid-morning and were greeted by a young doctor and a female attendant. We were shown into the main building which was a very big, yellow-brick edifice with arched windows that came to points and the roof was graced with a number of beautifully constructed dormers. Just the sight of such a grand building began to dispel my fears for Eunice's treatment.

Once attendants had helped Alex offload Eunice's trunk and our hand baggage Alex bade me farewell and turned his wagon and team down the long lane toward Highbury. When we were finished and I was ready to leave, someone from the asylum would drive me back to the train station in time to catch the last westbound train.

Inside the grand foyer of the main building, the female attendant saw to our needs. Even though we were expected, the registration process was going to take some time and so a walk on the grounds was suggested for Eunice. She did not see the point in becoming too familiar with the establishment, as she believed she was only there to receive some kind of treatment that would be over quickly enough for her to return home that very day. I am largely at fault for this because I suggested this might be the case in order to have her accompany me without fuss.

The female attendant, quickly discerning the strategy from our conversation, suggested it was such a wonderful spring day with the flowerbeds in full bloom that missing them would be a shame. Suspicious as she was, Eunice agreed to a tour of the grounds and left with the female attendant. In the meantime a hospital clerk with impressive moustaches brought me into an office where we set down the particulars of Eunice's confinement. Afterward he bade me wait upon Dr. Bucke to discuss her condition and possible treatments.

"I trust you had a good journey yesterday?" To which I replied that we did. Bucke is a good-looking man of medium height a long white beard and kindly countenance. His appearance is that of a scholar, which is added to by his slight English accent. The suit he was wearing was one of the new sack-style becoming popular in the bigger cities. I felt unfashionable and out of date, by comparison, with my frock coat, ruby waistcoat and wine-dark cravat.

"Dr. Abbott and I have discussed Eunice's case and it is perplexing in many ways. It seems similar to the condition of those veterans who have seen vicious fighting in battle. There is fatigue and exhaustion. Then there are the nightmares, which will not let her sleep. These are all similar to the symptoms of soldier's heart, but as far as you know, or tell me, your wife was never subject to a conflict or bombardment?" This was not meant as an insult. He seemed to have read Eunice very quickly.

Soldier's heart, or Da Costa's syndrome as it now more formally known, described the condition of frontline troops who could no longer take the strain of battle. Many simply walked away from their regiments. Officers deemed it cowardice and I observed an execution where nine riflemen shot a teenager who had dropped his musket and walked left a fight. Even after years of rest, many of the men who developed this malady during the insurrection, continued to suffer from it.

I answered Dr. Bucke's question as truthfully as I could in the negative.

"It is strange, strange indeed. Has she exhibited other behaviors that may have escaped your attention until now?" Again I answered in the negative.

Eunice had always been dark and unforthcoming about her experiences in America. I simply presumed she had followed Albert to Massachusetts then the Carolinas to make his life in camp easier by mending his uniforms and washing his clothing. But perhaps I was wrong. Maybe there was something I missed.

Promising to delve into the mystery, we continued our discussion of the treatments he would attempt. Among them was rest and moral therapy. Moral therapy was the daily regimen of light work, so the patient could feel they were accomplishing something productive; Christian instruction; a healthy diet; and recreation. It was felt this would help them to shake off the melancholia that plagued so many. Women did sewing and knitting and they were also permitted to garden on the grounds. Men worked on the farm producing the food consumed by the patients.

Eunice would have her own room in the main building. She would be separated from the indigent who were there on charity. There were also common areas she would share with other paying guests. Her room and meals would cost two dollars a week. A sum we could well afford.

It was nearly lunchtime before we were finished with the confinement details. Dr. Bucke invited us to join him for lunch in the main dining room and I was surprised the noise in the mess hall was such a happy one. Patients sat in small groups at four-place tables and shared conversation. Attendants circled the room, speaking to this patient and that one as if they were long time friends who had dropped by to pass the time of day. Everything was orderly and neat. This was not the hell I imagined from the stories I had heard or the wretches I had seen working the fields near Fort Malden.

Our meal was not sumptuous, but healthy. Asparagus, the first of the year's fresh vegetables along with potatoes and cuts of pork graced our plates. There was an abundance of milk, tea and coffee. After lunch, Dr. Bucke suggested a tour of the grounds and various industries they undertook with the patients.

We strolled the grounds until I could see that Eunice was starting to become agitated. I was ready to administer another dose of paregoric, but Dr. Bucke stopped me. Instead, he suggested to Eunice that she might like to lie down. He did it in such a pleasant manner that Eunice surprised me by accepting and thanking him politely.

Her room was on the second floor and when we arrived there, her trunk had been unpacked and her clothing hung in the cupboard. It was at that moment she became conscious of my intention to place her in care. Her eyes filled with tears.

"Oh God Frederick. Please don't leave me here. I'll die. They'll kill me here. If you let me come home, I'll be good. I won't be any trouble. Please take me home Albert..."

"Who is Albert?" Dr. Bucke interceded.

"Her first husband. He was killed in the war."

A low moaning broke from her lips and she began to sway. I caught her before she could fall and eased her onto the bed. She began rambling and would not look at me. Instead she began talking to Albert telling him not to go, that she needed him, and cursing the army.

I held her stroking her hair and face. What could I do? I loved her and had all my life. Even in those times when I would gladly have struck her or wished she would quietly die, I loved her. Now I felt the Judas, the betrayer, worse than some faithless husband who spends his time in the taverns and bawdy houses. The hole in my soul became a pit I was tumbling into. For a brief second the room spun then grew dark, threatening to become completely black. Bracing myself on the metal headboard of the bed I gulped air until I felt the calm hand of Dr. Bucke on my shoulder. He turned me toward the bedside chair and bade me sit.

"Are you alright?" he asked looking deep into my eyes as if to see something that might be amiss. But sitting assuaged the dizziness and within seconds I returned to normal.

Turning from me to Eunice, he took her wrist and checked her heartbeat then felt her forehead to determine if she had a fever. In a quiet, friendly voice he said her name. "Eunice, can you hear me? If you can please tell me."

Her only response was a skein of drool leaking from the corner of her mouth onto the pillow.

"Please fetch the women's attendant." He commanded me. "And tell her to bring Dr. Millman." Millman was the assistant superintendent whom I had not yet met. I left the room, relieved to be away from the scene, and rushed down the corridor to find the designated staff.

It took five minutes to find the attendant who dispatched a junior to locate Dr. Millman. I returned to Eunice's room with the woman only to be met at the door by Dr. Bucke.

"I think now is the best time to leave her in our care. She won't know you have gone and it will be better that way. It will seem like a dream when she regains her senses." Dr. Bucke's suggestion stunned me. I imagined a gradual parting or even violence occasioning our separation. Slinking away like a skedaddler made me cringe.

Not knowing what to do or where to go, I left the main building and went into the gardens hoping the afternoon air would refresh me. Making my way to a bench that I remembered from our earlier tour, I wanted to sit, but a gentleman already held possession of the seat.

At first glance he resembled Dr. Bucke, but his beard was a little wilder with the bottom edge growing down his throat and the moustache overgrowing his upper lip. When the man looked up at my approach, his eyes were of the kind that permanently questioned life, where Dr. Bucke's held a fullness of confidence. There was something about him I recognized. I knew his face, but from a long time ago.

At first I thought he had been a soldier in one of our regiments. Not able to recall him as a brother in arms, I wondered if maybe he wasn't even a Confederate officer we had captured, but the thought fled the instant he spoke. He had a sharp and unmistakable New York accent.

"You appear to be in distress." He said looking around to verify there were no other resting places in the immediate vicinity. "Please sit."

When I did, he glanced at my clothing and continued, "You are obviously not a patient, so I assume you are either visiting or placing a relative in Dr. Bucke's care."

I nodded gracelessly. Sitting was the thing I most wanted to do to get my strength back so I could flee the grounds and the hospital and the city. I had no thought other than for myself. Thinking of Eunice and her collapse caused me to weep again. But the man was insistent.

"Take a moment and catch your breath. Dr. Bucke is one of the best men I have ever encountered and I have known a lot of doctors over the years. Who is it you are placing in care here?"

"My wife," was all I could manage.

"Well, she will be well looked after. But you must now look after yourself. Do you live in London?"

I told him where.

"Ah. Buxton. You traveled up from Chatham with my friend Dr. Abbott? I doubt if more than one patient a day is admitted from Buxton." He said this with a great deal of warmth and a hint of inoffensive humour. "My name is Walt. I would guess you are Frederick?"

Strangely, it pleased me to be known. When I admitted my identity he continued, "You may not remember, but we met once at the end of the war in the Contraband hospital in Washington." That was why I remembered him.

"You have the advantage of me. I am sorry to say you are very familiar, but I do not recall meeting you. But if these were different circumstances, I might not have to make such an embarrassing admission."

He patted my hand kindly and observed, "I understand completely, so I will spare you further discomfort. We met when you passed through Washington after the war was finished and you were mustered out. You stopped to see Dr. Abbott at the Contraband Hospital. I was there visiting with him, upgrading, if you will, my education on Canada. Being so close, you are still a very mysterious country to many Americans." Then, as if to spare me further strain, "I believe you went to school together?"

"We did, but Dr. Abbott was one year ahead of me."

He hemmed and said, "I suppose at the time it seemed like such a large gap. But now, it is nothing."

To speak of anything other than Eunice, even for a few minutes, was a great relief. Before I sat down, I could feel a massive headache starting below my ears at the base of my neck. I've had them before and they almost blind me with pain. More than once they have caused me to be sick to my stomach. But now, the headache was vanishing faster than it came on.

"It was a small school and we looked up to the bigger lads. Anderson and I remained friends while he was away at university and have become closer since the war. I was afraid he might see a permanent attraction in Washington and not return home. As it is, when my family doesn't require his professional services, we meet for tea to talk about the world and music and books."

"Yes. I remember now. He told me you were a journalist at one time. Do you still write?"

"I correspond with several friends and keep a diary. Nothing more. Since my wife became sick, I have not had much time for anything."

"You should come back to it. It is good for the soul. When I worked in the Union hospitals around Washington, I used to think that poetry was the antidote for those dark nights when my choice was either the pen or the bottle. I am glad now I had poetry because after some of those big battles, the bottle would never have sufficed. Now, I keep my travel diaries and write an essay here and there."

"I have thought about it," I said avoiding any discussion of my own diary, "but I don't know if I've anything to say."

"You were with Sherman? I would think that, without the jingoism we Americans embrace, would be a fit subject for an unbiased historical perspective. You should give it a try."

It was like he knew my mind and its deepest secrets. Even Eunice was not acquainted with the fullest extent of my correspondence with the General and Mrs. Lincoln.

"At Christmas, I received a pamphlet from a group of linguists in London who are trying to create a comprehensive dictionary from sources drawn out of English literature since the time of Chaucer. They are seeking readers who can identify words and the context they are used in to collect and submit them. I thought it sounded challenging and if circumstances permitted, I would write to them offering my services."

"You should."

"I may. I just don't know what will happen with Eunice. Oh. I am sorry. That's my wife's name."

"No need to apologize. I already assumed that to be the case."

"Everything is so uncertain right now I hesitate to make plans. I am not sure if she will ever again see the outside of this place."

Speaking with Walt was too easy. It was like we were old and firm friends who had a habit of regularly meeting in this pleasant garden to catch up on the events of our lives.

"Frederick. Life is never certain. After the last quarter of a century we should have come to know that. I often think about God and what he has planned for us, but I know if there is a plan, he isn't revealing it. I sometimes believe he placed us here on this earth and left us alone to see how we would do and it is we who fool ourselves into believing there is some divine plan," he paused for a moment passing his eyes over the bright quilt of flowers. "What ever happens you must start moving forward for the good of your own soul. If you let yourself become mired in your wife's sickness, then you risk losing the divine spark that makes you who you are. I don't mean to tell you what to do and this may sound cruel, but you may have to deal with your wife the way you dealt with the battle death of a comrade you loved. You preserve his memory then pick up your gun and keep moving forward into the fire of the enemy. When it is all over, you still cherish the memory of your friend and not the final wreckage of him that you last saw during the fight."

I was stunned. This was not expected advice and not the depth of counsel a stranger should be giving, but he was right. I needed to go ahead with my life. My life with Eunice had been all but a sham, a fantasy on my part. She had not loved me and could never love me in the same way I loved her. By all accounts I had done the best for her that I could and would continue to do so, but now I must think about what I will do with the rest of my own life.

"Oh Frederick," he said turning his knees so they pressed against mine and then he reached up and placed his hand lovingly on my cheek. "I can see I have hurt you. I am so sorry. I…"

"But you haven't Walt. You have addressed those things I am probably too cowardly to consider."

"Well, you are saddened by the day my friend. So let's change the subject and bring some joy back into our meeting." And we did. We spoke of old times and new ideas for the next hour until Dr. Bucke sent for me. The asylum's carriage was ready to convey me back to the railway station in time for the evening train.

We left Walt waving in the garden as I went in to sign the final papers before departing.

Not having anything more than my holdall bag, I was ready to go a few moments after signing the commitment papers. Someone had already brought the bag down from Eunice's room and left it in Dr. Bucke's office. He walked me to the main door and remained in the doorway while I took my seat behind the driver.

As we readied ourselves to pull away from the hospital, Dr. Bucke called for us to wait. The attendant rushed out and placed a hastily wrapped package in my hands. "Walt wanted you to have this."

Looking up past the smiling Dr. Bucke, I could see Walt in the foyer window to his right. I waved and as we rolled down the drive, I placed Walt's package in my bag.

March 1, 1879

I received another letter from Mrs. Lincoln today. This letter was a return to her normal self. After receiving her last note, I grew quite concerned and wrote the General about it. He was quick to reply that we must wait until she returned to America before the proper help for her could be obtained. I sincerely hope she is healthy and there is no problem real or imagined. Learning from my experience with Eunice, I know the real problems are easier to remedy than the imagined ones.

Mrs. Abraham Lincoln,
Pau, France

Mr. Frederick Macdonald
C/O General Delivery,
Buxton, Ontario
Canada

January 26, 1879

Dear Mr. Macdonald,

The manuscript of your memoirs arrived on January twentieth and I was delighted to receive it. I wasted no time in reading the complete work and enjoyed it so thoroughly I am reading it once again.

I am very surprised Secretary Stanton even bothered to talk to you. He rarely addressed underlings and not with any degree of kindness when he did. Mr. Lincoln commented more than once on this. Normally he made up his mind about things and went ahead with what he thought and would not listen to anyone else. I would like to have seen his face that night in Savannah, when the Negro preacher let him have it.

Secretary Stanton certainly behaved that way with my husband, particularly when it came to the issue of slavery. My husband fought the election of 1860 on the basis that the Union had to be preserved and the idea that slavery be eliminated was a negotiable afterthought. How he was going to accomplish the preservation of our country alone was a hard question to which he was not sure he had an answer. Slavery was pushed to the back of his mind except when he was asked directly about it.

We discussed this problem at great lengths many times. Mr. Lincoln felt he had to listen to all voices, from slaveholder to Quaker, in order to make a plan for the peaceful dismantling of that institution. It became obvious to him that there was no consensus and never would be. Each state and group had its own opinions, which took precedence over every other point of view and Mr. Lincoln did not know which way to turn or who indeed was in the right.

The war occupied much of my husband's time. It did not appear at first as though we could win it. Only in the second year could he return to the question of slavery. Still, he had to maintain the balance with the slave states that remained loyal to the Republic for we could not do without them.

Stanton had no such considerations to deal with. He was a dog that saw only the wagon going by and had to charge. He did not care who rode in that wagon nor what their opinions were. Because of this, he made promises to a great many people that were beyond his ability to keep. The only promise he meant to keep was the one to make himself president in place of Mr. Lincoln.

It is too bad my husband could not consult closer with General Sherman. From your description of him he appears to be a man of great common sense. I now understand why my husband liked him. Mr. Lincoln planned to get to know General Sherman better once the war was over and hoped he would become a personal friend.

Your description of the conspiracy of Secretary Stanton and General Halleck leads me to believe they kept General Sherman as far from my husband as possible, and as the war wound down with the General gaining his rightful fame, they then found it necessary to try destroying his reputation. I would not put such meanness past either man.

In early 1862 Mr. Lincoln called me into his office and sent his secretaries, Nicolay and Hay, away.

"Mother, what shall we do?" he asked.

"About?"

"About the slaves. You have always held strong opinions on the subject and right now all I receive is bad advice. Tell me what you would do."

His request dumbfounded me. I asked for some time to think about it and two days later made the following proposal.

"Father, this is what I would do. I would win the war."

At which he laughed and said he had already thought of that.

"No. You do not understand. I would win the war by first freeing the slaves in the renegade states, then enlisting Negro troops to help in the fight. Once I had brought the Confederates into line, I would free every Negro whether in the South or the friendly slaves states. You need the border states on your side Father. But remember, the people in Maryland, Delaware and the others are simply pandering to avoid losing their slaves. They have no real love for the Union, but they know we will win the war."

"Secretary Stanton would free them all immediately and give them the vote," was Mr. Lincoln's reply.

"And he would cost you all you have worked for and in one fell swoop giving himself not only the presidency, but the votes of the Negroes to sustain himself in that position for as long as he wants. He could become King Stanton."

"That's very harsh mother. I doubt if Mr. Stanton sees himself as king…"

"You wait and see," I said. Sometimes Mr. Lincoln could be exasperatingly naive.

"I will wait, but in the meantime I do like your idea of freeing the slaves in the Confederate states. That would cause a lot of confusion for Jeff Davis to deal with. The slaves have caused me a lot of sleepless nights, why shouldn't Jeff have some trouble too? Then, by letting the Negroes enlist, we would have a people grateful for the opportunity to fight rather than have to beg for or draft unwilling citizens."

So you see, it was me who actually freed the coloreds. You need to write that into your history. I can make several suggestions as to where this would best be inserted. But please do not ignore my great contribution.

I hope this letter finds you and your family well.

Sincerely,
Mrs. Abraham Lincoln

CHAPTER SIX

June 17, 1879

Last night when I arrived home the silence of the house had a hollow quality. Not the quiet that signifies a home is simply sleeping, but the ringing silence that shouts of the absence of the people who should rightfully fill the space with their breathing.

After tossing and turning in my bed, I arose and filled in my diary with all the events, which took place in London.

Despite the nature of the day, the train trip home was empty of noteworthy news. Nonetheless, by the end of my writing I was so tired I was barely able to complete the entry. In the meantime I had forgotten about Walt's present and it wasn't until this morning that I opened the package.

Once on the train I was tempted to open it but resisted, guessing the package contained some literary gift, which I was not in the mood to read. Some spiritually uplifting tome filled with kindly platitudes, so it was easy to forget I even had it until this morning.

After taking care of the animals I set about making breakfast for myself. While I turned the coffee mill, I decided I would check the fields then go to Benjamin and Mary's to report on my journey. Whilst planning my day, I was shocked to realize I was already thinking of myself in the singular.

Placing the coffee pot and a muffin I had made several days ago on the table, I sat down to open the package. Inside sat a handsomely bound book and my heart almost stopped. It was "Leaves Of Grass", the poems of the great American poet, Walt Whitman.

I could scarcely breath as I opened the front cover and looked down upon the inscription… "To Frederick Macdonald, an old friend from sadder days. May your days brighten from this day forward. Walt Whitman."

June 27, 1879

After church Mother came to help me organize Eunice's room. I received word from Dr. Bucke that she would probably never recover her senses to the point she could come home without a permanent companion to look after her. Even then he doubted her condition would remain as it is, but would deteriorate until she would not know where she was, what day it was or even who I was.

I had not been in Eunice's room since she left it. I felt it would have been like stepping down into her grave. Sitting on the bed, I did not know where to begin and was on the point of dissolving into tears when Mother bustled in and took command.

"After lunch we will go into the village and buy a trunk for her clothing.

Then you can move it up into the attic or leave it here as you wish. Before we do that, I'm going to sort through everything to see what we need to keep and what we can send up to London. Then we will either give or throw everything that is left over away..." Without thinking of the cruelty she was committing, she added "... Although I don't know anyone who would choose to wear a mad woman's clothes."

Dumbfounded and wounded by her assumption that I now shared her contempt for Eunice, I stormed out of the room seeking refuge in the barn.

Just before lunch, when my rage subsided somewhat, I returned to the house and looked in on the room where Mother had already removed practically all traces of my wife.

"I'll make some lunch. Everything here is just about done. All we have to do is get the trunk and pack these things in it," she told me indicating a pile of neatly folded apparel. "But there are some letters and papers you need to go through. I left them in her secretary."

When Mother departed for the day, I placed the new trunk with Eunice's things at the foot of her bed. Despite Dr. Bucke's admonition, I still expected to bring my wife home sometime.

The rest of this day has thankfully been filled with farm work. Toward sunset, I filled the tub in the yard with water and sat soaking as evening fell like the first gentle snowflake of a storm.

Inside, I made tea and lit the lamps in the kitchen. Going once more into Eunice's room I returned with the letters from her secretary. They were mostly tied in a bundle. One, however, was not. It was addressed to Mrs. Lincoln.

CHAPTER SEVEN

Each line was neatly written, but the hand was parsimonious. This new hand formed its characters straight up and down. There was something also oddly feminine about the curls and flourishes that started and ended each letter.

Mrs. Eunice Macdonald
General Delivery,
North Buxton, Ontario,
Canada

Mrs. Abraham Lincoln,
Pau, France

November 28, 1878

Dear Mrs. Lincoln,
I wish to write to you because I also lost my husband during the war. Although I am now married to Frederick and he is a good man, he is not and will never be my real spouse. Before him, I was married to a man named Albert Johnson and he is still my true love. You asked Frederick to tell you about the coloured troops. Albert and I were soldiers and it is our experiences I will tell you about.

You start by the intelligence I was also a soldier. There is nothing unnatural in it, as you will presently see. This story I write is true, but it is the first time I have divulged all of the details, even to Frederick.

The reasons why I feel I must break a silence, which I planned to carry to my grave, by writing this letter have come close to eluding me, but a voice in my heart tells me that, race notwithstanding, you and I are sisters in grief and I must talk to you, even if only through pen and paper. In truth, I can no longer bear this knowledge on my own and must share it with someone who will care.

Your letter to Frederick describing how you felt Mr. Lincoln's life shudder out of him when that coward shot him from behind is another reason why I feel compelled to address you. However, I will write more about that later.

Mr. Lincoln was no secret to us Negroes. We knew his height and breadth. We knew his eyes and his lips and his ears. We knew every hair on his head and chin; and every wrinkle in his face and can imagine the worries that put them there. If the unthinkable happened and were it suddenly proved tomorrow that there is no God, then we would believe in Mr. Lincoln instead. Words are not very good for telling you how we felt about your husband, but they are all I have.

Only my father lived as a slave. All our lives, first as children from our dad, my brother and I heard about life under slavery, then from other residents of Buxton as we grew older. Our happiness that those days have been brought to an end is marred by the actions taking place today in the South. Still, it was our victory but not without a terrible cost.

Albert was born a slave in Missouri and escaped with his parents to Canada West. Slavery left its mark and it was a mark that neither love nor time could erase.

Let me describe Albert.

When he died he was one month short of his twenty-third birthday. I would have loved to see him grow old. His face contained all the secrets of what he would become as the years passed. Many of our race are embarrassed by their dark skin, but not Albert. He was very black and I expect he did not have any white blood in him. Someone once told him that there were black kings and queens and he delighted in it. As for myself, I am not so sure about that. Some people create these imaginings to make themselves feel better about unhappy situations. I never saw the need. Whether or not there was some kind of African royalty in our past did not affect our condition when we were slaves nor does it affect us today. Many Negroes hate the white race because you brought us into bondage. But the way I see it, you also took us out of it. If it were not for men like Mr. Lincoln and the good soldiers who fought against the Confederacy, we would still be there. So I cannot hate your race, nor attempt to raise mine over yours.

But if anyone should know this history it is you, so there is no need for me to dwell on it any further.

Albert was also very handsome. His face looked like some gifted Frenchman had carved it. He had high cheekbones and a prominent forehead that told anyone meeting him for the first time how intelligent he was. When he looked at you, there was light in his eyes. Light and warmth and humour. He laughed a lot and loved jokes. Never have I met a man who was so continually happy. I could imagine him sitting down with your husband to trade pleasantries and those stories men love so much.

Both of our husbands seemed very strong to me. The stories I hear about Mr. Lincoln include his younger days as a farm hand and you do not do that without great strength of arm. Albert loved to show how strong he was. He would often lift two sacks of seed weighing a hundredweight each or he would work from first light through the heat of the day and into the night by lantern-light.

It sounds like he was showing off, and he was, and I loved him for it. I am sure you'll agree that it is the man who goes out of the way to win your heart, that you are most likely to give it to.

Albert and I first met when I moved with my family to Buxton. My father tried to make a living farming in the bush northwest of Toronto but the ground was hard and stony, so he failed. At Buxton land was being offered to fugitives with favourable rates, causing our move there. Albert and I attended the same school. Because his owners had denied him any kind of education, Albert strove to read and write and perform mathematical equations. He would hurry through the morning chores and go to school early just to talk with Mr. Rennie and Reverend King. Both had traveled and Albert desired to hear tales of places like London and Edinburgh. Had it not been for me, he would have joined a ship's company to explore these. I am not sure he was that eager to hear about Washington or Charleston, however. As it was, he went off and joined the army.

I long knew that given the chance, he would do whatever damage he could to the South and its slaveholders. He almost went with John Brown, but I screamed and cried, making him promise that he would never do anything so foolish. It broke his heart, but I was happy he was safe.

From the start, Albert followed the war through the newspapers. He subscribed to all the newspapers from Detroit. They were delivered to Buxton by the Windsor train and he never missed going to the depot to pick them up. I knew what he was planning and understood that once Mr. Lincoln began using Negro troops, I would lose Albert to the war. I just did not want to lose him forever.

That sounds foolish and greedy when you think of the number of women who lost their husbands on the battlefields, but I cannot help feeling that I, personally, was somehow cheated out of my love by the fates before we had our chance at life.

Frederick has always been my friend and has told me time and again that I was the only woman he ever loved. Sometimes, he made such a nuisance of himself that I shooed him away. Like me, he was married once before, but his wife died in childbirth. Her name was Helen and I knew her as well. Frederick told me he only married Helen because he knew that I would never willingly separate myself from Albert. In that he was right.

You will understand that it was loneliness and the confusion of loss that brought me to Frederick. I imagine you endured the same emotional fog and were accused of being crazy for it. But, you had children and the memory of children to help you through it. If someone were to accuse me of being crazy right now, they would be correct. Since Albert died, my life has been lived in a fog. Recently the haze has been getting thicker. Sometimes I awaken in the middle of the night and am not sure where I am. Whether I am in my old bed in my father's house or the bed Albert and I shared or in some distant camp waiting for the drum to call us awake.

It seems as if I am wakened to await Albert's return, which will happen at any moment. Does this happen to you? Do you miss Mr. Lincoln this way? Most recently I have been waking up to find that I have wandered. Sometimes the dreams that precede these awakenings are filled with the sounds of battle and canon fire. They frighten me terribly. Then when I can stand it no longer, I awaken someplace other than my home. Kindly neighbours have brought me back here to Frederick.

I have tried everything to cease these journeys. They don't happen every night. In fact they are more infrequent than regular. Still they frighten me.

The newspapers carried accounts of your internment in a mental sanitarium at the behest of your son. What caused him to force you into such an inhuman and publicly humiliating condition?

My condition and yours are undoubtedly the result of the cruelties we suffered during the Insurrection.

But this is not why I write to you. The story I wish you to know begins with Albert and ends with Frederick.

All through 1861 and the spring and summer of 1862 Albert read the newspapers and followed the battles in West Virginia and Virginia. More particularly he attended to those that happened in Missouri at Dry Wood Creek and Lexington, which was country he knew. Whenever a big battle was conducted he read all the details and kept them in his head. Then, he would look at me and say, "I want to fight. It's my duty and if I were to be killed then it would be for a great cause. I don't understand why Mr. Lincoln won't free us and let us fight. We've seen the worst and stood up to it for centuries."

Starting in the spring of 1862, we began hearing rumours black regiments were forming in the east and south. I never knew how these rumours started or who passed them on, but he suddenly had this knowledge and I knew the time when he would leave me was getting closer. In advance of that day I had a desperate plan forming.

People who wanted to be recruiters were making it known they would sign up any man willing to fight when the time came. Dr. Delany, who had returned to Chicago, had broadcast through his correspondence that he would be a recruiter for the Union cause. There were other famous and less famous people who were waiting to be drawn into the war. Mary Anne Shadd worked to enlist men from Buxton, Chatham and Dresden.

The difficulty was the uncertainty caused by the government's reluctance to recognize us as potential allies who would gladly carry the fight to the enemy. In fact, the Fugitive Slave decision was still law and many of our men were frightened to set foot in the United States in order to support the Union.

"I don't need to fight both Washington and the Confederates," was how Albert looked at it. "I would go as the meanest labourer if they would let me, but as it stands, they would make me a criminal should I set foot over that border. Once I get to Michigan the slave catchers can pick me up and spirit me South, and nobody will care. Then I will have to kill who ever it is that tries to catch me and that will make me an outlaw instead of the good soldier I want to be."

Regardless of how much we wanted your husband to prevail, we needed to be accepted by the government before we felt it safe to move. The threats by Jefferson Davis that any Negro caught fighting for the Union would be killed did not frighten us. If that was to be our lot, then so be it. But, we would not countenance a new United States that, through a compromised peace, still held to the empty future of slavery.

Albert sought to sign up anyway.

I don't remember correctly when it was we heard General Hunter was recruiting black soldiers in South Carolina, but the news fired Albert. Behind my back he went to Mrs. Shadd and made to enlist. Nothing was said to me, but Albert took several trips to Chatham in September and early October. He was his usual kind self, offering to pick up anything I needed while he was there, but did not invite me along with him.

Frederick had not yet disappeared. His mother told me that after his wife and baby died, he went south into the States to help the Contrabands as a teacher. It was like Frederick. Although I did not love him, I admired him in many ways and one of them was his devotion to those still trapped in bondage.

When he did go, if he wrote it was to Albert and not to me. I had done my best to send him away and because of that I imagine he did not feel very kindly toward me.

The day Albert left I knew something was on the wind from the moment we woke up. He usually leapt out of bed and hastened out to the barn before I had the chance to awaken fully. Instead, he lingered and stole a private husband and wife moment with me. Only then did he go to the barn to feed the animals and that took much longer than usual. It was like he was saying goodbye for good. Back in the house we had breakfast and over coffee, he asked me what I had planned for the day. This was so unusual it took me aback and I could only stare at him for the moment. Instead of looking away to avoid my gaze, his eyes swept across my face reading every line. I started to cry. He reached out his hand and placed it gently over mine without saying anything and we sat there in kitchen with our coffee growing old. There was nothing to say. I knew he was about to leave and had known for weeks that he would be leaving. Still, it came as suddenly as a dagger's thrust. The room went cold in spite of the fire in the stove and warm sunlight pouring in through the windows. In the stillness of the kitchen a wind that only I could hear raged in my ears.

"When will you go?"

"On the noon train."

"Where will you end up?" It sounded foolish. I had meant to ask where he would be going to join the army but it did not come out that way.

"I hope back here with you." His face was calm.

"No. No. No. I mean what part of the army are you going to join? How will I know where you are and how will I find you? How will my letters find you?" Desperation commandeered my voice.

"I'll have to write to let you know. I'm going to Boston first. They are forming a regiment of freed men there. When I know where we will be going after that, I will write to you and let you know..." There was a long silence after that. Then he looked at me. I had never seen him cry and my heart broke for him. "Please don't worry. I will be all right and will not put myself in any more danger than I have to, to get the job done. And when it is all over, I will come straight back here."

There was little more to say. Pleading and screaming worked to keep him from joining Brown, but we all knew in the secret corners of our hearts that Brown was destined to fail and anyone with him would die. Now, a great army was getting ready to move and I could not keep Albert back from that. Your husband announced that we would finally be free and that all the slaves were to be freed. We now had the law, but we needed to fight to make that law more than just paper words.

It's funny how some things you have come to love suddenly become your enemy. I used to love travelling anywhere by train, but now the westbound train became my enemy. We sat throughout the morning talking occasionally, but more often just touching whenever it seemed right. Albert had already packed his bag in secret and hidden it in the eaves where he knew I would not find it because I hated to go up there. There were bats under the eaves and I did not want them nesting in my hair.

Albert's plan was to take the afternoon train to Windsor where he would stay with his friend Daniel Hall, another fugitive who escaped from New Orleans some years before. Then he would cross over the Detroit River to the recruitment officer's gathering place thence to Boston by train.

"We have to make that journey in secret as there are still a great many people in the North who would gladly sell us to the Confederacy. So please, I ask you, do not tell anyone, even your brother, where I have gone or how I am getting there."

It was rare for the sun to shine so intensely in December. Usually we have thick cloud or watery sunlight, but on that day the sun came out and warmed the world as if there was something of great import going on. But, I only was losing my lover. The world was stealing him from me and the sun was making it seem a small thing.

When it was time to leave for the station, I rode with Albert. He was planning to leave me behind in the house, but I refused and vilified him until he allowed me to go as far as the railway. Perhaps that was a mistake. As he drove our mule and trap up the road, he did not look away from the traces and his face was cold and set. The sun spangled his cheeks and the hard, manly beauty was caught in it. I made quick sidelong glances to watch him. I know he didn't want me to do so. It made it hard for him to leave me, but I wanted to make it harder even still.

CHAPTER EIGHT

At the station he set the brake on the trap and tied the mule to a hitching post then swung me down. The stationmaster just nodded at us. Without my knowledge, Albert had purchased his ticket several days before. Within minutes of our arrival the locomotive pulled into the station and slowed to a stop at the platform. Albert swung his carpetbag up onto the train, turned and hugged me tightly. I could feel his tears and pushed my own down onto the collar of his coat so he would not feel them. He whispered how much he loved me then climbed the steps onto the train.

The conductor was polite enough to wait until Albert was aboard. With a nod to me, he signaled the engineer his readiness to leave and the train commenced moving.

I watched the carriages rock from side-to-side as they gathered momentum until they were so far down the track the train blended into the horizon. I climbed into the trap and drove it home by myself. The silence of the house became too much to bear, so I went out to the barn just to hear the animals moving about. That night was the first time I had the dream in which I heard the sounds of battle.

Over the next few weeks I developed my plan and commenced it by organizing the sale of our cattle and the feed in the silo. The seed for next spring's planting went as well because I knew there would be no more crops grown by our hand on this farm. While I busied myself with this, I waited for news from Albert.

My plan was to enlist Morgan in a deception that would see me safely away without rousing any suspicion. I took it for granted that Albert had probably told several friends he was enlisting. Now I would use that myself telling any who asked what I would do while Albert was away, that is, I would follow him from camp-to-camp to be near and to help him. Several women from the area had already followed their men so this would not be unusual. Morgan would act as my defender, but not even he would know the real purpose of my journey.

The last time I spoke with Frederick, when he told us that he was going South, I asked if he were not afraid. If he had been, it might have influenced Albert to stay with me, but Frederick responded "I've been afraid all my life and now I can no longer live with that fear. It's time to do something to wipe the fear out."

Finally a letter came from Albert. He was in Readville, Massachusetts at Camp Meigs. He had enrolled in the new black regiment that Governor Andrew authorized and the white officers were training them hard. Albert was particularly proud of his skill with his rifle. His letter said he could hit the mark from one hundred yards nine times out of ten and had even scored the occasional bull's eye. "This," he assured me, "will stand me in good stead when I finally meet up with a rebel." The letter went on to say he would be at Fort Meigs for two more months. He wasn't sure how long, but until at least until Easter. That gave me until April 4 to fulfill the plan that was solidifying in my mind.

Midway through the week his letter arrived, I sat down in front of my mirror and cut off all of my hair. It seemed strange to see my face so starved for the curls that made it beautiful to Albert. I resembled a young boy, which is what I wanted. I just hoped not too young.

With the last of the animals gone, I locked up and walked the four miles to the train station carrying a small holdall. I didn't even turn around to look at the house. There was nothing to see with Albert gone. If I had cried then I would have turned back to wait for him to come home. The tears did flow, but I would not allow myself to weep, for weeping would have been crying.

After purchasing a ticket, I boarded the Windsor train following in Albert's tracks like a hunting dog on the scent. My bag contained everything I would need for the journey including our savings. I was sure Albert would forgive my using this money. He would be upset at first, but then he would see how this would bring us together so that come what may we would share it.

We had friends in Windsor I could have stayed with, but I did not want to be seen by anyone I knew.

When I reached Windsor, I lingered until all of the passengers had left the station then went into the ladies' cloakroom and quickly changed out of my dress into a pair of Albert's trousers and one of his shirts. I had cut both down to fit me. Quickly I laced on a pair of men's boots and left all of my women's clothing hanging on a peg in the hopes some unfortunate might profit from what I was about to do. I was worried that I would be challenged on leaving the cloakroom, but the stationmaster had his head down and was busy with his deskwork.

In the street, I flipped on a rounded felt hat of the type men wear for work and hoped my disguise would carry me through. At first I discreetly watched the faces of passers-by to determine if any noted my personating a man, but there was no change in their demeanor. As I walked along toward the river, my stride became more confident. I watched the men as they moved along. Some shuffled as if reluctant to arrive at their destination, others rushed toward it. Of the few Negroes I saw, the women kept their heads down and moved along quickly minding their own business. The men were more sure of themselves and undertook a manly stride, still being polite whenever they encountered a knot of people in front of a store or an office. I tried to emulate them.

In Sandwich I found a boarding house that was run by a family of Negroes I did not know. There was a community of fugitives there centered around the Sandwich First Baptist Church on West Peter Street. Many of the community's members were unfamiliar to me so I felt safe enough although it was expensive. I spent a dollar to have a room to myself.

My plan now was to travel as a man. A Negress traveling alone might arouse curiosity and even invite unwanted attentions from male passengers. But there were still hundreds of miles to go before I could join Albert and the best way was by lake steamer and train.

I have read your friend Elizabeth Keckley's book "Behind The Scenes" and often wondered how she managed to move about so freely. Her journal was studiedly delicate on the matter. Did she ever confide in you that she suffered from undue attentions?

On the following morning after my arrival, I addressed a shipping agent for passage to Buffalo and was told that a propeller would be arriving late that afternoon to fuel before continuing on across the lake. The captain of the ship was always willing to take a Negro passenger if I did not expect to be housed the in same accommodations as the whites.

There was nothing but to accept this and I set out with my bag to find a meal and the foodstuffs I might need for this journey. I was not sure that the captain would feed me, even though I had money and was willing to pay.

At four o'clock the steamer arrived and tied to the wharf. Within minutes the crew was loading the cords of hardwood that would fire her boilers. The ship was the *J.B. Howe* and her master, I learned, was Captain Wilfred Buckingham of Buffalo. I approached the captain and he agreed to carry me for a price, then turned and asked if I would help to cook and wait on tables.

"We lost our steward in Port Huron and I need someone until we get to Buffalo. If you're willing, I'll forgo your fare and feed you to boot." Rather than part with money we might need later on, I agreed.

"Capital. You'll bunk with the cook on the mess deck." Then walking out onto the wing bridge, he bellowed down to a man catching a breath of air near the bows. "Cook, I got you a replacement for the steward. Come up and get him."

The cook was a heavyset man who obviously ate well because of his profession. "Come on. We'll get you stowed then we got to get supper rolling. There are eleven passengers aboard who need to be fed at five thirty."

Suddenly I was seized with a fright. What would I do if the room contained only a big double bed? How could I keep this cook from discerning

I was a woman? Maybe I should have paid my fare to guarantee my privacy. Then, I calmed a bit with the understanding that if I kept paying extra to protect my secret, I would be destitute before I reached Albert.

Carrying my small bag, I followed the cook to the back of the ship and down some stairs to a room that adjoined the kitchen. It was tiny and smelled of oil and damp. There were two bunks, one over top of the other and a small writing desk with an oil lamp hung from the wall. On the wall opposite the beds, there was a small chest of drawers and on the back of the door a coat hanger which I did not see until I was left alone in the room. With the two of us inside, there was barely enough room to turn around. Cook, whose name was Hobson, told me, "You're up there. Swing your bag up and get changed into your best clothes then meet me in the galley." I didn't have any "best clothes". All I had was another pair of trousers and they were nowhere nearly as clean as the ones I was wearing. I did have a better shirt and would put it on as soon as he left. But, he didn't leave.

"What are you waiting for?"

"I'd like some privacy to change."

"Well, I never heard the like… a shy nigger. Don't that beat all," which he said with a bemused humour. So he left and I quickly slid into the clean shirt. I thought it would be so much easier once I found Albert.

The voyage passed without incident and three days after leaving Sandwich, I was entering the United States at Buffalo. I had never been to the United States before and was nervous about it. I did not know what would happen once my foot touched its soil. I was a little scared there would be slave catchers on every corner. But all that occurred was a man asked me where I was going and when I told him I was on my way to Boston to join the army, he wished me good luck and turned to the next person in line behind me.

I should not have been frightened. My journey went smoothly as I remembered to stay in the coloured section of the different trains I needed to take. These travels took me from Buffalo to Attica and thence onward to New York City and from there to Boston. I had to stay overnight in New York, but I met a coloured man and his wife on the train and they offered me accommodation in their home. The next morning, I proceeded on to Boston and Readville where Camp Meigs was.

In New York, the people I boarded overnight with, Alvin and Eleanor Carter, advised me to be careful. There was much unrest among the poorer residents of that city. They were against the war and hated Negroes. The Irish and Italians felt blacks were in competition for the few low paying jobs available.

"You'll be safe as long as you head directly to the station and board the first train you can…"

"Our friend Marshall Ellison was cornered and badly beaten last week by a bunch of Irishmen. He wasn't doing nothing wrong. They just stopped him in the street…"

"Honey," Alvin interrupted, "Marshall was in a side street without many people around. He shouldn't have been there."

I accepted the warning as a serious piece of advice and quickly walked the seven city blocks to the train depot.

It had been my intention that upon arriving in Readville, I would march up to the post and demand to enlist in Albert's company, but it was late in the day and the soldier on duty at Camp Meigs told me to come back tomorrow.

My immediate need was a room for the night. The soldier directed me to a tavern in the centre of town where I could find a bed. It was noisy, smoky and full of men. I had never been in such a place. The landlord rented me a bed in the big room on the upper floor. There would be two other tenants sharing the room for the evening and, he said, he hoped they wouldn't snore too loudly. Supper was included as part of the cost and I was told to hurry or I would miss it.

People sat at long tables and a young woman who could have been white brought me a bowl of stew and a spoon. When she came close I could see her eyes were gold in color and there was a slight frizz to the hair. She stayed close to our table, which I assumed was because she either wanted to clear up my plate and spoon as soon as I finished or because she liked to listen in on other peoples' conversations. The rest of the tavern's patrons were Negroes, as was the man across from me who asked what I was doing in Readville. I told him I came to sign up.

"You a bit skinny."

"I can hold my own, sir."

"Well, they be taking anybody right now. Union's losing too many so'diers. You not afraid o' dyin' boy?"

"No sir. I just want to do my duty."

"You don' sound like you from aroun' here. Where you from?"

"Canada West."

"You safe. Why the hell you want to get mix up in this?"

"My father and mother were slaves. I owe it to them to help others out who weren't lucky enough to get away."

"You read?"

"Yes."

"Why you want to t'row d'at away? You could have a good life up north d'ere," he said while he sopped up the remainder of his stew with a piece of bread. "You should have read yo'se'f 'bout some of there big fights and many men's kilt."

"As I said, it's my duty to help others and my education may end up being of some use to the Contrabands our troops encounter."

"Hope you know what you doing." Then he laughed and said, "... and I hope you can pass the doctor check to get in."

"What do you mean doctor check?"

"You got to go see the doctor and they look you all over before they let you join the army. Jus' like a horse."

It never occurred to me that I would have to have a medical inspection. I assumed you swore an oath then changed into a uniform.

The problem vexed me. As long as I was dressed, I could pass for a man, but there was no way I could undergo the scrutiny of a doctor. I asked a few more general questions about enlistment, but steered our conversation away from the subject of medical examinations. My dinner companion finished his meal before me and left the table to stand next to the bar where ale was served.

Finally, with my own supper done, I rose to leave. The girl with the golden eyes who had been close by all through our meal came and stood by my side and addressed me in a low voice.

"Missy, what do you want to join that army for?" When I looked at her with shock that my costume had been descried she continued. "I knew you were a woman from the way you came in here. You looked around this room like there wasn't a man in it good 'nough for you. Then when you sat down and I served you, I could smell the fear in you. Men don't smell that way. So I listened and sure you said what I already knew. But you don't want to sign up, there's camp fever there and if you don't cough your lungs out, then the Rebels surely will kill you. Must be something pretty strong to make you do this."

I was caught short and did not know what to say. But her bright eyes and quick mind went right to the heart of the matter. "It's a man, isn't it? Your man is in there and you think you can go with him." She paused for a moment. "My man in that regiment too, but I could never pass at what you're trying to do." With this her hand drifted across her bosoms and I knew what she meant. "You don't have my two problems," she laughed. "But I can help. In truth I can."

How could she help? Even if she was a witch she could not just fly me over the medical tent and into a uniform. There was no magic spell that could grow the necessary appendages that would pass me for a man. The smoke in the tavern made sick to my stomach and I wanted to get away from her as quickly as possible. "I'm sorry, but I do not know what you are referring to. Now if you will excuse me miss…" I said trying to sound as manly as possible.

But she would not be undone in her course. "Sister you a stranger here and you don't know your comin' from your goin'. Let me help. I know how to get you past the doctors."

I stopped myself from going any further toward the door and turned to her. "Okay, what can you do that I can't for myself?"

CHAPTER NINE

"Oh sister. What you need is a man to stand for you. He can take you test and give you the papers. Once you got the papers, nobody wants to look down your pants again. You knows a man hereabouts?"

I was embarrassed, as any proper lady would be, at this talk. It did not seem appropriate to have at any time, but especially with a room full of men. Still, her comments intrigued me enough to ask her quietly for more.

"I have a young frien' who can he'p and he can use the money. He tryin' to buy hisse'f." I did not know that a man in Massachusetts still had to buy his freedom. Only later did I learn this was not true. "You do got some money, don' you?"

Cutting to the heart of the matter like that set my mind and heart in two different directions. It would be a substantial sum that Albert and I would never get back. Secretly, I had hoped to preserve enough of the money from the sale of the farm animals so we could start again once the war was over. In my deepest dreams, I hoped by the time the Insurrection was done, we would have saved even more and could resume our lives where we paused them. This new demand would prevent that. Still my heart bade I do this no matter the cost. I counted on Albert's forgiveness for the money I would spend to be with him, whatever fate decreed.

"What will this youth demand for doing this?"

"Why money of course!" was her surprised answer. She did not comprehend my question so I rephrased it.

"No. No. How much money will he demand?'

"Not much. He be willin' to do this for the bonus money."

Rumors had reached me that the government paid a bonus to any able-bodied man who enlisted. This money now became part of my plan. By agreeing to part with the enlistment bonus, I could maintain our savings and accomplish what I wanted. Still, I was not sure I wanted to leap straight ahead into anything without having a chance of backing out if I didn't like the young man or something did not seem correct.

Her golden eyes sparkled as she told me when and where to meet her the next morning. She would bring the young man, whose name was Peter, "… like the apostle", to meet me.

I mounted the steps to the upper room, which was more a ladder than a staircase, and by the light of a single candle found the bed I was to occupy. Except for the bedbugs it was empty.

Up until I embarked on this journey, in all my life, I had only slept in the same room with one man and that was Albert. By the time my brother and I were old enough to notice the difference between boys and girls, I was already given a small room and Morgan slept in the kitchen on a mattress he rolled up every morning. Now, I had shared a room with a ship's cook and was about to join two strange men and after that an entire army of strange men. The Lord must think me a very strange and determined woman.

From the darkened corner of the sleeping room, I could hear heavy snoring and an occasional, wheezing flatulence. I do not know why men cannot comport themselves in a civilized way even when their company is limited to other men. They paid no attention to me and I used my fingers to stop my ears.

I have read in one of the journals we receive that Mr. Lincoln dreamt of his own murder. Please forgive me if this sounds cruel, but I must ask if there is a kernel of truth to the story. You see a horrid dream haunted me from the moment Albert left and still does to this day. Sometimes it is just the sounds of battle, but at others I watch the faces of my friends and enemies dissolve into death.

With the first light of morning I left my bed and collected my slim possessions. Neither had been disturbed, as I was afraid they might be. A girl of ten or eleven brought a pitcher of water and a basin. Because I was first to arise, I had the private use of these and turning away from my sleeping male companions, I washed as thoroughly as possible without revealing myself. Bathing felt good and reminded me that a full bath with hot water and soap would be wonderful. Once I was enlisted into the regiment, the opportunity for a bath would probably not offer itself again for a long time.

Golden Eyes, whose name I still did not know, arranged to meet me at the front of the town's general store. It was an easy enough place to find, but there were a lot of white people and very few Negroes when I arrived. I did not want to appear to be waiting on trouble so I walked toward the end of the main street then turned back. On my return sweep I could see Golden Eyes and a slight young man waiting nonchalantly in front of the store and they descended into the street to join me. Golden Eyes quickly introduced the young man, who looked to be anywhere from seventeen to twenty-five years old, as Peter. We were of a size. He was slight and, like mine, his face was narrow and delicate. Since butchering my hair I kept it short by passing shears over it weekly. Peter's hair was longer than mine.

We were starting to attract unfriendly attention. Even in a state as determined to find a place for us among Christian men as Massachusetts proclaimed itself, many people did not accept us. Thus far, on this journey, I had learned not to say anything about my plans to enlist, except to other blacks. Hobson, the cook aboard the J.B. Howe, was surprisingly kind to me, but cursed Negroes in general for instigating a war that was costing large numbers of white men their lives. "No ten niggers 're worth the life of a white man. You got to agree with that."

I did not agree with that, but it is the way many people felt.

It was obvious Peter had experience in this type of activity. He asked me what name I would like to be known as. This was something I had not thought about so I blurted out "Everett Jordan," hoping to keep our family name intact.

Everything, Peter promised, would be easy. He would take the test, which he would pass without problem then pretend to wander off inside the camp where I would meet him and he would pass the necessary documents to me and I could assume the name of Everett and would give him the bonus.

"You know honey, they don' give you the bonus right away. It take some time to come from Washington. So what you gonna do is give me the same as what they gonna give you and then you keep the bonus when it come."

No mention of this arrangement had been made. I started to protest, but Peter hushed me with "It take maybe six weeks to get here. That time you could be anywhere and I don' got nuthin' for my trouble. No honey. All I want is you give me the same as the bonus when I do this for you. That way we both happy."

The bonus, he said and Golden Eyes assured me that he bespoke the truth, was three hundred dollars cash. Giving this over to him would just about drain my purse, but I could see no other way and I had overheard from people talking on board the Howe that there was a bonus of the same amount. Because I did not want him to see me delving into my purse I told him that the money was in a safe place and I would go get it while he began the medical check.

Peter looked toward Golden Eyes who regarded him with wariness. I determined to hold fast and not let them treat me ill. For now, because of their exchange of glances, I did not trust them. It was obvious that Peter was in command because he made the decision that appeared to be final for both of them. "You go fetch the money and I will get started. I won't be finished by the time you get back, so you visit with Anna here and when everything is in order, I'll come and find you in the camp."

So her name was Anna. It was rather drab for someone so exotically beautiful. I had observed the reaction of the men to Anna last night. They may have talked to each other, but they watched her move around the tavern with great lust in their eyes.

Leaving the pair, I walked back toward the tavern and then, after following a curve in the street, I found a side street and left the main thoroughfare. My route had no definite direction, but I did want to know if their intentions might be dangerous, so I traced a square coming completely back to where I left the main street and watched to see if I was being followed. The fact that I was not bode well for this adventure and I withdrew the three hundred dollars from my purse and slipped it into my coat pocket.

Peter did not emerge from the regimental surgeon's office for two hours, but he had a sheaf of papers that he clutched high on his chest as he walked toward us then straight past into the camp.

Camp Meigs was not what I expected when I first saw it the night before. I thought it would be castle-like or surrounded by earthen works like Fort Malden in Amherstburg. Instead, it was a mere ten rows containing maybe a dozen tents each. On three sides the camp was bordered by woodlot. In the front there was an open patch of ground where soldiers marched about singing gaily while groups of mounted men pranced their horses around them like they were dancing to the same rhythm. All of this was accomplished under the watchful eye of a tall flagpole and the accompaniment of orders shouted by hoarse-voiced men. I would come to learn that these were battle drills on which my life might depend and within hours I would join the men on the parade ground.

We strolled into the camp trying to look like a family reluctant to say goodbye. Then, Peter hissed at me "Okay, give me the money."

"I want to see the papers."

'You a fool girl? Nobody gonna let us stan' 'round while you read these papers.'

"I don't want to read them," I interrupted, surprised at my own brazen determination. "I just want to make sure they are from the army and not just some bundle of scrap you put together."

He started to protest but Anna chimed in loudly asking to see the government papers that would commit her dear brother to the life of a soldier. She held them as if looking at the information inscribed upon them, but it was really me who observed and confirmed the papers were what Peter said they were.

Very slowly, I slipped the money out of my pocket and placed it on the sheaf of papers. Peter took the documents and before I could blink the money disappeared. He then asked me to hold the papers while he stooped to tie his bootlace.

"Tha's good. Tha's good. You in the army now girl... for better or worse, you a soldier."

"What do I do?"

Straightening up he told me to run along and find any sergeant from the 54th Massachusetts and present myself for duty. "They tell you where to go from there."

Anna clasped me to her bosom and bade me good luck. Peter shook my hand and we parted as any family would take leave of each other.

CHAPTER TEN

It did not take long to find a corporal who gave me directions to the orderly tent. From there it was a whirlwind of activity. All of the time I kept expecting to see Albert. Three days passed before he marched past me in a company of men and it took a supreme effort to keep from calling out, or worse, crying.

The clothes I was issued did not fit well yet so many of the men in Company K, where I had been placed, thought these were the best clothes they ever had. I could see that from the point of view of a slave who had been dressed in rags; and I understood the attachment to the uniform which stood for our cause; but as a woman these clothes were rough in their making and ill-fitting. Vowing to re-cut my battle blouse when the opportunity presented itself, I satisfied my urges to make the blue flannel suitable by drilling another hole in my belt to keep my pantaloons up.

You should know, Mrs. Lincoln, that the first men who joined the 54th were well uniformed. They were something to be proud of. The regiment received funds from many of Boston's leading Abolitionists and it was spent on our equipment. However, as time went on and our ranks grew with men clamoring to be taken in for the fight, these monies were insufficient. With the creation of the 55th Massachusetts, there was even more need to spread this purse further. My blouse was what was referred to as an arsenal coat. In other words, its manufacture was under the direction of the government at one of our federal arsenals. These blouses were at least lined to fend off some of the cold of the New England winter. Later equipment was commercially made and so shoddy, I would have commanded the firing squad myself to shoot the men who filled those contracts.

Mr. Lincoln must have been aware of these conditions. Was there nothing he could do?

It took the better part of the week to find Albert again. He was in Company C and although we drilled together on the same field, we never came into contact. Learning how to shoot and use a bayonet and regimental manoeuvres took up a great deal of my time as a new recruit. Finally Sunday came and we had half a day to do our laundry and visit around the camp. I immediately went off in search of Company C's tents.

When I saw him, he was standing at a washtub scrubbing a pile of wet clothing. Five other men were gathered around laughing and joking with each other. Two of the men were sitting on benches at a knock-up wooden table sewing on their uniforms. The other three appeared to be waiting on Albert to finish so they could take their turn with the tub.

Albert had the sleeves of his shirt rolled up on his arms. It was cold out, but that didn't seem to matter as he attacked the washboard vigorously all the while joking with the others. I did not know how to approach him without giving myself away. Surely the others would read his surprise and everything I had done so far would be for naught.

Standing there was purely foolish on my part, so I carried on, willing to satisfy myself with having seen him. I turned and began walking up the line of tents when I encountered one of the drummer boys from our regiment. Soldiers were not supposed to be recruited any younger than sixteen years of age, but this boy could not have been any older than twelve. I told him I needed to see Private Albert Johnson on a personal matter and offered him ten cents to run the errand. "Tell him an old friend from Buxton has just enlisted and I want to surprise him. If he's happy he may just give you another ten cents. I'll be waiting by the flagpole on the drill field."

Ten minutes later Albert made his way out from between the rows of tents and onto the parade ground. I could tell he did not recognize me, it being often easier to recognize someone you are expecting than someone you are not. He squinted at me trying to place my silhouette and I could see from the consternation on his face that he was having no success. As he approached, I turned my back to him, pretending I had yet to discern his presence, and waited for him.

"You..." or "Eunice," my ears were so stopped with tears and I could not tell which he uttered. "What are you doing here? Why are you dressed in uniform?"

At first I could not reply. I just needed to look at him. He moved toward me to take me in his arms, but I moved back away. No one could see us in the habit of man and wife. Then he realized this and stopped just staring at me.

"What are you doing here?"

"Please don't be mad. I have enlisted to be with you. I could not stand the thought of being alone on the farm for a moment longer or losing you in some battle so I have dressed as a man to share our fate whatever it is."

Tears welled in his eyes and it was all I could do to keep from bursting out myself, but I contained my feelings and pointed out to him that we could not let anyone see us or have someone suspect my secret. He had a lot of questions and I was willing to answer them all. But not at this time, nor in this place. Quickly we made an assignment to meet in the east woodlot after the camp settled down for the night.

I was flushed at the thought of the hours we would spend together. When the time came, I stepped over two of the three other men sleeping in my tent. When one of them stirred I uttered one word "latrine," counting on it to carry me to safety.

The night was the blue black of the hour preceding moonrise and held no threat of snow. I felt the Massachusetts seasons were about to change. Emerging from the night, the white canvas rows of tents glowed like the spirits of dead soldiers lined in their final ghostly ranks. All of the wind we had during the day had dropped and the still air held that crystalline chill of a night anticipating spring. Grippe was running through Camp Meigs and the occasional cough of a soldier suffering from it disturbed the silence. Otherwise the evening was quiet. The halyards hung loose, draping straight down on their flagpole and waiting for the morning when they would once again lift our flag. Sentries, knowing there was no enemy within five hundred miles, only moved when the cold penetrated their coats, but otherwise paid no attention to the lone private heading in the direction of the latrines.

My plan for getting into the woods was simple. Allowing the door to slam told the picket I had entered the latrine. Inside, I found one other soldier, nearly invisible in the dark, squatting on a hole. From the sounds he made he was suffering from dysentery. After a few minutes I rose, told my companion I hoped this would pass and closed the door quietly as I left. From the latrine, it was a simple matter to turn back into the trees after first checking there was no one walking the line.

Albert was already there and his arms wrapped me and held me tightly. I could smell his skin and feel the warmth of his breath on me, but I could not see his face. My fingers traced the lines of his shoulders, then his ears and finally his face. I needed to absorb every bit of him like a thirsty man needs to absorb water. He must have felt the same way, because his hands coursed through my hair and over my eyebrows. They drifted to those spots on my chest only a husband should be allowed to touch, then returned to my cheeks. But, he could not touch my lips because they were pressed upon his.

With his arms wrapped around me I did not feel the chill. I am sure you must have felt the same way with Mr. Lincoln. It is remarkable how we feel this way when we are with the right man. No cold can harm us when we are wrapped in their embrace; no danger is present; nor is there any sadness that cannot be overcome.

On the ground behind us, Albert spread his ticking and bedding making a nest. The comfort it gave me to finally ease myself into this small home was immense. I needed nothing else but him and a pallet to lie upon with him. And so we passed the night.

Reveille was cruel. We had not slept a wink. Instead we had mostly talked the night through. Albert wanted me to return to the farm and there await him. He did not want me to share his dangers, but I would not countenance this. I forced him to consider any alternate plan that would keep us together by telling him "… my efforts will not be for nothing. I am here and I am staying so you had better get used to it."

"I could disclose you to the captain. He will send you home in short order."

It was then I told him about selling our livestock and feed then giving the money over to Peter and Anna.

"Oh God!" was his reaction. "How much did you give them?"

"The three hundred dollars I will receive in bonus. It will take at least a month to…"

He stopped me.

"Coloured soldiers only get one hundred dollars and our pay is shorter than the white soldiers by three dollars a month. Some of the boys are saying they ain't even taking that. They figure if the army can't treat us the same as the whites, they won't take nothing at all."

Minutes ticked by as this news bored its way into my heart. I lost everything we worked for because I could not control my feelings. How could I have not seen what they were doing? At that point I started to weep. I betrayed him, unwittingly, but nonetheless I caused more grief and consternation than I knew I could correct.

Albert was quiet for a time, I am not sure how long, then he stroked my hair and told me we'd get along.

"But we can go after them and get the money back."

"No. That money is gone and so are they. They're probably in Boston or New York. They won't have gone far to start spending it, but they've gone far enough we'll never find them."

What he spoke was true. The money was gone and no tears or screaming imprecations would return it. Now, we would have to save up the money to restart the farm when we finished our service. He could not reveal me to the captain now, because we would need both pays to rebuild what I lost. So I wasn't sad the money was gone. It forced him to let me stay.

"We are both going to accept the pay, no matter how little it is. We need that money Albert."

"But the only way we're going to be recognized as being as good as the whites is if we refuse to accept anything less than what we're due. I became a soldier to fight for the slaves who still need to be free, not for the United States government."

"Be that what it may, Albert, we still need to save whatever money is available to us. It is my fault we lost it, but now I need your help to replace it. I will not be going home and I will not be turning down what's due to me for being a soldier and neither will you."

We continued to meet at night. Albert went to his company commander,

Captain Grace, and asked that I be transferred into Company C. "Private Jordan was a friend of my family back home in Canada. I promised his mama I would look after him if I could."

Grace, who was a nice man granted us permission if my own captain would accept the move. So it was that I became a member of Company C.

On a Sunday, just before April, Albert and I made arrangements to have our photographs taken. An itinerant ambrotypist set up his tent on the edge of our camp and offered pictures with our regimental flags and the Stars and Stripes. We had to bring our own muskets. For that we needed permission from an officer. All of our officers were white and most of them were strict, but good-natured. Others, not many, treated us with contempt. They were supposed to be Abolitionists and supporters of the notion that Negro troops could be as effective as white troops. I did not doubt this to be true. Albert found Lieutenant Dexter and asked his permission which was gladly given.

We took our place in line with a dozen other members of the 54th. The rifles we carried were the old Harper's Ferry muskets. The new Enfield rifles had just started to arrive in camp and as such were deemed too precious for pictures.

The interior of the artist's tent was set up with the flags and banners. What is never seen in these pictures is the smell. Acid permeated the interior air and it washed upon us whenever the leather-aproned assistant moved about creating a draught. It was not offensive, but not a normal smell we encountered. I now imagine it to be very much like the odor of the embalming tents set up on the edges of the great battlefields.

We were offered the choice of a white pillar to stand beside or a short table to lean against, but we chose to stand straight and at attention as if on duty. This was a common pose and the ambrotypist was used to it being requested. I went first and the assistant brought a brace up behind me and inserted my head and neck into it then clamped me so I was unable to move. Telling me to hold my breath, he took the cap off the lens of his apparatus. I watched his lips move silently as he counted the seconds to himself. I dared a small exhalation and inhalation, which brought the admonishment "… do not move." Finally it was over and I found myself trembling from the exertion while the assistant whisked the machine's magazine away only to return with another for Albert's portrait.

The photographs were a success. Albert's made him look fierce and handsome, but mine only accomplished a look of terror in me. I still have those pictures. The one of Albert is the only one of him left to me and I keep it in my linen drawer sneaking it out whenever Frederick is out of the house. I often stroke it and think of those things that might have been.

April broke fair and sweet. The air was beginning to warm with each passing day. We were up at five every morning to perform close order drills with our squads until late in the afternoon when we would have a full dress parade. Colonel Shaw was our regimental commander and he made us work hard. He was supposed to be from a big Abolitionist family in Boston and a friend of Governor Andrew's, but I occasionally heard him describe us to the other white officers as 'nig's' and 'darkies', which I was not in much appreciation of. In spite of this, I was becoming extremely proud of my regiment and the men in it. Strength I had never known was building within me and I could lift, haul and shoot with the best of the men.

It did not take long before we had the full complement of companies and orders came down that we were to move south to take our part. First, though, we were to be paraded in Boston so the public could see we were well disciplined and trained beyond what much of the public believed Negroes capable of. I suspect some of our original officers would have been amazed at what we became.

The parade through the streets of that eastern city was as thrilling a moment as I have ever known. After travelling by train into the heart of Boston early on the morning of May twenty-eighth, we formed up on the parade ground at Park Square and began to march in a column preceded by our regimental band. Governor Andrew presented us with our regimental colours and for the first time we unfurled the battle flag we would campaign under. I will admit now, as both a woman and soldier, that my eyes filled with tears at the sight of that splendid bunting. Nor, was I alone in this.

Before leaving for the city, we were issued six rounds of ball cartridge. No one knew what would happen when we marched through the city. Many of Boston's police were Irishmen who were not above beating a soldier in their country's uniform and had proven their willingness to do this on several occasions. Orders also came down from our commanding officers that the men of the rear guard companies would march with fixed bayonets.

We all prayed we would not need these appliances.

Hither to I did not appreciate marshal music, but marching becomes very much like dancing to an easy rhythm when a band plays an air like "The Northern Star" or even "Dixie". But the song we loved above all was "The Battle Hymn of the Republic". It explained everything that graced our hearts in those moments. From the gusto with which we voiced it, anyone listening would immediately understand our ambition.

Whenever some brave lad hiding among the crowd spat invective at us, we responded with John Brown's Body and in particular the stanza that announced we would "... hang Jeff Davis from a sour apple tree." This was usually enough to make the hidden speaker cower behind some woman, especially when he realized these sable men in blue uniforms meant it seriously.

When we detrained, the preparations of the early morning hours weighed upon us. The trouble we expected was like a forecast of rain that does not fall. Instead, a wonderfully strange thing occurred. Shock was evident on the faces of the people. They had known there were two regiments of Negroes preparing to join the Grand Union Army, but this seemed more a myth about an event that was occurring in some other country rather than right in their home county. Then someone, I did not see who, cheered.

'Three cheers for Colonel Shaw… Hip, hip hurrah! Hip, hip hurrah! Hip, hip hurrah!'

By the time the final cheer sang out, I could no longer hear the speaker. His voice was lost in a sea of wild cheering. From there the day grew in momentum. We performed drills on the Common with people rushing up and touching us and shaking our hands. Our movements were precise and impressive as we looked straight ahead: proud in our bearing. Shopkeepers closed their stores and schools shut up for the day. I later heard, the railroad ran more trains to bring in the crowds that wanted to see us.

Albert marched by my side and would occasionally turn his head to give me a happy wink or his largest smile. He was happy and so was I. As our right arms swung in time to our step, our left arms were occupied with our rifles. Still, he would move close to me and brush me with his swinging hand sending an immense thrill through me.

A few ruffians made the mistake of harassing the companies at the tail end of our column and were given short shrift by our soldiers as we marched down to the harbour that had seen so much.

A camp rumour made the rounds during the day that we were to be transported to New York and marched along the entire length of Broadway, but rumour was all it was. The people of New York proved themselves to be murderously less willing to accept Negroes than were the kindly people of Boston.

CHAPTER ELEVEN

The troop ship we were on nudged along in a southerly direction. Many of the men, who had escaped from slavery, could use the stars and had no need of a compass. I had never been interested in the heavens and so the North Star looked very much the same as the South Star to me. Several of the men, including George Stephens had been sailors and knew what to expect. As we passed the bell buoy at the northeast end of The Graves, the ocean swell commenced and almost the entire regiment became seasick.

Our destination was unknown to us. I had heard it argued that Negroes would be better suited to the southern climes because we had been broken in the heat of the cotton fields and rice plantations. The officer who espoused this view should have known better as most of the men in his company were from the northern states where winter snow was more familiar. Daily, some expert would prophesy our destination. We would invade Charleston or Savannah or we would strike at Richmond from the sea. In truth only Colonel Shaw and the ship's officers knew our landing place.

This worried those of us who had no opinions one way or the other. Many held the private belief that we would be given over to digging and constructing rather than fighting.

Mrs. Lincoln, I could not imagine the change that had come over me. I was now a soldier and I was overjoyed at the mere thought of it despite my womanhood. There is no gender under a uniform, but there is a heart and I had the heart of a soldier.

The 54th and 55th were not the first coloured regiments to be mustered into service. General Butler had recruited a regiment in New Orleans from the free population of that city and the First Kansas Coloured regiment was recruited before us, but not mustered in until after. General Hunter had started recruiting Negroes the summer before we were allowed to fight and that was when Albert made up his mind to return to the United States. I don't know why, but at the time your husband disbanded Hunter's unit.

Early one morning four or five days after we left Boston steaming southward we began passing a stretch of islands off the ship's right side. Near the mouth of a broad channel between these islands a fleet of Union ships lay at anchor. The air was becoming hotter and thick with moisture, which set up a haze, and we could not see much further than the ships. Stephens told me this was the mouth of Charleston Harbour and that is where this whole war had started. The islands themselves looked low and unwelcoming. From what I had learned in my career as a soldier, I could see that the land was good for defense if you were the first troops there and could entrench. If not, the open stretches of beach on the islands' outer shores would make it nigh unto impossible for troops to try to seize anything by frontal assault.

While I ruminated on this, Stephens pointed to a small steamer and exclaimed, 'That is the *Planter!*'

The *Planter* and her Negro pilot, Robert Small, were well known to many of us. His act of heroism in stealing that ship had helped to convince many of our white detractors that we were not simply Topsies to be humoured and patronized, but serious people who could act on our own and accomplish great things. Still, the majority of my comrades had not heard the story and asked Stephens what it was all about.

I did not like Stephens. He was arrogant about his ability to write and read. I could not reveal my own equal accomplishments in those disciplines for fear that I might be forced to reveal my womanhood. Thus far I had been cautious, continually wearing a singlet beneath my shirts and blouse. I bathed late at night when no one would see me and I developed a reputation as being strangely shy. My woman's attributes are not large, but they are large enough as to leave no doubt about my sex. Albert teased me about this often when we had a moment of privacy. The one thing he never taunted me over was my education. In school I always scored higher on tests and got more of Reverend King's questions right and he respected me for this. Albert knew I could not confront Stephens with this, and so could not defend me when Stephens never missed a chance to lord his education over those in the regiment who never had the opportunity of an education. He impressed some and hurt others. Many took him for what he was.

'One year ago, very near this day,' he began 'Robert Small stole that ship and presented it to Commodore DuPont.

'Pilot Small was the best pilot on Charleston waters and knew every sandbar and snag in the surrounding rivers. For his owner he was a real boon. I have heard it said that he was smarter than the man who owned the ship. It does not matter. Over the years he performed exceptional services for the people of Charleston and the ship captain who used his skills. A good waterman.

'Small could have been content with his lot. He had a house in Darktown and his wife and children were safe from being sold off as long as Daddy performed well. Still, he wanted to be free. You see he was part of the inventory of that ship, just the same as the engine or the capstan or ship's wheel. If the owner decided to sell the Planter, Small would have been a part of the arrangements.

This did not appeal to Small. I do not know if this was the case Mrs. Lincoln. Small may have had other motives for pirating the vessel. I understand that Congress voted to award Small and his crew half the value of the vessel as a prize for its delivery. Later in the evening I asked Stephens if he had ever met Small and in a moment of truthfulness he acknowledged that he had not actually met the man. I queried him no further, but his response helped set my opinion of him.

'Late one night, when the *Planter's* captain had gone ashore to see his wife, he left Small in charge of the ship. Other than the captain and mate, the rest of the crew were bondsmen. The captain did not believe Small and his fellows capable of such an act of treachery. I presume they thought he was just another happy darkie. So even though captain and the mate were not supposed to go ashore while they were at dock in Charleston, the white crew went home.'

One of the listening soldiers looked at Stephens with admiration for the tale being told and asked 'How them niggers know that was the night to steal that ship?'

"Easy. Small was treated as a gentleman would be. It was widely believed he was trustworthy and the plans for the next voyage were divulged so he could prepare to navigate the passages among the harbour islands. The *Planter* was to take four canons and a large cargo of balls and shells from Coles Island to Fort Ripley with the overnight stop in Charleston.

'Long before first light, Small put his plan into action. Their families had already made their way to a warehouse ship tied up at the North Atlantic wharf. Their strategy had been laid out weeks before and would be carried out as soon as they knew when they would be sent to fetch the canon.

'As bold as brass, Small sounded the whistle and hoisted the Palmetto then, with a lot of noise to convince the sentries on the wharf that they were leaving on their proper business the Planter left the dock heading out into the stream.

'Each time they passed a signaling point where they were required to sound the whistle they made the necessary signal and received recognition from shore and a friendly wave to speed them on their way.'

The soldiers on the deck were listening to the story as if Stephens were writing a new gospel. Some of them were moving from one foot to the other with excitement at Stephens' retelling and I confess, I was enjoying the story.

'How that ship get away? They flying a Secesh flag so if the Reb's didn't shoot 'em then the Federals would have.' It was the same soldier asking another question. Several of his friends hushed him impatiently so Stephens could get on with his story.

"Well that's where they were really smart. Once they passed Fort Sumter they hoisted a bed sheet to the flagstaff, but it almost did not work. The first of our blockade ships that they approached at dawn loaded a broadside ready to fire because they knew it was Confederate ship. The Secesh don't have good coal and so it burns with a lot of smoke. Look at our stack,' he pointed upward and every face followed his arm. There was heat and a small bit of white smoke coming from the two big vents. 'Our coal burns clean while the Rebs' burns black and you can see them coming from ten miles off.

'Anyway, the Union ship was about to fire when her captain saw the bed sheet and bade his men hold their fire.

'When the *Planter* pulled alongside, Small addressed the captain as one equal to another and this surprised the Federal man. 'My name is Robert Small,' he yelled between the two wheelhouses 'and I bring you the ship *Planter* and four Carolina canons as a gift. We have our families with us and beg to be free.'

'With that the captain sent troops aboard the *Planter* and, after searching her, welcomed the Contraband families. He then sent Small and his crew on to Commodore DuPont who received him as a hero.'

It was stories like these that gave us spirit and convinced us that when our test came we would be up to it, no matter the cost.

Later, I heard that among the canons carried by the ship was one of those that fired in the barrage on Sumter that started the war. Little did we suspect our own test would come on the very shore the Planter had sailed by and which we were now passing.

The heat became almost intolerable. Many men stripped to their shirts wrapping their woolen battle blouses in their kits below decks. I doffed my blouse, but kept my shirt and singlet on and by the first bell in the forenoon watch I was so wet it looked like someone had doused me with a bucket of water. A few minutes after I noted this, someone did in fact douse me with a bucket of seawater and general mayhem in the form of a water fight broke out on deck. Men used deck buckets to haul up gallons of water for their play and the sailors who should have been using those same buckets for work stood back watching and laughing.

The officers let us play until we had all cooled off then brought order back to the deck.

Two days later we steamed into the river off Hilton Head Island.

Hilton Head, Mrs. Lincoln, is low and marshy. It is absolutely plagued with mosquitoes and flies that do not hesitate for a moment to tear a chunk of living flesh from your arms or neck. When the tide went out we could smell the rot of the bottom and the sense of decay reminded us we were in the South and why we had come.

Colonel Shaw and Lieutenant-Colonel Hallowell did not give us a moment's peace. It was 'git-and-go' as we would say, from dawn until dark. At first we set up our tents upon the raw ground as there was no lumber for flooring, but that was soon remedied. Most of what we did was labour and drill. We all wanted to fight. Myself included in that school.

By now, I thought of myself more a man than a woman. This feeling was marched into my feet and slammed into my shoulder by the recoil of my rifle. I thought of nothing else than finding a rebel in my sights and pulling the trigger. I wanted to watch as my Minnie balls would tear him into fragments and anticipated the elation I would experience when the opportunity arose. My longing was now as much for the destruction of a barrage as it was for Albert. This was a blood thirst no woman should experience and expect to stay a woman. Yet, as I say, this was the emotion that overcame me.

For a brief period rumours floated through our camp that we would be armed only with pikes and used as defensive troops and labourers. Whatever became of that plan or if it was even true, I do not know. If it was indeed afoot, I believe Colonel Shaw quashed it because in the second week of June we were loaded on troop ships with the 2nd South Carolina under Colonel Montgomery. We steamed up what turned out to be the Altamaha River into Georgia and anchored in the stream while our naval guns unleashed a veritable hell of shells upon the small town of Darien.

While the cannonading was going on, we lined the rails of the ships cheering as each shell landed blowing apart a home or mill. Even hog pens suffering the indiscriminate destruction brought on manly hurrahs. When the bombardment was finally over, we made our way to the shore in ships' boats and fanned out through the town. Col. Shaw, mounted on his horse, directed us. There were a few scattered musket balls from the trees, but the town was ours from the moment we arrived.

The 54th behaved as soldiers. We held our lines, returned fire where directed and enveloped the town with our presence. All was in good order and I heard Col. Shaw speaking above the noise.

"Go through the town to ensure no Rebels are left behind. Spare the women, children and old men. Sergeants, your troops may enter private homes, but they are to take only what we can use in camp. Any man seeking profit for himself from our enemy's misfortune will be dealt with."

Lt.-Col. Hallowell repeated the orders and they passed down through the ranks. I doubt that any man would have disobeyed them because this is what we had come to do.

Col. Montgomery's troops were less than disciplined. Some of our soldiers called him Bushwhacker Montgomery. This term was one we learned from members of his own regiment. He believed, like General Sherman, in all-out war, and turned his troops loose to rob and burn.

They worked at frightening the women of the town and, I believe, may have even forced themselves upon some of these ladies. Nothing could have sickened me more than being lumped in with the brutishness of these men. Later I was gladdened to hear my fellow soldiers in the 54th also viewed this conduct as unsoldierly.

Upon our return to Hilton Head, Col. Shaw was said to have written a letter to Governor Andrew decrying the acts of Montgomery and asking for a real chance to prove our mettle in battle. Whether it was this letter that authored our next expedition or it was already being planned I do not know, but less than a month after Darien we were loaded once again onto ships and sailed north.

Our order of battle for the upcoming campaign saw the 54th placed with General Gilmore. We were still under General Terry, but he was subject to Gilmore's orders and planning. Our one constant was Col. Shaw. Except when we were preparing to fight or on manoeuvres I did not see much of Col. Shaw. What I did see and what I heard made me think he was starting to change his appreciation of us. He no longer called us 'darkies' and Topsies to our face and the word 'nigger' seemed to have been eradicated from his vocabulary. As he was becoming happy to serve with us, I was becoming content to serve him.

CHAPTER TWELVE

The day we read about the victories of July fourth at Vicksburg and Gettysburg was one of celebration and we almost took the entirety of James Island at the mouth of Charleston Harbour. There were more than five thousand of us and we felt like we would be in Charleston in the morning. Even this far out from the city, we imagined we could hear the city's bells toll the hours of the day. The island was infested with sand fleas that made us miserable in their voraciousness, so I was relieved when our company and two others were ordered back to picket duty on a small island between the mainland and Morris Island.

We were guarding the end of a causeway that led directly to the mainland. It was easy duty and we were able to rest for several days. I would be more specific in this Mrs. Lincoln except that I can no longer remember something so insignificant. Do you remember the entirety of the day on which Mr. Lincoln was murdered? I would be surprised to hear you do. The momentous events that occur on a day overshadow all we know of commonplace actions with their enormity. I cannot even remember the date my father died. I have to look in the family bible or at his gravestone to find it. All I have is a fleeting memory that it was a fine late-spring morning when he passed on.

One of the things I do remember of that day before the fight is the fact Albert and I were able to steal some time to be together as man and wife.

Our lives had changed since we joined the army. Some of it was for the better. I can think of no stronger bond to a man, any man, than sharing mortal danger with him. By the end of the Darien action I felt closer to George Stephens that I did to my own brother Morgan and I did not like Mr. Stephens in the least bit.

Dear Mrs. Lincoln. You shared your husband's trials and dangers and so you must have some inkling as to how I felt about Albert.

It was taking a chance, but while we were on picket duty together one night, just after the change of the midnight guard, Albert and I had private time in a thicket with our rifles leaning against a tree. We reckoned dawn was too far away for the Secesh to commence an action and our officer had come by on his inspection and opined the same wishing us a peaceful evening.

As far as we could see, the island we were on was little more than a bump in the salt marsh. There were two causeways connecting it to another island, or the mainland, we were not sure which. But whatever it was, it looked to have more substance than our pitiful patch of ground. The entirety of the region was darned with creeks and rivers while the nights and days were sewn with mosquitoes. On our island, there was only low scrub and the occasional tree with those broad, fan-shaped leaves that prosper in salted soil. When the tide was out, the mud flats all over the island gave off a consumptive odour. There was nothing about the pleasant seashore in it.

I have looked for the name of that island in the history books Frederick keeps and even asked Reverend King about it, but it seems to remain a piece of ground so luckless it does not bear a name.

Albert bade me to sleep for the rest of our watch. I was most grateful for this and the night seemed very calm. He was a good man, always thinking of me and when privacy allowed, Albert would show it in any number of ways.

He had been like that from the time I met him. I first remember how, in school, he tolerated boys who were his age, but not quite so robust. He could have ruled the schoolyard with one mild threat, but instead used his gentle strength to move our play and schooling in ways that benefited all. For this, all the boys admired him, as did more than a few girls. I don't know what he saw in me. I was, by my own truth, ugly and skinny. Morgan told me later I was unpleasant to most folks and could be very mean if people did not accord me my wishes. Still, Albert's eyes grew bright and so full of light when we first met you would think him possessed.

I was sent to fetch Morgan to tend to some chores. The village boys were playing at war, running in and out of the oak and hickory thicket to attack and withdraw from the imagined battle. Today I see how these were not games but training for the higher calling of men. At the time I thought it a vainglorious waste of time. To me, those boys were so insignificant I would not allow them to even speak to me. Then Albert stepped out from behind a tree carrying the stick he fancied as a sword.

His hair was cut close to his skull and his scalp glistened through it, but the strands of hair were tightly curled. What you Americans call nappy. Albert's skin was the color and fine grain of stained black walnut. It shone even on the coldest day as though he had been working hard. But his eyes were what captured me. They were liquid with irises of such a deep brown that if you glanced quickly without really looking, you would simply say they were black. But they were not. They changed with the position of the sun. The whites of his eyes were brilliant and enhanced by the perfection of his teeth. The only time I recall ever seeing him without a smile was sometimes when he was talking or singing. He knew a world of hymns and popular songs, but as much as he loved to sing, it was an even greater pleasure for him to talk intelligently about any topic. As I have already told you how much he valued his education, I will not go into that again.

Suffice it to say, he could hold his own with George Stephens and often the two ended, not in discord, but in agreement. Although Stephens had never been a slave, he came close to being one once and the experience gave him a binding sympathy with Albert's past. On the occasion they could not come to an agreement on a topic, Albert gave as good as he got, often winning the arguments. I think he would have been delighted to write about our experiences in the Insurrection had he survived. Stephens wrote for a Negro newspaper in New York or Boston, I am not sure which, but it was a popular thing for our men to do and even Frederick contributed stories to the newspaper in Chatham. Not a lot of what has since been written about the war was authored by Negroes, but if you desire knowledge of our experience Mrs. Lincoln, then you would do well to read what they wrote. This is particularly true today as I see new laws and public actions mentioned in the dispatches that curtail the American coloured's freedom once again. I believe that once General Sherman is finished killing the Indians, our turn will be next and then the Chinese and then the Jews and then the Catholics until there is only one type of American left.

But I have strayed from my path here. Just before dawn on the island Albert and I were set to defend, we heard the commencement of a cannonade. The Rebel batteries strung along the Stono River were opening on the gunboats that protected us. We did not know it, but the fusillade was furious enough to drive the ships away leaving us to the mercy of the Secesh ground forces.

With the explosion of the canons and their shells, I came fully awake and took up my musket. Albert and I were a small out-picket of a larger group. Captain Grace had set us there to make sure the Confederates did not cross over to harry our main encampment. We were still convinced our position was secure, but we did not count on General Hagood sending more than three thousand men from his camp at Secessionville.

As the dark dwindled to be replaced by hazy, dawn light, we heard the voices and yells of a sizeable force approaching our position. Moving within the trees on the other side of the causeway were hundreds of men. Albert stood stalk still watching them in awe.

'Albert. We can't stop them. We have to get our captain.' He stood there until I pulled him by the arm and we ran back to our main bivouac to fetch more men.

Returning to the causeway, we were just in time to see the first ranks start out to cross. Enfilading fire came from across the river against both our right and left flanks, but our men held true, waiting. We waited as the tread of their step drew closer. They were not the undisciplined mob some of us had convinced ourselves they were. I was among those whose newfound soldierly posture convinced me there were none like us in all the world and that any Rebel who dared confront us would feel the heat of my Minnie ball and cold of my steel and I would escape unharmed.

But here was a true army marching in practiced files toward us with death in their eyes. Not their demise, but ours. My whole body began to quake. Sweat trickled out from under my kepi and the salt of it stung my eyes. Then the order to take aim came from the sergeants behind us. With that, I ceased shivering and looked down the barrel of my rifle toward our attackers and waited, only this time measuring the wait not by their footfalls, but by counting my own heartbeats.

This was the first time I sighted on a man with the intention of ending his life. The soldier I chose was dressed in a baggy brown rig and looked to be about thirty years old. His face showed no fear of the imminent fight, but his eyes flashed with hate when he saw that he was facing a Federal company made up of Negroes. It was like I could read his mind. How dare we pick up a musket? This was a white man's war, about white men's affairs. When the order came to fire, I felt no sorrow in erasing that thought from his mind and this earth.

Our first volley staggered them, but the press of men guaranteed their momentum. We loaded and fired and loaded and fired. Powder, ball, cap, fire; powder, ball, cap and fire. After the first organized musketry from our lines, we began loading and firing without direction. It was to good effect, but not enough to stall their surging and they were on us.

As they swept the causeway killing all the defenders, they broke ranks and loped to a charge shrieking that horrific Rebel yell which I wish never to hear again. The air was so thick with smoke I aimed at the sound, not at any one person, for I could not make a body out. Behind, hidden by the smoke some evil machine began a dull roar that grew in its intensity until it sounded like the doorway to Hell had opened and all of Beelzebub's demons were spewing forth. Despite the blinding fog, we knew horses and their malicious riders armed with sabers and carbines were the composers of that terrible beat.

"Cavalry," was the one word shouted by our men above the din.

To my left and right, many of our soldiers began to turn away. The officers and NCOs were yelling to hold the line, but panic set in and more men began fleeing. The ones who still had some control over their terror kept their rifles. Others just fired them and dropped the empty guns before fleeing.

I had reloaded when a group of three men broke out of the smoke. I took aim then stopped from pulling the trigger. The man bearing down on me was not white. He was a Negro, just like me, but dressed in butternut. He saw me but did not stop. I wanted him to stop. I wanted him to see that I was coloured as well, but he was blind. All he saw in me was my blue blouse and Enfield rifle. He had no business attacking me. I was there to free him. Still he came on. I wished him out of there, pleading silently that he turn round. My prayer was that he would turn back when he realized who we were, or that he would at least stumble. But, still he came on. When he was ten feet from me and I could see the pitting in his skin and individual strands of his beard I pulled the trigger and he dropped. Then I too fled.

I ran completely across the island to a boardwalk that was threaded through the salt marsh. It was only when I started across this that I realized I lost Albert in the fray. He was not beside me as I expected. My heart wanted to turn back for him, but fear drove me forward. On the other side of the boardwalk, I paused to look back and saw ten of our men slowly retreating. It was Albert, George Stephens and eight others turning and firing at hidden attackers. One-by-one, eight of those Spartans died. Albert made it across and Stephens was the last man to escape.

Our training had made me keep my rifle. Before leaving camp the day before, I loaded forty rounds into my cartridge box and when I reached our camp where a defensive line was set up, I found there to were only two left.

We managed to slow the onrush, which let the rest of our regiment arm for battle and allowed a Connecticut battery bring their guns to bear. The gunboats were able to shoot their way into Stono Creek and give us supporting fire, but in spite of all this, the surviving Secessionists persisted and fought us back onto Battery Island where we created a perimeter and small redoubt. The men and one woman of the Massachusetts 54th now knew what our senior comrades already did – Southern soldiers would not avoid a fight and were not cowards, but we hoped they now knew Negros were cut from the same harsh fabric.

That evening we re-established our camp on the unnamed island where our forces were massed. The Connecticut artillerists who rescued us with their guns were almost trapped on James Island at Grimball's Landing. We learned the next day, when they came forward to our camp, that our actions in that battle had saved them and they were profoundly grateful and sorrowful for our losses.

Confederate soldiers continued to snipe our pickets, but the battle was over. We knew that there would be more fighting within a day or two, but for the moment we could rest and repair our equipment. Albert was transfigured by this fight, as were Stephens and many others. They had come to fight and prove we were capable of being soldiers and citizens. This, and more, was accomplished. For me, I had come to look after Albert and share his fate, not his glory. I could not partake of their glory or risk a wound. If I did, someone would discover my secret and I would be forcibly separated from my husband.

The morning of July 18 was a day so perfect I would have loved to be home on our farm. I remember imagining its fields with their maize and wheat all neatly laid out and Albert walking among his fields, stooping to pull a weed or open an ear to check on the progress of the crops. I drank several canteens of coffee, dipping my hardtack into them, rejoicing that God had made just such a day.

Before long, word came down the line that we should be ready to move. All day we waited in camp, then early in the afternoon the drums began calling us and we marched east among the dunes toward Morris Island.

The sand was soft making our march hard and slow. The dunes were covered with grasses and little else. I remember thinking 'it's a good thing there is no wind because these granular waves would have had an irritating spindrift'. Beyond the dunes the blockade ships began a rolling barrage. Hopefully men were dying and breastworks were falling somewhere further north on the island. Our troops had not been able to advance past the big earthen fort that straddled the island protecting the top third of it. No one said as much, but we knew our attack would be made on this.

Called Battery Wagner by the Secesh, none of us had ever seen it, but we knew all about it. Descriptions flew up and down the lines as we marched. Some thought it would be an easy victory, reasoning that we must have taken the fight out of the Rebels two days earlier. Others predicted a devastating failure from which no one survived. I could not countenance that. Our generals, Gilmore and Terry, were not wasteful men and would not spend our lives without some gain. Another rumour had it that General Gilmore singled out the 54th specifically for this assault. How a private soldier would have come by this intelligence still baffles me, but I found it later to be true.

Then we assembled on the beach with our officers. Albert and I were too far back to hear any of the speech made by Colonel Shaw, so I simply watched the shell bursts dapple the sky with smoke above an island without trees.

After a while, the shelling lifted and the corporals and sergeants ordered us forward. We had a mile, maybe a mile-and-a-half to cover before we reached the embankments of the fort. At first we were beyond canon range and so it was like a pleasant walk along the beach. Then we were ordered to quick time and it became a pleasant trot.

Someone on the ships must have been watching us through a telescope for as we closed on the fort our shelling lightened and lifted. We were still far enough away that the figures scrambling on the ramparts were small and indistinguishable. They were out in the open without fear, being well beyond rifle range. Could I shoot at them? I would have gladly. Their comrades had killed more than forty-five of my friends during the battle on the small island, but the lessons of that battle stuck with me. I wanted to save my cartridges until they would do the most good.

Our trot broke into a run and with the start of that run, we issued our own manly "Hurrah" to frighten the enemy and give strength to our own legs.

Those men in the fort were cool. They took their time depressing the muzzles of their guns and aiming to do the most damage to us. I guess when all was ready according to their needs an unheard voice must have given the order to fire.

At first we did not hear anything. A wave of smoke roiled out and up from the gun emplacements along that wall. In the next instant, men in our front ranks began to fall, then that debilitating sound reached us. It brought me up sharp for a second with its mass. Mrs. Lincoln, sound like that truly does have weight and I felt it strike me. Other soldiers were now running past me and I could see Albert striding ahead with his rifle at port. We were still too far for our muskets to do any good. Not wanting to lose him, I began to run along the beach. Shells from the fort were now bursting in the air over top of us and men were being driven straight into the ground as though hammered by some unseen mallet.

They say that time slows down in battle. It does, but you are not aware of it. Those movements you perform with alacrity seem casual in their execution as you accomplish them. You do one thing after another in perfect order and it all seems very natural. I held my rifle in front of my chest and ran as fast as I could to catch up with Albert.

Drawing near to him, I saw the strangest site. The sand of the beach we were charging was hard-packed making it easy to advance. The rebels in the fort knew this from having control of the island for so long and used it to their advantage. While some batteries continued to fire shells to good effect over our heads, others were loading balls and firing them so they skipped off the sand. Dozens of balls came bounding toward us and in our frenetic state, we could see where they would strike and could dodge them. It was after they passed the front ranks, who managed to avoid them, that they caught some hapless foot soldier in the leg or arm shearing off that appendage. I watched horrified as men had their heads torn from their bodies and all of this only inspired me to run harder to be with Albert lest something should happen to either of us.

Albert, like many of the other soldiers, had misjudged the distance of the charge and was now slowing his pace. I was finally catching up to him when a ball came skipping down the beach kicking up small sprays of wet sand. It struck him below his ribcage and sheared him in half. His blood and parts were dashed over me. I stopped and looked at him on the sand.

There was only the top half of him there. His hips and legs were gone. I never saw them again.

It was like the ball had taken me. I always felt it would be better for me to die than Albert, but it was he who now lay on the sand. Dropping my rifle I skidded to his side. His eyes were already half closed and unfocused in the death stare. I am sure I screamed something at him but I do not know to this day if I did. Holding him to me in the midst of that battle, I rocked back and forth, weeping. Why I was never hit, I do not know. Maybe I had been such a bad person to everyone except Albert, that God was taking him away from me leaving me to endure unscathed as a punishment.

There was a lull in the fighting and our soldiers began to regroup. George Stephens, crouching low to avoid the occasional musket ball that strayed our way, found me and yelled at me that we were attacking again and that I needed to fight, '...everyone needs to fight in this charge.' He took me by the arm and tried to pull me away from Albert, but I resisted. Then he threatened to shoot me with a pistol he was carrying.

Nothing could now make me fight. Spinning away from Albert's body I stood up to him and ripped open my blouse and shirt showing him my breasts. He stopped then walked away. I needed to say nothing more.

After dark, I left the fight. It was still going on when I made it to the dunes where I lay down and slept.

The next morning, I threw away my cap and blouse leaving only my shirt. I went back to our camp, but not to our regiment in case Stephens had survived. From there I was placed on a transport back to Port Royal and when the opportunity presented itself, transformed myself into a woman once again and began making my way north. I will not tell you how I raised the money for that return journey, as it is shameful and I had no shame. Suffice it to say, I arrived in Buxton and had to depend on my brother Morgan for my living.

That is my story Mrs. Lincoln. You and I have shared the sad harvest of the war, and reap no future because of it. I will live on with Frederick until I die, which I sincerely hope is soon, but I wanted you to know there are others who feel what you feel and cry the same tears you cry.

Sincerely, your friend and soldier
Eunice Johnson,
(who is also known by the name Everett Jordan)

EPILOGUE

June 30, 1879

It has been three days since I read Eunice's letter to Mrs. Lincoln. It was so stark and frightening that my first inclination was to burn it, but I have seen too much dissembling and lying around this war to destroy such a historical document. No, I will place it here in the diary with the letters from General Sherman and Mrs. Lincoln then decide what to do with it at some later date when my heart is clear and I can think straight and honestly.

Not wanting to leave off writing to Mrs. Lincoln without an explanation, I prepared the following letter and forwarded it to her yesterday. I could not bring myself to burden her with Eunice's letter as the poor widow has had so much grief already.

> Frederick Macdonald,
> C/O General Delivery
> Buxton, Ontario
> Canada

Mrs. Abraham Lincoln,
Pau, France

> June 29,1879

Dear Mrs. Lincoln,

Because of the tragedy to befall you and your family, the war wound down beyond your view and I can add nothing more than what was in my memoirs, which were forwarded to you in January.

This is likely to be my last letter to you for some time as sorrow has struck my own family. My wife is ill and this illness now has forced me to place her in an asylum. I realize just the idea of placing someone in such an institution must gall you and I can only imagine what you may think of me for taking such drastic action, but I assure you it was not done with malice or lightly. My wife has a condition, which has seen her become increasingly violent toward those around her. I did not wish to take this decision on my own so I consulted Dr. Abbott closely and he recommended a good facility in London, Ontario, where we hope treatment will be successful.

She will be under the care of Dr. Bucke who is very well regarded in the treatment of psychiatric disorders. We do not understand as of yet what has happened, but I believe it may be a result of the war.

My wife wanted to write to you, but her illness has prevented such an undertaking. She regards you as a personal friend, a friend to our family and a friend to our race.

It has been a great honour to be your correspondent and I will always feel indebted to you and the president for freeing my people from bondage. When our current situation has been resolved I will endeavour to once again be of service to you. Until that time I give to you with all the warmth of my heart, my best and fondest wishes.

Sincerely
Frederick Macdonald

This morning I wrote to the General accepting the invitation to the Chicago Convention in the autumn. Then I addressed the dictionary writers in London offering my services. We will see where this journey will take me. I just wish I had some company for it…"

Notes On Historic Facts and Fiction

The Fugitive's Son is based on historical fact and so are many of its characters. The period from 1829 to 1865 was an intensely interesting era affecting both British Canada and the United States and the joint histories of North America did not stop flowing at the borders.

Our third family member, Mexico, was the first country in North America to outlaw slavery in 1829 - more than seven years before the Alamo battle was fought. When Texas won its independence from Mexico it reinstituted slavery in 1836. France and Britain worked their way through various permutations of bans before England banned slavery at home in all colonies except in territories controlled by the East India Company and Ceylon (today's Sri Lanka). Britain instituted numerous bilateral agreements to curtail slavery and dedicated a good portion of its naval forces to patrolling the waters off West Africa where numerous slaving voyages originated. Before the Civil War a number of U.S. states like New York, Illinois and Pennsylvania reduced slave holdings to indentured servitude and eventually full freedom.

In Canada a number of historic actions took place. During the War of 1812 a group of black soldiers who fought on the British side in the American Revolution was formed. It was called The Black Corps (also known as Runchey's Company of Coloured Men) and it fought at the battles of Queenston Heights and Fort George. In the post-war period a mixed group of blacks and whites did free a captured slave from a railway carriage near St. Catharine's. Slave catchers did periodically make their way north into Canada in the hope of easy prey. Many black Canadians did return south to fight in the Civil War. One of the most important regiments in the U.S. Colored Troops was the 102 Michigan. It contained a number of men from the Buxton Settlement.

Many of the people used in this novel (and remember it is a work of fiction) were real. John Brown, Martin Delany, Rufus Stephenson, George Brown, Elizabeth Keckley, Dr. Anderson Abbott, William Tecumseh Sherman and his officers, Ulysses S. Grant, Osborne Anderson, Mary Ann Shadd, Thomas Wentworth Higginson, Laura Towne, Ellen Murray, Charlotte Forten and many more are recorded in the pages of history.

John Brown really did work in and around Chatham. He organized a series of meetings, held at the British Methodist Church, the Princess Street School and on May 8 1858 at the First Baptist Church in Chatham. His men were drilled in Tecumseh Park. He also visited several other Southern Ontario towns to raise funds and recruit soldiers for his raid on Harper's Ferry later that fall. One of the men he recruited for what he called his "Kansas work," was a white Canadian, Stewart Taylor, from Uxbridge, Ontario, who died in the final assault by federal troops on the Harper's Ferry engine house. He is buried alongside Brown at the Brown Family Homestead (National Historic Site) near Lake Placid in upstate New York.

I did, of course, make up characters like Frederick, Eunice, Martha and Absolom. It would be hard to move the plot of a book like this forward without some license in that area. To advance the plot I took the liberty of putting words in the mouths of the historic figures.

Many of the settings in the book come from first hand observation while writing stories about the African-Canadian Trail in Southern Ontario, travels in the United States and interviews with historians.

I tried to make this novel as historically accurate as possible so the reader will have a real sense of the pre-Civil War period, the Civil War and the lives of the fugitive's slaves. The descendents of this last group I am extremely proud to call my brothers and sisters in the Canadian family. Their ancestors who made good their escape from the dark night of slavery were intelligent, talented and most of all determined to find a life for themselves they could control and a good one to leave for their families.

And On The Language...

I used both English and American spellings in Fugitive's Son. When the letter writer was American, as in the case of General Sherman, I spelled words like colour without the British "u" as he would have done.

I have also avoided the use of contractions as much as possible in the narrative portions of this story, but allowed them to slip into the vocabulary of the dialogue so the speeches flowed rather than stumble over awkward construc-tions. Growing up in the Southern Ontario school system where we were heavily influenced by England and our own Canadian Broadcasting Corporation, contractions were frowned upon in our written work. I believe students of the Anderson Abbott and Frederick Douglass Macdonald era would have been taught the same codes of expression.

In the dialogue I tried to avoid going too far in the direction of attempting to mimic all nuances and cadences of the different accents and dialects present in the old south. I tried to retain some of the flavour and abandoned any attempt to be historically accurate. First because I had no way of determining what words and pronunciations the Gullah language of the 1860s may have been comprised of. Secondly, as with all the world before mass communication took a firm grip, there were too many variations to deal with.

For a list of books and websites used in researching this book visit:
www.brucekempphotography.net/civil-war-resources

Also by Bruce Kemp

Weather Bomb 1913: Life and Death on the Great Lakes

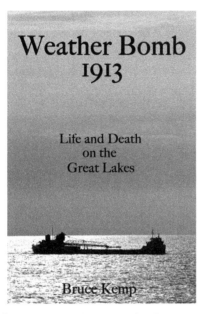

In the dark hours of November 9th, 1913, death screamed across the Great Lakes in the guise of a rare, white hurricane. The storm brutalized the region for the following week. It left in its wake cities crippled by devastating snowfalls, paralyzed communications, mysteries that remain unsolved to this day and the corpses of 256 men and women from twelve of the largest ships on the fresh water seas. Weather Bomb 1913: Life and Death on the Great Lakes is an accurate accounting of the causes and costs of the Storm as told by the few surviving witnesses who had a living memory of the carnage, courtroom testimony and newspaper reports of the day. Now modern ship captains and meteorologists contribute their expertise to help explain and define this horrendous "extra-tropical cyclone".

If you enjoyed The Fugitive's Son, send for
Weather Bomb 1913 today from Amazon.com

CPSIA information can be obtained
at www.ICGtesting.com
Printed in the USA
LVHW050817041119
636239LV00011B/1367